JUSTICE DELIVERED

JUSTICE
DELIVERED

PATRICIA
BRADLEY

Revell

a division of Baker Publishing Group
Grand Rapids, Michigan

© 2019 by Patricia Bradley

Published by Revell
a division of Baker Publishing Group
PO Box 6287, Grand Rapids, MI 49516-6287
www.revellbooks.com

Printed in the United States of America

Library of Congress Cataloging-in-Publication Data
Names: Bradley, Patricia, 1945– author.
Title: Justice delivered / Patricia Bradley.
Description: Grand Rapids, MI : Revell, a division of Baker Publishing Group,
    [2019] | Series: A Memphis cold case novel ; 4 | Includes bibliographical references
    and index.
Identifiers: LCCN 2018027438 | ISBN 9780800727192 (pbk. : alk. paper)
Subjects: | GSAFD: Suspense fiction.
Classification: LCC PS3602.R34275 J89 2019 | DDC 813/.6—dc23
LC record available at https://lccn.loc.gov/2018027438

ISBN 978-0-8007-3557-9 (casebound)

19 20 21 22 23 24 25   7 6 5 4 3 2 1

To the volunteers who give a voice to the
many victims of human trafficking.
And to my family who encourages me.
But most of all, to my Lord Jesus
Christ, who gives me the words.

PROLOGUE

JANUARY 2010

JASMINE EASED OUT of her cell-like room and down the dimly lit hallway. Two light raps on another bedroom door brought no response, and she turned the knob and slipped inside.

Moonlight filtered into the darkened room through narrow slats on the window. Labored breathing coming from the bed sent her heart spiraling to the floor. It was almost time to go, and Lily was still in bed. She eased closer, noticing that the thin blanket shook.

"It's me, Jasmine," she whispered. "You have to get dressed."

Lily didn't respond. If she wasn't ready when Blade came to get them, there would be consequences. Jasmine touched her shoulder, feeling the tremor in the girl's body. And the heat. Her hot skin made Jasmine wince.

"C-can't . . ."

She knelt beside the bed and smoothed the girl's hot brow. She was pretty sure from the way her friend had been coughing that she had pneumonia.

Lily's eyes fluttered open, and she turned toward the only window in the small room. "It's dark already?"

"Yeah, but don't worry—maybe they won't make you go tonight." Even as she said the words, Jasmine knew they would.

7

And if Lily didn't bring in her thousand dollars, Blade would beat her or worse.

"I-I have t-to. C-can't go in the H-hole again."

The Hole was why Lily was sick. A week ago she'd had a toothache and begged off hitting the streets. And for two days he'd shut her up in a tiny room in the basement of the house where they lived. With no lights and only the bare floor to sleep on, she'd come out of it disoriented and feverish.

"You're too sick to get out of bed." Jasmine swallowed and lifted her chin. "I'll tell Blade I'll see your clients tonight too."

"They won't let you," Lily said. She tried to sit up and fell back on the bed. Tears dropped from the corners of her eyes. She tried to take a deep breath and fell into a fit of coughing. When she got her breath, she slipped a bracelet from her arm and pressed it into Jasmine's hand. "I'm not going to make it, Jaz."

Jasmine clenched the thin chain in her hands as if holding on tightly would make Lily well. She didn't know what she'd do if Lily died. "You have to make it."

"I'm so c-cold." She squeezed Jasmine's hand. "Jaz, you . . . have to . . . forgive . . ."

"Lily, don't ask me to do that. These men don't deserve forgiveness!" she whispered fiercely. Someone had given Lily a Bible, and after she started reading it, she'd changed.

"None of us deserve forgiveness . . . and it's for . . . you. If you don't forgive . . . it will eat you alive."

She didn't have to ask if Lily had forgiven Blade or the one responsible for her being sold into prostitution. Peace showed on her face. Jasmine gripped the bracelet tighter. Her anger at Austin King and Blade was all she had to hold on to, and she wasn't letting it go.

Lily closed her eyes briefly. She tried to breathe deeper and triggered a spasm of coughing. When she got her breath, she turned, and her eyes pierced Jasmine.

"You have to find a way to get out of here. Find those women."

Last night four women from some shelter had brought coffee and doughnuts to the girls on the street. She'd ignored them, but Lily had talked to one of the ladies. Jasmine shook her head. "I can't leave you like this. I have to get medicine and bring it to you."

"No . . ." Lily's chest barely moved. "Can't breathe." Her feverish eyes locked on to Jasmine's. "Promise."

Jasmine wanted to promise, but after the "modeling agent" sold her to Blade, she'd tried to get away. Escaped three times. She rubbed the scar inside her forearm. The first time, a cop found her and took her back to Blade. He branded her with his initials and beat her until half her ribs were broken. The next time he locked her in a closet for a week. The last time, he'd beaten her and locked her in her room for three weeks with nothing but moldy bread and very little water. She never tried again.

They both jerked as Blade's voice thundered from the front of the house, ordering the women to assemble for the ride into town.

"Those women . . ." Lily's breathing grew shallower. "They . . . will . . . help."

Jasmine couldn't think about trying to escape again. "They may not be there. Blade will probably drop us off in a different part of the city," she said, looking toward the door when he shouted her name. Maybe if she told him how sick Lily was, he'd get help for her.

She turned to tell Lily she'd be right back and her heart stilled. Lily was dead.

◆

EARLY APRIL 2012

At a coffee shop near Nashville, Carly Smith typed "Lia Morgan" into the Facebook search engine, then chose Tennessee's second largest city for where to search. It had been ten years since she'd seen her sister, and she was probably married by now. Still, there couldn't be too many Lias in Memphis.

She hesitated with her finger poised over the enter key and closed her eyes. It had taken two years after she escaped Blade to get the courage to look for her sister. Two years and a name change. What if Lia wanted nothing to do with Carly? She wouldn't blame her. The feeling of worthlessness she struggled with daily washed over her. The psychiatrist she saw every two weeks had told her it would take time to put her past behind her, but Carly didn't believe she'd ever be free of her fear and shame. Opening her eyes, she pushed aside her hesitation and tapped enter.

While she waited, Carly fingered the gold bracelet around her wrist. Chains looped together with a locket dangling in the middle. She'd had an artist draw Lily's likeness for the inside of the locket. *Lily*. She would never have stood for Carly's self-pity.

She straightened her shoulders as only one Lia Morgan popped up on her screen. Carly studied the small image. The woman in the photo had shorter hair than she remembered . . . but it was definitely her sister. She clicked on the name, and Lia's Facebook page opened.

Oh, wow. Evidently her sister was a freelance photographer. That shouldn't surprise Carly, not the way Lia had always gone around with a camera in her hand. She studied the page. Portraits, sports, events, crime scenes—Lia covered it all. And based on all the awards she'd received, she was good. A phone number for her studio was listed on the sidebar, and Carly put the number in her phone.

Should she call her? She wished her friend Jamie was here—she'd know what to do. Her fingers hovered over the call button. What if Lia hung up when she told her who she was? Lia was bound to be angry with her for just dropping out of her life. Carly pressed her dry lips into a thin line. No. She couldn't do it. Not today. But she saved the number and slipped her phone in her pocket.

A week later, Carly sat in the same coffee shop, tears stinging her eyes as the barista set an oversized cupcake on the table. Another of the employees lit the one candle. "You shouldn't have done this."

Jamie Parker smiled. "I couldn't let your birthday go by without a celebration."

The barista cleared her throat, and Carly jerked her head up. "Please. Don't sing 'Happy Birthday' to me."

"No one is singing to you," Jamie said with a laugh. "I still remember last year at the restaurant. I thought you were going to have a stroke. Now make a wish and blow the candle out."

Carly paused, then leaned forward and blew out the flame. Everyone around her clapped and she nodded her thanks, resisting the urge to fan her heated cheeks.

"What did you wish for?" Jamie asked when they were alone again.

Carly busied herself with cutting the cupcake. All day she'd been thinking about birthdays past that she'd spent with Lia. "You have to help me eat this," she said.

"Of course, but what was your wish?"

"If I tell, it won't come true."

"Oh, come on. That's just for kids."

She put half of the cupcake on the extra plate and pushed it toward Jamie.

"Is it about your sister?" Jamie asked.

Carly nodded.

"You should call her."

"That's what my psychiatrist says."

"What's holding you back?"

Carly almost wished she hadn't told Jamie about finding Lia on Facebook as she thought of all the reasons she hadn't called

11

and settled on the main one. "What if she doesn't want to see me after she learns where I've been?"

"You're not to blame for what happened to you. Not like me, and if my family can forgive me for the mess I made of my life, your sister will welcome you with open arms."

Jamie reminded her of Lily. Always pushing her out of her comfort zone. No doubt the reason she'd bonded with her in the recovery home.

"Besides," Jamie said, "you had no way of knowing the man who offered to make you a model was into human trafficking."

"Even a seventeen-year-old should have known when something was too good to be true." She fiddled with the turquoise pin adorning the scarf around her neck. He'd been so convincing when he said she could make $10,000 a week.

"You're looking at it from ten years on the other side," Jamie said softly. "What's the worst that can happen if you call her?"

Rejection.

When Carly didn't answer, her friend said, "From what you've told me about Lia, she doesn't sound like someone who would reject you for something you couldn't help."

Jamie knew her well. Carly scraped at a chipped nail as memories of her big sister teaching her to swim and climb on a horse flashed through her mind. Lia had always looked out for her and never seemed to mind when Carly tagged along. *That* Lia would accept her. "You're right, and when you encourage me, I think I can do it . . ."

Jamie touched Carly's arm. "Call her right now." She nodded toward the patio. "You can have privacy out there."

Carly glanced through the window at the empty tables. Could she? She pulled her phone from her pocket. "Pray for me."

"You know I will."

Maybe God would hear Jamie's prayers.

On the patio, a cool breeze touched her cheek as Carly scrolled through her contacts until she came to Lia's name. Her thumb hovered over the number, and she almost returned the phone to her pocket. *No.* It was time, and she pushed the call button before she could change her mind.

"Lia Morgan Photography. How may I help you?"

Hearing Lia's voice took her breath away. *Say something.* She couldn't. Her vocal cords were frozen.

"Hello? Is anyone there?"

"Y-yes," Carly said.

"How can I help you?"

"It's me . . . Heather." The name felt strange on Carly's tongue. She'd discarded Heather years ago. Along with Jasmine, the name Blade had given her.

"I see," Lia said with an impatient sigh. "I suppose you need money for a plane ticket."

"What?" Her heart reeled at Lia's brusque tone.

"Don't act like you didn't read the article about Heather that came out in the *Commercial Appeal* today. Every time a reporter runs a story on her disappearance, at least half a dozen kooks call, claiming to be her. You're the third one today. The first one wanted me to fly her from California so we could be a family again. The second caller just plain wanted money. What do you want, the reward money?"

"Reward? What are you talking about?"

"There's a $10,000 reward posted on Memphis CrimeStoppers."

It took Carly a few seconds to process that someone had actually been looking for her. "I don't know about any reward."

"I've heard that before too."

"You mean people can actually claim a reward for turning themselves in?" This reminded Carly of the arguments they'd had as children at the breakfast table. Lia, older and more logical, rarely backed down. "Look, I'm sorry about your other calls, but this one is for real. I'm your sister."

There was a pause on the other end of the line. "You . . . don't sound like my sister. You don't even sound as though you're from the South, for that matter."

It hit Carly. While she'd recognized her sister's voice with its Southern accent right off, Carly had forgotten she'd lost her drawl long ago in New York and hadn't picked it up again when she was moved to Atlanta. "What if I asked you to meet me at the Natchez Trace State Park?"

There was a gasp on the other end of the line, then Lia asked, "Why there?"

"Because it's where we spent a week every summer with our parents until they died."

Silence filled the airwaves. "Oh my goodness," she whispered. "It really is you."

"Yes, it really is."

"Where are you? And where have you been? Are you all right?" Lia's voice rose as the questions tumbled out.

"I'd rather explain in person," Carly said.

"I can be at the state park in two hours."

"It will take me about the same amount of time. How about the restaurant there?"

"Okay, but how will I know you?"

"I'll know you," she said, glancing down at the clothes she wore. "But I'm wearing a plaid scarf and a white sweater over skinny jeans. Give me your cell number, and I'll call you if I'm running late."

Lia rattled off a number and Carly wrote it down. "You have my number on your caller ID." Then she said, "You looked good on Facebook. That's how I found you."

"Why haven't you called before?"

"I'll answer all your questions when we meet. And please, don't tell anyone I called or where we're meeting. Not even Gigi and Frank."

"But they'll be so happy to know—"

14

"No!" She bit her lip. Her aunt and uncle had never approved of her, and she could only imagine their reaction when they heard what had happened to her. Carly didn't want their reunion tainted with Gigi and Frank's disapproval. "You can tell them after we talk, if you still want to."

If they showed up with Lia, Carly would silently disappear.

Two and a half hours later at the Natchez Trace State Park, Carly sat at a corner table with a cup of dark roast and studied the people in the restaurant. She fingered the turquoise pin that held the GPS tracker she always wore somewhere in her clothing or her hair. Today she'd snapped it into a customized pin that held her brightly colored scarf in place. Tomorrow she might wear it in a barrette. Either way, she would not be without it—if she were ever kidnapped again, she wanted someone to be able to track her. Right now that was the people at RLT Security.

An overhead fan circulated cold air, making Carly shiver even with a sweater on. She rubbed her arms. Why did restaurants freeze you to death? She wished she'd told Lia she would meet her outside and turned to stare briefly through the bank of windows across the back of the room. The trees around the lake looked as though an artist had filled his palette with every shade of green known to mankind and dabbed it on the trees. Maybe they could move down by the lake once her sister arrived . . . if she came.

Restless, she glanced toward the door again. Lia wasn't coming. Carly unclasped her hands and five seconds later gripped them again, jumping as her cell phone announced a text. Maybe it was Lia. No. Jamie.

Did you make it safely?

Yes. She's not here.

Seconds later her cell phone rang. "Are you okay?" Jamie asked.

"Yes. No. What if Lia doesn't come?" The door opened and a Tennessee state trooper ambled into the room. For a few seconds, Carly struggled to breathe against the adrenaline pumping through her body. Some days it didn't matter how hard she worked, the sight of a policeman threw her into panic mode. "I have to go."

"What's wrong?"

Carly tracked the trooper as he walked to a table and pulled out a chair. "A s-state trooper just came in."

"Don't panic. Just close your eyes and picture a calm lake, with swans paddling in a circle . . ."

"You sound like my therapist." She glanced out the windows again. "And I don't have to close my eyes for that." A deep, cleansing breath stilled the fluttering in her chest. She could do this.

"You were getting better about that. What happened?"

Nothing had happened. She'd just gotten better at hiding her fear of the police. "I guess it's the stress of contacting Lia."

"Most cops are not like the ones in Blade's back pocket."

Carly wished she could believe that, but she'd seen too much corruption and too many instances of cops turning a blind eye to human trafficking and drugs. She looked up as the waitress stopped at her table and held up a coffeepot.

"Would you like a refill, honey?"

Still holding the cell phone to her ear, Carly nodded. As soon as the waitress moved on, she glanced toward the door again. Her breath stilled. Lia stood just inside, scanning the room. "She's here."

"Good," Jamie said. "Don't rush anything."

"I won't. And thanks for being a good friend." Keeping her gaze on Lia, Carly laid her phone on the table. The Facebook photo didn't do her sister justice. Unlike Carly, who had inherited their mother's ash-blonde hair and translucent skin tone, Lia had gotten their father's darker coloring. Dark brown hair, blue eyes, and skin that easily tanned. They looked as though they came from different gene pools.

She waved to get Lia's attention, and their gazes locked. Lia's face showed no recognition of Carly as she slowly approached the table. Doubt shrouded her face. The waitress stopped her, and after she nodded, the waitress sped toward the kitchen.

Then her sister stood at the table, her gaze still riveted on Carly.

She'd thought Lia might recognize her. But the last time her sister had seen her, Carly's hair had been jet-black, and she'd been super thin, almost anorexic. While she wasn't overweight, she'd filled out in a healthy way. The weight gain had changed her face, softening the sharp angles of her jawline and rounding it out.

"What did you call me at the breakfast table when we argued?" Lia demanded.

Carly laughed that her sister still remembered their morning arguments. "Gorilla. You called me Stinky." Then she inhaled deeply. Lia still wore the same perfume. "And you're wearing Joy. Just like me." She held her wrist up.

Lia bit her lip, and her eyes widened. "It's really you. All the way here, I kept preparing myself for disappointment." She pressed her fingers to her lips as her eyes turned shiny. "You don't know how long I've prayed for this, and down deep I knew one day you'd come back."

Maybe Carly should try praying more often. But it was hard to trust that a God who allowed her to be sold into slavery would hear her. She brushed the thought away as the waitress returned with a cup and filled it with coffee.

"Can I get you two anything else?" she asked.

They both shook their heads. "We'll order something later," Lia said, then she turned to Carly and studied her again. "I would not have recognized you if we'd passed on the street." She cocked her head, and Carly shifted her gaze away from Lia's scrutiny. "Unless I saw your eyes, and then I might wonder if it was you."

It'd been a while since Carly had worn the colored contacts that dried her eyes but effectively hid the gold starbursts ringing her irises. Maybe she should start wearing them again.

"I would have known you, and thank you for coming." Carly cringed. Her voice sounded stilted, and an awkward silence fell between them. Now that Lia was here, Carly didn't know what to say. Even though they were sisters, the years apart had made them strangers.

"I'm so sorry I didn't ask you to move in with me," Lia blurted.

"Move in with you?"

"Yes. I knew it was bad with Gigi and Uncle Frank, but I was living in the college dorm with a roommate. I didn't have anywhere to put you." Her chin quivered. "It was my fault that you ran away."

The pain in Lia's face pierced Carly. All these years her sister had lived with guilt? "Didn't they tell you? I'd moved out and was staying with whoever would give me a place to sleep until I could get a job." It was one reason no one had reported her missing right away. She took a deep breath. "I didn't run away, either. I was kidnapped and sold into sex trafficking."

Lia paled. A gasp escaped her lips, and then she dropped her gaze to the table. "No," she whispered.

"I didn't mean to upset you."

Placing her hand on her chest, she brought her gaze back to Carly's. "Please, tell me that didn't happen."

"I wish I could."

"How?"

She'd known Lia would want to know, but that didn't make the telling easier. How to start? "I met a modeling agent. He promised me a job and lots of money if I would go with him to New York. You know how much I wanted to be a model." She paused to take a breath. How stupid she'd been. The memories of those first days assaulted her, and she sought the gold bracelet around her wrist.

"When we got to New York, he turned me over to a man called Blade, and the modeling job turned out to be in adult entertainment. When I said no, Blade kept me locked up in a tiny room with no food until I agreed. That's when I found out the modeling agent had sold me to Blade."

No need to mention the beatings she endured or what happened the times she tried to escape. Especially since her matter-of-fact words had evidently stunned Lia into silence. The once-cold room suddenly felt like a sauna, and Carly peeled the sweater off. "I finally got away from him two years ago. By then he had moved me to Atlanta. There were some ladies there who ran a shelter for trafficked women. They got me out of Georgia, otherwise Blade would have found me."

"Who is this Blade?" Color had returned to Lia's face, and her jaw clenched. "What's his last name?"

"I have no idea." The scar on her left arm throbbed, and she rubbed it with her thumb. "Blade is the only name I ever knew."

Lia shifted her gaze to Carly's arm. "How did you get that scar?"

She glanced down, remembering the smell of her seared skin when Blade pressed the red-hot *B* just below her elbow. "The first time I ran away and Blade caught me, he branded me with his initial. A surgeon removed it earlier this year."

Lia winced. "Who was the New York agent?"

"He went by the name Austin King, but I'm sure it was fake. I've searched the internet and there's no New York agent by that name. None of the photos I found matching Austin King turned out to be him."

"How did you meet him?" Determination crept into Lia's voice as she took out a notebook and pen.

Every moment of their meeting was stamped in Carly's memory. "Logan Donovan had taken me to a party at his mother's, and she was not at all happy I was there, so I was kind of staying under her radar and sitting in a corner. King approached me and said he'd been watching me all night, and had I ever considered being a model. I should have checked him out, but I was seventeen and stupid."

"If he was at one of Jacqueline Donovan's parties, I'm sure you thought he was on the up-and-up."

"That's exactly what I thought. We set up a meeting for breakfast to iron out the details, and then he left the party. I should have asked Logan about him."

"Why didn't you?"

Carly made a face. "It's going to sound dumb, but King told me not to mention him or the modeling gig. That someone would try to mess it up." She shook her head. "That should have been a warning flag, but he told me how that had just happened. Another girl was all set to go to New York with him and she told someone. Her parents got wind of it and wouldn't allow her to go. I was the lucky girl who got to take her place. Pretty sure it was all a lie and there never was another girl."

"Oh, honey, he knew how to manipulate you."

"Do you think Jacqueline could have set me up with him?"

Lia paused in her note taking. "I've been to Jacqueline's parties. Some of her guests can be a little offbeat, but she'd never knowingly associate with someone dealing in human trafficking. Did you know anyone else at the party?"

"There were a lot of people there, even Gigi and Frank." She searched her memory bank. "Jared Donovan . . . and a couple of friends of Logan's I'd met . . . I haven't thought about them in years, so I'll have to work on remembering their names."

"Yes. I'll need them. But I really have a hard time believing Jacqueline had anything to do with it."

"She didn't like me." Carly played with the gold chain around her wrist. "She wasn't pleased that Logan had brought me, or that he was even dating me—I wasn't upper class enough for him. I used to think that was one of the reasons he took me out—he liked irritating his mother. I don't know if she would have gone that far, though."

"He was too old for you," her sister said.

"You're probably right. Logan didn't know I was only seventeen. If he had, he never would have asked me out."

Lia rubbed the handle of her cup with her thumb. "I barely remember you dating him, but I was working to finish my bachelor's, totally swamped."

"I didn't understand why I rarely saw you, but I do now," Carly said with a rueful smile. When Lia looked puzzled, she added, "I'm getting my bachelor's now."

Lia grinned, her smile stretching big. "Oh, Heather, that's wonderful."

"Yeah, it is. And I don't go by Heather anymore. After I escaped, I changed my name to Carly Smith."

"Carly?" Lia's lips curved into a smile. "That's a wonderful name. It means strength."

"How do you know that?"

"Because I almost named my little girl that."

"You have a daughter?" Carly had missed out on so much. "Tell me about her, and what's been going on in your life."

"My daughter is five. I met David when . . . you went missing. I kept running into him whenever I went to see the detective that worked on your case. We were married a year later, and Alexis was born three years after that."

"Alexis." Carly liked the way it rolled off her tongue. "Did you choose it for any particular reason?"

"I liked that it means helpful or defender, and Lexi is certainly both—even as a five-year-old, she makes sure no one bullies her friends. I wouldn't be surprised if she didn't follow in her daddy's footsteps."

"What do you mean?"

"He's a sergeant with the Memphis police department."

A shiver chased over her body. Of all the men Lia could have married, why did she have to choose a policeman? "I'm sure he's nice." It was all she could think of to say. "But I'm glad you hadn't changed your name on your Facebook page."

"That's my photography page. My married name is Raines."

"Are you happy?"

"I am now that I've found you." She stared down at the table, then raised her gaze. "Why did you wait two years to contact me?"

Another question Carly had known was coming, but it was still difficult to explain. "I wasn't a nice person that first year. I was really messed up and living at a recovery home."

"Recovery home?"

"Drugs had been the only way I could cope while I was . . ." Carly looked down at her clasped fingers. "Anyway, after I was clean, well, let's just say when you've been in the situation I was in, it's hard to face people, especially those you care about."

"But it wasn't your fault."

"That's what my psychiatrist keeps telling me, but it doesn't change the shame."

"You shouldn't feel shame over something you had no control of."

Almost the same words Jamie used. Carly looked up into Lia's tender gaze. "One day I hope to believe that, but I'm not there yet. Just now, it took every ounce of courage I had to tell you what happened."

"Why? Did you think I'd turn away from you?"

"I didn't know how you would react."

Lia's face hardened. "Whoever is responsible needs to pay, and I'm going to find out who it is. Can you describe this Austin King?"

"No!" Lead settled in her stomach. She hadn't dreamed Lia might go after King. Carly leaned forward. "Please, just let it go. It's too dangerous for you to get involved."

Her sister lifted her chin. "I've been trying to find you for ten years. I can't let it go. What happened to you might happen to someone else. And what if I'm coming in contact with him every day or even occasionally? Austin King probably wasn't even his name, and I wouldn't know him."

"He wouldn't look the same."

"He couldn't have changed that much. What did he look like?"

Carly should have seen this coming. Lia had always been her champion and protector, and once her sister set her mind, there was no changing it. Slowly, she took a sketch from her purse. "I had a forensic artist draw this from my description, and it may not even look like him now. I was pulling from eight-year-old memories. He would have been maybe forty then, so he'd be close to fifty now."

Lia studied the sketch then raised her gaze, her eyes round. "*This* is Austin King?"

A cold chill ran over Carly's body. "Do you know him?"

"I don't know for sure, but he looks so . . . normal, and I was expecting a monster, I guess."

"But you do think you know him?"

"Maybe. I'm not sure."

"Who is he?"

Her sister shook her head. "If I accuse someone without being certain, it could ruin his life."

"How will you find out?"

"We have a shelter for women who've been on the streets. I'll talk with the person running it. Either the director or one of the women might recognize the sketch. Or maybe the name." Then Lia leaned forward. "Why haven't you returned to Memphis and taken this to the police? They're equipped to find this man."

"Cops don't care about victims of human trafficking," Carly said.

"The ones I know do. Please, come back with me, give this information to David."

Lia's husband probably wasn't on the take, but he could be. So many she'd met in her past were. Her fear of cops wasn't the only reason Carly hadn't pursued finding Austin King. Going to the police meant reliving every day she was on the streets. She worried a hangnail on her thumb. "I just can't."

1

The nip in the air invigorated Carly as she cantered the Arabian mare on the smooth lane. Getting up an hour early to ride Angel had been so worth it. The horses at Tabula Rasa had been a deciding factor in accepting the recovery center's job offer.

Carly's earliest memories had involved horses, and after her parents died, her mare, Candy, had been her biggest comfort. She'd like to know if the horse was still alive . . . horses lived thirty years sometimes. But to see her would mean revealing who she was to the world. What if Blade tracked her down?

No. For now she'd have to settle for the horses at the center. She brought the mare down to a trot then to a walk, and then she leaned over and patted the horse's neck. "Good girl. Are you ready to go back to the barn?"

Carly didn't know what she'd do if the mare answered her with more than the toss of her head.

She reined Angel around and nudged her into a trot, rising out of the saddle to match the one-two beat of Angel's rhythm. Her mind turned to the counseling sessions for later in the morning. Over the weekend a new girl had arrived at the center, and Carly

25

was anxious to meet her. No one had said exactly what her problem was . . . probably drugs. That was the majority of the girls' problems here.

An hour and a half later, Carly lit a lavender candle then turned as the door opened and girls filed in for their session. She made eye contact with each girl as they handed her a sheet of paper that listed their name and what they wanted to discuss. Most smiled and nodded, but not the new girl. Carly had learned from one of the other counselors that her name was Jenna Carson.

After she collected the last sheet, Carly scanned the room, searching until she found Jenna sitting in a rocker with her knees pulled close to her chest, ignoring the activity around her. Brassy blonde hair almost covered a pixie face. Carly hadn't had an opportunity to look over the girl's paperwork, so she knew nothing other than her name. By noon, that would change when she plowed through the stack of folders on her desk.

She nodded to the two assistants who would sit in on today's session and then turned to study the other girls in the group. All recovering addicts, and all still in their teens. She skimmed the papers the girls had handed her. Jenna had only written her first name and age, seventeen, on the sheet. Evidently there was nothing she wanted to talk about.

Typical of a new girl who was still hiding from her past. After eight years, Carly understood that better than anyone. But it was her job to get Jenna to realize the past did not define her. Here at Tabula Rasa she had a clean slate. That's what *tabula rasa* meant in Latin. Carly had to remind herself daily that she had a clean slate because not a day went by that she didn't struggle with her past, and especially with her sister's death.

She hadn't discovered Lia was dead until almost six months after they'd met at the state park. When a week went by and her sister hadn't contacted Carly again, she figured once Lia had time to think about what she'd learned, she'd decided Carly had too

26

much baggage. And Carly didn't blame her, but she wasn't about to contact Lia again and suffer more rejection.

It had been Jamie who had tracked down Lia's unsolved murder case that the police termed a random act of violence. Hers was similar to three other unsolved shootings on the 385 bypass.

"Ms. Carly, when we getting started?"

"Shortly," she said, blocking the memories. She turned to Trinity. The eighteen-year-old would graduate from the program in two weeks, an accomplishment that had been hard to envision five months ago. Surly and uncooperative, she'd only been there because the alternative was prison. But somewhere around two months into the program, Carly had broken through the hard shell encasing the girl and helped her see her worth, freeing the prisoner inside. Breakthroughs like she'd had with Trinity kept her going.

Carly scanned the room again. Jenna now stood facing the window with her arms wrapped around her thin body. Carly stepped closer to Trinity and lowered her voice. "Could you try and engage Jenna? Let her know she's in a safe place?"

Trinity glanced toward the other girl. "She's been through a lot. Not going to be easy for her to trust."

Carly queried her with her eyes.

"She's been trafficked."

The bottom dropped out of Carly's stomach and her knees threatened to buckle. Instinctively, she fingered the chain around her wrist. Why had Jenna been put in her group? The director knew she didn't counsel victims of human trafficking. "How do you know?"

Even as she asked, she recognized the symptoms in Jenna—avoiding eye contact, isolating herself, like now at the window, arms crossed over her body for protection. She'd heard the facility planned to take in rescued women who had drug and alcohol problems, but she thought they'd be in their own group. Trafficked girls dealt with more than addiction and would need specialized treatment.

The director didn't know Carly's history, only that she wanted to focus on counseling victims of substance abuse. No one knew her story except her psychiatrist, Laura Abernathy, and her friend, Jamie Parker. Carly rubbed the scar below her left elbow, feeling the ridge that surgery had not been able to completely erase. Her first impulse was to call Dr. Abernathy or maybe Jamie.

No. Both women would only tell Carly to face this challenge head-on, even though she didn't want to. Not right now.

She had two weeks of vacation coming. Maybe now was the time to take it. But what if it was too short notice? She wouldn't know unless she tried, and as soon as this session ended, she'd put in for her leave.

But there was nothing to be done for this session except see it through. She turned to Trinity. "Call the girls together," she said, her voice cracking. "I'm going to grab a water bottle and my pen and pad."

The teenager shot an odd glance toward her then arranged the chairs in a circle and announced the start of the meeting.

One by one the girls took a chair while Carly sipped her water. It did little to relax her throat. *Focus on getting the meeting started and then let the girls take over.* Maybe she could plead a sore throat . . . no, she could do this.

Jenna was the last to take a seat at the far side of the semicircle. Turning to the opposite side, Carly scanned the waiting faces, stopping at a girl who'd been at the facility two months. Taylor was inches from a breakthrough. Could be today. Her gaze finally rested on the new girl. Jenna never looked up from studying her fingers.

"Good morning," she said and received mostly mumbles from the girls. It was going to be a long day. "Tell me how you feel today. What are your P.I.E.S.?"

Each session started with the patients telling where they stood physically, intellectually, emotionally, and spiritually. No one spoke up. Carly waited. Finally, Trinity nodded toward the girl sitting next to her with her head ducked. "Birdie's upset."

The girl elbowed Trinity. "My name's not Birdie. It's Holly."

The girls had nicknamed her Birdie because of her small frame and quick movements. "But are you upset?" Carly asked.

Holly lifted her shoulder in a shrug.

Carly waited again.

Huffing a breath, Holly said, "My mama came to see me Sunday afternoon."

That explained a lot. Her mother's visits usually left the girl angry for days. "You want to talk about it?"

"Not really." She picked at her thumb. "When she left I was wiped. She told me if I wasn't so dumb I'd already be out of here."

Carly's jaw tightened. She'd counseled with the woman, asking her to be positive when she came to see her daughter. Maybe it was time to let the director deal with her. Before she could encourage her, Trinity spoke up.

"You're not dumb."

"She said I had to get new friends when I got out too."

"She's right about that," another of the girls said.

Holly pressed her lips together. "I know it's what I have to do, but I don't have to like it."

"You'll be right back here if you don't find new friends," Trinity said.

Carly nodded. "That's right. Who can tell me why?"

"Because they'll want you to party with them," Trinity said. "They'll tell you that one drink or a snort won't hurt you."

Another girl agreed. Jenna never spoke up as the group batted the question around, and Carly directed the discussion back to their P.I.E.S., asking each girl to talk about how they were feeling. She kept an eye on Jenna, noticing her agitation when the discussion turned to God.

"God is my best friend," Trinity said. "He had a good plan for my life, and I messed it up, but he's gonna take my mistakes and make something good from them."

"Oh, give me a break! What if you didn't make a mistake and you were just at the wrong place at the wrong time!" Jenna stood and palmed her hands toward the group. "Y'all can sit here and listen to this baloney, but I'm out of here."

She turned and bolted from the room.

Carly took a deep breath. Everything in her wanted to let the girl go.

2

CARLY GLANCED AROUND, looking to see which counselor she could send after Jenna. *Go yourself. You can help her.*

Not fair, Lily. And in the end, Carly had been no help to Lily at all. She felt the girls' eyes on her. They were waiting to see how she handled Jenna's outburst.

Someone had to go after her. No. *Carly* had to go—her session, her girls, so she had to deal with the situation. "I'll be right back," she said and called one of the other counselors to take over the discussion.

When she didn't find Jenna in her room, she searched the grounds, starting with the park area and walking trail. No Jenna. She stopped an aide. "Have you seen a girl with blonde hair? About so tall." She held her hand shoulder high since Jenna was at least half a foot shorter than Carly's five nine.

"Saw a girl about that size headed toward the stables."

Of course. One of the girls, probably Trinity, would have shown Jenna the horses. They were a big part of the treatment at Tabula Rasa, and like Carly, most of the girls were drawn to the big animals.

She walked toward the barn, almost hoping Jenna wouldn't be there, that another counselor would have found the girl, but when she turned the corner, sniffling came from Beau's stall. The most troubled girls gravitated to the golden palomino that Carly liked almost as much as Angel, and she understood why. Beau's gentle spirit could calm her on her worst days.

The sweet scent of hay from the bales stacked in the hallway met her as she eased to the stall door, her rubber-soled shoes barely making a sound. Jenna's back was to her as she brushed Beau's coat. She stopped once and buried her face in the horse's mane.

Carly struggled to get out the words she needed to say, but they stuck in her throat. She couldn't do this. Just as she turned to find another counselor, Jenna spoke.

"I know you're there. And don't try to tell me there's a God, at least not like they were talking about."

She saw so much of herself in Jenna—how many times had Carly said or thought those same words? She knew the pain behind them. And because of that, she wanted to run. Even as she wanted to, her feet refused to cooperate.

You can help her, Jaz. Lily had been the one who helped the new girls when they came in, and sometimes she asked Carly to join in. Then it hit her. Jenna didn't just remind her of herself. Physically, she reminded her of Lily.

That was why Carly's feet would not move. She couldn't leave Jenna, not with the girl in so much pain. She found another brush and slipped inside the stall. Beau nickered, and Carly rubbed his muzzle, his whiskers prickly on her palm. "We can't ride today, old boy."

She ran the brush over the gelding's sleek belly, silently asking God for words that would help Jenna. "I felt that way once, so I understand how you feel," she said.

A derisive snort came from the other side of the horse. "You don't have a clue."

But she did.

The walls of the stable closed in, and she grabbed the horse's mane, steadying herself. Thoughts sucked her into the past as scene after scene flashed in her memory. Nights standing on street corners. Beatings when she didn't bring in enough money. Fear. Humiliation. Shame. She closed her eyes and tried to make the nightmare go away. *Tell her . . .*

"I'm afraid I do." It was as though Lily had taken over her mouth.

The brushing stopped. "That's not possible."

"I was on the streets for eight years." She closed her eyes again, remembering the way it was. Walking the streets, hungry most of the time, the bruises. Never in the face, though. Blade didn't want a girl with marks on her face. "Tried to escape a couple of times, but my pimp always found me."

"How did you get out?"

"He'd moved us to Atlanta. It was January and my legs about froze off. There was a women's shelter not far from where we worked the streets, and the director and three of her volunteers set up in the middle of our territory with a tent. After eight years, he didn't think I'd run, and he wasn't keeping as close a watch on me. His attention was mainly on the new girls that he hadn't put the fear of his fists in yet."

Carly shook her head. "I thought the women were crazy, standing out in the cold, handing out coffee and doughnuts and Jesus tracts. They told us they'd help us get out. I took their coffee, but I didn't buy anything else they said. I knew he would find me if I tried to run again. But after . . ."

Carly's throat tightened, and unshed tears burned behind her eyes. She didn't know if she could get the words past her locked jaw. Besides her psychiatrist, Jamie was the only other person who knew about Lily.

"What happened that made you risk trying to escape again?"

Carly concentrated on brushing the horse. Finally she said,

"Lily. She was the only friend I had, and she pushed me to go to the women and get help."

"Why didn't she go?"

The back of her eyes burned. "Because . . ." She drew in a deep breath and blew it out. "She died."

Jenna gasped. "I'm sorry."

"Me too." She wiped her tears with the back of her hand. "I didn't tell you that story so you'd feel sorry for me. I told you so you'll know you can start over. You can go to college. Like I did. Your past doesn't define you."

Jenna had moved, and Carly could see her face and looked for signs that her words had reached the girl. The scowl was gone, lifting her heart.

"You really think I can start over?"

"Yes. From this day forward, you have a clean slate."

"Will you help me?"

"I can guide you, but it's going to be up to you to claim your freedom."

For the first time, hope shone in Jenna's eyes. Maybe she would make it after all. "How long were you on the streets?" Carly asked.

"A month. I ran away from home. Went to Memphis—"

Jenna was kidnapped in Memphis? The buzz in her ears drowned out the rest of the girl's words. Carly tried to swallow, but cotton filled her mouth. The age Jenna had written at the top of her page flashed in her mind . . . seventeen. Same age as Carly when Austin King sold her to Blade.

"All I wanted to do was become a model. This guy told me he was an agent—said he could get me started in New York. He was nice, like my grandpa." She squeezed her eyes shut. "It couldn't have been his first time to do this. So why hasn't someone reported him and warned girls about a modeling agent who was trafficking women? One who looked so . . . so safe. If someone had just told me . . ."

34

No. The strength in Carly's legs dissolved, and her peripheral vision narrowed. She fought off the encroaching blackness as she backed up to the wall and slid to the floor.

If Carly had gone home and told her story to the police and anyone else who would listen, maybe she could have spared Jenna and no telling how many other girls what she went through. Maybe if she had made enough noise, Blade would have been afraid to come after her.

Instead, she'd hidden away, and others had suffered for it.

3

DAVID RAINES PACED the carpet in his den, then turned and stared at Georgina and Frank Wilson. "You've got to be kidding."

"No," Georgina said softly. "You know how fond we are of Alexis. The Academy in Senatobia is one of the best private schools in the state."

"We want her to come live with us at the farm," Frank said. He sat beside his wife on the plaid sofa, his ramrod posture giving evidence to his early years in the army. "Their mathematics curriculum will prepare her for the Mississippi School of Math and Science her junior year. Not to mention their girls' soccer team is ranked in the top ten."

"And we're happy to pay her tuition—it's the least we can do for Lia's daughter," Georgina said.

"She could come home on weekends," Frank added.

"No! My daughter stays with me." It was enough that he'd lost his wife six years ago. "The school she's in is a good school. I'm not losing her."

"You wouldn't lose her," Georgina said. "You could see her anytime."

"I know, because she's staying here."

She crossed her arms. "Well," she said, her voice hardening, "the fact of the matter is, you're so busy, you've already lost her. You don't attend her parent-teacher meetings. You don't go to her soccer games. And unless we're here, most of the time she has to eat dinner with Mrs. Baxter. Besides, she wants to come live with us."

He stood perfectly still. That couldn't be true. Could it? No. Lexi would never leave him, at least not until she was ready to go to college. While David freely admitted he was a workaholic, what Georgina said wasn't quite true. He didn't go to all of her parent-teacher meetings because early on, Georgina and Frank wanted to be involved in all aspects of Lexi's life, including school. He'd seen no need for all of them to go, but he never missed an important one. As for Lexi's soccer games, he attended more than he missed. He liked to think he and his daughter had quality time together. "I don't believe she wants to leave me."

"We're not trying to take your daughter from you, but she needs more attention than you're able to give her," Frank said.

Uncrossing her arms, Georgina leaned forward. "David, we understood when you buried yourself in your work after Lia died, and I truly appreciate that you've tried to find my niece's killer. But it's been six years. You're consumed with solving not just her case, but every cold case in Memphis. Alexis is suffering because you're never here. As much as I hate to say it, Lia is gone. Nothing you do will bring her back, and it's time you let it go."

"I can't." He knew finding whoever shot Lia wouldn't return her to them, but at least he would have closure. They all would. "I want justice for Lia and for all the other families like us. As long as these murderers remain free, there is no justice."

"But at what cost? Your daughter needs you to spend more time with her, and since you can't seem to do that, she should be with someone who can." She gave him a pointed look. "When was the last time you took her to church? Or spent even half a day with her, just the two of you?"

"Plenty of times." Just last week a water main broke at the school, and he'd picked her and Hannah up, and they'd gone for root beer floats at a fast food place.

Evidently there was no pleasing Georgina. She'd complained right after Lia was murdered that his helicoptering of Lexi's activities had bordered on obsession. Since he'd made lieutenant and formed the Cold Case Unit, he'd stepped back and given his daughter room to breathe. Okay, so maybe he'd exchanged one obsession for another, but if he hadn't argued with Lia about her missing sister the night she was murdered, his wife would never have been on the Bill Morris Parkway alone after dark. Now every cold case he solved gave him a measure of peace and provided closure to a family.

"She'll soon be a teenager and you have to put her first."

"I have two years before that happens." A slow burn crawled up the back of his neck. He was doing the best he could as a single dad with a demanding job. He was home every night, even if he didn't always make it in time to eat. And yes, she did spend a lot of weekends with either the Wilsons or her best friend, Hannah, but he usually joined them at church and then afterward they went out to eat.

David rubbed his forehead. He'd always had a good relationship with the Wilsons. They'd never had children of their own, but Lia had talked about how they took her and her sister in after their parents were killed in an auto accident. He'd have to admit they'd done a good job with Lia, but from what he'd gleaned, it had been a different story with her sister, Heather.

Maybe he'd made a mistake depending on them so much after Lia died. But the Wilsons had always been involved in Lexi's life, taking on the role of surrogate grandparents from the time she was born. Lia's death had hit him hard, and when they stepped into the void left by her death, he'd been thankful for Lexi to have someone to turn to.

Georgina slid to the edge of the sofa and laid her hand on his knee. "Would you at least consider letting her go to the Academy? The school will accept her in January, at the beginning of the next semester."

The front door slammed and David jerked his head toward the entry hall. "I don't want to discuss this in front of Lexi."

Before either of them could respond, Lexi burst into the den. "Dad! You're home!"

She dropped her book bag to the floor and hugged him then turned to the Wilsons. "Gigi, I didn't know you and Uncle Frank were coming today! Can you come to my soccer game next Tuesday? And can we all go eat pizza tonight?" She turned to him. "You'll be here for supper, won't you, Dad?"

"Whoa," David said. Lexi looked so much like her mother with her heart-shaped face and easy, natural grin. "Catch your breath."

She rolled her brown eyes and made a big production of taking a breath, then asked, "Can we go to Pizza Corner tonight?"

The pleading in her voice got to him. How could he tell her he was going to Madeline Starr's for dinner at six? The Wilsons had found him at home only because he'd stopped by the house to finish a report and change clothes.

"I, ah . . ." He faltered.

Georgina raised her eyebrows, and David checked his watch. If he and Lexi ate at five and he could get Maggie to delay their dinner an hour, he could make it work. He went on faith that Maggie would go along with him. "Sure. Why don't we go before the crowd hits? Say in about an hour?" He glanced toward the Wilsons to include them in the invitation.

Frank cleared his throat. "We hadn't planned to stay at the condo tonight."

"Then it looks like it's just you and me, kiddo," he said. She high-fived him.

"We hadn't mentioned it to you yet, David," Georgina said with a glance at him, "but we actually came up to see if Lexi would like to spend the weekend at the farm with us."

He bit back the no he'd almost snapped. She'd spent three of the last four weekends with them either at the condo or in Senatobia. "I'm off this weekend," he said, "and I thought Lexi and I would hang out together, maybe go fishing."

"Really? Fishing?" Lexi's face lit up and she turned to the older couple. "Gigi, you and Uncle Frank won't mind if I don't go this time, will you?"

"Of course not, honey," Georgina said. But the look she shot him over Lexi's head said otherwise.

"We'll tell Midnight you'll see him soon."

Briefly, Lexi's face fell at Frank's mention of her horse. David tightened his jaw. He'd never noticed how manipulative Frank was.

"Tell you what," David said, smoothing his hand over his daughter's brown hair, "we can fish in the morning and then drive down and see Midnight tomorrow afternoon."

"Awe-some!" Lexi pumped her fist. "I can show you how good he takes the jumps."

He mustered a smile toward the Wilsons. "I guess we'll see you tomorrow afternoon."

After they left, David turned to Lexi. "Take your books up to your room and work on your homework until it's time to go."

While Lexi hurried upstairs, he called Maggie. Up until a year and a half ago, he'd known and respected Madeline Starr only through court cases—her on one side and him on the other. But that all changed after they worked on a case together and she stirred emotions he never expected to experience again. He'd realized just how much he cared about her when she was kidnapped and he thought she might die.

When he explained the situation, she told him it was no problem. But that was Maggie. Flexible and understanding. The yearning in his heart when he thought of her always caught him by surprise.

After Lia's death, he never dreamed he'd fall in love again. He and Maggie were an unlikely pair, he a cop and she a criminal defense attorney, but so far that hadn't been a problem.

He busied himself with a report, and forty-five minutes later, he looked up as Lexi clomped down the stairs.

"Are you ready?" he asked when she stopped in front of him.

She cocked her head and then pointed to the gun on his waist. "You're not wearing *that*, are you?"

He glanced down at his automatic. It would bring a lot of stares at the family pizza place, but wearing it had become second nature. "How about I wear a jacket over it?"

She thought a minute and then nodded. "That'll do it."

After he slipped on a jacket, he took his daughter's hand as they walked from the house. At the car, he opened the right rear door.

"Can't I sit in the front?" She raised her brows, encouraging him to say yes.

"What's the rule?"

"Not until I'm thirteen or five feet tall," she said, drawing the words out.

"And you don't fit either condition."

"I think it's a silly rule."

He swallowed a grin. "I don't, and my opinion is the one that matters."

Once they buckled up, David backed out of the drive. He couldn't get Georgina's words out of his head. *"Your daughter needs you to spend time with her."* He couldn't deny he'd buried himself in his work since Lia died, but Alexis appeared to be happy. Maybe he didn't make it home for supper much, but he almost always arrived in time to tuck her into bed and say good night. Still, she was eleven now . . . he figured it wouldn't be long before she considered herself too old for the tucking in.

David glanced in the rearview mirror at her. "Lexi, honey, you're happy living with me, aren't you?"

Her brown eyes widened. "Mmmhuh."

"I mean, you'd tell me if you weren't, right?"

"Oh, Daddy, you're being silly."

"So, if Gigi and Uncle Frank offered for you to come live with them . . ." He swallowed. He didn't have a horse to offer or unlimited time with her. "Would you like to do that?"

"Of course not. You're my daddy."

Relief made him weak. He flashed her a smile in the mirror. "I'm glad."

Alexis frowned. "Besides, who would make sure you got enough sleep? Mrs. Baxter says if it weren't for me, you'd work day and night."

Great. He had to do something about his schedule if even the housekeeper remarked on how much he worked. "Lexi, I'm sorry. It's my job to take care of you and protect you, not the other way around."

"But you do, Daddy. I always feel safe when you're around 'cause I know you won't let anything happen to me."

His heart swelled almost to bursting. He would die protecting his daughter if it took that. But, the good Lord willing, that would be a test he'd never face. "How would you like it if Maggie went fishing with us tomorrow? And maybe went with us to Gigi's?"

"Really? Cool."

Idling at a traffic light, he glanced at her again. Lexi's eyes were round and filled with . . . hope? "What?" he asked as she continued to stare at him.

"When are you going to ask Miss Maggie to marry you? I could use some help keeping you from working all the time, you know."

He almost swallowed his tongue. He'd been very cautious not to let Lexi know how involved he was with Maggie, but she must have sensed it. And he and Maggie had never discussed this subject, mainly because he wasn't sure how Lexi would react. "You'd like that?"

"Yeah. You're not getting any younger, you know. If I'm ever going to have a brother or sister—"

A horn honked behind him and David jumped. Lexi wanted a brother or sister?

Having kids was another subject he and Maggie hadn't discussed.

4

MAGGIE OPENED the glass door to her balcony and stepped outside as the contrails from a jet streaked across the purplish-red sky. She never tired of the view from her condo overlooking the Mississippi River. Too bad it was too cool to eat on the balcony, but the warmth from earlier in the day was already evaporating as the sun went down.

She leaned on the rail and followed the jet trail as the plane bypassed the Memphis International Airport. Probably a flight from Nashville to Dallas. She checked her watch as twilight set in. Six forty-five. When David had called and asked that they move dinner from six to seven, she'd been glad for the extra time. Now that she had everything ready, a tiny case of jitters set in. The past few weeks their relationship had suddenly moved at warp speed, and she wasn't sure she was ready for the next step.

Or if David was. He'd never told her he loved her, not the actual words. And while she wasn't the kind of woman who had to be told all the time that a man loved her, she needed to hear it at least once.

Her cell phone rang and she glanced at the caller ID. Jared Donovan. She thought about letting it go to voicemail. They'd gone out a few times . . . he was one she wouldn't have to wait on long to say the L-word. And probably the M-word. But she didn't love him, not like she loved David. She pressed the green button. "Hello?"

"Maggie, how are you?"

His well-modulated voice could calm an angry cat. "Good. You?"

"I'll be better if you'll go to dinner and a concert in St. Louis with me next week. We'd fly up Saturday afternoon and come back Saturday night."

Her heart sank. Jared had not given up. "That is so sweet of you to ask, but . . ."

"It's David Raines, isn't it?"

"Jared, you deserve someone who is free to love you. I'm not."

"I really care about you, and I think we could have something good."

Maggie held back a sigh. "I really like you as a friend."

"I had to give it another shot—no harm, no foul. If you ever ditch that police lieutenant, give me a call."

"Good night, Jared."

Shivering, she slipped her phone in her pocket and walked back inside her condo, where Vivaldi's *Four Seasons* played through her stereo system. Jared was everything a woman could want. Handsome, rich, confident. But the magic just wasn't there. And it was with David.

Maggie put aside thoughts of Jared and glanced around the room. A fire would be cozy, and she used a remote to light the gas logs. She loved her place on Riverside Drive. Was she ready to give it up if David should ask her to marry him? She couldn't see him and Lexi moving away from her school . . . not that they had exactly discussed marriage . . . maybe danced around the subject a little, but still, she sensed that might be about to change.

The scent of rosemary potatoes lured her to the oven, where she checked the dish. Should be perfect by the time he arrived. As should the two filets waiting to be pan grilled—it wasn't often she actually had time to make his favorite meal.

The doorbell chimed. She checked the video feed, and his six-two frame filled the screen. As always, her heart fluttered as he grinned at the camera. He looked almost as good tonight as he had the day he'd rescued her when she and Andi Hollister had been under siege in the hills of middle Tennessee.

She sighed. Her heart was definitely in love with David Raines. It was her head she had trouble with, and the change a permanent relationship would bring to her life. Maggie swung the door open. "'Come into my parlor,' said the Spider to the Fly," she said, dropping her voice an octave.

He grinned at her. "It's actually 'will you walk' into my parlor."

"And you know this, how?"

He stepped inside her living room and shrugged out of his jacket, hooking it on the hall tree by the door. "It's Lexi's favorite poem."

Figured. He was a good dad. And Lexi was a good kid. She should know—Maggie occasionally taught the girl in Sunday school. "You should have brought her."

"She was into pizza." David sniffed the air. "Is that rosemary potatoes?"

"And cheese biscuits," she said. "Come on back into the kitchen while I prepare the filet mignon."

"Filets? I must rate higher than I thought." He followed her through the dining area. "We're eating here?"

"I thought it'd be nice." When they ate at her place, which was rare, they always dined in the breakfast nook off the kitchen. She walked around the island and turned on the eye under the grill skillet. "Dinner should be ready in a few minutes. Would you like something to drink while you wait?"

"Tea would be great, but I'll fix it."

A few minutes later, she slid the sizzling steaks into the hot oven. Sensing David's gaze, she looked up. He was leaning against the island, studying her. Heat spread through her chest and into her cheeks. "What?"

Grabbing a paper towel, he pushed off from the island. "You have flour on your cheek," he said and dabbed her face.

Flour from the biscuits. And here she thought he was admiring her.

An hour later, he sighed and pushed away from the table. "You could open a restaurant, you know."

"I'm glad you enjoyed it," she said. David was in a strange mood tonight, and it was good to know it had nothing to do with her cooking. "Do you want to watch TV?" she asked, nodding toward the sofa.

He shook his head, his gaze intense again. "Is it too cold to go out on the balcony?"

"Not if I put on a wrap."

She slipped into a woolen cable-knit sweater and slid open the door. The night air was crisp with a faint aroma of barbecue from a nearby restaurant. Her condo was high enough that they were above the streetlights, giving a beautiful view of the quarter moon and stars twinkling against an inky-black sky. To her right, the lights on the double-arched Memphis-Arkansas Bridge reflected on the glassy waters of the Mississippi.

"It's a beautiful view." David's voice was husky as he slipped his arm around her waist.

"Definitely." She leaned into him, and he turned her to face him, his eyes glinting in the light. "The river is always—"

"I'm talking about you," he said softly and stroked the side of her face with his thumb.

The clean, cottony scent of his aftershave wrapped around her, increasing the longing in her heart. He lowered his head and captured her lips with his own, his arms bringing her close. When he released her, she sighed and laid her head against his chest. His galloping heartbeat matched her own.

"I've wanted to do that ever since I got here," he said.

Maggie smiled even though he couldn't see her lips. Then she lifted her head and looked up into his eyes. "What's put you in this mood?" she asked. "Is anything wrong?"

He shook his head. "I hope not." Then he took a deep breath. "What do you think about getting married?"

Her legs turned to jelly. "What?"

Of all the questions he could have asked her, she did not expect this one, at least not like *this*. She moved out of his embrace and gripped the balcony rail.

He joined her. "Are you that surprised?"

"Y-yes."

"I thought you felt the same way I do."

He hadn't mentioned the L-word. "Exactly how *do* you feel?"

David stared at her a long moment. "I messed this up, didn't I?"

She released the breath caught in her chest. "Depends. That wasn't a proposal, was it?"

"No!" He rubbed his forehead. "I mean, sort of."

Now she was confused.

"Maggie, I'm in love with you . . . I thought you knew that."

"It helps to be told sometimes." A sudden gust of wind off the Mississippi made her shiver.

His mouth twitched. "You're right. But you're getting chilled. Why don't we go back inside and talk about this."

She followed him and warmed her hands by the fireplace as she tried to collect her thoughts. *He loves me.* And she wanted what her parents had—after almost fifty years of marriage the looks they exchanged when they thought no one was looking were pure love. Maggie could see it being that way with her and David . . . so why did she only see obstacles?

He took her hands. "Your fingers are cold," he said, rubbing them. "Sorry I didn't make myself clear. I guess I was asking if marriage was even on your radar screen. I mean, we've never really talked about the future."

"No, we haven't. Until tonight, I didn't really know how you felt."

"Aw, come on, Maggie. You had to know I love you."

She supposed she did, and maybe she was being silly about him saying the actual words. "Do you think it would work with me being a criminal defense attorney and you a detective?"

Her sudden switch made him frown. "Why wouldn't it? It has so far."

"But . . . what if you were the investigating officer and I represented the person you were investigating?" she persisted.

"I work cold cases, so the likelihood of that happening is remote, but even if it does, we'll work around it."

She stared at her hands that he still held. All sorts of "buts" flooded her mind. He released her fingers and lifted her chin until she was staring into his blue eyes. Eyes tender and filled with longing.

Her heart throbbed in her throat until she wanted to melt into his arms. David traced his thumb along her jaw and then brushed it against her bottom lip, outlining its shape.

She slipped her arms around his neck, his aftershave once again working its magic on her. The fire in her bones flamed when he pressed his lips against her forehead, then her closed eyes, until finally he lowered his mouth against hers, claiming it.

When he released her, his gaze held hers. "The question is, do you love me?"

If she had doubts before, they were gone now. "Yes," she whispered. "I love you."

"And I love you." Smiling, he wrapped his arms around her waist. "I'm glad that's settled. Does that mean you'll think about marrying me?"

"Definitely."

5

MONDAY AFTERNOON Carly slowed as she drove past the Memphis Brooks Museum of Art. Alexis's Facebook page indicated her soccer game was on the Greensward across from the Georgian marble building at Overton Park. She pulled around to the side and put the car in park. How many afternoons had she and her mother spent wandering those rooms filled with art? On the occasions Lia hadn't joined them, it'd been their time together, just her and her mom. Carly swallowed down the lump in her throat and blinked away the moisture that filled her eyes. There was hardly a day that went by that she didn't think of her. And of Lia.

She sat up straighter and squared her shoulders. Sixteen years since she'd been back in Memphis, and while Carly had thought there might be landmines, she hadn't counted on them being quite so painful.

The theme from *Star Wars* blasted from her phone, and Carly smiled. Jamie always seemed to know when to call. "Hello?"

"I checked the RLT Security app and saw you made it okay. But are you all right? I mean, it has to be hard going back to Memphis."

"Yeah. I'm glad you called. My thoughts were going down the wrong side of memory lane." Carly adjusted the barrette where she'd hidden the GPS tracker. Jamie was on the RLT Security account and had the app that could access her location at any time.

The tracker worked like the family locator apps, only it was much more accurate, and besides Jamie, she had a team of technicians tracking her every move. If she was ever kidnapped again, the kidnappers would not pay any attention to the barrette, unlike a cell phone that would be the first thing they would find and take.

"Always glad to be of help. But why are you parked at the art museum?"

"Because I'm going to watch my niece play soccer, and the soccer field is across from the museum."

"I thought you were going to Haven House."

"I am—at six."

"I'm still not sure trying to find this Austin King on your own is a good idea," Jamie said.

"I don't trust anyone else to do it," Carly said.

"Your sister's husband is a detective with the Memphis police department. Go to him."

"No! What if he killed Lia?"

"Come on, Carly."

"No one was ever caught for her murder, and the husband is *always* the prime suspect . . . unless he's a cop."

"I've seen all the research you've done on David Raines. There's nothing there that indicates he might be her killer. He can help you."

Another call beeped in and Carly checked the caller ID and frowned. "Can I get back to you? RLT Security is calling," she said and clicked off. "Hello."

"Ms. Smith, Jason Marshall here. I see you're in Memphis. Is that correct?"

"Yes." She caught her breath. "I forgot to let you know I was coming here, didn't I?"

"Yes, ma'am. So you're all right?"

"I'm fine. Just taking a few days' vacation, but thank you for checking." It was good to know they were keeping close tabs on her.

"Do you know your itinerary while you're in the city?"

Carly massaged her neck. She had no idea where her search would take her. "I should be in a twenty-mile radius of Memphis at all times," she said.

"I'll note that. The other reason I'm calling is our records indicate you haven't changed your password lately. I strongly suggest that you do that ASAP."

She'd meant to change it before she left Stillwater. "I'll do it right away."

"Good deal, Ms. Smith. And do you know how long you plan to be there so I can note that in our records as well?"

"Probably no longer than two weeks." She thanked him and disconnected. Sometimes her phobia about being kidnapped again was a pain, but if the worst happened, she was prepared. She dialed Jamie back. "They called to remind me to change my password," she said. "I'll do it when I get back to the hotel and let you know what it is."

"Do you think you'll ever feel safe enough to discontinue the service?" Jamie asked.

"Not in the foreseeable future." Jamie was as bad as Dr. Abernathy, always pushing her to get past her phobia.

"I do have you on Find My Friends," she said.

"And the last time you tried to trace me on it, you kept getting the location unavailable message," Carly retorted. If she trusted those family apps, she wouldn't have hired RLT Security to keep tabs on her.

"Maybe someday you'll feel safe again." Jamie was silent for a moment. "I've been thinking while I waited for you to call back. Do you think you should go to your niece's soccer game? What if your aunt and uncle show up? Or someone recognizes you?"

"Frank and Gigi aren't coming. Saw that on Facebook. And

Lia's husband has never seen me. The only ones I really have to worry about running into are Blade and Austin King, and Blade's probably still in Atlanta—Memphis would be a step down for him. Besides, if my own sister didn't know me six years ago, I don't think either of them will recognize me."

"Just be careful. And call me if you need anything."

"Thanks." Carly slipped her phone in her jeans pocket and climbed out of the car. A brisk October wind blew, bringing the musky odor of the lions from the nearby zoo. She zipped her jacket and felt inside her right calf-length boot and made sure the small dagger was secure. The GPS tracker wasn't her only security measure.

Satisfied, she checked her surroundings. A couple of joggers were on the trail to her right and a tourist bus was offloading its passengers at the art museum. She glanced toward the Greensward, where Facebook said the soccer game would be held. People were already gathering, but instead of going straight there, she meandered along the walking trail—at least she hoped it looked like meandering in case anyone followed her. Carly tried to shake off the fear dogging her.

She'd fought it the whole two weeks it took for the request for time off to go through. It shouldn't have taken her so long to get back to Memphis. Carly should have returned when she learned Lia had been killed. At the very least, she should have contacted David Raines or her aunt and uncle, but she couldn't. With her sister dead, Carly had spiraled into another depression and by the time she surfaced, six months had passed. And then another six months . . .

Questions niggled in the back of her mind, questions that had been there for years. What if David Raines *had* killed Lia? Or her sister had contacted some of the people Carly had mentioned? Like Jacqueline Donovan, or her sons, Logan and Jared. What if Lia had questioned the wrong person and paid with her life? The questions had overwhelmed Carly, so she'd done nothing until Jenna had come to Tabula Rasa.

Now she was looking for absolution. It didn't matter that looking for Austin King could be dangerous. Living with the truth that she had done nothing to stop him was worse. The very least Carly could do was warn other women about a man posing as a scout for a modeling agency. Surely someone would listen.

Maybe that someone would be Vanessa Driscoll. Carly looked forward to meeting the director of the safe house who had placed Jenna at Tabula Rasa. If Austin King was still operating in the area, Driscoll should have heard. But could Carly trust her? She'd wrestled with this question before she made the appointment. The woman helped victims of human trafficking. If she couldn't trust her, Carly might as well find a cave and hide in it.

A police cruiser rolled into view as she angled toward the Greensward. Her muscles tensed. The beat of her heart drummed in her ears and shallow breathing made her lightheaded as she slipped back sixteen years, running to a police car for help, only to be put in the back seat like a criminal and taken back to Blade. Had to do better than this. If she passed out from hyperventilating, she'd draw attention she didn't want.

Carly reminded herself to breathe like Dr. Abernathy had taught her. Inhale slowly. Release the fear. She repeated the process until her heart stopped racing and the cruiser passed, the officer not giving her so much as a glance.

She had no control over when the mini panic attacks happened, but her psychiatrist's technique always helped. Carly took another cleansing breath, then another, and resumed her trek toward the soccer field in a roundabout way, just in case someone was following her.

6

LIA MORGAN RAINES. The folder lay on David's desk, left there by
Brad Hollister after he cleaned out Alan Patton's desk and moved
all his unsolved cases to the Cold Case Unit. Alan had pretty well
given up on solving Lia's murder long before his own untimely
death two weeks ago from a heart attack.

David had a duplicate copy in the top drawer of his desk. Darts
of guilt stung his conscience. It'd been months since he'd revis-
ited Lia's case. He leaned forward in his chair and picked up the
folder to check for anything new Alan hadn't passed on to him.
He scanned through the information, recognizing most of it.

When he came to a photo of Lia's sister, who had gone missing sixteen years ago, he paused. Heather Morgan. Lia had met
with the alleged sister and hours later she was dead. His gut said
Heather was the key to whoever murdered Lia—if the woman
was still alive.

Every time he thought he'd put that day to rest, something happened, like getting this file, that brought it back fresh. If he could
rewind time, he would be more understanding when she called to
talk about the woman she'd met with. He would drop what he
was doing and insist that they meet so she could tell him what had
happened. He would find out what she'd learned that made her

excited and angry at the same time. He would know what was so important that she'd called Georgina to come and babysit Lexi.

But because he'd been in the middle of a homicide case and dog-tired, instead of being understanding when she promised to be home by eight and explain everything, he'd demanded, rather than asked, that she wait until the next day. Lia had blown up, and the bitter words they exchanged haunted him even now. The irony that he had accused her of being obsessed with her sister's case was not lost on him. It was the same thing the Wilsons had accused him of.

They were only partially right. In the beginning he'd spent every waking moment searching for her killer. But after a while, he'd come to realize unless something new appeared, the case would never be solved.

He studied the photo taken of Heather at seventeen. Heaven help him if in a few years Lexi started wearing black clothes and dyed her hair jet-black to match her fingernails. According to the Wilsons, Heather had been rebellious and determined to become a model. The report indicated she was five nine and super thin, making modeling a possibility. In addition to the height, she had the looks for it. Even with the garish hair and dark eye shadow, her unblemished skin and high cheekbones were not diminished. She had something else—the camera liked her. Or maybe it was the photographer. Lia had written where and when she'd taken the photo on the back, and even sixteen years ago, she'd been a talented photographer.

David placed the photo back in the file and wished he'd paid more attention to Heather's missing persons case back when she disappeared, but it had been assigned to someone else. Even so, it was the reason he'd met Lia. She was at the CJC so often that they kept bumping into each other. One day he'd asked her out for coffee, and they had clicked. He sighed. At least they'd had a few good years together.

If Lia had truly met with her sister that day, why hadn't Heather come forward after Lia was killed? If he could just find her, he might get answers. He picked up the sister's photo again. It'd been a couple of years since he'd sent the picture out to different law enforcement agencies around the area. Maybe it was time to do it again. Maybe turn it over to the forensic artist MPD had recently contracted with and get her to sketch how Heather would look after sixteen years.

He looked up the artist's number and dialed. When she agreed to create sketches aging the photo along with a few sketches with different hairstyles and color, he scanned it into his computer and emailed it to her. As soon as she returned it, he'd send it out. Then he picked up the file and Lia's photo that he'd provided for Patton six years ago. In the picture, her dark hair hung past her shoulders, framing a face that could have been on the cover of the magazines where her photos appeared.

It was the same photo that graced his desk now. Blue eyes that could freeze fire when something angered her or soften when she held Alexis. Full lips that . . . He closed the file and stuffed the folder back in his desk. How many cold cases had he solved or helped solve now? Ten? Fifteen? Yet this one had gone nowhere.

He turned at a knock at his door and said, "Come in."

Maggie came through the doorway with a smile on her face. Calmness filled him. She had that *something* that made everything better. Like Lia. That wasn't the only similarity between the two. Personality-wise, they were a lot alike—quick wit, generous, and a soft spot for children. They also shared a stubborn trait and would not give an inch when they were in the right, at least their perception of right.

"Ready to go to the soccer game?" Maggie asked.

"Just about." He tilted his head. "Are you sore from riding Saturday?"

He and Lexi had picked up Maggie and they'd forgone fishing

for a late breakfast, and then had driven down to the Wilsons' farm. David had been surprised at how good a horsewoman Maggie was. And a good shot. Frank had gotten out his rifles and they'd practiced target shooting. Even Lexi had shot Frank's new rifle, hitting the target every time.

"Not too much." She glanced at her watch. "The game starts in thirty minutes, and you said something about getting there early to talk to her coach . . ."

"Oh, that's right." He did want to talk to Logan Donovan about the upcoming tournament in Nashville. "Give me a minute to get the rest of these folders put away."

Maggie's eyebrows rose, clearly sending the message there wouldn't be enough time to discuss anything with the coach. Not only were he and Maggie usually on opposite sides of the courtroom, they were on opposite ends of the time spectrum. She always arrived early at appointments, and while he was rarely late, barely on time was more his speed. "I can talk to Logan after the game," he said.

"Good idea."

He placed the other files on his desk in a drawer and then tossed an empty coffee cup in the trash. He looked up and caught her smiling. "What?"

"I wish my desk looked like yours."

He stood and they walked out the door. "No you don't. You know exactly what's in each stack in your office, and if you organized it, you couldn't find anything."

"But they are organized."

He laughed. "Yeah, right."

She laughed with him. "I'm looking forward to watching Lexi play today."

It would be Maggie's first game to watch. "She's excited about you coming."

"How about Georgina and Frank?"

58

"They won't be there. Said they had other plans." He and the Wilsons didn't travel in the same circles and had little in common other than Lexi, so he rarely talked with them unless it pertained to his daughter. And they didn't know how serious he and Maggie were, something he would just as soon they not find out. He wasn't ready to answer their questions. So far they hadn't mentioned Lexi coming to live with them again, but he was certain they hadn't forgotten about it.

7

ONCE CARLY WAS CERTAIN no one was following her, she angled toward the field where portable bleachers had been set up. She was pretty sure Lexi's soccer game would be held at the same field she'd played on as a kid. A rush of euphoria added bounce to her step. She was alive and today she might actually get to see her eleven-year-old niece. Carly had fallen into the habit of thinking of her as Lexi rather than Alexis.

Someone needed to warn Gigi about posting photos and information about Lexi on Facebook and Pinterest. Carly had found out about the soccer game when her aunt posted Lexi's photo in her soccer uniform along with the team's schedule for all the world to see. Either she didn't realize her photos were public or she was very naive. But then not everyone viewed the world as a dark place the way Carly did.

When she reached the field, the game hadn't started. A couple of girls in blue-and-white uniforms practiced their kicks on the field along with a man she supposed was their coach. Something about him struck her as familiar, and then Carly caught her breath as she looked closer at one of the girls and recognized Lexi from the photo on Gigi's Facebook page. Once again she was struck by how much she looked like Lia at that age.

Carly scanned for her aunt and uncle to make sure they hadn't changed their minds and decided to show up. She didn't see them and ambled over to the two sets of bleachers. She chose to sit in the nearest one on the second row close to the end just in case she needed to leave in a hurry. As other people arrived, she searched for someone who might be Lexi's father. There'd been no comments from him on the Facebook page indicating he was coming to the game, but surely he was. She'd also searched but hadn't found him on Facebook, and he wasn't in any of Georgina's photos.

Suddenly, Lexi ran toward a man and a woman, and for a second, Carly's heart dropped to her stomach when she thought it might be Gigi and Frank. A closer look revealed it wasn't them. The way the girl wrapped her arms around the man, it must be her father— Carly just hadn't expected him to be with anyone. David Raines appeared to be in his midforties and stood a head taller than the woman, who was not petite herself. With his rugged features and dark hair, she understood why he'd attracted her sister. Carly liked the quick smile that he bestowed on his daughter.

She studied the woman. About his age, straight honey-blonde hair. She hadn't found anything on the internet that indicated David had remarried, but from the way he rested his hand on the small of her back and she leaned into him, it was obvious the two were a couple. A feeling akin to yearning blindsided Carly. No man had ever looked at her with the tenderness David was now giving the woman. And never would.

She snapped her attention away from them as the coach approached the couple, but she couldn't get a good look at him. The woman said something to Lexi's father and then walked to the bleachers and settled on the row a few feet from her.

"Hi," she said. "Do you have a child playing today?"

Uh-oh. A talker. She hadn't expected anyone to ask why she was there and hadn't thought about what she'd say. "I, ah . . . no, I don't have anyone playing. I was walking in the park and stopped here to rest and saw they were having a game. I decided to watch a minute." *Stop talking so much.*

"I never played soccer. I wasn't very coordinated when I was a kid." The woman scooted closer and held out her hand. "I'm Madeline Starr."

"Carly Smith," she replied. The woman's grip was firm, and the warm smile that radiated from her face put Carly at ease. "You looked graceful enough when you walked to the bleachers."

The woman laughed. "That was the result of my mother making me walk around the house with a book on my head. Believe me when I tell you no coach would have wanted me on his team."

Surprisingly, Carly found herself drawn to the likeable Madeline Starr. Quick connections never happened with her. "So one of the players must be yours?"

Madeline shook her head and pointed to the man. "My friend's daughter is playing. She's the one with the brown braids. Lexi Raines."

Carly tried not to hold her breath. She'd been correct—the man was David Raines, Lia's husband.

"Lexi loves to play soccer."

"I was watching her. She's pretty good."

Pride showed on Madeline's face as she looked toward the field. "She has natural ability. I didn't know her mother, but her father is pretty athletic."

"The mother isn't around?" It was a question Carly felt she would be expected to ask.

"I'm afraid she died several years ago. But David has done a great job with her." Madeline tilted her head. "You're not from around here, are you?"

"No. I'm from up around Nashville. But how did you know?"

"You don't have the Southern drawl for Memphis . . . or for Nashville, either."

"I've spent a lot of time traveling the country."

"Army brat?"

"No." Why was the woman so interested in her? Could she be a cop?

"What brings you to Memphis?"

Evidently her short answers weren't going to deter David's friend. The flash of discomfort Carly felt must have shown on her face, because suddenly Madeline's face turned red.

"I'm sorry. It must sound like I'm interrogating you," she said.

"I *was* beginning to feel I was on the witness stand."

Madeline gave a soft groan. "I'm doing it again. But I'm an attorney, and asking questions is second nature to me."

An attorney? She wasn't a cop, and Carly relaxed a little. "That's okay. I'm a counselor and have taken a couple of weeks to visit rehabs in the area."

She didn't understand this rapport she had with the attorney. She didn't make friends easily, and even with her friend Jamie, it'd taken a couple of months before Carly had let her guard down.

Madeline had turned to watch Lexi on the field and Carly followed suit, glancing toward the field in time to see three people join David Raines. She almost quit breathing. Gigi and Frank? And not just her aunt and uncle, but Jacqueline Donovan as well.

Coming to her niece's soccer game had been a mistake. She'd only meant to slip in and get a look at Lexi and then be on her way. Gigi and Frank weren't supposed to be here. And who would have thought that Jacqueline Donovan of all people would be at a soccer game?

What if by some fluke one of them recognized her? She had to leave. Now. David had ended his conversation and the group was walking toward the bleachers. Carly stood. "I-I actually need to be going—I have an appointment with the director of Haven House at six, and I need to swing by my hotel room."

Madeline's eyes widened. "You know Vanessa? I'm a founding board member of Haven House."

"Really?" Carly hadn't meant to blurt out she was meeting with Vanessa Driscoll. Nothing was working out like she planned.

"Yes," Madeline said. "I have to pick up some papers later tonight. But you'll probably be gone by the time I get there."

If the attorney was on the board . . . "Have you ever heard the name Austin King mentioned?"

Madeline tilted her head in thought, and then she shook her head. "No, that name isn't familiar."

It'd been worth a try. The group on the field stopped and talked with another couple, buying her a few seconds. Madeline was an attorney and a board member of Haven House, and Carly needed someone she could trust. "Do you have a card? I'd like to talk with you again."

"Sure."

She accepted the card just as David left the other three and climbed the bleachers, his questioning gaze pinned on her. Her heart thumped wildly. Her brother-in-law would pick up on any sign of nervousness, and she pictured swans on a lake to calm herself.

Madeline turned to him. "Did Logan agree that he needed at least four chaperones for the tournament?"

"Not at first." He shot another questioning glance toward Carly.

She fought the impulse to bolt and instead held out her hand. "I'm Carly Smith. From what little I saw, your daughter has talent."

"David Raines," he said, shaking her hand. Then he glanced toward the field. "I think so."

"Hate to run off," she said, checking her watch. "But I have to be somewhere. Good to meet you both." She glanced down at Madeline's card in her hand. "I'll call you."

"Tell my secretary we met at the soccer field and I gave you my number."

"I will." She turned to leave and looked right into Frank's eyes. She thought he was still with Gigi, but no, he stood not ten feet from her while Gigi and Jacqueline stopped to speak to someone. *Stay calm.*

She swallowed down her panic and nodded, first at Frank then at the other two before stepping off the bleacher. Once on the sidelines, she glanced back. Frank was talking to David, but now Jacqueline stared at her, a frown on her face. Then Carly crashed into something solid and stumbled. Strong hands caught her.

"I've got you," he said.

"I'm sorry. I didn't see—" She looked up, and his amber eyes held her captive. Logan Donovan? He was the Logan that Madeline had mentioned? Lexi's coach? Jacqueline Donovan's son? Heat flushed her face. This day had just gone from bad to worse.

Logan's eyes widened. "Do I know you?"

Carly stepped back, breaking contact. She glanced over her shoulder to see if anyone had followed her. His mother stood on the sidelines, her gaze still riveted on Carly.

"Are you okay?"

She forced her attention back to Logan. "Yes, I'm fine."

He held her gaze, and her heart stuttered. Invisible cords clamped around her chest and squeezed. *Act natural.* "Thank you for stopping my fall."

"My pleasure." He frowned, still studying her face. "Are you sure—"

She tried to brush past him. "Excuse me, but I have an appointment."

"Wait. You seem discombobulated."

The use of a word she hadn't heard since she left Memphis halted her. "I am not addled, but thank you for your concern."

"Are you sure?"

The twinkle in Logan's brown eyes sent shivers through her body, just like years ago. But not because she was attracted to him. Her years with Blade had left her with nothing but shame and numbness. "I said I'm fine. And I need to be going."

"I can't let you leave without getting your phone number. Just to check on you later."

Same old Logan. The grin on his lips said he was flirting, but the question in his eyes bothered her. "You don't need my number."

She sidestepped him and hurried across the Greensward to her car.

"I saw you talking to Madeline Starr," he called after her. "Maybe she'll know how to get in touch with you."

Thank goodness she hadn't given Madeline her number.

8

MAGGIE'S GAZE FOLLOWED CARLY, and she winced as Carly slammed into Logan Donovan. The coach was quick, steadying her when she stumbled.

"Do you know her?" David asked.

"I didn't until ten minutes ago," Maggie said and nodded at Frank Wilson as he sat down on the row below them.

David scratched his jaw with his thumb. "She looks familiar . . . but I can't remember anyone by the name Carly Smith."

"I agree with you, David," Frank said as his wife joined him on the bleachers. "She looks like someone I've seen before."

"I noticed her when we first arrived," Georgina said. "She's very striking. Did she say where she's from?"

The woman would keep prying if she didn't give her some sort of answer. "Somewhere around Nashville."

Then Maggie turned to David and lowered her voice. "I'll probably see her again. She has a meeting with Vanessa Driscoll at the safe house at six, and she may still be there when I drop by to pick up some papers. I'll ask if there's any reason she should look familiar to you."

"Good. There's something about her that makes me think I should know her. Does she have family in Memphis?"

"She didn't say. Although she did ask if I'd heard of someone named Austin King."

"Madeline," Georgina said, raising her voice.

Maggie looked around and found Georgina staring at her, a slight frown creasing her brow. "Yes?"

"I didn't realize you would be here."

Maggie was skilled at reading body language, but even a novice could tell by the woman's pinched face she wasn't pleased that Maggie was at the game. Evidently David hadn't told Lexi's surrogate grandparents much about their relationship. Not that she could exactly blame him. The Wilsons owned a farm not far from where Maggie grew up in Senatobia, Mississippi, and she'd heard her mother talk about how prickly Georgina could be.

Maggie learned it firsthand when she served on a couple of committees with Georgina, and when things were going her way, she was apple pie and sweetness. When things didn't go to suit her, she was blunt to the point of rudeness, which could be very annoying.

"So did Alexis invite you? It's very commendable that you would take your valuable time to attend a child's soccer game."

"*I* invited her," David said.

The lines around Georgina's lips deepened. "I see. Well, unless you two plan on getting married, I suggest you not let Alexis know you're dating. The girl wants a mother, and it wouldn't be fair to get her hopes up."

Heat flashed up her face, burning Maggie's ears. A retort formed on her tongue, but before she could get a word out, David blew out an exasperated sigh.

"Georgina, mind your own business." He took Maggie's hand. "Lexi is my daughter, and I'll be the one who decides what to tell her and when."

The warmth of his fingers shot straight to her heart, but even more so his words were like armor, protecting her from Georgina's disapproval.

"And," he said, "she'll be returning to her regular school for the second semester in January."

"You mean you would actually rob her of the opportunity to attend the Academy?"

Oh, boy. Maggie sensed they were on the brink of all-out war. "Oh, look, the game's started," she said, pointing toward the field. "And Lexi has possession of the ball."

The tension dissipated as Georgina turned and yelled, "Go, Alexis!"

David squeezed her hand, and she gave him a quick smile before turning her attention to the game. She noticed Jacqueline had opted to cheer from the sidelines, encouraging her granddaughter when she made a good play. Georgina and Jacqueline were both independent and opinionated, but of the two, Jacqueline was easier to get along with.

The game moved quickly, and an hour and a half later, they were on the field congratulating the team for playing with great sportsmanship.

"Only two goals, Alexis," Georgina said. "What happened? I've seen you play better than that."

"You did great, honey!" David hugged her small shoulders.

Maggie noticed he looked over her head and gave Georgina a silencing glare. "You handled the ball like a pro," Maggie added.

"She sure did," Logan said as he and Jacqueline joined them. "Lexi is my star player, but I think all the girls were awesome against this team."

"Why in the world did you allow them to play older and more experienced girls?" Georgina demanded.

"For practice," Jacqueline snapped as her granddaughter joined her. She smoothed the girl's hair. "I've been reading up on the teams they'll play next weekend, and our girls needed to know the kind of competition they're facing."

Lexi didn't seem to notice the tension and beamed at Maggie.

"Thanks for coming. Will you come to Nashville and watch me play?"

"I'll try," she replied. "But it'll depend on whether I can change my schedule."

Logan turned to Maggie. "The woman you were talking to earlier. Do you know her name?"

"She didn't tell you?" Maggie had seen them talking, and if Carly hadn't shared her name, Maggie wasn't sure she should. She wasn't in the habit of freely sharing information, anyway. Not even with a Memphis homicide detective and someone she'd known and trusted half her life.

"She said her name was Carly Smith," David said, answering for her. "And she's looking for someone named Austin King."

"Never heard of him, but something about her reminded me of someone." Logan shook his head. "Can't quite place who."

"You too?" Frank said.

"Yeah, but I could be wrong. She didn't sound like she was from around here." Logan shifted his attention to Maggie. "Do you know where she lives? Or her phone number?"

"Why are you interested?" David asked.

The coach grinned and lifted his shoulder in a half shrug. "A knockout like that? You have to ask?"

David laughed and tilted his head toward Maggie. "Did she say?"

She didn't like being put on the spot, but Carly wasn't her client. Besides, she didn't know exactly where the woman lived. "Somewhere around Nashville, and no, I don't have her phone number."

"She was quite the looker," Frank said. "And if you really want to see her again, Logan, I heard Madeline say she'd be at Haven House over on Walnut Grove at six."

Frank must have been straining hard to overhear her conversation with David. If Logan showed up while Carly was at the safe house, she would assume the information came from Maggie. She'd make a point of getting there before Carly left and let her know about Logan's interest in her and that Maggie hadn't broadcasted her plans. "Your niece did great, Logan," she said, shifting the conversation. "And I know you're proud of your granddaughter, Jacqueline."

"I think between her and Lexi, we'll take our division next week," the proud grandmother said.

"Yeah." Logan nodded. "We have a great team. It's fun to coach them, and speaking of that, we have a few things to work on before we go to the tournament. Practice will be at this field tomorrow at four thirty."

"I say we get something to eat," Frank said. "My treat."

"Mrs. Baxter is making pizza, and the rest of the girls are coming," David said. "You're welcome to join us."

Georgina touched her stomach. "I think not. I've been having heartburn and pizza is a no-no. Next time tell Mrs. Baxter we'll be taking Lexi and the team out to eat after the game."

David nodded, then turned to Lexi. "Why don't you round everyone up? Jacqueline, you and Logan are welcome to come as well."

"Unfortunately the employee who usually stays until nine to close the store needs to leave early," Jacqueline said. "So I need to get back."

"And I'm pulling the night shift this week, but thanks."

Maggie hoped Logan's "work" didn't involve stopping by the safe house.

"You ready?" David asked.

She checked her watch. "I can come for a short while."

David's place wasn't too far from Haven House, so it wouldn't take long to make the drive. She walked to her car and was surprised when Jacqueline joined her.

"I think I'm parked behind you," Jacqueline said as they walked across the field to their vehicles. "You and David seem close."

Maggie nodded without replying, and the older woman sighed.

"I'd hoped you and Jared might . . ."

Oh, boy. Jared was the older of the Donovan boys, and Maggie didn't want to touch that subject. How did you tell a mother you weren't interested in her son? Her very successful son. "Jared will find someone better suited for him," she said as they reached their cars.

"Hmm." Then Jacqueline smiled. "Just don't let Lexi's aunt mess things up for you. Georgina means well, but she can come on strong."

Maggie swallowed a smile. Georgina and Jacqueline's personalities meshed like two pieces of industrial-strength sandpaper. She said her goodbyes and climbed into her car and drove to David's East Memphis home. If he asked her to marry him, she wondered how Georgina would take it.

9

CARLY CLOSED THE HOTEL DOOR behind her and leaned against it, her heart hammering against her ribs. Normal coping techniques were not working, and she crossed the room to her suitcase.

If she had it to do over, she would not have gone to the soccer field. But Gigi and Frank weren't supposed to be there, and who would have dreamed Logan Donovan would be Lexi's coach or that his mother would be there? She was pretty sure no one knew her, although there had been a flicker of recognition in Logan's eyes. The Logan she remembered was a detail person—he wouldn't be satisfied until he figured out how he knew her.

She found the bottle of medicine her psychiatrist prescribed for her when biofeedback failed and took the bottle to the bathroom, where she quickly downed half a tablet. Hopefully, the pill and a relaxing shower would be enough.

After Carly showered and changed clothes, she thought about ordering in a sandwich, but her stomach rebelled at the thought of food. Instead, she booted up her computer and changed the password on her RLT Security account and then called Jamie with the update. Jamie was the only person she trusted to keep track of her other than RLT Security. She stared at the mixture of letters and numbers. Good thing she didn't have to remember it.

After she hung her remaining clothes in the closet, Carly picked up the fully charged GPS tracker and snapped it into the one-inch holder built into the barrette. Then she pulled a section of hair away from her face and secured it with the barrette. She was all set.

In the hallway, Carly checked to make sure the door was locked, then hurried to the elevator, her thoughts on the disastrous visit to the soccer field. Had she done anything that might give her away to the people she'd seen today? A mannerism, maybe? Or the starburst in her eyes? She almost returned to her room to put in blue contact lenses, but she didn't have time. It was nearly five thirty now, and the drive to Haven House would take at least half an hour. The elevator doors lumbered open, and she joined two other women for the ride to the lobby. No one spoke beyond a nod as Kenny G played from the speakers.

A traffic pileup caused Carly to be half an hour late when she pulled into Haven House and found a parking space. The glow from the setting sun cast a dusky light over the area. The gloaming, her dad always called it. It wouldn't be long until it would be pitch dark at this time, and she dreaded it. She hated the long, dark nights. But Blade had loved them since he made more money. Carly pushed the past away—hating how it always intruded into her thoughts.

After she climbed out of her car, she made the usual scan of her surroundings. Trees lined either side of the property, their branches still covered with yellow and red leaves. Several cars were parked in the lot. Employees, probably. She walked the hundred feet or so to the steps, where an imposing man guarded the entrance. "Leon" was stitched above his left pocket.

"I have an appointment with Vanessa Driscoll," Carly said.

"Your name, please."

"Carly Smith."

"Yep, I see you on the list." His kind smile warmed her. "Ms.

Driscoll isn't here yet, but Bethany will make you comfortable—she's at the desk."

The door scraped the floor as he opened it for her, sending a shiver down Carly's back.

"Need to get that fixed," Leon said, wincing.

Inside the building, four brightly painted hallways converged at a circular desk, probably a busy area in the daytime, but right now only one person sat there. Bethany, who appeared to be in her midthirties. Carly approached and repeated that she had an appointment.

"I'm afraid Vanessa is running late," the woman said with an apology in her voice as she came around the desk. "Would you like to wait in our activity room? There's a TV in there."

"Sure." Carly followed her to a room off to the right. Muted sounds came from somewhere in the back of the building. Probably where the residents were. "How many girls do you have here?"

"Several. I'm sure Vanessa will fill you in on our operation when she arrives."

In other words, don't ask Bethany. The director had trained her staff well. Bethany halted abruptly, and Carly barely kept from bumping into her.

"Dr. Adams. I didn't know you were still here."

A man looked up from his laptop. "Finishing up paperwork and trying to hang around until Vanessa returns," he said. "I wanted to see her before I left for my hunting trip."

"Good luck on that," Bethany said with a chuckle.

After the receptionist left, the doctor studied Carly over the top of his glasses. "Are you waiting for Vanessa too?"

She nodded. "I gather she's usually late."

He laughed. "You could say that."

"Bethany called you doctor. Are you part of the staff?"

"I volunteer. One of the girls has bronchitis and I was following up from my visit Friday." He removed his glasses and tucked them in a case before he closed out of whatever he was working on. Then he stood and said, "I don't think we've been properly introduced. I'm Henry Adams, semi-retired physician."

Carly guessed him to be midsixties and only slightly taller than she was. She shook the hand he held out. "Carly Smith."

He released her hand, settled in the chair again, and slid his laptop into a bag. She wandered around the room, admiring the pictures that looked as though amateurs had painted them. Perhaps even the women who came through the shelter.

Dr. Adams cleared his throat, and she turned to face him.

"If you're here to see Vanessa," he said, "you must be involved in the anti–human trafficking campaign."

"No." When he continued to wait expectantly, she said, "I'm a substance abuse counselor at Tabula Rasa in Stillwater, up around Nashville."

He nodded, apparently satisfied, and she relaxed her guard. Dr. Adams reminded her of the pediatrician who'd taken care of her as a child. The one who gave her lollipops when she didn't cry. She approached the chair across from him and sat down.

"Stillwater is a great fishing spot on the Tennessee River up there." The pale blue eyes in his round face twinkled. "One of the state's best-kept secrets."

The skin on the back of her neck prickled. He'd been to Stillwater? It wasn't a town you passed through to get somewhere else. You had to be *going* to Stillwater to get there. Carly fingered the gold bracelet around her wrist. "Do you drive there often?"

"It's been years, but the wife and I used to camp on Brandywine Creek."

She breathed a little easier and wished she wasn't so suspicious of every man she met. But old habits were hard to break.

"Are you here about the counselor position? We desperately need someone. So many of the girls we get come here with substance abuse problems."

Carly hadn't been aware there was a position open. "No. I have a different matter to discuss with her." Why not show Dr. Adams the sketch? She hesitated. It wouldn't be necessary to disclose her story . . . but what if he pried? But what if he could give her a lead? He probably had a wide range of acquaintances. Carly pulled a sheet of paper from her bag. "I'm here because I'm looking for this man."

She handed him the paper then watched for his reaction as he studied the drawing.

He raised his gaze from the paper. "Why are you looking for him?"

Exposing her past was tantamount to climbing the Himalayas, and while she was prepared to disclose her story to Vanessa Driscoll, Dr. Adams was a different matter. "He's someone I knew once, and I'd like to reconnect. Do you know him?"

He shook his head. "It's hard to say from a sketch, but some of the man's features trigger a sense of familiarity. Does he live in Memphis?"

"I'm not sure. Memphis is where I met him."

"And is he the reason you're here in Memphis?" he asked before he glanced at the sketch again. "Does he have anything to do with human trafficking?"

Carly swallowed the panic that rose in her throat. Dr. Adams was either very perceptive or . . . She brushed her paranoia away. The doctor appeared to be a good man who wanted to help abused women . . . and he *was* here at a safe house full of trafficked women. "Why do you ask?"

He shrugged. "Haven House is a home for women who have escaped the streets. You may not be part of the anti-trafficking campaign, but I believe you're not being quite truthful. Why else would you come to see Vanessa?"

She edged a step closer to the mountain. "I think he may pose as a modeling scout or agent."

"I see. We have a girl who came to us not long ago who described being sold into the trade by a modeling scout. Was it this man?"

She was certain he was talking about Jenna. "I don't know. It's what he did sixteen years ago. I thought I'd ask Ms. Driscoll to show this sketch to the girls here, see if any of them recognize him."

"Do you have a name for him?"

"Back then he went by Austin King." She faltered under the doctor's intense scrutiny.

"I hope you're not trying to track him down on your own."

"I have backup," she said. Jamie and RLT Security qualified as backup. "And when I know for certain he's still operating in this area, I'll involve the proper authorities." If she could find someone she trusted.

"Just be careful. The people involved in human trafficking are dangerous."

He didn't have to sell her on that.

Dr. Adams checked his watch and sighed. "I can't wait any longer." He stood and nodded to Carly. "It was nice meeting you, and do be careful with your search."

"Don't worry, I will."

David's house rocked as sixteen girls and a few of the parents crowded around the kitchen and overflowed into the den. While the sounds were happy ones, Maggie could barely hear herself think. It was after six when she caught David's attention and tapped her watch. "I have to go," she mouthed to him across the room.

He nodded and motioned toward the front door. "Meet me there," he mouthed back.

They met in the foyer. "Thanks for coming. I wish you didn't have to leave so soon," he said.

"I have a long day tomorrow, and I need to drop by Haven House on my way home to pick up papers Vanessa has for me."

"Can't it wait 'til tomorrow? That's not the safest area of town after dark."

She was well aware of the crime in the area around the shelter—it was one of the reasons they had an armed guard at the front door. "I need the papers first thing in the morning."

"I wish I could go with you, but . . ." He looked toward the den.

She laughed. "You have a lot of cleanup to do here. Besides, I'll be fine."

He took her hands. "It meant a lot to Lexi for you to be at the game."

"I enjoyed it." She tilted her head to the side. "What Georgina said—"

"Don't pay any attention to her. She can be a pain sometimes."

"She's right, though, about Lexi. Don't you think we should talk with her before we make a lot of plans?"

David gave her his slow grin. "I actually thought we might do that tomorrow night after soccer practice. We can pick up burgers and bring them here."

"Perfect." Her heart fluttered thinking about how Lexi might react. Maggie thought she would approve, but one never knew with children.

"You want to meet me here? Unless you want to watch soccer practice."

"I have court tomorrow afternoon, so don't count on me to be there for practice."

He nodded, and their gazes met, and her breath stilled in her chest as he dipped his head toward her.

"Dad! Where are the lemon cookies?" Lexi's voice yelled from the kitchen.

They both jumped, and she stepped away from him.

"I better get back to the kitchen," he said. "See you tomorrow.

And be careful when you leave the safe house—get the guard to walk you to your car."

A few minutes later, Maggie hummed as she pulled from the drive and turned her car toward the shelter on Walnut Grove. She couldn't shake the feeling her life was about to do a 180. The change would be a challenge, but one she looked forward to.

10

BLADE'S PHONE DINGED an incoming text from Grey. The message along with a photo elicited a frown.

> We have a problem. I believe Heather Morgan is back in town and she's going by the name Carly Smith.

He clamped down on his jaw, shooting pain all the way to his ear. He'd been looking for Heather, Jasmine to him, for eight years now. She was the reason he looked over his shoulder daily, checking with his contacts in law enforcement to see if his likeness was on their radar. He'd never figured out why Jasmine hadn't gone to the authorities with a description of him after she escaped. Had to be her way of punishing him, making him wonder if today was the day.

Blade studied the photo, taken some distance from the subject. It'd been eight years and memories tended to fade, but not his first glimpse of Heather Morgan's Goth-like image. Twiggy-thin with spikey hair, black lipstick, and over-made eyes. Of course she would have aged, but the woman in this photo looked nothing like the Jasmine he remembered. Even from a distance, the woman in the photo possessed a quiet beauty, almost elegant.

Blade picked up the phone and dialed. "This cannot be Heather Morgan," he said when Grey answered.

"Trust me, it's her. She's asking about Austin King. Meet you in an hour? Our usual place?"

Still studying the photo, Blade didn't answer. He didn't see the likeness between the photo and Heather, but it had to be her if she was asking about King. Heat sparked in his chest, and he gripped the phone, his fingers turning white. She'd made him look like a fool when she escaped. She would pay for that. And not just with her life. He wanted her to suffer.

"Well? Are you meeting me or not?"

"Yes. Give me thirty minutes, and I'll see you there."

After the phone call ended, Blade slid the phone back and forth in his hand. He had a shipment of girls going to Miami this week. Heather Morgan had a niece. What better way to exact his revenge than to add the girl to his shipment—Heather would know what was in store for the girl, but he would remind her before he snuffed her life out.

He made a quick call to a hacker friend. "I need a cell phone number. Name is Carly Smith and her service is probably out of Nashville."

"That all you got?"

"Afraid so. Can you do it? Or do I need to get someone else?"

"Nah. Might take half an hour, but you'll have the number. Cost you though."

Blade didn't care what it cost. He would have his revenge.

Traffic had thinned as Maggie drove farther east, allowing her thoughts to wander, and they turned to the shelter. She was a board member of Haven House as well as their attorney, and the documents waiting for her had to do with the board meeting tomorrow.

She checked the clock on the dash. Almost seven. Carly's meeting with Vanessa should be over. Or not. Vanessa was notorious for being late, always with good reason. At any rate, Carly Smith had captured her interest, and Maggie hoped she didn't miss her since she wanted to know more about the woman. Not to mention if Logan Donovan showed up, she didn't want her to think Maggie had told him where he could find her. Maybe she would catch Carly before she left.

When she turned into the shelter, Maggie scanned the dimly lit parking lot for Logan's BMW and was glad when she didn't see it. Wait . . . he'd said something about working tonight, but thankfully she didn't see his police vehicle, either. Logan as a police officer. She shook her head. He came from old money and privilege, and she'd been surprised when he joined the police academy. But according to David, he made a good officer.

Maggie parked as close to an overhead light as she could. They really needed more lighting around the building. She would bring it up tomorrow at the board meeting. A security guard stood sentry at the front entrance of the converted church building. At six four and well over three hundred pounds, he provided their first line of defense. "Evening, Leon," she said, nodding. "Is Vanessa here?"

"No, ma'am, not yet."

They both turned toward the door as it scraped open and Dr. Adams came out. Someone needed to realign the door before it wore grooves in the floor.

"Good evening, Madeline, Leon," he said.

"Is someone ill?" Maggie asked.

The rotund doctor pocketed his phone and shifted the bag he carried to his other hand. "One of the girls has bronchitis, and I wanted to check on her before I left town. I had planned to see Vanessa as well, but of course she's not here." He gave Maggie a wry grin.

Typical Vanessa. "Do like I do—call before you come," Maggie said as she removed her volunteer badge from her purse.

"I did get to meet the lovely woman who is also awaiting our director's arrival—Carly Smith. Do you happen to know her?"

So, she was still here. "No, although we did meet earlier today at a soccer game."

"Really? That's a rather strange coincidence since she's not from here."

Maggie had thought so too. "It almost felt like she was reconnecting with her roots," she said.

"You think she lived here at one time?"

"Possibly."

He tipped his head. "Well, you have a good evening, my dear."

"You too." Maggie caught the door before it closed and entered the building. In the lobby, one woman manned the desk, someone she didn't recognize. She introduced herself and learned the volunteer's name was Bethany. "Do you know when Vanessa will arrive?"

"No," she said. "But there's someone waiting to see her in the front room, so it should be soon."

When Maggie walked into the room, Carly stood at the window, looking out. "I'm glad you're still here," she said.

Carly startled at her voice and turned around. "Yes. I'm waiting for Vanessa."

"Oh, before I forget—I saw you and Logan Donovan talking, and you caught his attention. If he shows up here tonight, I want you to know I didn't tell him you'd be here."

Maggie hadn't known what she expected her news would bring, but she hadn't expected Carly to faint.

11

SOMETHING COLD AND HARD pressed on Carly's back. A woman's voice broke through the darkness that filled her mind.

"Are you all right?"

She blinked her eyes open. The blurry image of Madeline Starr came into focus. Carly blinked again and her vision cleared enough to see another woman hovering behind the attorney. The receptionist. Apparently Carly had fainted and caused quite a stir. It explained why she was on the floor. She struggled to sit up. "What happened?"

"Here, drink this, and we'll talk about it later." Madeline took a cup from the receptionist and handed it to Carly.

The cold water felt good going down her dry throat. When she drained the last drop, she handed the cup back and held out her hand. "If you could help me up."

Once she was on her feet, Madeline guided her to a chair against the wall. "Sit here until you get your bearings."

Suddenly the attorney's words came rushing back. *Logan Donovan.* He knew she was at Haven House. Sweat broke out on her face. What if he'd figured out who she was? What if he had been working with Austin King? She had to leave. And not just Haven House but Memphis. She jumped up. Bad choice.

"Oh!" Carly pressed her hand to her head and plopped back in the chair.

"Take it easy," Madeline said. "And breathe deeply."

Slowly everything stopped spinning. "You don't understand. I have to leave."

"But you haven't seen Vanessa yet."

"Excuse me," the receptionist said, "but that's why I came in here. Vanessa encountered an emergency and will be delayed at least another half an hour. She said if you wanted to reschedule, she could see you in the morning at nine."

Thirty minutes? Carly rubbed the bridge of her nose. What if Logan showed up while she waited? Reason wormed its way into her thoughts. She was allowing fear to dictate what she did. *Think rationally.* If Logan had recognized her, he would have already been here.

Just go back home to Stillwater. Let this go. Focus on taking care of the girls in the group. What could she do anyway? She was one person against no telling how many, and everything about this trip had gone wrong. Maybe God was trying to tell her something.

"If someone had just told me . . ."

Jenna's words echoed through her heart. If Carly went home, fear would win. Austin King or his clone would win. He was still operating in Memphis—Jenna's capture mirrored Carly's too closely. She couldn't return to Tabula Rasa without at least trying. She straightened her shoulders. "Do you think Ms. Driscoll will actually be here in thirty minutes?"

"We can only hope. Is there anything I can do to help?" Madeline asked then tilted her head. "You look like you could use some fortifying. Have you eaten today?"

When had she last eaten? The sandwich she'd picked up at a truck stop around noon was long gone, and her empty stomach was probably why she'd fainted. "It's been a while."

Madeline turned to the receptionist. "Is there anything left from supper?"

"The girls made pizza earlier. There might be some of that and salad left over."

The thought of a greasy pizza turned Carly's stomach. "Thanks, but I think I'll pass."

"Come on back to the kitchen," Madeline said. "There should be eggs in the fridge. I'll make you an omelet."

"You don't have to do that."

"But I do. You're too shaky. If you leave now, you might pass out and have a wreck."

"I'm sure you're busy. I'll be all right—I can grab something to eat at my hotel."

"I have the time, and if you want to see Vanessa, tonight is much better than tomorrow. We have a board meeting at eleven thirty and she'll be distracted."

Thirty minutes wasn't that long, *if* Vanessa actually showed up. A hunger pang stabbed her stomach. An omelet sounded pretty good. "Okay, if you don't mind, I think I'll take you up on it."

She followed Madeline down the hall. When she'd first arrived, she noted the shelter had once been a church. Looking around, she decided the kitchen area had probably been the fellowship hall. It was much smaller than the one at Tabula Rasa, but then Haven House was much smaller than the center where Carly worked.

"Did you have any trouble finding the shelter?" Madeline asked.

"No. I lived in Memphis a long time ago," Carly said as Madeline took eggs from the refrigerator and cracked them over a bowl. "How many girls do you have here?"

"Last time I checked, we had twenty-three, but that number changes weekly." She whisked milk into the eggs. "Sorry I don't have any ham or peppers, but I did find cheese."

"Oh, cheese is fine."

Madeline continued to chat as she made the omelet. "Too bad

you had to leave the soccer game. Lexi's team played a good game, although they lost."

Would it be normal to remember the child's name? Especially when she hadn't even met her? Or was the attorney testing her? "Lexi?"

"You met her father, David."

"Oh yeah. The name slipped my mind." She was so tired of dodging questions. And she would love to warn Madeline about the dangers of Gigi posting her great-niece's information on Facebook. *Tell her.* Carly studied the geometric pattern in the floor. Madeline was an attorney, and she was on the Haven House board. Surely she was trustworthy, and she might have information on who was behind the human trafficking in Memphis. But the words stuck in her throat and the moment passed. A few minutes later Madeline set a delicious-looking omelet in front of Carly. Her mouth watered as she stared at it.

"It's not fancy," Madeline said, "but it will tide you over. Would you like a cup of coffee?"

"Yes, and thank you for making this. My mom used to make omelets." She took a bite. Velveeta. Exactly what her mom always used. She ate slowly, savoring the taste.

"This is so good," she said and took another bite. "You're not going to make yourself one?"

"I had pizza before I came here." Madeline placed a cup under the pod coffee maker. The machine churned through its cycle, and she handed Carly a steaming cup. "Sugar or cream?"

"Black is fine."

Madeline popped another pod in the machine.

"So you work in a recovery cen—"

"Madeline—"

They'd both spoken at the same time.

"Sorry," the attorney said. "And why don't you call me Maggie? Outside of business, that's how almost everyone knows me."

"Maggie? Not Maddie?" she said, jumping on the diversion. Maybe they could just stay on superficial subjects.

"Yeah. Don't tell David, but my grandfather wanted my folks to name me Margaret. My mother preferred Madeline. Grandfather shortened it to Maggie and it stuck. So, essentially, he got his way."

"Maggie suits you better than Madeline," Carly said.

"Except in the courtroom," Maggie said.

"Why not tell David?"

"Oh, when we first met I wouldn't tell him, so it became sort of a game," she said, grinning.

"I see," Carly said, remembering the way David had looked at Maggie. She ate the last bite of omelet and looked up. "What made you become a lawyer?"

She told herself she wasn't evading the subject, just getting to know Maggie better. When a pained expression crossed the attorney's face, Carly almost wished she hadn't asked. "If you don't want to talk about it, it's okay. I'll withdraw the question."

Maggie chuckled, and that was the response she'd been going for.

"What kind of lawyer are you?"

"Criminal defense."

Carly blinked. Never in a hundred years would she have guessed that.

"The look on your face is the response I usually get when I tell people that."

"Someone close to you must have been wrongly accused."

Maggie gaped at her. "I thought I was good at reading people. What made you say that?"

She didn't know. It was the thought that jumped into her head. Carly searched for an answer. "You don't seem to be the type to be in it for the money, so it had to be something personal."

"I'm glad you didn't think it was the money." Maggie arranged and then rearranged the silverware in front of her. "My brother was wrongly accused of a crime. He died before DNA proved his innocence." She rubbed a spot on the counter. "A lot of my work has been with death row inmates. I know all prisoners say they're innocent, but the two I've helped set free really were innocent."

Madeline Starr was on a crusade. She'd be a good person to have in her corner. And it didn't sound like she trusted policemen any more than Carly did. So it puzzled her that she'd be dating a police detective.

"What made you want to work in a recovery center?" Maggie asked.

"I want to help people. Drugs and alcohol are a major problem in our society."

"So you are a counselor?"

She nodded. "I'm working on my master's in addictions counseling."

"Why addictions?"

When most people asked that question, they were usually asking if she chose that field because she'd had a problem with drugs in the past. Carly rubbed her fingers over the gold chain on her wrist. The urge to tell her story to Maggie hit her again. Even though she barely knew the woman, during her years on the streets, she'd developed the ability to read people, and her intuition said Maggie was trustworthy. "I had a problem with drugs at one time."

"Then your girls will have a hard time conning you."

"Exactly."

Maggie sipped her coffee. "I know you want to see Vanessa, but is there anything I can help you with? I'm pretty hands-on with the activities at Haven House, in addition to handling the legal work."

"What do you mean, hands-on?"

"About once a week I'm out on a street corner with three other women, handing out cookies and coffee to the local 'girls.' We try to dialogue with the ones we encounter, offer them a better way of life."

Carly's breath stilled in her chest. Just like the women in Atlanta. It was the kicker she needed. "Are you familiar with a man who poses as a model scout or an agent?"

"Several of the girls have mentioned they fell for that scam."

"Did they mention the name he used?"

"I don't think it's the same man each time. From what I gather, it's a common ploy with these traffickers."

Carly opened her purse and took out her checkbook. "Earlier today I said I might be calling you. Would you be willing to take me on as a client?"

"You believe you need a criminal defense lawyer?"

"No, not a criminal defense lawyer." Although she might if she found Austin King. She really didn't need a lawyer at all, but once Maggie knew who Carly was, the attorney would want to tell David Raines. But if she hired her as her lawyer, Maggie would be honor bound to keep anything she told her private. "At least not yet. But I trust you and I have a problem I'd like to discuss with you." Her face grew warm under Maggie's scrutiny.

Maggie laid her arms on the counter and leaned forward. "I don't know if I can help you, but I'm intrigued to know why you need a lawyer. You can put your checkbook away until we decide if you need to retain me."

Carly hesitated. Even though she'd connected with Madeline Starr almost immediately at the soccer game, she wasn't sure if God was nudging her to share her story with the attorney . . . On the other hand, maybe that was why Vanessa had been delayed. Maybe Maggie was the one he'd brought her here to meet, not Vanessa.

She bought time by closing her checkbook and returning it to her purse before she took out a ten-dollar bill and slid it across the granite. "I want to make this legal, so would you accept this as a down payment on your services?"

Maggie picked up the money. "You're really serious about this."

"Yes." She didn't want anyone to know what she was about to

share and had only ever shared with Jamie and her psychiatrist. Carly wrapped her hands around the still-warm coffee mug. The light caught the locket with Lily's picture in it, reminding her of what she must do. She shifted her gaze to Maggie. "Will that be enough to keep whatever I say here in strict confidence?"

12

CARLY'S QUESTION about confidentiality gave Maggie pause. Usually when a client asked that question, it wasn't good, but she had a feeling if she didn't accept the money and agree to keep what they said private, the conversation would end. And she didn't want that.

Carly had piqued her interest, and besides, as an attorney, she routinely kept matters private. She couldn't imagine Carly having information that anyone outside of Haven House would be interested in.

"A dollar would have sufficed," she said. "And as a prospective client, you receive the same pledge of confidentiality a current client receives—unless you intend to commit a crime. Otherwise, whatever is said here stays here."

Apparently satisfied, Carly took a deep breath. "I'm looking for a man who poses as an agent or scout for a modeling agency. Sixteen years ago, he was very . . ." She appeared to struggle for the right word. "Average looking, but he had this air of confidence that instilled trust. Thinking back, that was the scariest part about him—his ability to make me think he was what he said he was. I'm sure he's had plenty of opportunities to perfect that talent over the past sixteen years."

"Sixteen years ago suggests a story," Maggie said.

"Yes," she replied. "I'll get to it shortly."

Carly took a sheet of paper from her purse and unfolded it, then laid it on the counter. "An artist friend took my description and created these drawings of what he *might* look like now."

Maggie picked up the paper. Four different images reflected a man in his fifties, and she understood what Carly meant. He wasn't handsome, but neither was he bad looking. Nothing stood out—oval face, regular nose and lips. No dimples. He was just . . . like she said, average. "Is this the man you asked about earlier? Austin King?"

"Yes. The sketch really doesn't capture him," Carly said. "When he talked, he became animated and it changed his looks, which is hard to reproduce in a sketch."

She studied the different hairstyles. In one, the man had a full head of dark hair, another showed how he would look with a receding hairline, and the other two reflected salt-and-pepper and solid white hair. Maggie tilted her head, focusing on the man with a receding hairline. He was somewhat familiar. "And you say his name is Austin King?" She didn't recall anyone by that name. "Don't you think he's probably changed it?"

Carly fingered a gold bracelet around her wrist. "I'm sure of it. A girl you probably know thought one of the sketches *could* be of the man who sold her into prostitution. Told her that his name was Gordon Armstrong. Have any of the girls here mentioned that name or a man who would fit any of these sketches?" She tapped the ones with the full hair. "He may be dyeing his hair."

What kind of man lured young girls into a life of prostitution? The pizza in Maggie's stomach soured. "Since we started the shelter ten years ago, model scouts and agents have been a recurring theme—one of the girls rescued last week talked about being taken in by a man recruiting actresses."

"Do you think I could speak with her, show her the sketches?"

Maggie checked her watch. "How about in the morning? It's

late and the girls are into their quiet time." She tapped the drawings. "I'll leave a note for Vanessa to show these to the girls at breakfast."

She brought her cup to her lips only to discover it was empty. "Need a refill on coffee?" she asked as she popped a pod into the coffee machine. Drinking another cup would probably keep her up until after midnight, but she needed a little boost.

Carly held out her cup. "That would be wonderful."

Maggie made Carly's coffee first and then while she waited for hers to brew, she turned her gaze toward Carly. "What's your connection to this man?"

Carly's hands squeezed into fists, then she flexed her fingers and lifted her chin. "Sixteen years ago, Austin King promised to make me a model, said I'd earn more money than I could ever imagine. But when he took me to New York City, instead of what he promised, he sold me to a man I only knew as Blade. I was seventeen years old."

Maggie pressed her lips together in a tight line. The words said so matter-of-factly created a vacuum of silence. "How long—"

"Eight years."

Half an hour later, after Carly finished telling of her years in trafficking, Maggie's shock had turned to horror at what the woman had gone through. And what her friend Lily had endured. She closed the locket Carly had handed her and gave the bracelet back.

"The night Lily died, the women from the Atlanta shelter were at their booth again. I didn't think I could try to escape again, but with Lily gone, neither could I go back to that house. I asked them to help me." Carly fastened the bracelet on her wrist again. "Thanks to them, eight years after my capture I was free."

"Why didn't you go to the police?" Maggie winced, remembering what had happened the first time Carly escaped. "Never mind. I understand."

"I didn't think it'd do any good." Her eyes hardened, and she slowly shook her head. "Most of the cops I've known would sell you out for a hundred bucks."

For once in Maggie's life she was at a loss for words as she absorbed Carly's story. She could not imagine what Carly had experienced. "Not all police officers are crooked. David—"

She palmed her hands. "I don't trust *any* of them."

When someone was as adamant as Carly about something, Maggie had learned it was better to bide her time. "Your parents . . . why did they let you go to New York with a man they didn't know?"

"My parents were killed in an auto accident when I was eight, and my aunt and her husband became our guardians."

"And they had no reservations about you going?"

"I never told them. My uncle and I didn't get along, and I had recently moved out and was staying with first one friend and then another."

It appeared Carly had a hard life even before she was sold into trafficking. "I don't see how you survived," Maggie said. "I admire you for trying to help others who are dealing with substance abuse, but have you ever considered counseling victims of trafficking?"

Instead of answering, Carly slid off the stool and walked to the microwave with her mug. "Do you mind if I warm this?"

"Help yourself," Maggie said.

Once the microwave dinged, she returned to the counter and cupped her hands around the mug. "It takes a certain amount of empathy for a victim's problem in order to counsel them, and I have that." She focused on the cup, absently rubbing her thumb over the handle. "But when I was first rescued, I had to get off drugs."

Carly paused and pressed her lips together. Then she began again. "I wasn't on drugs because I liked them. When I was with Blade, I had no choice. It was the only way I could get through the night. Disassociation only goes so far. So, in those early months after I escaped, I went through a drug treatment center, a lot like where I work now. When I first decided to go into counseling I thought about focusing on trafficked victims, but just studying the cases threw me into panic."

Maggie could see how that could happen. "Yet you can counsel substance abuse addictions?"

"I was never emotionally addicted to drugs or alcohol." She looked up from the mug. "I know that sounds strange, but a doctor once explained the difference to me. He said that it was similar to a heart patient with chest pains who is being treated with morphine. Once the heart is fixed and the pain is gone, if the person isn't an addict, he doesn't crave the morphine. I don't crave pills or alcohol, so I can counsel addicts, but revisiting the trafficking part of my life sends me down a dark hole."

"So what changed? You had to know Haven House was a shelter for trafficked women when you came here."

Carly closed her eyes briefly, then she opened them and clasped her hands on the table. "Two weeks ago, a girl came into Tabula Rasa and she was put in my group session. I hadn't read the report on her and almost had a panic attack when I learned she'd been trafficked. In the middle of the session, she bolted from the room, and I had to go after her."

"Couldn't you have sent someone else?" Maggie asked.

"She was my patient, so my responsibility." Beads of perspiration dotted her face. She took a deep drink of the coffee and then set the cup down.

"You don't have to tell me anything more if you don't want to."

"Yes, I do." She took another breath. "I discovered she'd wanted to be a model and had been lured into trafficking with the promise of a modeling contract, right here in Memphis. She was seventeen, same age I was when Austin King took me to New York under the same pretense. Looking at the girl . . . it was like looking at myself. If I had gone to the police eight years ago and given them a description of King, they *might* have listened, and he might have been arrested. But I didn't even try. If I had, she might not have endured what she did—"

"You don't know it was King."

"It could be."

"The man who sold you."

"Yes."

The fluorescent light overhead illuminated the dark circles under Carly's eyes. Telling her story had drained her. Given the same circumstances, Maggie didn't know if she could have shared such a story. "You've done the right thing," she said. "Coming back to resolve your issues."

"I can't stop thinking how many girls might have been saved from trafficking if I'd stepped forward years ago. And my sister . . ." Her shoulders drooped, then she squared them. "That's a story for tomorrow. I'm too tired to relive it tonight. If it's all right, I'll come back in the morning at nine and talk with Vanessa and the girl who came in contact with the scout. Maybe if we can get a good description, the police can find and arrest him."

Just then the kitchen door swung open, and Vanessa entered the room.

"You look tuckered out," Maggie said. Usually Vanessa looked at least ten years younger than her sixty years, but tonight fatigue lined her face and her linen suit hung limp and wrinkled.

"You won't believe the night I've had. My granddaughter fell playing basketball and broke her arm." She turned to Carly. "You must be Ms. Smith."

Carly held out her hand. "Yes. I hope your granddaughter is okay."

Before she could answer, Maggie said, "That's terrible. Was it Caroline?"

"It was. That girl gets hurt more than anyone I know. And yes, she's all right." Vanessa glanced at Carly's plate, where remnants of the eggs remained. "Did you make her one of your famous cheese omelets?"

"Yes, would you like one?"

"Bless you, Maggie—that is, if you don't mind." Then Vanessa turned, and her gray eyes bored into Carly's. "Sorry to keep you waiting."

Carly waved her hand. "Thank you for seeing me. Especially with your granddaughter—"

"She'll be fine. Her mother is with her now."

While Maggie prepared the omelet, Vanessa pulled up a stool to the counter. Her cell phone dinged a text, and she spent the next five minutes responding as texts flew back and forth. "That was my daughter. Caroline is now sleeping," she said, putting her phone away. Then she turned her attention to Carly. "How is Jenna?"

"Coming along when I left," Carly said.

"Jenna?" Maggie asked.

"She's the girl I told you about in my counseling session," Carly said.

"You remember . . ." Vanessa held her hand out, indicating a short person. "The tiny girl with the pixie face. I was so surprised when I learned how old she is."

"Oh yeah," Maggie said. "She looked like a kid."

"Sadly, that's what the traffickers want," Carly said. "Pimps will starve the girls to keep them skinny and young-looking."

Vanessa nodded. "I arranged for Jenna to go to Tabula Rasa because it was best suited for her needs. Carly is her drug counselor." She turned to Carly. "So how can I help you?"

"There are a couple of things I need to discuss with you, but why don't we wait until tomorrow? That is, if you can give me a few minutes of your time then."

"I'll make time," Vanessa said. "And I am sorry for being late."

"I do have sketches that I would like for you to show the girls in the morning. It might save time tomorrow if you pass them around before I arrive."

"Sketches?"

Maggie pushed the paper Carly had given her to where Vanessa could see it. "She's looking for this man. He's recruiting girls for trafficking, pretending to be a model scout."

"Then he's a scumbag, and I'd like to put him and every one of the other recruiters in jail," Vanessa said grimly as she perused the sketches. "I've never seen him, but that doesn't mean one of the girls hasn't. How about getting here around nine thirty? The girls have a nine o'clock group session, and I'll pass these sketches around. You can talk to them the last fifteen minutes of their meeting. Perhaps one of them came into contact with this man. Then we can talk afterward, before the board meeting," she said, glancing at Maggie.

Carly took her cup to the sink and washed it before she turned and faced them. "Good." She turned her gaze to Maggie. "Thank you for listening and . . . for not being judgmental."

Maggie put her arm around Carly. "I admire you for sharing. I don't know that it's something I could have done."

When Vanessa queried her with questioning eyes, Maggie said, "She'll explain tomorrow."

Vanessa held up the paper with the sketches. "I'll make copies for the girls. Do I need to make you one?"

"No, I have several," Carly said and picked up her purse. "I'll see you tomorrow."

"Wait, and I'll walk out with you," Maggie said.

Outside, a few cars passed on the street that fronted the old church. Leon was on his cell phone, and she almost asked for Carly to wait and let him escort them to their cars. Maggie surveyed the parking area. Her car wasn't far from the front of the building and Carly was already striking out across the lot. "Wait up," she called.

Carly waited by a silver Chevrolet that was parked on the other side of Maggie's. She'd taken a barrette from her hair and was examining it.

"That looks Celtic," Maggie said. "Is it an heirloom?"

Carly opened the barrette. "No. It's actually a GPS tracker. I'm terrified of being kidnapped again, so I found a company that can track me through this," she said, showing Maggie the back side of the clip.

"How does it work?"

"This chip"—she pointed to a tiny square—"gives the tracking company my location at all times. If I go missing, either the company or a friend I have on the account can find me."

Maggie didn't even know a tracker that small existed. "I've seen the kids' watches that have GPS capabilities, but nothing like your barrette."

"I thought about a smart watch or phone, but that would be the first thing a kidnapper would look for and get rid of. I can put the chip in a piece of costume jewelry or this barrette. I wish it had a panic button or two-way communication, but those trackers are so large, it'd be hard to hide or carry all the time. I've tested this one and it works." She clipped the barrette in her hair again and then dug her keys from her purse. "I've also taken a few self-defense classes, not that I'm all that great at the moves."

"Knowing how to defend yourself is a good idea," Maggie said. "Where are you staying?"

"Downtown at the Westin, across from the FedEx Forum."

"Nice place. It's not far from where I live," she said. "Do you know how to get downtown from here?"

"Yes."

"Oh, that's right, you lived here once. Do you still have family in the area?"

Carly hesitated. "Is what I say still confidential?"

"Should it be?" Carly Smith was either hiding something or very afraid.

"Yes. There's one more thing I'd like to tell you, but I don't want anyone else to know it just yet. It could prove dangerous to them."

"Dangerous? What . . . who are you talking about?"

"My sister's family."

"Why would it be dangerous to them?"

"My sister died. Two years after I escaped, I contacted her instead of going to the police and told her about Austin King. Now I wonder if what I told her might have gotten her killed."

Her heart went out to Carly. That was a lot of guilt to live with. Then Maggie frowned. A woman murdered six years ago would have hit the news big-time. "How was she killed? Was it here in Memphis?"

Carly's cell phone lit up, and she fumbled for her phone, dropping it. As she bent to catch it, the crack of a gunshot split the night air. Carly's eyes widened, and then she crumpled to the ground.

13

DAVID HELPED HIS DAUGHTER gather up the paper plates and pizza boxes in the den and take them to the kitchen. "Pretty good party," he said and tweaked one of Lexi's braids. Having Maggie here had made it almost like family time.

"Yes." She sighed and looked around the kitchen. "And if we don't get this mess cleaned up, Mrs. B. will skin us alive."

"That she will." David had sent Mrs. B. home, telling her he'd help Lexi clean up. He pulled a large black garbage bag from under the sink. "You grab the Solo cups, and I'll get the other trash."

"I'm glad Gigi and Uncle Frank came to the game." His daughter dumped her stack of paper plates in the bag.

"Yeah." He hoped they got the message that Lexi would not be going to the Academy. She attended an excellent school in Memphis.

"Can you take me to soccer practice tomorrow afternoon?"

What time had Logan said practice would be? Four thirty? David should be able to get away from his desk by then since he wasn't working on a major case. "Sure."

"Can you pick Hannah and me up at school too? If we have to ride the bus, we won't get home in time to walk Max before it's time to leave." When he hesitated, she said, "That's okay. I can call Gigi and see if she's in town."

"No, don't call her." He'd forgotten their next-door neighbors had hired Lexi to walk their dog every afternoon. Since they lived in a safe neighborhood with little traffic, he'd encouraged the job to teach her responsibility. "Let's see if Mrs. Baxter can pick you up, and if she can't, I'll manage it."

She beamed at him. "I'm so glad you're going to practice with me. Do you think Miss Maggie will come?"

"I doubt it. She's awfully busy."

"Like you," Lexi said with an exaggerated sigh. "Why do grown-ups have to be so busy all the time?"

"So we can buy things like pizza and ice cream," he said, tapping her on the head. "You go on and get ready for bed. I'll finish up here and then call Mrs. Baxter and let her know she can sleep in her own bed tonight since I shouldn't be going out again."

Having a housekeeper who lived in the garage apartment behind the house was a bonus. After Lexi went to her room, he finished cleaning the kitchen and then rang the grandmotherly Mrs. Baxter and asked if she could pick up Lexi and her friend from school.

"I am so sorry, but I have a doctor's appointment tomorrow afternoon. Any other time would be no problem."

"That's fine, Mrs. B. I'll take care of it."

And he'd have to do just that. No need to give Georgina more ammunition. An hour later, he'd tucked Lexi in, and as he descended the stairs, he wondered how much longer she would allow him that ritual. He couldn't believe she was eleven and in less than two years would hit the teen years. His cell phone rang, and he answered without looking at the caller ID. "Raines."

"David, someone shot Carly."

Maggie's distant voice sent his heart spiraling. "What? Where are you?"

"Haven House parking lot. I've called 911."

"Are you hit?"

"No. Just Carly."

Carly? The woman at the soccer field? Faint sirens sounded in the background. "I'm on my way."

David took the stairs two at a time as he speed-dialed Mrs. Baxter's number. "I have an emergency. Can you stay with Lexi?"

"I'll be right there," Mrs. Baxter said.

He stuck his head in his daughter's room and flipped the wall switch. A soft light from the lamp by her bed flicked on. "Lexi, I have to go out. Mrs. Baxter will be here in a minute. Don't open the door for anyone." Evelyn Baxter had a key to the house.

Lexi bolted up in bed, her brown eyes round. "What's wrong?"

"I don't know yet. I'll fill you in tomorrow morning. Okay?"

"Is anyone hurt?"

"No one you know." His mind raced, connecting the dots, and he didn't like the way they connected. A woman he'd just met a few hours ago was now a gunshot victim. Coincidental? Perhaps, but highly unlikely.

"Is the person going to die?"

David crossed to his daughter's bed and smoothed back her hair. He was tempted to say no, but he'd always been up-front with Lexi. "I hope not, sweetie."

She nodded. "I'll say a prayer for them."

"That's a good idea. I'll check on you when I get home."

Mrs. Baxter was entering from the back door as David hurried down the stairs. "I'll be back as soon as I can."

"Don't worry. I'll sleep in the guest room tonight."

In the garage, David climbed into his pickup and remotely raised the door. Fifteen minutes later, he pulled into the Haven House parking lot amid the flashing blue lights. Maggie stood a few yards away from her car, talking to Det. Logan Donovan. David's heart slowed for the first time since her call. She really was all right.

He parked out of the way and hurried over to Maggie. Up close, judging from her colorless face and the red stains on her clothes, she might not be as all right as he thought. She gave him a wan smile, and he pulled her to his side in a hug. "You okay?"

"Not really. Why would anyone shoot her?"

"What happened?"

"We were just standing here, talking. Suddenly I heard a rifle shot, and Carly fell to the ground." Maggie rubbed her hand over her face, and then she shook her head as if to clear it. "If she hadn't been trying to catch her cell phone, the bullet would've hit her in the center of her chest instead of her shoulder." She glanced toward the spot where he assumed Carly had fallen. "She lost a lot of blood. The paramedic . . . he said using my jacket stopped the blood flow, otherwise . . ."

She shuddered and he hugged her closer. "I don't understand how a woman visiting Memphis comes to a soccer game where the three of us are, and then ends up getting shot."

"Me, either," Logan said, looking up from his search through a wallet. "What was this Carly Smith doing here?"

Maggie hesitated and stepped out of David's embrace. "She had an appointment with Vanessa, and Vanessa was late, so I waited with Carly until she arrived."

Logan raised his gaze. "What did you talk about while you waited?"

Maggie stiffened. "She told me a little bit about her history, what she does."

"And . . . ?" The detective waited.

Maggie stared at her feet.

Why was she reluctant to share what she and the Smith woman had discussed? "What's going on, Maggie?"

14

MAGGIE SHIVERED and rubbed her arms as she mentally separated what Carly had told her in confidence and what she'd said in front of Vanessa. When she shivered again, David took his jacket off and put it around her shoulders. She turned to Logan. "You spoke with her at the soccer game. Did she tell you anything at all about herself?"

The detective shook his head. "Something about her was familiar, but she shut me down before I could ask her anything."

"That's what I'm talking about," David said. "I get the feeling Carly Smith was hiding something this afternoon. And *Smith*? Even the name sounds fishy." He turned to Maggie. "What did you two talk about?"

"Yeah," Logan said. "I'm still waiting for the answer to that question too."

"She's a substance abuse counselor."

"And?" Logan asked. "What else did you discuss?"

"She's looking for someone involved in human trafficking." Maggie dug her hands into David's jacket. "And I'm not at liberty to discuss anything else she told me."

David folded his arms. "What do you mean, you're not at liberty?"

Maggie lifted her chin. "She's a client, and what we discussed was told in confidence. Until she gives me permission, I can't reveal what it was."

"You mean between the soccer game and before she was shot, she hired you as her attorney," David said.

"Yes."

Logan tapped his pen against the notepad. "Maggie, we need to catch whoever did this, and what you discussed may have a bearing on the case."

Carly had been in town less than twelve hours, and she'd been so certain that no one knew she was in Memphis. That made the odds that her shooting had anything to do with her past very low. "The information we discussed was personal."

Carly had been adamant that the information she shared remained confidential, and Maggie had agreed to her terms. Unless Logan came up with a direct connection between the shooting and trafficking, she had to honor her commitment. "Like I said a minute ago, she's here looking for someone, a man involved in human trafficking."

Both men turned and stared at her. "Why didn't you say so before?" David asked.

"I did. You just weren't listening." The look David shot her way indicated he was not happy with her. Well, she wasn't happy with him either if he thought she'd break a confidence. She was glad when Vanessa joined them.

"Do you know if they've reached the hospital yet?" Vanessa asked.

Logan nodded. "The uniformed officer I sent with the ambulance texted a few minutes ago that they had arrived."

David turned to the Haven House director. "What can *you* tell us about Carly Smith?"

"Not much. I was delayed for our appointment after my granddaughter broke her arm. When I did arrive, it was late and Carly decided to come back in the morning for our meeting."

"So you have no idea what she might have discussed with Maggie?" David asked.

"No. Is it important?" Vanessa asked.

"We have a victim with a gunshot wound, and whoever did it may try again. I would *think* the circumstances warrant overriding any confidentiality agreement." Logan's sharp tone matched the frustration in David's face.

"The only thing she told me that might tie in with her shooting is the man she's looking for," Maggie said. "Austin King."

"Did you tell them about the sketches?" Vanessa asked.

"No, because they're not listening to me. Why don't you fill them in?"

"What sketches?" David asked.

Vanessa turned to the two men. "Over the years, a man posing as a model scout has been a recurring theme with traffickers. About a month ago a girl came through Haven House—her name was Jenna. She said that she'd been abducted when she answered an ad for a modeling job. I placed her at a drug treatment facility, and Carly is her counselor."

"So you're saying the girl told Carly about this man, and she came to Memphis to find him?" Logan appeared skeptical.

"I believe that's correct, but you really need to ask her," Vanessa said. "The sketches she provided are in the kitchen. Would you like to see them?"

"Definitely," Logan said.

The four of them walked inside the building and Vanessa handed the men the drawings.

David and Logan studied them. "The name Austin King does not ring a bell," Logan said. He tapped the drawing of the man with the receding hairline. "But he looks vaguely familiar. Can you make copies of this sheet?"

"Of course," Vanessa said. She took the paper and disappeared down the hall.

David folded his arms over his chest and Maggie tamped down her frustration and returned the hard gaze he leveled at her. Her years in front of a jury had conquered her tendency to blush.

"You've had a few minutes to think. Is there anything from your conversation you can share?" he asked.

She thought back to when Vanessa joined their conversation. From that point on, she was released from her promise. Unfortunately, not much had been said after the director joined them. "I'm sorry, but we left right after Vanessa arrived."

"So you're saying Smith hired you as her lawyer?" Logan asked.

"Yes, she gave me ten dollars and—"

"Only ten dollars? That's not a real contract," David said.

"Excuse me? Since when did you become a lawyer?"

"Blast it, Maggie!" It was evident that David had not mastered the ability to keep *his* face from turning red. "The woman was shot at. What if the person goes after her again? Or comes after you?"

"If they were after me, they would have taken care of that when they shot Carly. And she's in the hospital, so I assume you'll put a guard on her room where she'll be safe until I can talk with her. I'm sure, given the circumstances, she'll release me from my promise, but until then I have to honor my word. Besides, what if this was random gang activity?"

"You don't believe that, do you?" David asked.

Since Carly was certain no one knew she was here, it made as much sense as anything. "It could be a gang initiation—there've been a couple of instances of that happening lately."

"What if the shooter goes after her in the hospital?" Logan asked. "Will you be able to live with that?"

"Don't make this any harder than it is," she said, palming her hands up.

After Vanessa returned and handed Logan several copies of the sketches, Maggie grabbed her purse. "I'm going to the hospital to wait until they let me in to see her. Do you think one of us could take her purse to her? I'm sure she'll need it."

David took the purse from Logan. "Keep me up to date," he said and turned to Maggie. "I'll follow you."

Maggie kept him in her rearview mirror, unable to shake the heaviness in her heart. She'd known the day would come when she and David would cross swords over a case. Criminal defense attorneys and police lieutenants didn't always play well together, and they'd been fortunate to go as long as they had without a problem. The ten dollars may have only been a token payment, but David simply had to understand—when she gave her word, that was it.

At the hospital, David caught up with her outside the ER, and they approached the receptionist at the desk. "Could you give me information on Carly Smith?" Maggie asked.

The woman typed a few letters and waited. "Ms. Smith is in surgery," she said, looking up. "The surgery waiting room is on the second floor. Just follow the yellow line."

As they took the stairs, Maggie struggled with how to mend the rift with David. She loved him, and she didn't want to lose him. But she was an attorney. If a client asked her to keep information confidential, she had no choice unless revealing what she knew kept a crime from being committed. And nothing Carly had told her fell within that parameter. "I'm sorry I can't give you any more information on our discussion. I just can't break her trust."

His mouth twitched. "Not even off the record?"

Her shoulders drooped. "You know there's no such thing as off the record." At his scowl, she added, "It's not like I don't want to. We talked about this before, remember? About how our careers might clash."

He raised skeptical eyebrows.

"You know it's a possibility," she said. "What if you arrest my client, and I ask you what evidence you have against him? How would you feel about that?"

"It's not the same thing. Ten dollars does not make Carly Smith your client."

"You're wrong, it does. While we didn't sign a contract, once she gave me money, she was a client and the rules of confidentiality apply. But forget about the rules. I gave her my word that whatever we discussed would be confidential. And that's the end of this subject."

David held her gaze and then ducked his head. "Actually I do understand . . . to a point. But I don't have to like it," he said as he pushed open the stairwell door on the second floor and let her go first. "And I do respect your integrity."

"Thank you." At the desk, she inquired about Carly again and was given the same answer. She was in surgery.

David stepped up to the desk and showed his badge and identification. "Would you ask the doctor to come out and give us an update when he's finished?"

The receptionist looked closely at his ID and then back at David. "I'll tell him," she said. "Do you know if she has any family in the area?"

David turned to her, his eyes questioning her, and Maggie said, "Carly never told me the name of any family around here. But you have her purse. You might check in it to see if there is anyone to call in case of an emergency."

15

THE RHYTHMIC SOUND of beeping penetrated Carly's consciousness, pulling her from a murky world. Voices hovered around her, and she wanted to tell whoever was talking to go away.

"I think she's waking up."

"I'll call Dr. Simms."

"Ms. Smith, can you hear me?"

The voice was commanding, and Carly tried to answer, but her lips wouldn't obey. Nodding her head was even harder.

"You're going to be all right. Can you open your eyes for me?"

No wonder it was so dark. She barely opened her eyes and quickly squeezed them shut against the bright light. "C-could you . . . the light . . ."

"Sorry." The kindly voice again. "The light is off now. Can you open your eyes?"

Carly cracked her lids enough to see the room was darker, and she opened them wider. "Where am I?" she croaked. Her mouth tasted like turpentine.

"You're in the hospital."

Hospital? Memories flooded her mind. Talking to Vanessa . . . Maggie . . . walking to her car . . . Carly moved, and burning pain shot through her left shoulder. "What's wrong with my shoulder?"

113

"Someone shot you . . ."

I was talking to Maggie. A noise . . . falling . . . She felt her wrist for her bracelet. No! It couldn't be lost.

"Are you in pain?"

"Yesss."

"Would you like something for it?"

"Tylenol."

"You can have something stronger," her nurse replied.

She was tempted, but pain medication fuzzed her brain and would delay getting out of the hospital. Besides, she'd developed a high threshold for pain during her years with Blade. "Just Tylenol."

Carly took the two pills the nurse gave her, and her mind drifted as she tried not to move. Who could have shot her? And why? How did anyone know she was in town?

"There's a lady in the waiting room who would like to see you. Madeline Starr. She's very worried about you."

Maggie? Other than Jamie, no one worried about her. Felt kind of nice to have someone else to add to the short list. "How long have I been here?" She glanced at the clock on the wall. It read nine, but she had no idea whether it was morning or night in the windowless room.

"About ten hours. You were brought in around eleven last night."

Vague memories of drifting in and out of sleep came to her. At one point, she thought she remembered a man bending over her, asking questions. Logan Donovan, maybe? But why would he be here? And how did he get in her room? Carly's heart rate accelerated and a low honking came from over her head.

"Ms. Smith, are you all right?"

Her head swam. If she was all right, she wouldn't be lying in a hospital bed. "What's that noise?"

"It's your monitor. Your heart rate increased. Take a deep breath and try to relax."

She knew how to do that. Carly pictured her favorite lake, swans paddling lazily, and the honking stopped. Maybe she'd just dreamed Logan was there. "Did someone question me last night?"

"The report indicated you roused a little around two, and a police officer tried to question you. When you became agitated, your doctor put a stop to that. I'm surprised you remember him."

Carly wasn't. It couldn't have been Logan Donovan, though. She assumed he worked for his mother in her jewelry store. "Has anyone else been in to see me?"

"No. The friend I mentioned just buzzed the desk again, asking if she could see you for a few minutes. Would you like to see her?"

Maybe Maggie could keep Logan out of her room. "Yes, thank you."

Carly rested her eyes while she waited for Maggie. When she opened them, she realized she'd dropped off to sleep again. She tried to move and groaned as pain shot through her shoulder.

"You okay?"

Carly jerked her head toward the voice. Maggie.

"Do I need to get the nurse? She's right outside the door."

"No. It only hurts when I move."

"You're alive and that's what counts," Maggie said. She placed Carly's phone on the bedside table and scooted a chair next to the bed. "I think that phone saved your life. If you hadn't been trying to catch it, the bullet would have done more damage."

She hadn't even thought about her phone. "My barrette—"

Maggie opened the purse she held and took out the barrette and pressed it into Carly's hand. She felt the inside of the barrette. The chip was still there.

"I have something else for you," Maggie said. She pulled Lily's bracelet from her purse. "I knew you'd want this."

"Thank you." Carly thought she'd lost it forever. She held out her right arm. "Could you . . . I can't—"

"Sure." Maggie stood and fastened the bracelet around her wrist. "This means a lot to you, doesn't it?"

"Yes." Lily may not have been blood kin, but she'd been as close to her as Lia. "Thanks." She checked to make sure the bracelet was secure. "Would you put my purse in the drawer here by the bed?"

Once Maggie closed the drawer, they both spoke at the same time.

"I—"

"I need—"

"You go first," Carly said.

"I hope you don't mind, but I gave the hospital your insurance cards to copy and your ID."

"No, that was fine. I really appreciate everything you've done." She fingered the white sheet on her bed. "You haven't told anyone what we discussed, have you?"

"I want to talk to you about that. I'd like to share your story with David. Just in case anything you told me is pertinent to your case."

"No!" Carly didn't need the low honking the monitor emitted to know her heart rate had jumped. She took a deep breath and forced her body to calm down. She couldn't let Maggie leave until she promised not to reveal what they discussed. Her heart rate increased even more when the nurse hurried into the room.

"I'm afraid your guest will have to leave," she said.

"Don't go! I'm all right," she said as Maggie stood. She pictured the lake with the swans. *Focus.* Soon the alarm stopped and the blood pressure cuff inflated, squeezing Carly's good arm. When the cuff released she craned her neck to see the monitor. One-thirty-five over eighty-five. "See. That's not bad for where I am."

"If your heart rate jumps again, she'll have to leave."

Carly nodded that she understood. Once they were alone, she turned to Maggie. "Please tell me you haven't disclosed anything we discussed."

Maggie sat back down. "I haven't, but I've thought about this all night. What if the person who shot you is this Austin King? He or someone he works with could come after you again. The police can protect you better if they know the whole story."

"No!"

"Your heart rate is climbing again."

"Then promise me you won't say anything to anyone."

"Okay, I won't say anything for now. Just calm down—I don't want you to code. But I don't understand why you want to keep it a secret after you've been shot."

"Thank you." Carly sank into the bed. "It's not that I want to be difficult, but you don't know who you're dealing with. Human traffickers can be anyone—judges, the mayor, even cops. Especially cops."

"Not David."

"Please, just give me a little time. No one knows me here, or why I came to Memphis." Her own sister hadn't recognized her, so surely no one she met yesterday had either.

Maggie leaned back in the chair with her arms folded. "We'll talk about it again later."

"You're coming back?"

"Yes, to check on you."

"Would you do me a favor?"

"If I can."

Carly hated being indebted to Maggie, but she didn't know anyone else to ask. "Except for my boots, I'm sure the clothes I wore are ruined. I'm staying downtown at the Westin. Would you go by and pick up a change of clothes for me to wear when I leave the hospital? I'll get the rest of my things then."

"You mean you don't like hospital chic?" Maggie asked with a laugh. "Of course I'll go by your hotel room and pick up something. Probably be five or later before I return—I have the board meeting this morning and court this afternoon."

"I'm not going anywhere." But she would get out of here today or tomorrow, and she would need something to wear. "Hand me my purse again and I'll give you a key."

Maggie pocketed the plastic card Carly handed her and then returned to her chair. "What are you going to do once you get out of the hospital? You're not going to continue looking for this Austin King, are you?"

The heart alarm went off, and Carly jerked her gaze toward the door. The nurse was not at her desk. "Can you silence that thing?" she asked.

Maggie obliged, and quiet filled the room except for the beeping of her heart that slowed back to normal.

"I want to talk to Jacqueline Donovan, see if she recognizes the man in the sketches."

"At some point you'll have to trust David, or Logan Donovan," Maggie said.

"Why Logan Donovan?"

"He's the detective investigating your shooting."

"What?" Logan was a cop? It had been him in her room. "He's the person who took me to the party where I met Austin King. What if he's in cahoots with him? I saw enough corrupt cops when I was on the streets to not trust any of them. And it goes from the lowest cop on the beat all the way to the higher-ups."

"But this is now. Logan would never be involved in trafficking."

Maggie just didn't understand. "You have no concept of what true evil is. Money makes people do things no one would dream of." Carly narrowed her eyes. "Trafficking women brings in billions of dollars every year, even more than drugs. I heard Blade say one time that he could only sell drugs once, but he could sell his women over and over. So, no, I can't trust David or Logan. I'm sorry."

"You *can* trust them," Maggie insisted.

"Can I? I'm not sure Logan wasn't in on my kidnapping. And David—what if he killed my sis—" Carly clamped her hand over her mouth. What had she done? She hadn't meant to let that slip, even though Maggie probably would have put the pieces of the puzzle together eventually.

Maggie jerked. "What are you talking about? David Raines would never murder anyone. Wait—" Her face turned the color of paste and she swallowed hard. "You said your sister was killed six years ago. That—that's when Lia Raines was killed. Are you saying . . ." She frowned and then her eyes widened. "Lia is your sister, and you're Heather Morgan?"

She scrambled for an answer that would satisfy the attorney. There wasn't one, and Carly sucked in a deep breath. "Yes. Lia Raines is my sister, but Heather Morgan died sixteen years ago when Austin King sold her to a man called Blade. I'm your client and you can't tell anyone, not even David Raines."

She felt her pulse rising again as Maggie crossed her arms and stared at her. Carly pictured the lake again, but she couldn't let go of the anxiety this time. Just when she thought she would lose it, the lawyer uncrossed her arms.

"All right, I won't tell David right now, but I just don't understand why you want to keep it a secret. If it's because you believe he'll judge you, I can assure you he won't. What happened wasn't your fault."

The sincerity in Maggie's voice reminded Carly of the women in Atlanta who had taken her in the night Lily died and then helped her start over. "You have no idea what it's like to have lived my life. Only someone who has lived through what I have can understand."

"Carly, at some point you have to start trusting again."

"I haven't reached that point." She bit her bottom lip as fatigue seeped into her muscles. Her pain level had grown as well, probably a ten now, and she might have to ask the nurse for something stronger than Tylenol. "I can't release you from your promise," she said and pressed the call button.

The attorney's eyes narrowed. "I don't normally go back on my word, but if I can't convince you to tell David—" Her phone chimed, and she glanced at the screen. "I have an appointment in thirty minutes, and I don't have time to stay and persuade you now. But I'll be back this afternoon. We'll discuss it further then."

Maggie could discuss all she wanted, but Carly wasn't changing her mind.

16

At her building, Maggie took the stairs until she reached the fifth floor, trying to get in a little exercise. She took the elevator to her twelfth-floor office and went in through the back entrance, just in case the lawyer she had a conference with had already arrived. She needed a few minutes to get her head together.

If that was possible. Carly Smith was Heather Morgan. David's long-lost sister-in-law. The one person he'd been looking for all these years. And she couldn't tell him.

Why had Maggie taken the ten dollars from her? Because the chances of Carly disclosing anything that would put her in conflict with David were a million to one. She leaned back in her chair and pressed her fingers to her eyes. What was she going to do?

Abruptly, she sat up straight. The only thing she could. Keep Carly's confidence until Carly released her from it. Or Maggie could convince Carly to tell David who she was. But how?

Her door opened, and her brightly attired administrative assistant startled. "I didn't know you were back. I was bringing the mail."

"That's fine. I came up the back way. Where did you get that caftan?"

A broad grin spread across Shawna's face. "A little boutique on Main Street. It was made in South Africa. You ought to try shopping there sometime. Oh, and Jim Rankin is here."

"I just might sometime." Maggie checked her watch. Ten thirty. Good, the city councilman-slash-attorney was early. She shouldn't have any trouble making the Haven House board meeting. "Give me five minutes, then send Jim back."

Shawna stopped at the door. "How many flights of stairs did you take?"

"Five. It's probably all the exercise I'll get today since I don't see much chance of getting to the gym."

Once the door closed, she opened the file and quickly scanned her notes. It was a simple civil case—something neither she nor Rankin normally took. But when friends asked for help . . . Rankin's client had accused her client of attacking him in a dispute over boundary lines. With no witnesses, it was a matter of one person's word against the other. What Maggie hoped to do was settle the dispute without going into court.

She looked up as the casually dressed criminal defense lawyer ambled into her office. More than one district attorney had underestimated Rankin's unassuming manner to their detriment. A born politician, he had a way of captivating a jury, and she did not relish going against him in the courtroom in this civil case.

"Good morning," she said, rising and offering him her hand. "I'm glad for this opportunity to discuss the case with you."

"So am I." He offered her a broad smile and firm grip then nodded toward the bank of ceiling-to-floor windows behind her chair. "I like your view."

"It's one of the reasons I chose this office." She leaned back in her chair as the older man took the wingback opposite her desk and crossed an ankle over his knee. "But you're not here to admire my office. Is your client ready to drop the charges?"

"I'd hoped we were meeting to iron out a financial agreement," he said.

She shook her head. "My client insists he was only defending himself."

"His word against my client's."

"But *my* client doesn't have a history of assault and battery."

"Irrelevant."

"Not if the judge allows it, and we're going before Judge Braddock." That was her ace in the hole. Judge Braddock had tried the assault and battery case against Rankin's client and would remember him.

He glanced up at the ceiling.

Maggie leaned forward. "My client wants to counterfile an assault charge, but so far I've been able to talk him out of it. I propose that your client drop the charges, and my client will sign a waiver agreeing not to file counter charges."

Jim ran his hand over his bald head and then nodded slowly. "I think I can get my client to agree to that if we can establish the creek as the northern and southern boundaries, respectively, between the two properties."

Her client had already agreed privately to allow the creek to stand as the boundary line since his deed only took in ten feet on the other side of the creek. "I think that's fair," she said.

"Good. Draw up the papers and my client will drop the charges."

They both stood, and this time Jim offered his hand first. "Pleasure doing business with you, Madeline."

"You too, Jim." She walked to the reception area with him. "You have a good rest of the day."

"Oh, I will. It's going to be busy. I'm going from here to Regional One to donate a pint of blood, and then an appointment I'm not looking forward to."

"Oh?"

"Yeah. It's another case I don't normally take. An heir wants to break a trust fund. Inheritance cases aren't my favorite."

"Mine, either," she said. "I admire you for donating blood."

"I'm O negative so it's always needed." Then he chuckled. "They've set me up with a standing appointment."

Maggie needed to think about donating blood since she'd read recently there was a shortage. She wasn't even sure what blood type she was. Mentally she put that on her to-do list and walked back to her office, mulling over an idea.

Jim's mention of a trust triggered something David had told her once. Lia had set up a fund for Lexi using money her parents had left her. And if Lia had an inheritance, then more than likely, Carly did too.

She turned around and walked back to Shawna's desk. "I need you to check Shelby County court records for a trust fund set up for Heather Morgan," she said. "And check Tate County, Mississippi, records as well."

That was the county Georgina and Frank Wilson lived in. They had been awarded guardianship of Lia and Heather after their parents died, and more than likely the couple had been put in charge of any inheritance the girls received.

17

Voices in Carly's room roused her from a deep sleep.

"Ms. Smith is sleeping now," her nurse said. Carly had learned her name was April.

"If you don't mind, I'd like to wait here in the room."

Carly opened her eyes enough to see that her visitor was Logan Donovan. He towered over the nurse, but she didn't appear to be intimidated.

"I'm afraid not, Detective. It might frighten my patient to wake up and find a strange man in her room."

Detective? Oh, wait, Maggie had said he was a cop. Now the gun on his belt made sense. When did he become a cop? She always figured he'd go into the jewelry business with the rest of his family. And what was he doing coaching a girls' soccer team? She'd like to know the answers to both questions.

"Would you at least call me if she wakes up in the next fifteen minutes? I need information from her."

"If she wants to talk to you," April replied.

You go, girl.

"What if someone tries to kill her again and succeeds because I don't know where to start? I know you don't want that on your conscience."

His words were softly spoken, and even though Carly couldn't see his face, she knew he was totally focused on April, drawing her into his confidence.

"I suppose it wouldn't hurt . . ."

"I don't want him in my room," Carly said.

They both turned, evidently surprised she'd heard them.

"You're awake," Logan said.

His gaze held Carly prisoner, only it wasn't Logan she saw, but the cop who took her back to Blade and then took the money her pimp handed him. Suddenly a wave of tremors shook her body, and Carly wanted to curl into a ball, but the IV and blood pressure cuff made it impossible. "G-get h-him out of h-here."

April took one look at her and turned back to Logan. "I'm sorry, sir, you'll have to leave. Maybe a little later."

"I'll be in the waiting room."

As soon as Logan left, Carly took a ragged breath. This would not do. If she didn't talk to him, he would only be more persistent . . . even might wonder what she was hiding. Right now it didn't matter what he thought. She couldn't talk to him. Carly startled when April touched her arm.

"I need to check your blood pressure." She pushed a button on the overhead monitor, and the cuff inflated. "It's a little high. Would you like something to help you calm down? The doctor left an order."

Carly shook her head. "I'll be okay. But I don't want to talk to him . . . or any policeman."

April's eyes softened. "I'm afraid he'll be back. He's investigating your shooting."

Her heart sank. April was right. Maybe it would be better to talk to him and get it over with. If he got too close to the truth, Carly could ask him to leave, and April would back her up, unless her nurse was totally taken in by him. Based on what she remembered about him, he had that effect sometimes. Besides, how long could she avoid him? Probably not long. "If I see him now, will you stay in the room?"

"I'll be right outside, although I don't think you have anything to fear from him. He seems really nice."

Yeah, and Austin King seemed nice too.

A few minutes later Logan stepped back into the room, and Carly didn't miss the grin that spread across his lips, revealing the straight white teeth and dimples she remembered. Her gaze traveled to his amber eyes. Eyes she could lose herself in. That she even noticed surprised her. It'd been so long since a man's features got her attention.

"Thank you for seeing me." He approached the bed and nodded toward the chair. "Do you mind if I sit?"

"Suit yourself." She pulled her gaze from Logan to the nurse. "Could I have a cup of water?"

Carly hoped he attributed her shaky voice and the increase in her heart rate on the overhead monitor to being shot and not the case of nerves that had suddenly taken over.

"Sure." April tossed the foam cup Carly had been drinking from into the trash and filled a new one. "Here you go. I'll leave the door open, and I'll be right outside if you need me."

Carly sipped the cool water through a straw, soothing her dry throat. She hadn't missed Logan's gaze that followed the cup to the trash. "I thought you were a soccer coach, not a cop. How do you fit in coaching a girls' team?"

The look he gave her said he saw through her delay tactic.

"I have a backup when I'm involved with a case, like today."

"So you have a kid on the team?" Not that she was interested.

"Nope. Never married, so no kids." His amber eyes twinkled. "Any other questions?"

"If you don't have a kid, why would you spend your free time coaching these girls?" If he was part of the trafficking ring, maybe he used coaching to scout out his next victims. His boyish grin had just the right look to gain any female's confidence. Except hers.

"I kind of got roped into it by my niece. My sister's kid is on the team. But I didn't come here to talk about me."

So that was why Jacqueline was there yesterday. To watch her granddaughter play. Carly's face warmed under his steady gaze. "You have some questions, then?"

"Yes, ma'am." Again he gave her that boyish grin and took out a notebook. "The address on your driver's license—" He rattled off her address in Stillwater. "Is that correct?"

Her heart rate jumped, and Logan glanced up at the monitor. Carly had thought she was prepared, but evidently not so she practiced calming herself. Gradually, her heart slowed. "Yes," she replied.

"How long have you lived there?"

"I'm sure you already have the answer to that question."

"Six years? And before that you lived in a small town in Kentucky. And you're a substance abuse counselor working on your master's."

"Yes."

He looked up from the notebook, his face unreadable.

She held his gaze, unflinching. If that was the best he could do to intimidate her, she wouldn't have any problem hiding her thoughts. Carly had learned to stand up to men far more menacing than Logan Donovan.

He broke eye contact first, looking down at his notebook again. "Where did you live prior to Kentucky?"

Her monitor shrieked a warning that her heart rate had jumped, and she concentrated on breathing in and out. She had to do better than this. She might as well be taking a lie detector test. *Think.* How would a normal victim respond?

"I don't mean to upset you," Logan said. "But I need any information that will help me find whoever did this to you."

"I appreciate that, but what does this have to do with who shot me?" She winced at her sharp tone and tried again. "I'm really tired, so if we could get to your investigation . . ."

Logan tapped the pad with his pen, and then he raised his head and smiled. "We seem to have gotten off on the wrong foot," he said, his voice soft.

"I don't know why you would think that."

"Maybe because I sense hostility in you?" He gave her a pointed look. "I've been assigned to your case, and if you could trust me, it might go a long way in solving who shot you. At any rate, it certainly won't hurt the case."

Trust you? Her monitor buzzed again. If only it would stop giving her emotional state away. She took a deep breath and was rewarded with a slowing of her heart rate. Logan might be a detective, but she wouldn't let her guard down until she was certain he wasn't part of the trafficking ring. Carly could count on one hand the people she trusted and have most of her fingers left over.

She took another sip of water. "I have no idea who shot me. I only arrived in Memphis yesterday, and very few people even knew I was coming. Is it possible this was a random shooting? I read about that happening all the time."

"We're not dismissing that possibility, but if that were the case, then Madeline Starr should have been shot as well. Look, you'll be getting out of the hospital in the next couple of days. Are you prepared for someone to come after you again?" He leaned closer. "Ms. Smith—if that's your name—you need police protection, and I need your cooperation."

He seemed to really care. It was hard to reconcile the serious detective with the wild, fun-loving man she'd dated. She was almost tempted to confide in him. Almost. Carly shivered and closed her eyes. "Like I said, I'm very tired. Could we finish this later?"

The chair squeaked as he shifted his weight. "I only have a couple more questions. Shouldn't take more than five minutes."

She opened her eyes and gave him what she considered a long-suffering grimace. "Okay. Shoot."

"That's a poor choice of word, Ms. Smith."

The twinkle in his eyes gave her pause. What if he had nothing to do with Austin King? Sixteen years ago they'd gone out for a short while, and she'd have to admit she'd been smitten with him from the first time they met on the University of Memphis campus. Logan had been twenty and unaware that she was a minor since she looked much older than seventeen. Flattered by the attention of a third-year college student, she'd let him believe she was a freshman at the university, when in reality, she was only visiting her older sister.

She remembered the party where she met Austin King vividly. The party wasn't long after Logan had taken her to a family picnic at their cabin in Shelby Forest where she'd met his family for the first time. What a disaster. Jacqueline Donovan had taken one look at Carly and her Goth look and turned up her rich nose. What in the world had made Logan become a cop?

"I like helping people."

Carly froze. She hadn't meant to voice her question. She shook the cobwebs from her head. Then she frowned. Logan had the sketches of Austin King in his hand. "What did you say?"

"You asked why I became a cop and I answered you." He held the paper up. "Vanessa Driscoll said you were inquiring about this man. Austin King, I believe you called him. Why are you looking for him?"

"Do you know anyone by that name?"

Looking a little taken aback, he started to shake his head, then hesitated. "No one comes to mind, but the older man with the receding hairline does look a little familiar. You didn't say why you're looking for him."

She had not asked Vanessa to keep their conversation confidential, and since Logan had the sketches . . . "The director didn't tell you?"

"I'd like to hear it from you."

Since he already knew, there was no reason not to tell him.

"He pretends to be a scout for a modeling agency, but instead of the girls getting a contract, they're sold into human trafficking. Two of the women from Haven House reported a man posing as such an agent—in fact, they fell for his scam and were sold into prostitution. This morning Vanessa intended to ask if any of them recognized the man in the sketches."

"Unfortunately, she didn't get around to it."

Carly sagged against the mattress. She'd counted on Vanessa showing the sketch and at least one of the women recognizing King. Fatigue seeped into every muscle in her body.

Logan tapped the paper with his pen and cleared his throat. "Why are you searching—"

"Could we finish this later? I've gone my limit."

He put away his pad, then cocked his head and appeared to be memorizing her features. "You have very unusual eyes. I still believe we've met somewhere before. Have you ever lived in Memphis?"

It took every ounce of willpower Carly possessed to not look away. *There is no way he can recognize me.* If he ever even thought about her, he would remember a skinny girl with black hair and Goth clothes. The only thing that hadn't changed was her hazel eyes with gold starbursts. She should have taken the time to put in her colored contacts yesterday.

"I'm sure you've checked your databases and haven't found a record for a Carly Smith in Memphis." She lowered the head of her bed, wincing as pain ripped her shoulder. "I'm done for now."

"Do you mind if I return this afternoon?"

Fuzziness encroached the edges of her mind, and she slipped into sleep without answering him.

18

LOGAN STOOD OUTSIDE Carly Smith's room. The woman was hiding something. But what? He couldn't shake the sense that somewhere, sometime they'd met before. The way she tilted her head sometimes when she talked, and then those eyes.

He'd only ever met one other person who had such vivid starburst eyes. Heather Morgan. And in the time they'd dated, he'd stared into them often enough. But there was no way the Goth-loving seventeen-year-old could have morphed into the quiet elegance that was Carly Smith. Or could she? Heather had grit, and he sensed Carly did as well. But if she was Heather, why didn't she acknowledge it? They'd had something special back then, at least he thought they had.

Logan rubbed the back of his neck. He'd been up all night, and his muscles ached and his head hurt. He needed to catch a nap, but first he had paperwork to catch up on. Then there was a sofa in the break room with his name on it.

"Logan, how are you?"

He looked up, surprised to see Jim Rankin in the hallway. "Good. You?"

"I'm good too," he said, removing a bandage from his arm. "Just got finished donating a pint of blood."

Logan remembered Jim was a regular donor and they sometimes ran into each other at the blood bank. "Is there a special need here today?" he asked.

"Always a need for O negative, but yes, I got a message this morning saying a patient here at Regional One was in need."

"I think I'm scheduled for next week." Logan nodded. "Good seeing you, and keep your buddies on the city council out of trouble."

"Impossible," Rankin replied, chuckling. He turned to leave and stopped. "Oh, before I go, can I count on your vote in the election?"

"Absolutely," Logan said. The city councilman was a shoo-in for reelection.

A few hours later and feeling fresher, Logan checked to see if the ballistics report on the bullet taken from Carly Smith's shoulder had been processed. When he didn't see the report in the computer, he picked up his phone and called the analyst. "Can you give me a timeframe for getting the ballistics results on a bullet I turned in earlier today?" he asked.

"You might get it by Friday. We're backlogged and short-handed."

Logan groaned. "Can you give me a preliminary?"

"Give me a sec." A second rolled into a minute, then two before the tech returned to the phone. "It was a .22 long."

"You're kidding."

"Nope."

"Okay, thanks." This case was getting stranger and stranger. While .22 caliber long rifle ammunition worked as well in a short handgun, Maggie had described the sound of the weapon as a rifle shot. Who used a .22 rifle to kill someone?

His phone rang within seconds of disconnecting. His mother again? He'd noticed she had called when he was interviewing Carly Smith and he'd meant to call her back. "Hello?"

"Have you had lunch?"

It'd been such a crazy morning that Logan had to think a second. "No."

"Come by the store. I'd like to talk to you about next week in Nashville since your sister is flying to New York for the fall jewelry show and I've been elected to fill in as chaperone."

"I'm glad you're going." His mother was great with the girls. "But I'm not sure I can take time to drop by the store right now."

"I picked up Chinese."

His favorite, and he needed to eat something anyway. "You got it."

It would also offer him a chance to ask his mother about Carly. He was pretty sure she remembered Heather Morgan, and if she'd gotten a good look at Carly yesterday, perhaps his mother could put his question to rest.

The drive to his family's jewelry store was short, and wonder of wonders, there was a parking space out front. He hurried through the posh showroom that shouted luxury from the marble floor and crystal chandelier to the glass cases of fine jewelry.

His mother had been disappointed when he hadn't gone into the family jewelry business like his brother, Jared, and his sister, Geri, but his decision hadn't caused any big waves. Logan secretly suspected his brother and sister were glad they didn't have to deal with their younger brother. Logan, the screwup.

All his life he'd walked in his brother and sister's shadow, never quite good enough whether it was academics or sports. Jared and Geri were straight-A students, valedictorians their senior years, while he struggled to maintain a C average in high school. And even though he'd been a decent running back, the coaches always reminded him how good Jared had been and how his jersey had been retired when he graduated. It was enough to make him want to quit, but if he had, then everyone would have known how much the comparisons hurt. So he was always the jokester, never taking anything seriously . . . until he joined the police academy.

Everyone had been surprised when he'd excelled at the academy, even Logan. It was like he'd found his niche, and he'd risen steadily through the ranks until he was now a sergeant in Homicide.

"Good, you're here."

He turned at his mother's voice and hugged her. "There wasn't much traffic. Where's the food?"

"My office," she said, opening the door to the hallway. "I hope you don't mind eating out of containers."

He followed her to her office, where the spicy aroma of Szechuan shrimp tickled his nose. His mother sat on the striped sofa, and he joined her, picking up a container of food.

After they exchanged the normal pleasantries, she asked, "How many rooms do you have reserved for next weekend?"

"Seventeen, counting mine. And thank you for agreeing to be a chaperone."

"It'll be fun. Besides, who needs sleep?"

They laughed, and then they discussed the details of the trip while they ate Szechuan shrimp with chopsticks. "How do you think the girls will do in Nashville?" she asked, expertly scooping rice from the box.

"They should take their division," he said.

"I think so too. If you're coaching this afternoon, I thought I'd stop and watch on my way home."

"Afraid I'm not. I'm working a case. Billy Taylor is taking over for me."

"Is it that shooting I heard about on Walnut Grove last night?"

"Yes." He concentrated on eating without dropping shrimp on his shirt. "The victim was at the soccer game yesterday. She bumped into me. Did you happen to talk to her?"

"No. I do remember seeing her, though."

"Did she look familiar to you?"

"When I first saw her, there was something about her . . . but then David said her name was Carly Smith, and I definitely have never known anyone by that name."

"Do you remember Heather Morgan?"

His mother rolled her eyes. "How could anyone forget Heather? Honestly, Logan, that had to be your worst girlfriend ever. And so young."

His face blazed. "If you had looked past her appearance, you would have found a very intelligent and caring girl," he said. "The Goth look would not have lasted. And for the record, I didn't know she was only seventeen until she went missing."

"Ran away, you mean. Frank said that girl was a handful. And Georgina concurred."

"So you don't think the woman at the soccer game yesterday could have been Heather?"

His mother gaped at him. "Uh. No. That woman had poise that Heather would never in her lifetime acquire."

Logan wasn't so sure. The more he thought about it, little things like the way Carly finger-combed her hair and lifted her chin just so reminded him of Heather. When he left the jewelry store, he planned to swing by the hospital again and point-blank ask her.

"The TV reporter said the shooting might be a gang initiation— do you agree?" she asked.

He'd never known a gang to use a .22 rifle in a shooting. "No."

She placed the chopsticks in the bag the food had come in and shook her head. "From what the reporter said, the victim wasn't from around here, so why would anyone shoot her?"

That was the million-dollar question.

19

A LITTLE AFTER TWO THIRTY, David hurried toward the elevator in the North Main building where the police department had just moved their offices. He should have left ten minutes ago. His daughter's school let out at three and if he didn't double-time it, Lexi and her friend would be the last ones left in the parent pickup group. Something she hated. And something Georgina would never let happen.

But he was still trying to get his department organized, and time had gotten away from him. He punched the down button with a little more force than necessary.

"David!"

He turned at the sound of Brad Hollister calling his name. "Can it wait until morning? I have to pick up Lexi."

Brad held a black book. "Found this when I finished emptying Alan Patton's office. It's Lia's planner."

"What?" He stopped in his tracks and waited for Brad to catch up with him. He'd asked Patton about it a year ago, and the detective couldn't find it. "Where was it?"

"In a box in his office."

The detective had been way overdue for retirement. David took the planner and flipped through it, his heart catching at little notes Lia had written. *Alexis's birthday - 3 days. Don't forget to pick up steaks for dinner tonight.*

The elevator slid open. "Thanks," David said and stepped through the opening. He'd look at it closer once he got home. "See you tomorrow."

A few minutes later he pointed his car toward East Memphis and the school. Patches of blue poked through the clouds that had hung low most of the day. Once he turned in to the school, he checked the time and winced. There wasn't a car in line. He pulled into the circle drive and recognized Lexi's art teacher, who eyed him like he was a candidate for worst father of the year before she motioned Lexi and Hannah forward.

"Running late, Lieutenant Raines?" she said as he got out and opened the door for the girls to climb in the back seat.

"A tad. Thanks for watching them for me."

"No problem." Her words said one thing, her tone another.

"I was afraid you weren't coming, Daddy," Lexi said as they pulled away from the school.

"I told you I'd be here. Have I ever failed you yet?"

"No." She ducked her head then looked up again.

"And I won't." He winked at her and both girls giggled. As he drove to the house, their light mood continued as they laughed and talked about the trip to Nashville for the tournament. He'd already put in for time off so he could drive one of the cars. The sun broke through the clouds, matching his mood.

"We're going to change," Lexi said when he pulled in front of the house. "And then go walk Max."

"Do you have time?"

"We'll only walk him around the circle once," Hannah said.

"And Mrs. Frasier is counting on us," Lexi added. "Since she broke her leg, the only time Max gets to walk is when we take him."

"Okay. I have something to check on, so I'll be in my office when you're ready. You have your phone, right?" David had activated one of his old iPhones for her birthday. Just for emergency use.

She rolled her eyes at him. "Of course."

"And it's booted up?" Lexi's school prohibited cell phones being turned on.

"Not yet. It's in my backpack. I'll turn it on after I change."

When the girls came back downstairs, Lexi had braided her hair and tied the braids with pink bows. "Cute," he said and got another roll of her eyes. Ignoring her, he said, "It's three thirty. Be back here in fifteen minutes."

She saluted. "Yes, sir!"

When the door closed behind them, David took the planner to his office and settled in the chair behind his desk. He'd given Lia the leather binder for Valentine's Day. Not exactly a romantic gift, but she'd loved it. He slowly turned the pages, pausing at May 18. Their wedding anniversary. Lia had marked through her afternoon appointments and written "date with David" in large letters.

Seeing the date in black and white brought it all back so clearly. They'd left Lexi with Georgina and Frank and had driven to Pickwick Lake for the day, stopping at the antique shops Lia loved along the way. One of the shops was adjacent to a little country store, and they picked up sandwiches for a picnic by the lake. He pulled his bottom lip through his teeth. It'd been the last anniversary they'd spent together. David slammed the book closed. *Why did she have to die?*

He rarely questioned God about her death these days—he was beyond that. Oh, his head knew the world was full of evil, but why had it touched his family? He and Maggie discussed that question sometimes. Maggie. He thought of something Gram had said not long ago—he needed to fish or cut bait, meaning it wasn't fair to keep stringing her along if he wasn't serious about her. And if he was, then he needed to ask her to marry him.

His grandmother was a wise woman. Tonight, after he and Maggie talked with Lexi and they got the go-ahead he knew she would give them, he would pop the question. If she said yes, Donovan Jewelers was only a few miles away and was open until nine.

David checked his watch. The girls had been gone almost twenty minutes. He'd better hurry them along or they'd be late for practice. Before he reached the door, he heard Max's sharp barks. They were back. He opened the door, but only the dog sat on the porch with his leash dragging on the ground. David scanned the sidewalk in front of the house for his daughter and her friend. A chill raced down his spine. Where was she?

Hannah rounded the curve several houses away and he relaxed. Lexi had to be right behind her. When she didn't appear, he took a closer look at Hannah. Her eyes were round and tears ran down her cheeks. Something was very wrong. David sprinted toward her.

"Where's Lexi?"

"Mr. David! Lexi—" She turned and pointed toward the far side of the circle. "A man—"

He unbuckled the strap on his holster. "What happened?"

"W-we were w-walking M-max—"

"It's okay. Take a deep breath," he said, "and tell me what happened."

"A white car stopped and a man got out. Lexi grabbed Max and started running. So I ran too. Then the man caught her, and she dropped Max. I told him to stop," she wailed. "But he didn't. He put Lexi in his car and drove off."

20

CARLY HAD BEEN MOVED to a step-down unit with a window and a day bed, as well as the recliner she sat in, and a guard stationed outside the door. The doctor had said she could go home in a couple of days but to take it easy for two weeks. She had no idea where she would go, only that she wasn't ready to return to Stillwater yet.

The nurse had gotten her out of bed, and a physical therapist had walked with her down the hall, where she met the guard stationed at her door. While the Tylenol didn't completely ease the pain, Carly tolerated the discomfort to keep her head clear. She'd spent most of the afternoon trying to figure out why anyone would shoot her.

When Logan asked if she had any idea who her assailant was, she'd told him the truth. Only a few people knew why she was here, and Maggie and Jamie were the only ones who knew her actual identity.

Earlier the nurse had brought a fruit cup and Carly picked at it. When she couldn't take another bite, she set the cup on the table and blotted her lips with a napkin while she mentally retraced her actions yesterday and everyone she came into contact with. Other than Logan, no one showed any sign of recognition. Could her shooting be no more than a random act of violence? She sighed. When she left the hospital in a couple of days, she would no longer have a guard at her door . . . What if it wasn't random and the shooter came after her again?

Carly didn't have unlimited funds. Not unless she accessed the trust fund in Heather Morgan's name. If there was still a trust fund. She figured it had been dissolved long ago and the funds disbursed to Gigi and Lia.

She'd thought about the trust when she first escaped but didn't see any way of even getting information about it without revealing her identity. She'd realized once she did, she would open herself up to the possibility of Blade finding her. Not to mention, she would have to deal with her aunt, who was the administrator, and when you dealt with Gigi, you dealt with Frank.

She'd managed without the money because of the generosity of different organizations and then grants that helped to put her through college. Now she gave back to the ones who helped her. She'd gotten by without it all these years . . . Carly pressed her hand to her head. She'd have to think about it later, when everything wasn't jumbled in her mind.

A soft knock drew her attention, and she glanced at the clock as she turned toward the door. Only a little after four, so it wasn't Maggie. Logan had probably come back to bug her. "Come in," she said.

The door swung open. No, it was Maggie, and she had Carly's small overnight case in one hand, and for that, she was glad. But the attorney's briefcase in the other hand reminded her of their earlier conversation. Just because she was indebted didn't mean she had to comply with everything Maggie requested. Especially if it meant divulging her identity to David Raines. "I didn't expect you so soon."

"The case was postponed." She opened the suitcase and took out a bottle of lotion and a perfume flask, handing them to her.

"Thought you might like a few creature comforts while you're here."

Carly uncapped the perfume and dabbed a little on her wrists. Joy had been one of the first things she had bought after she escaped from Blade. It had taken a while to save up enough money to buy it, though. Her mother had worn the scent and so had Lia, and having that connection was important to Carly. The lotion had the same floral scent, and she rubbed it over her hands, wincing a little when the movement caused pain. "I appreciate you taking your time to help me."

"No problem, although I was tempted to use your hand cream," Maggie said. "Oh, here's your room key."

"You keep it—I may need something else. Besides, I have another one in my purse."

Maggie slipped the key into her purse and surveyed the room. "Nice quarters."

"Yeah. I like the window—at least I can see the sunshine. And feel free to use the lotion."

"Thank you." Maggie set her briefcase on the sofa. "I hope you've given thought to allowing me to tell David and Logan your story. They have no leads on who shot you, and if they knew your background, it would help."

Like she could forget what they'd talked about. Telling Maggie last night about her past had been difficult but doable since the information was confidential. Even now the shame of those years lingered over her like storm clouds. It was one thing for strangers to pass judgment on her, but to have her brother-in-law and niece look at her like she was dirty . . .

"I know David, and he won't judge you, Carly."

"It's not that simple." She blinked back the unexpected tears that sprang to her eyes. Carly picked up the napkin she'd dropped and concentrated on folding and refolding it and forced her thoughts away from her niece. "You don't know what it's like to see people's expressions and know they're wondering why I didn't keep trying to escape."

She glanced down at the napkin that now lay shredded in her lap and focused on picking up the pieces and stacking them in a neat pile. She raised her gaze, and the compassion in Maggie's face almost did her in. "Not everyone is like you," she said softly. "And I hear what you're saying, but I'm not sure I believe it."

"David won't judge you—I promise."

"Maybe so, but I can't do it today." Carly bit her bottom lip. She didn't know how much more of this conversation she could take. "I don't want him to know who I am."

"But he's been looking for Heather Morgan for six years."

"Why?"

"What do you mean, why? You were probably the last person who saw his wife alive other than the teenaged girl who helped her in the photography studio. He really is trying to find his wife's killer."

Was he? Or was he the killer? Remembering the tender way David Raines had looked at his daughter made it hard to believe he'd killed Lia. Carly raked her hand through her hair. She didn't really think David was Lia's killer, even though it was preferable to thinking the information she'd given her sister may have been what had gotten her killed. Heat crept into her cheeks. "I thought the newspaper said her death was gang related," she blurted.

"David has never bought that theory. Do you remember what you and Lia talked about when you met?"

Carly didn't have to search her memory. "We talked about Lexi. How much she loved her daughter . . . and her husband."

"Anything else?"

"Then we talked about . . ." Carly shrugged. "Basically what I told you last night—"

"Did you mention Austin King to her?"

"Yes . . ." Her stomach threatened to toss what little she'd eaten. "I showed Lia a sketch similar to the one I showed you."

"Did she recognize him?"

"I don't know. Maybe."

"You have to let me tell David who you are."

"No." What if she *was* responsible for Lia's death? He would hate her. And Lexi would hate her.

Maggie leaned forward and placed her hand on Carly's knee. "You are not responsible for your sister's death."

"But maybe if I hadn't told her about Austin King or showed her the sketches, she might still be alive." Pain pounded through Carly's head, and she massaged her temple with her good hand. Coming on the heels of being shot, this was too much. "I can't do this right now," she said, lifting her face. "Don't ask me to tell David Raines my story."

"Do it for Lexi. Don't you think she'd like to know what her mother told you?"

"Please." Carly pleaded with her eyes. "I can't. Not right now."

"Then let me tell him."

Carly didn't know . . .

"I'll stop pressuring you for now, but please consider it."

She barely nodded her head. "I'll think about it."

The attorney patted her hand and then asked, "Did the doctor say when he would release you?"

The pain in her head eased a little. "A couple of days."

"Where will you go?"

She lifted her shoulder in a half shrug. "Back to the hotel, I guess."

Maggie sat on the side of the bed. "Do you plan to stick around Memphis?"

"Maybe."

"You'll need someone with you for at least a week after you leave the hospital. Have you considered staying with your aunt? I'm sure she'd want—"

"No! I won't be staying with Gigi." Maggie was just coming at her from a different angle. "I'll be fine. I've worked after beatings that were tougher than this gunshot wound."

Admiration flashed in the lawyer's face, then she said, "There's an aspect to this you haven't considered."

"I doubt there's anything I've overlooked," she said, splaying her hand. "I've looked at this problem from every direction for eight years."

"Really?" Maggie took a legal pad from her briefcase and scanned the top page before she returned her attention to Carly. "This morning I remembered David mentioning once that Lia had set up a fund for Lexi's education from money she'd received when she turned twenty-five. Money that came from a settlement when her parents died in an auto accident. That got me to thinking—if Lia had a trust fund, then Heather would as well."

"I haven't forgotten the trust fund, but I doubt there's anything left. I'm sure my uncle discovered a way to get his hands on it."

"That's where you're wrong." Maggie tapped the yellow pad. "My assistant did a little research this morning and discovered your part of the insurance settlement is still being held in the trust. I spoke with the person at the bank who is in charge of it, and while he wouldn't divulge the amount, he did indicate it was substantial."

Carly could use the money to track down Austin King. She pulled her lip between her teeth. "It's so tempting, except it would mean coming forward and revealing that I'm Heather Morgan, and I've already told you, I can't do that for so many reasons," she said, then frowned as Maggie's words penetrated the fog in her brain. "Wait . . . did you say someone at the bank is in charge of the trust? My aunt was the trustee, not a bank."

"That changed a couple of years after you left. Evidently, your aunt became ill and Frank requested that he be made trustee of the trust fund. Lia must not have been comfortable with that because her lawyer asked the court to set up the bank option. Once she turned twenty-five, she received her portion of the settlement, but yours stayed in the trust."

Maggie held the legal pad where Carly could see the name of a bank. "My personal opinion is that Lia always believed you would return, and she wanted to make sure your money was protected."

Remembering her sister the last time she'd seen her pierced Carly's heart. Those had been some of the first words Lia had spoken to her. *"I knew you'd come back."* Why hadn't she mentioned the trust that day? "I don't understand. Removing Gigi just doesn't sound like something Lia would do."

"She wasn't removed, but I think your aunt had some health problems. It looks as though Lia thought there needed to be another safeguard in place."

It still surprised her. Gigi and Frank were always tight with Lia. Whereas Carly's run-ins with them had been legendary, especially with her uncle. As a kid, she hadn't understood why Frank never liked her. But then, she hadn't exactly been likeable, and her Goth lifestyle had certainly rubbed him the wrong way.

"You'll never amount to anything."

He'd told her that so many times that Carly wondered if proving him wrong had been one of the reasons she'd so readily fallen for Austin King's line. She could just see the I-told-you-so smirk on Frank's face if she came forward and revealed her story. "What will happen to the money if I don't claim it?" Maybe it would go to Lexi. Carly could live with that.

"Since you had no will when you disappeared, if you were somehow declared dead, it would go to your heirs—Lexi and your aunt."

It was one thing to give up her inheritance for Lexi . . . but for Gigi and Frank to share in it . . . not after the way they had treated her growing up.

Maggie sat back in the chair. "Where you've been the past sixteen years is actually no one's business but yours."

Was it possible? Could it be that simple? Just come forward

and make a claim? The original settlement had been for a half million dollars. After twenty-two years of sitting in an account and drawing interest, her part should be at least—she tried to do the math, but it was too much for her brain today.

"What if no one believes that I'm Heather?" Carly said. It'd be just like Frank to throw up that roadblock.

"There's always DNA," Maggie said. "A test would show you're a close relative to Lexi and Georgina."

Carly chewed her bottom lip. "You said my aunt had health problems. What kind?"

"It appears your aunt had a bout with depression, but I could ask David—"

"No." Carly turned the information over in her mind. Maggie's cell phone rang, and she excused herself and stepped out of the room. Carly wished she could do what Maggie asked. Maybe it would give her closure. And Lexi. She was certain her niece would like to know how proud Lia was of her and how much she loved her.

Her phone dinged a text and she frowned. She rarely received messages, since few people had her number other than the staff at Tabula Rasa. She grabbed the phone off the table and opened the screen, and a photo of Lexi appeared.

Her heart slammed against her rib cage. The door jerked open and Carly quickly hid her phone.

Maggie's face was white. "Lexi has been kidnapped! I'll be back."

Carly struggled to speak. "Wait," she said as Maggie wheeled around to leave. "What happened?"

She stopped at the door. "I don't know. I'll call you when I do."

Numb, Carly could only nod. Once she was alone, she opened the screen on her phone again and read the text.

Keep your mouth shut or your niece will die.

The photo of Lexi gripped her attention. Her niece was on her side with her hands tied in front of her. Some type of scarf had been wrapped around her head as a blindfold, and gray tape covered her mouth.

The room faded as darkness encroached Carly's vision.

Keep your mouth shut or your niece will die.

Barely breathing, she stared at the photo. The message chased through her head until she thought it would explode.

How did they get her phone number?

21

AT FIVE O'CLOCK, David paced his living room. An Amber Alert was being broadcast every fifteen minutes on the airways, and Kevin Scott with the Missing Persons Unit was doing everything possible to find the two men who'd taken his daughter. But why did they take her?

Hannah had described one as having a bushy beard and a tattoo of a snake on his neck. She hadn't seen the driver because the SUV they were in had dark, tinted windows. But without a license number, looking for the white SUV was like looking for a minnow in a pond full of small fish.

His third phone call had been to his brother, Eric, and the FBI agent had come immediately. A command post had been set up in record time. While Eric spoke with the technician assembling equipment for a phone trace in case the kidnappers called, David checked his locator app again. The message had not changed. Lexi's location was still unavailable.

Hannah had confirmed that Lexi forgot to boot up her phone after David reminded her. Pocketing his cell, he crossed the room to where the girl huddled next to her mother, Elaine. "You don't have to stay," he said.

"Hannah doesn't want to leave," Elaine replied, smoothing her daughter's red curls. "She wants to be here when Lexi comes home."

He knelt in front of the girl. "It'll be all right," he said. "Lexi would want you to go home and rest."

"Why did that man take her?" The girl's voice broke.

"I don't know, honey. But you've been a big help."

"But I couldn't tell you what the other man looked like!"

"It's okay. You remembered the one with the beard and that he had a tattoo. When we catch him, we'll be able to identify him from the snake on his neck." He figured the beard had been fake, but at least her description of the white SUV narrowed the vehicles somewhat. Unless they changed cars. He stood, catching the fear in Elaine's eyes. The same fear he felt in his heart. "Take her home," he said. "I'll call as soon as we have any word."

As the two walked out the door, David was thankful Hannah had been spared. But why did the men want Lexi? Eric had asked him to review his cases, but it'd been over two years since David had worked an active homicide investigation. He hadn't been able to think of a single one involving a criminal who would kidnap Lexi to get back at him. And she was definitely targeted. Otherwise, Hannah would have been taken as well.

He turned at a hand on his shoulder. Maggie. He hadn't seen her come in, and he drew her into his arms and held tight. The shock was wearing off, leaving a hollow, sick feeling in the pit of his stomach. "Thanks for coming."

"I'm so sorry," she said.

"Why didn't I make sure her phone was on?"

Her arms tightened around his waist, then she released him and stepped back. "You couldn't have known something like this would happen. Do you have any news at all?"

"No."

"Do you think it's for ransom?"

He nodded toward his brother. "Eric is preparing for it, just in case I receive a call demanding money."

Her blue eyes darkened. "Can I do something? Make coffee, maybe?"

"Mrs. Baxter made a pot." How could they be talking about everyday things like coffee? His daughter was missing. His cell phone rang and he looked at the screen, then at his brother. "It's Kevin Scott," he said. Scott was a good officer, thorough, and he paid attention to details. Eric joined him as David answered. "What have you found?"

"Uniformed patrol discovered a white SUV that had been reported stolen on the Target parking lot half a mile from you," Scott said. "There was a pink bow stuffed under the floor mat, like someone may have hidden it."

An image of his daughter with her hair braided popped in his mind. "Lexi had pink bows in her hair."

"The Crime Scene Investigation team is on its way."

"I'll be there in five minutes."

"I think you should stay here and let the professionals do their job," Eric said.

David exhaled a breath. "Scratch that," he said to Scott.

"Yeah," he said. "I heard. You don't have to be there—the CSI team will be thorough."

Perhaps, but he wanted to be on-site, going over that vehicle himself. "What if they miss something?"

"They won't. And I'll be with them. We're going to find Lexi."

"Thanks." He hung up and slid the phone in his pocket and tried not to think of how scared Lexi must be. But she'd left them a clue in the SUV, and if she got a chance, she'd turn her phone on.

His brother approached and put his arm around David's shoulder. "I'm so sorry. I wish there was something I could do."

His brother loved Lexi like one of his own. "Thanks. It helps for you to just be here."

David had been on the other side, telling parents how sorry he was for whatever happened to their child. He balled his hands. He didn't know how to be the victim. "You haven't told Gram yet, have you?"

Their grandmother had practically raised Eric and him, keeping them while their parents worked. She loved Lexi with the fierceness only a grandmother could have. How was he going to face her? Tell her he hadn't kept Lexi safe?

"Yes. I didn't want her to hear about it from someone else—Lexi's name is on all of the alerts. How about Georgina? Have you let her know?"

Georgina. David hadn't even thought about her. He quickly dialed her number. It went straight to her voicemail, and he disconnected. No way was he going to leave her a message saying that Lexi had been kidnapped.

22

THE MAN HAD SHOVED LEXI onto the floor of the van, and she lay curled into a ball. He sat on the seat above her, and even though the blindfold pressed tight against her nose, she could smell him, like he'd been working and gotten all sweaty. Tape covered her mouth, making it hard to breathe. Her hands were bound tightly with the same kind of tape.

Sounds bombarded her ears—the tires hummed on the road, changing to bumps, and she counted them. One, two . . . ten. A bridge, maybe? Then a horn blared. Were they still in the city? It seemed like they'd been driving forever. Far away, she heard the faint wail of a siren.

Daddy, please come get me.

Something tickled her cheek, and she raised her hands to brush it away.

"Don't move again, or I'll kill you." The voice was gravelly, like he was working to keep it low.

She shivered as flat, cold metal touched her neck. He had a knife. He must not have seen her when she tucked her bow under the floor mat. *God, help me!* He'd saved Daniel from the lions' den, surely he could send her daddy to find her.

The knife eased away from her neck. Lexi rolled as the van made a sharp turn.

"Be careful up there," the man said, forgetting to keep his voice deep. "Stop slinging us around."

"You wish to drive? No? Then shut up."

It was the first words she'd heard from this kidnapper, and she tucked his heavy Spanish accent into her memory. When she got away, she would need a way to identify her captors. She'd heard her dad talk about that.

The van made another sharp turn. Where were they taking her? Lexi lost track of the many turns they made until finally the van stopped. Rough hands pulled her upright, and then her captor slung her over his shoulder. As he walked, the blindfold inched loose, allowing her to see they were walking through tall grass. The air had a chill in it along with the scent of burning wood. They climbed stairs and then keys rattled and a door creaked open.

The man carrying her stood her on the floor and ripped the tape away from her mouth. "Ow!"

"Shut up, or I'll tape it shut again."

Lexi pressed her lips together. She did not want that tape over her mouth again. With the blindfold on, she couldn't tell what kind of house they were in, but it had an old-house smell, like the cabin at the lake. One of the men clamped a hand on her collarbone, and she bit her lip to keep from crying out.

"If you do what I say, you'll live. If you try to run, I will catch you and you will die. Do you understand?"

Certain he could hear her heart hammering against her ribs, Lexi bobbed her head.

"Good." He opened another door and shoved her inside the room. "Sit here."

She felt for a chair. "I c-can't see. C-can I t-take the b-blindfold off?"

"No! Sit on the floor."

When she was slow to do what he ordered, he shoved her, and she cried out as she landed facedown on the hard floor.

"I told you to shut up."

"You hurt me." The words surprised her and she ducked, expecting a blow.

"I'll do worse than that if you give me any trouble."

Then his footsteps crossed the room and the door slammed shut. Maybe he was trying to fool her into thinking he'd left. Lexi scrambled backward until a wall pressed against her shoulders. She stilled herself as faint voices came from another part of the house, too far away for her to understand what was being said. Another sound reached her ears. Someone was crying, and it didn't sound like a grown-up.

She pushed the blindfold up, but darkness still surrounded her. Lexi brought her bound hands close to her face but still couldn't see them. Her breathing came faster as the darkness closed in, and she started shaking. *Stop it*. If she fell apart, she'd never escape. Taking a deep breath, she held it for a few seconds like her dad had shown her once when she had a nightmare. Then she released her breath and pushed all the air from her lungs. It took two more breaths before she quit shaking. If only she had her phone, she could call her dad. But the man had found it and taken it away from her.

Suddenly she became aware of someone knocking on the other side of the wall. Three knocks and then a pause, then three more. Cautiously, Lexi rapped her knuckles on the wall. The person tapped again—one, then four quick taps like a tune that Lexi had heard her grandmother do. *Shave and a haircut . . . two bits*. She responded with the first part and stopped. Two knocks quickly came back.

"Can you hear me?" she whispered.

Nothing. The walls must be too thick. She tapped again and the person returned it, but not in the same place. Whoever it was had moved to her right. Lexi followed the taps until she came to a door. No light shone under it, so the room must be as dark as hers. If only she could get her hands loose. But the tape was too tight, so using both hands, she felt along the frame until she came to the doorknob. It turned easily, but the door wouldn't budge. Either it was locked with a dead bolt or it was stuck. She ran her hands down the frame to the floor. A finger-width space ran along the bottom of the door and she knelt close to it.

"Are you there?" she whispered and held her breath.

"Yes." The faint voice was a girl's. "My name is Natalie."

She wasn't alone.

23

FOR WHAT SEEMED like the hundredth time, Carly checked the clock on the wall. Almost three hours since Maggie had left and not a word from her. If she called the attorney for an update, Maggie would push Carly to release her from her promise, and that could get Lexi killed. But at least now she had an answer for her shooting—someone *had* recognized her. But who? And how?

She didn't think Jacqueline and her aunt had been close enough to get a good look at her, but she'd been up close and personal with Logan. And David and Frank. They had been close enough to get a good look at her. Was it possible one of them recognized her? Frank never liked her, but try to kill her? That was hard to fathom. She pressed her hand to her forehead. Did she have a mannerism that held over from sixteen years ago?

Carly searched for a common thread in the people she'd met, and caught her breath. Austin King. His name flashed in her mind like a neon sign. What if he'd used that name only one time? That had to be it. She sank back on the pillow. She'd given herself away. *Stupid. Stupid. Stupid.*

If the connection was Austin King, then she needed to add Vanessa and Dr. Adams to her list. And Jamie and Maggie. Immediately she discarded the last two. Carly pulled the message up again. *Keep your mouth shut or your niece will die.*

Lead settled in her stomach. It was all her fault Lexi had been kidnapped. And Lia—icy bands tightened around her lungs, squeezing the breath from her. Without a doubt the information she'd given her sister had gotten her killed. If she'd just stayed away from her family, none of this would have happened.

Carly threw back the sheet. If she was the cause, then only she could fix it. She eased out of bed, feeling the cold floor under her feet, her mind whirling with questions. Who had the most to gain from her silence?

Whoever kidnapped her sixteen years ago.

A knock at the door froze her. Carly did not want to see anyone right now, but the door opened without her invitation, and Logan stepped into the room. Her mouth dried. Logan thought he recognized her at the soccer game. And they had talked about Austin King.

"You're up?"

She reined in her thoughts and pasted a faint smile on her lips. "Yes. Even walked down the hall," she said, climbing back into bed. "Did they find David Raines's daughter?"

"You know about that?"

"Madeline Starr was here when David called and told her. Have they found Lexi?" Immediately she regretted using her niece's name.

"I'm afraid not." He gave her a curious gaze. "You don't know the girl, so why the interest?"

"That's a stupid question. I would be interested in any child who had been taken."

"Touché." He tilted his head. "I can't figure you out."

"I don't understand."

Logan pulled a straight-backed chair near the bed and straddled it, then propped his arms on the back. "I sense this connection between us, like I know you. At the soccer field, you reminded me of someone I once knew."

She didn't flinch under his steady gaze.

Logan raised his eyebrows. "Are you Heather Morgan?"

In her first few months with Blade, he had beaten her every time she'd glared at him, and sometimes when he just didn't like the expression on her face. Lily had made Carly stand in front of a mirror and practice keeping a poker face while Lily yelled obscenities at her. That practice served her well now. She rubbed her hand over her friend's gold bracelet. "Like I told you, my name is Carly Smith. Would you like to see my driver's license?"

"Not right this minute."

"Then what's your problem?" She returned the intense gaze he'd pinned on her. Carly had stared down meaner cops than Logan. She wasn't about to admit anything to him. Not until she was certain he wasn't crooked.

"When I did a background check, I found no records older than eight years for a Carly Smith living in Stillwater, Tennessee, not even for a credit card. It's like you didn't exist prior to then."

She lifted her good shoulder in a shrug. "What can I say? I've never been arrested or even gotten a ticket, and I paid cash for everything until I returned to college. Didn't even want a credit card until then." She smoothed her hospital gown and glanced toward her suitcase, wishing she'd changed into street clothes before Logan arrived. The cotton gown did nothing for her confidence, not when Logan Donovan's eyes seemed to see through her. Could he tell her heart was thumping in her chest? Thank goodness there was no monitor overhead trumpeting her racing pulse.

He'd always had that effect on her, but this time she didn't know if it was because she still had feelings for him or because of her aversion to cops. Curiosity stirred in her heart. She should tamp it down . . . "This Heather Morgan. What was she to you?"

Startled, he broke eye contact then glanced toward the ceiling while a tiny smile played at the corner of his lips. When he returned his gaze to her, the smile was gone. "We dated for a short time.

Then she left town and no one has heard from her since. She had unusual eyes, like you—hazel with gold starbursts—not something you see every day, otherwise I wouldn't remember them so well."

He continued to stare at her, and heat radiated up her neck into her cheeks. "Only a short time? I'm surprised you remember her at all."

Abruptly he stood and handed her his card. "In case you need me. And I'll let you know when we have the complete ballistics report on the bullet the surgeon recovered from your shoulder."

She took the card. "Do you know what kind of gun was used?"

"The crime scene techs believe it was a .22 rifle."

"That's a hunting gun," she said.

"Certainly not your usual firearm for killing people."

Goose bumps prickled her arm, and she shivered. It was hard to wrap her mind around the reality that someone wanted her dead. She cradled her wounded arm closer to her body.

"How is your shoulder, by the way?"

"Still hurts, but I'll live."

"When do you think you'll be discharged?"

"Tomorrow." That's what the last doctor had said, but she wasn't waiting until tomorrow. She had work to do and willed Logan to leave. But he continued to stand at the foot of her bed. A text dinged on her phone, and her gaze darted to the table where she'd placed it. What if it was another text from Lexi's kidnappers?

"Shouldn't you check that?" Logan asked.

"It'll wait." Nevertheless, she reached for the phone and slid it under the sheet.

"If you don't mind, I'd like to have your cell phone number. So I can keep in touch."

"I assumed Madeline Starr gave you that information."

"It's on the report, but I want to make sure it's correct."

Was that how the person texting got her cell number? From

the police report? Carly gave him her number. She didn't have to answer when he called.

"I gave you my card earlier. Will you put my number in your phone?"

"Why would I do that?"

"Because someone tried to kill you, and if they try again, you would need me," he said. "Do you want to do that now? Or I can do it for you."

She grabbed her phone. "I'll do it."

Once she had him in her contacts, he nodded. "So, where did you attend college prior to your time in Stillwater?"

He had caught her slip about returning to college, and his question caught her off-guard. It was so easy to slip up, and she scrambled for an answer. "I, ah, took classes when I was in high school."

"I didn't find a record of a Carly Smith attending high school in Tennessee."

"You know how those records can get lost." The skepticism sent her thinking for another answer. "Besides, I didn't attend high school in this state."

"Oh? Where did you attend?"

Carly searched her memory for a town she'd stayed in long enough to cover any questions he might ask. "I was in California for a while. Los Angeles." That city was big enough for it to take a few days to check her information and learn she'd never set foot in the state. By then she'd be gone from here.

Logan nodded and turned toward the door, stopping just when she thought she was free of him.

"I'll contact you if I learn anything about your shooting."

"Thanks."

As soon as the door closed behind him, she slid the phone out and opened the screen. A text from Maggie. For a second she relaxed, at least until she read it. *Call me.*

Carly knew what the attorney wanted, and she did not want

to talk to her. Her phone rang, and at the same time, another text showed up. The ringing stopped and her stomach churned as she read the text.

If you ever want to see your niece, you'll forget
you ever heard of Austin King or Blade.

Above the text another photo of Lexi filled the screen. This time she was sitting upright, still blindfolded and her hands tied.

She didn't have a doubt in her mind that if she told the police about either of the men, whoever sent the text would know. These people were powerful enough to get her cell phone number and anything else they wanted. Life meant nothing to them, not even the life of an eleven-year-old girl.

Carly glanced toward her suitcase. Did she have the strength to leave the hospital and get answers to her questions? She'd worked the streets with broken ribs after Blade beat her, and a flesh wound didn't compare with that pain. Her cell phone rang again, and Maggie's name showed on the screen. Ignoring it, she held her shoulder and eased out of bed and found her boots. She was surprised the dagger was still in the sheath.

Carly fished the barrette from her purse and, using her good arm, clipped it in a strand of hair. The tracker and the small dagger in her boot should keep her safe. Opening the suitcase Maggie brought, Carly pulled out a pair of jeans and an oversized pullover. She had to have answers, and the only place to get them was at the place it all started. Jacqueline Donovan. And for that, she needed her car.

24

MAGGIE HUGGED HER ARMS to her waist as David paced the living room. She understood his need to move. It meant he was doing something. She wished she had something to do besides dwell on where Lexi might be and why anyone would take her. Because of Maggie's work with trafficked girls, her thoughts veered places she didn't want them to. *No.* If that were the case, the men would have taken Hannah as well. This was personal.

"Do you have any clue why Lexi was targeted?" she asked.

David stopped pacing and shook his head. "I've made a few calls to my informants on the streets, and the other detectives have as well. There's nothing out there suggesting it's retaliation."

"Would they tell you if they had heard?"

"Yeah, I think so." He dropped on the sofa next to her and leaned his head back, staring up at the ceiling. "Why hasn't someone called if they want money?"

"Wearing you down," she said. What if Carly's true identity was connected to Lexi's kidnapping? But she didn't know how to bring it up without breaking her word to Carly. The area of confidentiality was sacred to a lawyer and not easily broken. There would have to be a clear-cut link between the two crimes or that the knowledge Maggie had would keep another crime from being committed. And so far, neither situation indicated that was the case.

He sat up and leaned forward, resting his head in his hands. "It's all my fault." His voice broke.

"You know better than that," she said. "You're a good father. You love Lexi. And you had no idea she was in danger."

"I'm her father. I should have known! I should have made sure her phone was on!"

"David, look at me." She pulled on his arm.

He lifted his head, and her heart broke at the pain in his eyes.

"Don't you understand? I didn't keep her mother safe, and now I've failed Lexi."

Maggie wrapped her hands around his. "She's not dead. They'll find her."

His cell rang, and he pulled his hands away to grab it. "Raines." After a minute, his face fell. "Okay. Thanks for letting me know." David pocketed the phone. "Preliminary report shows no prints other than Lexi's in the SUV. Whoever took her wore gloves."

"What about hair and fibers?"

"They're vacuuming the car now for any trace evidence." His shoulders drooped in a picture of despair. "If they find anything it'll be hours, maybe days, before it can be analyzed. No telling where Lexi will be by then."

"Did anyone see the car they switched to?"

He shook his head. "They're canvassing the area now and looking at security videos." David scrubbed his face. "It's been four hours and not a thing other than an abandoned car."

Was that all? It was as though every minute was an hour long.

His phone rang again and he winced when he looked at the ID. "Georgina."

Maggie felt for him as he reluctantly answered it.

The woman's frantic voice was loud enough for Maggie to hear even though he hadn't put the call on speaker.

"Why didn't you call me?" she demanded. "Do you know how I felt when I heard Lexi's name on an Amber Alert on the television?"

"I'm sorry, Georgina," he said. "I tried to call you, but it went straight to voicemail."

"Well, you should have tried again!"

"Is Frank with you?" David asked. Maggie missed whatever her answer was, and David spoke again. "I hate for you to be alone. Why don't you come over here until he finishes with his business meeting?"

Maggie pointed toward the kitchen, and David nodded he understood. She walked to the kitchen, where she texted Carly another note to call her then slipped her phone in her back pocket and poured a cup of coffee while she waited for an answer. She couldn't help but compare the last time she was here to now. Was it just last night the kids had made the place hop? They were all excited about the upcoming tournament. And now . . .

"She's upset," David said as he joined her and poured himself a cup of coffee. "But I think once Frank gets home, she'll be okay."

"So she's not coming here?"

"I don't think so."

Maggie cupped the mug in her hands. "I wish we could hear something new."

"So do I." He glanced toward the room where his brother monitored the phone. "I don't think I'm going to get a ransom call."

"It hasn't been that long," she said.

David walked to the patio door and stared out. "I bought this house because it's in a safe neighborhood. I thought I could keep the evil in the city from touching my family. And I failed."

"You haven't failed. Don't blame yourself for the evil someone else does."

"Who do I blame, then? I'm a cop, sworn to protect the people of Memphis, and I can't even protect my own family."

An elephant standing on her chest wouldn't be any more painful. "No one's ever been a better dad than you," she said. "You've devoted your life to Lexi."

"If only that were true." His voice cracked, and he sank onto one of the kitchen chairs. "I've been too wrapped up in my job, in solving her mother's murder."

Sometimes when tragedies occurred, family members got caught up in the why rather than moving past the tragedy. He'd never talked much about Lia's murder other than in terms of finding the killer, and sometimes he drew into himself, shutting her out and making her wonder if he really was ready to marry again. She swallowed down the acid from too many cups of coffee and set the mug on the counter, pushing it away. David loved her, she didn't doubt that, but would Lia's ghost always hover over them?

He stood, his hands clenched. "I should have walked the dog with Lexi and Hannah, but I'd just gotten Lia's planner, and I wanted to look over it." He pressed his hands to his temples.

"What do you mean, you'd just gotten Lia's planner? Haven't you had it all along?"

David stopped and turned to her. "No. I'd asked for it last year from the detective who investigated her case, but he'd misplaced it."

Lia was murdered after meeting with Carly, and now Lexi had been kidnapped the day after Carly returned to Memphis. Coincidence? "Is there any possibility that Lexi's kidnapping is connected to Lia's death?" she asked.

Shock registered in his blue eyes. "Why would you ask that?"

"I—I don't know . . ." Maggie had to tell him. If she didn't and it turned out she had information that would help locate Lexi, David would never forgive her. She'd never forgive herself.

Fishing her phone from her pocket, she dialed Carly's number again. Still no answer.

25

CARLY USED HER UBER APP to arrange for a driver to pick her up outside the hospital and take her to Haven House. She assumed that was where her car was, and while she was at the shelter, she planned to question any of the girls who happened to be around.

Gingerly, she pulled off her gown and slipped into the jeans Maggie had brought. Getting the oversized sweater on was another matter. Once she was dressed, Carly sat on the side of the bed to regain the energy she'd expended.

The nurse had unhooked her from the IV just before Logan came, leaving the catheter in. When Carly asked if she could take the whole thing away, she learned it would stay in until the doctor discharged her. With her lips pressed together, she peeled the tape back and pulled the port out. A drop of blood appeared on her arm, and Carly pressed two fingers firmly against the vein. Once the bleeding stopped, she wadded the tape and catheter into a ball and tossed it in the trash.

As soon as she felt stronger, Carly used her phone to check Donovan Jewelry's website to see what time it closed. Nine. Jacqueline would probably still be there. She thought about calling to make sure, but that might raise questions she didn't want to answer. She'd just take a chance on her being there, but if she wasn't, then Jared, her older son, should be. He'd been at the party. Maybe he knew Austin King.

Carly stuffed what she needed from her suitcase into her purse. She picked up the bottle of Joy and spritzed her wrists. Fortification. The other things Maggie brought would have to be left behind. If April, or any of the nurses, saw her with the suitcase, they would realize what Carly was up to. *What about the guard?* Maybe he wouldn't be there, but if he was, she would tell him she was doing what the doctor ordered. Hopefully he would not want to accompany her.

She took a deep breath and swung the door open and strolled out of the room. The chair beside her room was empty. The guard must be on a bathroom break, and she hated that he might get in trouble when she went missing.

Carly surveyed the hall. When she'd walked earlier, she'd scouted the floor and she now zeroed in on the red exit sign. She glanced left and faltered. The end of the hallway widened out to the round nurses' station she'd walked to earlier, and Logan stood with his back to her, talking to the guard and April.

Straightening her shoulders as much as possible, she hurried in the opposite direction toward the exit and pushed the metal door. It didn't budge. Couldn't be locked—it was an exit and exits were unlocked. She pushed again and it scraped open. Carly didn't look to see if anyone noticed her escape but instead held on to the rail and descended the steps.

At the next landing, the number five made her groan. The way her shoulder throbbed, she couldn't walk down another five flights. She exited the stairwell, looking for an elevator. The layout of this floor was the same as above. Carly would have to walk past the nurses' station. Somehow she had to pull off looking like a visitor. She slipped her purse from under her pullover and hung it on her right shoulder.

One of the nurses looked up when she passed the desk, and

Carly smiled. "Good evening. I've forgotten where the elevator is. Could you direct me?"

The nurse chuckled and waved a dismissive hand. "Oh, sure. It's down the hall and around the corner."

Without breaking stride, she followed the nurse's directions. Once Carly was on the main floor, she asked how to get to the front of the building, and again she had the impression the hospital was easy to get lost in. Twilight was fading when she stepped outside the main entrance, and she scanned the parking lot for the red Corolla the Uber driver would be in. A wave of weakness washed over her, and Carly steadied herself with the rail alongside the steps, almost missing the red car that pulled into the circle.

A young man hopped out. "Ms. Smith?"

She pushed through the weakness and took a hesitant step down. "You okay?" he asked.

"Yeah, but I wouldn't turn down a little help getting to the car."

"Yes, ma'am," he said, and tucking his arm under her elbow, he guided her to the passenger side. "Front seat?"

"Sure." Pain seared her shoulder as she slid across the seat and fastened her seatbelt. What if the wound started bleeding? She wouldn't think about that.

"So you want to go to this address on Walnut Grove?"

"Please."

"Yes ma'am," he said with a jaunty salute.

If he said "ma'am" one more time . . . She grabbed the armrest as he lurched out of the drive, and then she leaned her head on the headrest, saving her strength while she planned her next move to find Lexi.

Keep your mouth shut. The text would not leave her mind. She had no doubt that returning to Memphis and bringing up Austin King's name was the reason for Lexi's kidnapping. And the name Austin King was her only lead.

First she'd talk to whoever happened to be at Haven House

and show them the sketches. But her main objective was to get her car and catch Jacqueline before the jewelry store closed. She was Carly's only link to King.

Her stomach lurched when the driver zoomed in and out of traffic. When they arrived, she shot up a prayer of thanks for getting there safely and that her car still sat in the parking lot.

"Ma'am, are you sure you're okay? You're awfully pale."

"I'm fine," she said through gritted teeth. Her cell phone rang, and a quick glance at the ID showed Logan Donovan's name. She believed she'd pass. Carly silenced her phone and then turned to the driver. "Just pull in front of the building."

When he stopped, she used her good hand to push herself from the car.

"Thanks," she said and closed the door. Once he drove off, she walked to the front entrance, recognizing the security guard from last night. What was his name? "Good evening . . . Leon," she said, finally remembering. "Is Ms. Driscoll in?"

His eyes widened. "You're the lady who was shot. Shouldn't you be in the hospital?"

Probably. "Do you think I could see Ms. Driscoll?"

"Oh, I'm sorry. She isn't here."

"Do you think I could go inside and wait?"

"I'm not supposed to let anyone in unless their name is on the list." He glanced at a clipboard. "And your name isn't here."

"But I was supposed to come this morning."

Indecision played on his face. "Well . . . since you've been here before, don't suppose it would hurt to let you in. I'd hate for you to pass out while you wait for Ms. Driscoll to arrive." He pressed a button and then held the door open for her.

"Thank you," she said and stepped inside. The aroma of popcorn met her inside the building and her stomach reminded her she hadn't eaten since lunch. One of Maggie's omelets would be heavenly.

No one sat at the desk. Voices came from the front room where Carly had fainted, and she walked to the doorway. Several girls watched TV while others curled up with a book. Heads turned toward her when she entered the room, and she reached deep to pull out a smile.

One of the younger women said, "I'm Becca. Can I help you?"

"Just looking for a place to sit down and wait for Vanessa," she said.

"The recliner is comfortable," another girl said.

"I better not—I might go to sleep." She sat in a wingback chair, glad to be off her feet. "Does anyone know when Ms. Driscoll will return?"

Echoes of nos popped up from around the room, then one girl indicated Vanessa would return around nine thirty. Carly checked her watch. Forty-five minutes. Pain throbbed through her shoulder and down her arm. Leaving the hospital before she received a prescription for pain medication may not have been her wisest decision. *Focus on Lexi.*

She straightened her back and pulled a bottle of Tylenol from her purse and shook two pills into her hand. "Could I have a glass of water?"

Becca stood. "You want ice in it?"

"No, thank you."

"Be back in a sec."

After she returned and Carly downed the two pills, she pulled out the sketches of Austin King and handed them to Becca. "Have you seen this man?"

The girl took the sheet and stared at it. "Who is it?"

"A man I know. Have you seen anyone who—"

"Ms. Smith? Why aren't you in the hospital?"

The concerned voice came from the doorway, and she looked around. Dr. Adams.

Busted.

172

26

DAVID'S BODY had a mind of its own. No sooner did he sit down than he was up and pacing again. And the door. He couldn't stop looking for it to open and Lexi to burst through. *What if she never comes through it again?*

The mantel clock's somber toll of the quarter hour drew his attention toward the fireplace. Eight forty-five? Almost five hours since Lexi went missing. It seemed like longer.

"More coffee?" Maggie asked.

He shook his head. "I'm so jittery now, it'd be like throwing gas on a fire." David sat on the sofa beside her. She'd been so quiet. "Did you reach whoever it was you've been calling?"

She pressed her lips together. "No."

"From the look on your face, it must be pretty serious."

"Yeah." She rubbed her hands up and down her arms.

"Are you cold?"

"No. There's something—"

David's cell phone rang. "It's Logan," he said and answered. "Raines."

"Is Carly Smith with you?"

173

"Why would Carly Smith be here?" Out of the corner of his eye he saw Maggie lean forward.

"She's missing from the hospital. Has Maggie heard from her?"

"I'll put you on speaker, and you can ask her yourself."

Logan repeated the question.

"Isn't she still at the hospital?" Maggie asked.

"No. She's been gone at least half an hour. When I talked to her, she appeared very worried about Lexi, and I thought she might be there with you."

Maggie's face had been pale before the call, but now she'd turned pasty. "Her car is at Haven House. Have you checked there?"

"It wasn't towed last night?"

"No, it was still there when I attended the board meeting this morning."

"Thanks," Logan said.

"Call me if you find her," Maggie said.

David ended the call and laid his phone on the coffee table before he turned to Maggie. She wouldn't meet his gaze. "Why do you suppose she left the hospital?"

Maggie leaned back on the sofa and pressed her hands to her face.

"What's wrong?"

She didn't answer him right away. A chill raced through his body and a sour, metallic taste filled his mouth. "What does Carly Smith have to do with Lexi's kidnapping?"

With a deep breath, she raised her head, but she still wouldn't look at him. "I'm sorry—"

David's cell phone dinged and he looked down. "Hold up a minute. I have an email I need to check—it's from a forensic artist I contacted about updating Heather's photo."

"Before you open that, I have something to tell you."

"This won't take a second," he said and punched his email app and then stared at the phone, his body stiffening. *Carly Smith is Heather?* He pulled his gaze away from the picture. "You knew she was Heather, didn't you?"

Her shoulders sagged. "That's what I was about to tell you."

"Why didn't you tell me before? And don't say it was *confidential*. You know how long I've been looking for her."

Maggie bit her bottom lip and then shook her head. "Until five minutes ago, there was no way I could break Carly's confidence."

"What happened five minutes ago to change things?"

"When she left the hospital, she put herself in danger . . . and maybe Lexi."

David's blood pressure shot up. "What are you talking about? Do you think she's in on the kidnapping?"

"What's wrong?" his brother asked. "What are you yelling about?"

He ignored Eric and pinned his gaze on Maggie, waiting.

She palmed her hands. "Carly had nothing to do with the kidnapping, I'm sure of that. But . . ." Maggie took a deep breath. "Some of the things she's been involved in . . . If we don't find her soon, I believe the people who took Lexi will find Carly and kill her."

"What?" David and Eric spoke at the same time.

David paced the living room floor. Maggie had chosen Carly Smith over him? He stopped and turned to her. "Why are you telling me now?"

"I believe there is immediate risk to Carly and maybe Lexi. That frees me from my obligation to keep what she told me confidential."

Misery was stamped on Maggie's face. David didn't know what to say.

"I didn't believe what Carly told me had anything to do with Lexi's kidnapping, but now—"

"You could have let me be the judge of that. What did she tell you, and where has she been all these years after she ran away from home?"

"She didn't run away. She was kidnapped and sold into human trafficking."

The bottom fell out of his stomach. What if Lexi's kidnappers were human traffickers?

27

LOGAN HOOKED HIS PHONE on his belt. He should have known Carly would go after her car. That she even left the hospital blew his mind. From the looks of her, a feather could have knocked her down. She was one tough cookie.

He hopped in his car and pulled out of the hospital parking lot. His phone rang just as he exited off Union onto Walnut Grove. "Donovan," he said, answering hands-free.

"It's me, Maggie . . ." He heard her take a deep breath. "I've shared with David that Carly is Heather Morgan and that she was kidnapped sixteen years ago by a man who went by the name Austin King and claimed to be a model scout. She came back to Memphis to track him down. I'm not sure how this ties in to everything else, but I believe there's a connection. I thought you ought to know."

"You're kidding." So he'd been right. "Where has she been all these years?"

Maggie didn't answer right away, then she sighed. "She . . . The man who kidnapped her, sold her to a trafficker. She spent eight years on the streets before she escaped."

Logan's knuckles turned white on the steering wheel. That was what Carly had been trying to hide. "You said eight years. She's been gone sixteen. What happened after she escaped? Why didn't she come back then?"

"You'll have to ask her that, if you find her. It's her story to tell."

"Thanks for letting me know who she is," he said, his voice husky. After they disconnected he drove, barely aware of the traffic. His chest ached for Carly. No wonder she didn't trust him . . . or any man, for that matter. Logan dialed dispatch and asked to be connected to Sergeant Neely in Vice. Once he had him on the phone he asked, "What do you have on the human trafficking ring in Memphis?"

"Not a lot," Neely answered. "We've arrested some of the pimps, but none of them have rolled over on the higher-ups."

That was common. "Have you ever heard the name Austin King or anything about a man posing as a model scout?"

"King, no, but the model scout—hear that all the time. When I speak to groups, I warn about fake agents and scouts. Don't know how much good it does."

"Could you ask around, see if you can locate anyone who knows something about this Austin King?"

"Sure thing."

Logan hung up and checked where he was. Still a couple of miles from Haven House. What was Carly up to? She'd received a text and acted strangely. What if the traffickers kidnapped Lexi as a way to keep Carly from going to the police?

Carly turned toward the door. "Dr. Adams, I thought you'd left on your hunting trip."

"Something came up and I had to put it off a day or two." He set his bag on an end table. "So I came by and checked on my patient here. How did you get out of the hospital so fast? And what are you doing here?"

How did he know she'd been shot? TV, of course. She nodded to the paper Becca held. "I'm still looking for this man."

The doctor scanned the room. "Does anyone know him?"

"No." The dull ache in her shoulder increased. Carly stood. "It was good to see you again," she said and walked toward the door.

"You don't look very well," he said. "I'm not sure you should be driving."

Ignoring the pain, she straightened her shoulders. "I'm fine. I have a room at the Westin, and the hotel isn't that far from here."

No need to tell him she was not going to the hotel but to Donovan Jewelers to talk to Jacqueline Donovan. Austin King was at her party and she had to know him. If she found King, she could find out where Lexi was. A wave of dizziness swept over her and she fought to stay upright.

"Sit down."

While the doctor's words were not a request, Carly could not have made it another step. She plopped into the nearest chair, and he held her wrist with his thumb and forefinger.

"Your heart is racing. I think I should call an ambulance."

"No! I was just dizzy for a second. I'm fine now." She inhaled a long breath and tried to calm herself as he continued to take her pulse. "It's slowing, right?" she said. "I'm fine."

He released her wrist. "Maybe so, but I still think I should drive you to your hotel."

"I promise, I'm fine." Careful not to stand too quickly, Carly got to her feet. "See? No problem."

She kept her body straight until she was at the front door, and then allowed herself to relax. She was not fine, but she had to find Lexi. Glancing back, she caught Dr. Adams staring at her, and she hurried out the door and past Leon.

"Hold up, Miss," he called. "Let me walk you to your car."

"Thank you."

Her heart sank when a car rolled to a stop in front of her and Logan Donovan climbed out.

"I'll see Ms. Smith to her car, Leon." Then he turned to her. "You're a hard person to keep up with."

Carly kept walking toward her car. "I have no idea why you want to keep up with me."

"Maybe because you're going to so much trouble to get away from me," he said, catching up with her. He adjusted the gun on his belt. "Why did you leave the hospital?"

"I had something I needed to tend to."

"Maybe I can help you with whatever it is. Where are you off to now?"

She might as well tell him since he would follow her to the jewelry store. "Donovan Jewelers."

Carly almost laughed at the surprise on his face. Somewhere to her left a car door slammed, and she looked in that direction but didn't see anything.

"Why there?"

"I want to talk to your mother."

"My *mother*? Whatever for?"

"That's my business."

"Well, you won't talk to her tonight. She isn't at the store—she went home early."

Not at the store? Carly's legs threatened to buckle and she leaned against her car. "Then I'll talk to Jared."

She jerked her head in the direction of the road as a full-size dark SUV careened into the parking lot. Before she could react, two men jumped out. Pain ripped through her shoulder and her head swam as one of the men grabbed her and muscled her to the truck. Behind her, Logan traded punches with the other man. Then more pain as the other man shoved her into the back seat.

Carly clawed at the door handle. The door wouldn't budge. The men thrust an unconscious Logan in beside her, and she fell back as the SUV screeched away.

28

DAVID'S GRANDMOTHER buzzed around the room, frying bacon and making biscuits. At least *she* didn't glower at her every time their gazes met. Maggie hadn't been able to stand David's stony silence toward her and had retreated to the kitchen.

"You could have used the dishwasher, you know."

Maggie looked up. David's grandmother smiled. A small woman, she stood at the counter, her flour-covered hands turning biscuit dough. She reminded Maggie of her own grandmother.

"Thanks, Mrs. Raines, but this gives me something to do with my hands." She plunged the last cup into the sudsy water.

"Call me Linda . . . or better still, Gram like the rest of the family does."

But she wasn't family and after tonight probably never would be. She didn't fit here. And she had to believe that what she'd kept secret had no bearing on Lexi's kidnapping. Otherwise, Maggie wouldn't be able to forgive herself.

"This, too, shall pass."

She didn't know if Linda meant Lexi's kidnapping or David's anger at her.

"Lexi will come home."

Said with the optimism of a grandmother. If only she could believe that.

"When this is over, he'll understand your position, that you had to honor your word."

"You heard?"

"It would have been a little hard not to. When David gets upset, he gets loud." Linda used the back of her wrist to shove a strand of gray hair out of her face, and then she cut the dough into squares with a knife. "My grandson is wrong to be angry with you."

"I don't know. He shouldn't have learned Carly was Heather from someone else. Maybe if I'd told him . . ." What if human traffickers had Lexi? She shuddered. Could she have prevented the kidnapping? Maggie looked up, and Linda appeared to be waiting for her to continue. "What Carly told me initially had nothing to do with Lia. Last night I didn't even know Carly was her sister."

"You did what you thought was right, Maggie, and that's all you can do in life." Gram wiped flour from her hands and hugged her. "Stop worrying. I truly believe God is protecting our little girl."

God. She'd been so upset, she hadn't even prayed other than when she drove to David's house from the hospital. Neither had she dreamed Carly would leave the hospital. Where could she be? Maggie had tried to call her again, but the call went straight to voicemail. There'd been no further word from Logan, either. Why didn't he answer his calls? She wrinkled her brow. Something was wrong . . .

29

FOR THE LAST HALF HOUR David itched to take the list of names Carly Smith had given to Maggie and question everyone on it, starting with Logan, except Logan didn't answer his phone. Besides, even though Carly was Lia's sister, that didn't mean there was a connection with Lexi's kidnapping.

"Learn anything?" he asked his brother.

"Not yet."

Eric had used the number Maggie provided and put in a request to Carly's carrier for her cell phone's activity. David checked his phone to make sure he hadn't missed a text from Kevin Scott.

He'd called earlier with an update on the search for the vehicle the kidnappers had switched to. Evidently, the switch had happened somewhere other than the Target store. The security feed from the camera in the parking lot showed a tall man getting out of the SUV and walking away with his head down and collar pulled up, blocking his face.

"David."

He turned at his grandmother's voice.

"There's fresh coffee in the kitchen," she said. "Maggie made it."

He missed Maggie by his side and owed her an apology. David didn't like himself very much right now for the way he'd raised his voice, but he still couldn't wrap his mind around the fact that she'd withheld Carly's identity.

"I'll get some in a minute." He glanced toward the clock. Time had crawled to a stop.

"David . . ."

He shifted his gaze back to his grandmother. She barely came up to his chest, but when she folded her arms and spoke his name in that tone, he was a kid again, looking up at her, knowing he'd displeased her. "Yes?"

"You need to make things right with Maggie," she said.

He'd known she was going to say something he didn't like. David gripped the mug, the heat radiating to his fingers. "If she'd just—"

"Stop." She put her hand on his arm. "Listen to me. And scowling doesn't become you."

"But Maggie knew I've been trying to find Lia's sister. If she'd only told me last night who Carly Smith was, I would not have let Lexi out of my sight."

"Is that right? Why would knowing who Carly was make a difference in the way you took care of Lexi?"

He opened his mouth and closed it. How would that knowledge have changed anything?

"Besides, she didn't know last night."

Gram's soft words pierced him. "What? Why didn't she tell me that?"

"Maybe because you didn't give her a chance before you flew off the handle. She's in the kitchen."

David raked his fingers through his hair. Why hadn't she imparted that little bit of information when she related Smith's ordeal in human trafficking? Maybe because she was done with him? "She could have told me Carly Smith had been trafficked."

Gram raised her eyebrows. "What this Carly told her was spoken in confidence. What kind of person would Maggie be if she broke her word?"

"But—"

"No buts. Just don't ever forget she's a woman who honors her word, and she told you as soon as she honorably could. You owe her an apology."

David hated when Gram was right and he was wrong. He dropped his gaze to the floor, and his heart hitched when he caught sight of the tiny dents in the floor. He would never fuss at Lexi for wearing her tap shoes again.

Gram patted his arm. "She's coming home to us."

He raised his gaze. "How can you be so sure?"

"I feel it." She touched her chest. "In here. Now, go talk to Maggie."

"She probably won't give me the time of day."

"I think she will."

David wasn't so sure. He started toward the kitchen and stopped by the desk where his brother was on the internet. "Anything new?" he asked for the hundredth time.

"I just received the report from sixteen years ago when Heather Morgan went missing. It's like she fell off the grid."

Like Lexi. The entire police force was scouring the city, even setting up roadblocks, and so far nothing. "Everyone but Lia thought her sister had run away from home. I didn't work the case, but I even thought that."

"Don't beat yourself up about it. These traffickers know how to cover their tracks." Eric looked up from the computer. "Have you remembered anything else from what Lia told you six years ago about her meeting with Heather? Was she calling herself Carly Smith then?"

"She never mentioned that name." David rubbed the rock-hard muscles in the back of his neck. He'd get a headache if he didn't find a way to relax. "Lia called me after she met with her sister, but she didn't relay much of what happened at the meeting, just that there was something she needed to check out and she would explain everything that night. If we hadn't argued, she may have told me more."

Eric nodded toward the kitchen. "Let's get Maggie back in here and go over it again—maybe she'll remember something new."

He doubted she'd overlooked or forgotten anything. But he swallowed his objection. Sometimes new details surfaced when a witness repeated an account. "I'll get her."

He paused in the kitchen doorway. Maggie was at the island, scrubbing the counter. David hated the angry words he'd spouted, and it wasn't like they hadn't talked about this very thing. He just never imagined a situation like this would come up. Still, he thought Maggie would trust him with any information. Was that why he was so upset? Because his pride was wounded? Heat rose in his face. "Don't rub a hole in my counter," he said softly.

Her head jerked up. "I didn't see you standing there. Any word?"

David shook his head. "Maggie—"

"David—" She dropped her gaze. "You go first."

"I'm sorry."

"For?"

She was not going to make it easy. "For 'flying off the handle,' as Gram says. For the unfair words."

A curt nod and silence met his words.

"I'm sorry I blamed you for Lexi's kid—" He couldn't say the word. "I'm just sorry."

Her face softened. "I am too. I truly didn't know Carly was Heather last night. I didn't find out until today." She rubbed the same spot on the counter.

"I believe you."

Her lips formed a thin line, and then she raised her gaze to meet his. "But the problem is, I wouldn't have told you if I'd known last night. Not unless Carly released me from my promise."

He balled his hands. "But you knew I was searching for her."

"She told me her story because I'd given my word to keep whatever she said confidential. The only reason I broke her confidence was because I think she's in danger."

"Where is she now?"

"I don't know. She doesn't answer her phone and neither does Logan."

He hadn't tried Logan in the last fifteen minutes. "He's still not answering?" he asked, taking out his phone.

"No. I tried just a minute ago."

Eric burst into the room with his computer, and David paused in dialing.

"You're not going to believe this," Eric said. "But Carly Smith's text records show she received a photo of Lexi and a text warning her to keep her mouth shut and forget she knew an Austin King and someone named Blade."

"No." Maggie sat down at the island. "Can you tell where the text came from?"

"Probably a burner, but I'll check." He set his computer on the island and went to work.

"Have you gotten her call records yet?"

"No. Just her texts."

David gripped his phone. Lexi *was* kidnapped to shut Carly up. They had to find her. He dialed Logan again, but he still didn't answer. David turned to Maggie. "While he's doing that, let's go over Carly's story again. Who is this Austin King?"

"He's the man she met at Jacqueline Donovan's party. He promised to make her a model."

"And Blade?"

"That's the man King sold her to. She indicated he was operating out of Atlanta when she escaped, but in the beginning he was in New York City."

"Why did she suddenly decide to try and find this man?" he asked. "She'd been free at least six—" A band squeezed his chest. *Six years ago.* Lia hadn't mentioned the name Austin King, but did he give her a chance to? "Did she tell Lia about meeting him at Jacqueline's party?"

"Yes. She showed her a sketch similar to what you have, and she thought her sister might have recognized him."

Eric looked up from his computer. "What else can you remember?"

"Before she was shot, Carly planned to question Jacqueline about King. She wasn't certain he was still in the area, but he was the only lead she had. Personally, I think her questions about him tipped someone off as to who she is. Maybe he only used the Austin King name once—when he conned Heather into going to New York City with him."

If only Lia had mentioned some of this when she'd called him that day. He focused on what Maggie had said about Jacqueline. David didn't believe she had anything to do with Carly's kidnapping, but she might know the man in the sketch. "Has anyone talked to Jacqueline?"

"FBI hasn't," Eric said.

David dialed Sergeant Scott and asked him the same question and got the same answer. He added Jacqueline to his list of people to contact, but first he wanted to look at his file on Lia's murder again, especially her cell phone records for the day she was killed. David snapped his fingers. Her planner. "I'll be right back."

He raced to his office and grabbed the planner. Back in the kitchen, he sat at one of the barstools and opened it to the day his wife died. Maggie crowded next to him, her clean, floral scent enveloping him.

"It looks like she canceled everything after eleven o'clock," Maggie said.

"Yeah." Three afternoon appointments had been marked through in ink. "But are these what I think they are?" He pointed to numbers jotted in her notes and three names randomly written on the page—*Vanessa* and *Donovan Jewelers*, and *King* with a question mark.

"Looks like phone numbers," she said.

David turned to his brother. "Can you do a reverse check of these numbers?"

"Already on it," Eric said. "The first one belongs to Donovan Jewelers."

"And that one," Maggie said, pointing to the second number, "is Haven House. I just recognized it."

"How about the last one?"

"That one doesn't show up in my search," Eric said. "Let me dial it." A minute later he shook his head. "It's a tattoo parlor. Said he'd only had the number a few months. I'll request a search of phone records for the number, but it'll take a few days."

David nodded.

"It looks like she called Jared Donovan or Jacqueline after she saw Carly, or maybe she intended to," Maggie said. "And Vanessa."

"I didn't realize she even knew Vanessa," David said.

"Maybe she didn't. Carly told Lia about her years in trafficking. Lia probably would have known about the shelter, and Vanessa was running it six years ago, so maybe Lia thought she could help her. And the one with the question mark—"

"Didn't you say Carly thought Lia recognized the sketch?"

"Yes. She must have called him." David's mind raced, trying to connect the dots in this crazy story. If Carly was telling the truth, a man she met through Jacqueline Donovan had forced her into prostitution. And Lia had recognized the man in the sketch. If she called him, asking questions . . . maybe he set up a meeting with her . . . and followed her to the 385 Parkway. If only she'd written the name of the man she suspected.

He looked at the planner again. He needed to find Lia's phone records for the day she was killed. His cell rang. Sergeant Scott. "What do you have?"

"Someone shoved Carly Smith and Logan Donovan into a dark-colored SUV and drove off!"

His heart rate shot up. "When?"

"Fifteen minutes ago," Scott said. "The guard at Haven House reported the abduction, and I just arrived. There's a be-on-the-lookout for the vehicle."

"I'm on my way," he said and disconnected.

Eric looked up from his computer. "Where are you going?"

"Haven House. Logan and Carly Smith have been snatched from there."

"What?" Maggie cried. Her eyes widened. "Wait a minute! I should have thought of this before! Carly wears a GPS chip all the time. We can find her location—" Her excitement evaporated and she groaned. "But I don't know who monitors the tracker or how to access it."

David turned to her. "Does she have a computer?"

"I *think* I remember one when I picked up her clothes at the hotel."

"Then maybe she has software for the tracking program on it."

190

30

MAGGIE PRESSED HER FINGERS to her forehead. Had she seen a computer in the room when she picked up Carly's clothes? "She's staying at the Westin and I still have her hotel key. I'll check it out."

David looked at his brother. "I'm going too. Once you get her call list, start contacting the people on the list. Maybe one of them has access to the program."

"She did mention there was a friend who was on the account."

"Do you have a name?" David asked.

"No, she didn't tell me." Why hadn't she asked Carly?

Eric nodded. "I'm on it. I'll call you if I find anything."

"My car or yours?" Maggie asked, grabbing her purse.

"Mine," David said.

In less than two minutes, her fingers fumbled with the seat belt as he gunned the car out of his drive. "Do we need a search warrant?"

David shook his head. "In this case not really since you have her key and permission, but it's not a bad idea. I'll call Kevin Scott and he can take care of it."

She grabbed the armrest as he swerved onto the ramp at I-240.

"Tell me again what Carly Smith told you."

She repeated the story as David wove in and out of traffic. Even at nine thirty, the lanes on the interstate were full. He seemed to

191

be absorbing what she'd said, not speaking as he switched lanes and once again cut in and out of the line of cars. In no time, David pulled into the valet parking lane at the Westin and jumped out.

"Let's see what we can find in her room," he said.

She followed him through the front doors to the elevator. Once the doors closed she punched the button for the third floor. The room was just as she'd left it, with Carly's clothes hanging in the closet. Evidently she hadn't returned to get anything.

"Here's her computer," David said.

While he booted it up, she went through Carly's clothes in the closet, laying them on the bed. Nothing. David groaned, and she looked over his shoulder. "Oh no," she said when she saw the log-in screen. As security-conscious as Carly was, Maggie should have known the computer would be password protected.

"Come on," David said. "I'm taking this to the computer lab at the precinct."

"Hold up a second," she said. "Let's take a minute to make sure we're not overlooking something in the room."

She thought he was going to balk, but then he nodded.

"Good idea."

A quick search showed nothing out of the ordinary. Maggie stepped into the bathroom and scanned the counter. A prescription bottle sat beside a glass. She checked the bottle before tucking it into her purse and wasn't surprised it was something for anxiety.

"It was worth a shot," David said, his voice tight as he ushered her out of the room.

The drive to his office took less than ten minutes, the silence between them growing by the minute. Would things ever be like they were once? Maggie didn't want to think about the answer to that question. David parked on the street in front of his building, and she followed him inside and signed in.

"Who's working the computer lab tonight?" he asked at the desk.

The clerk made a few keystrokes. "Thompson."

David nodded and they hurried to the elevator. "He's one of the best," he said and punched the button for the seventh floor.

A few minutes later, he set the computer on a table in front of the tech. "I need you to get past the security code."

Thompson nodded. "I'm sorry about your daughter. Does this have anything to do with her?"

"Not sure, but it could. The owner has been kidnapped as well."

"She told me she has a GPS tracker on her at all times," Maggie said. "We're hoping she installed the tracking software on the computer."

The tech winced. "Most of the time it's on a person's phone, but who knows. I'll see what I can do."

Maggie hoped that wasn't the case. Given the message they'd found in Carly's phone records, if they found her, Maggie was certain they would find Lexi. While Thompson worked on the computer, David paced the room with his phone glued to his ear.

A few minutes later, Thompson looked up. "Got in!"

"See if you can find a tracking program," David said, pocketing his phone. Then he turned to Maggie. "Talked to Kevin Scott. Still no trace of Logan or Carly Smith."

"How about Eric? Has he located anyone on Carly's call list who knows about her GPS tracker?"

He shook his head. "He's still waiting for the company to come through on her calls."

Carly was so secretive, Maggie worried that she hadn't trusted anyone with the information. She shifted her gaze to the tech, who frowned at his computer. "What's wrong?" she asked.

"I've looked in every folder and there's no locator program on this computer."

"You're sure?" David hurried over to him and leaned over his shoulder, staring at the computer. Then he straightened up. "The call list is our only hope."

31

CARLY TRIED to keep from groaning when the SUV hit a pothole. She counted her heartbeat by the throbbing in her shoulder, surprised it wasn't off the charts, what with a man watching her from the front seat, his automatic pointed at her chest. Because of his Texas accent, she'd dubbed him Cowboy. The other man spoke with a Spanish accent, and when she stared into his flat black eyes that had no soul, he reminded her of a cottonmouth. Snake scared her more than Cowboy and his gun.

She should have fought harder, but it'd happened so quickly there hadn't been time to use any of the self-defense moves she'd practiced. Besides, she held out hope that the men were taking them to the same place Lexi was being held. Maybe she could bargain for her niece's release.

The SUV hit another pothole, and she stifled a groan as sharp pain jabbed her, making her lose count. When the pain eased, Carly moved her hands, testing the zip ties that dug into her wrists. Too tight to wiggle out of. At least her hands were in front of her. Sitting in the back seat had made it too difficult for their abductors to get her hands behind her back. Logan's hands were secured in the same manner, and he shifted beside her. He'd come around not long after they'd screeched away from Haven House, but he hadn't tried to communicate with her. She couldn't believe Logan had risked his life to help her. Maybe it was a ruse to get her confidence. It was the way traffickers worked.

The men were bold, for sure. Kidnapping them the way they had and not blindfolding them. Of course, if they planned to kill them, there was no need for a blindfold. Carly clenched her jaw. She wasn't ready to die. Her mind raced, searching for a way out of this mess. The knife in her boot offered little comfort. Knives were no match for guns. She'd thought she was prepared for another kidnapping, but she was wrong.

Focus on details to tell the police once we're free. Smelled like a new SUV. Chevrolet emblem was on the steering wheel. As big as the vehicle was, it had to be a Tahoe. But where were they taking them?

Her hair wasn't falling in front of her face, so maybe her barrette was still in place. She would check it except the kidnappers might get suspicious. How long would it take before Jamie was notified she'd been kidnapped? If only she'd told Maggie to get in contact with Jamie if something happened to her.

"You won't get away with this."

Logan's gruff voice startled her, and Carly pressed her leg against his, hoping he would shut up. Rule number one when you're kidnapped—don't irritate the kidnappers.

"I'm a cop, and you'll have the Feds after you now."

Cowboy barked a laugh. "I'm shaking in my boots."

"We're in the middle of nowhere, so pull over and let us go. You'd have time to get away."

"Enough with your talking." Cowboy raised his gun. "We don't need you anyway."

"Why do you want her?" Logan asked.

"She has a nose problem. Now shut up or I'll shut you up."

If Logan kept talking, Cowboy would shoot him, and while Carly still didn't trust him, she didn't want him dead. She elbowed him just as Snake made a sharp left turn, throwing her against Logan. Another groan escaped her lips as pain stabbed through her left shoulder. She managed to catch Logan's eye and shook her head. For a second, he looked as though he'd speak again, then he huffed a breath and gave her a slight nod.

The truck turned again, this time into a narrow drive, and Carly searched for markers, a gnarly tree, anything that could be used to direct a rescue team to their location. Provided she escaped. But it was so dark she couldn't see anything except lights and an old house at the end of the drive.

Snake stopped at the front of the house and opened the rear door on her side while Cowboy motioned them out. Carly eased from the seat, gritting her teeth when she moved her arm. Logan tried to help but he stumbled, slamming into her shoulder. Searing agony sent her world spinning into darkness.

When she awoke, she was still in darkness.

"Logan?"

"Yeah," he said.

The pain in her shoulder came back with a vengeance. Passing out had been a blessing. When the pain subsided, she felt for a blindfold. There wasn't one, and she held her bound hands close to her face. "Why can't I see? Am I blind?"

"No, evidently we're in a windowless room."

Like a shroud, the dark wrapped around Carly and plunged her into the past. *The Hole.* Days without seeing light. She fought the memories. *Picture the lake, swans paddling in circles.* The coping mechanism failed, and she curled into a ball. "No, please no," she moaned.

"Carly?" Logan's hand brushed the side of her face. "It's all right. I'm here."

His soothing voice broke through the terror. She wasn't in New York or Atlanta. And she was with Logan, not Blade. But what if Logan was part of the ring? No. He couldn't fake the gentleness

196

in his voice and touch. Slowly Carly relaxed. "Thank you," she whispered.

"You okay now?" he asked, smoothing her hair.

His hand snagged on her barrette and fear seized her again. She jerked her head away. What if she was wrong about him? "Don't touch that!"

"Sorry."

Even in the dark, she sensed his confusion. But she couldn't afford to trust the wrong person. Seconds later his feet scuffed the floor.

"What are you doing?"

"Trying to find a wall. Here it is," he said. "Scoot back and you can rest against it."

Gritting her teeth again, she used her right hand to push herself into a sitting position, and then she scooted back until she found the wall. Once her shoulder stopped throbbing, she could get the knife from her boot and cut the ties that bound their hands. "How far away are you?"

"I'm right here," he said.

He sounded close and it troubled her how comforting that was to her. What was going on? One second she thought he was the enemy, the next he was her rescuer.

"Coach Logan?" A child's hesitant voice broke the silence. "Is that you?"

Carly jerked her head toward the voice. Someone else was in the room?

"Lexi?" Logan whispered.

"Uh-huh."

Her heart slammed against her ribs. Lexi was here in the room with them?

"Where are you?" Logan kept his voice low.

"Right here."

"Keep talking so I can find you." His steps moved away from Carly.

"I'm scared. Can we go home?"

Carly raised her hands, feeling the empty air in front of her.

"I've got her," he said.

There was more scuffing, and then she sensed their nearness. Carly patted the air until her hands found the child. The girl scooted away from her.

"I won't hurt you," Carly said.

"W-who are you?" the girl asked.

"Her name is Carly," Logan said.

"I don't know anybody named Carly." Lexi's voice quavered.

"She's a friend." He bumped her leg as he sat down again. "Sorry."

"It's okay." At least it wasn't her shoulder this time. But her hands being bound together made the pain worse.

"I was scared," Lexi said. "But Jesus was here with me. He told me not to be afraid. And then he sent you, Coach."

Carly's heart hitched. The faith of a child. Maybe if she hadn't been so determined to find Austin King on her own, none of them would be in this mess. It was just so hard to trust. Even Jesus.

"They haven't hurt you, have they?" If only Carly could see.

"No. I don't want to be here anymore."

"I know, honey." Lexi fell silent except for an occasional sniffle, and Carly sought her niece's hands. Like hers, they were bound, not with zip ties but what felt like tape. "It's going to be okay," she said, squeezing Lexi's fingers. "We're going to get out of here."

"We have to hurry. I heard them talking and they're going to take me somewhere with the other girls."

Other girls? Carly's heart sank. They were definitely dealing with traffickers.

"Got to find a way to get these ties off," Logan said. He grunted. "The lock is embedded in the middle of my wrist. No way to move it so I can pop it open."

Bringing her hands to the side of her face, she ignored the pain and moved her hands until she located the lock on her tie. "Same here. Give me a second."

Carly brought her knee up so she could retrieve the knife in her boot. Leaning forward sent pain radiating from her shoulder to her fingers and she almost dropped the dagger as she fished it out of the small scabbard. "I have a knife. Where are your hands?"

"Where did you get—"

"I'm always prepared." When his hands rested on her knee, she pressed the knife into them. "Cut me loose, and then I'll get yours."

When the tie fell away, she dropped her left arm to her side and held her shoulder. "Give me a second." When the pain subsided, she used the knife to slice his restraint, and then she handed the dagger back to him. "You better cut Lexi's."

While he freed himself, Carly felt for Lily's bracelet and almost cried when she found it. She was surprised their captors hadn't taken it.

"She's free," Logan said. "I'm going to see if I can find a way out." He made very little noise as he moved around the room.

"Don't leave me, Coach."

"I won't. Why don't you snuggle next to Miss Carly?"

Carly batted the air again, searching for Lexi, and connected with her head.

"Ouch! That hurt."

"I'm sorry. Can you scoot next to me? That way you won't feel so alone."

"I'm good." But she inched closer.

Independent. Carly didn't have to wonder where that came from. She wrapped her good arm around her niece and pulled her closer, getting a whiff of her fruit-scented shampoo. "You've been really brave," she said, resting her cheek on Lexi's head.

"I'm scared."

"I know. Is that strawberry shampoo I smell?"

"Mmm-hmm. You smell like Aunt Gigi."

Carly had forgotten Gigi wore Joy. She sniffed her wrist, barely able to smell the perfume. The darkness must have enhanced Lexi's senses. "How did you hear they were going to move you?"

"When I was in the van. The men were talking."

"Do you know when and where they're going?"

"They said in the morning, then they quit talking. Is it morning?"

"I don't think so," Carly said. "Do you know how many other girls are here?"

"Uh-uh. But there's someone on the other side of the wall. If you find the door and put your face on the floor, you can talk to her. But she might not answer—she didn't just before you came. I heard a car leave, and they may have taken her somewhere."

Another room, adjoining this one? Maybe Logan could get the door open. "Did you hear what Lexi said about a door?"

"Yeah," he said. "I'll find it."

"I tried to get it open," Lexi said. "But it's stuck."

"Logan is stronger. Maybe he can unstick it." Carly couldn't quit thinking about them moving the girls. They had to stop them. She needed a plan in case she and Lexi were separated. Carly unclipped the barrette in her hair. "Lexi, I want you to listen to me."

"Yes, ma'am?"

The kid was polite. "Where's your hand?" she asked. When Lexi patted her arm, Carly placed the barrette in the child's hand. "This hair clip has a GPS chip in it. Put it in your hair, and whatever you do, don't lose it. If we get separated, if you have the barrette, we'll find you. Okay?"

She felt Lexi nod. "Good."

Once she heard the hairpiece snap in place, she breathed easier. If Carly and Lexi were separated, at least RLT Security could find Lexi.

32

DAVID PULLED into his drive and opened the garage door. His headlights caught Lexi's bike hanging on the wall, and an instant memory of him teaching her how to ride flashed through his brain.

"Don't let go, Daddy!" Lexi's eyes were big as she looked back to make sure he was running beside her.

"I've got you, honey. You can do it."

The video played in his mind. It hadn't been long until she was saying, "I can do it. You can let go now."

He gripped the steering wheel until his knuckles turned white. Where was she?

Maggie put a tentative hand on his arm. "We're going to find her."

"I don't know. Without a direction to go in . . ." He slumped against the seat. There were so many places to hide in Memphis—if they were even still in the area. The thought made him sick. David jerked the car door open and climbed out, then hurried to the back door.

"David, wait," Maggie said. She caught up with him before he entered the house. "We need to talk."

"No, not until this is over."

"Are you still angry?"

He shook his head. "Not angry. Stressed and frustrated. I get that you gave your word, but I keep going back to the information you had. What if it could have kept Lexi from being kidnapped?"

Blood drained from her face and her lips pressed together in a thin line. "We have no way of knowing that."

"But now we'll never know, will we?" He folded his arms across his chest. He didn't want to have this conversation now. "I worry that the law will always come first with you."

"It's not about the law." Her gaze faltered. "My word is all I have," she said, lifting her chin. "And my reputation. People know they can trust me. I can't change who I am."

"I understand that, but—" He unfolded his arms and palmed them up. "When this is over, I hope we can get back what we had." He hoped it with all his heart. David turned and walked through the door into the kitchen, blinking when he saw Logan's mother sitting at the island bar. "Jacqueline? I didn't know you were coming."

"Have you heard anything from Logan?" Jacqueline asked.

"I'm sorry but I'm afraid not."

"Can you at least tell me what's going on? Is Logan's disappearance connected to Lexi's kidnapping?"

She was asking questions he had no answers to. "I don't know a lot more than you do."

Jacqueline tucked a strand of platinum hair behind her ear, and the emerald-cut diamond ring on her right hand flashed in the kitchen light. "I understand he was with the woman from the soccer game yesterday. Who is she and what does she want?"

"Yes," Georgina said as she entered the room. "I want to know who she is too."

David glanced toward Maggie, sending her a silent plea for help. Georgina would not take the news about her niece well. "Where's Frank? Is he still at that business meeting?" The man needed to be here for his wife.

Georgina pressed a hand to her mouth. "I forgot to leave him a

202

note telling him where I am. He doesn't even know Lexi is missing yet." She pulled out her phone and walked to the window with her back to them.

"Why don't you explain about Carly Smith," David said to Maggie, with his gaze on Georgina, catching her frown when she turned around.

"He doesn't answer, so I left him a message to call me." She bit her lip. "His meeting wasn't supposed to go on this long. I hope he hasn't had an accident."

"He'll call you when he gets your message," David said. "Maggie will fill you in on the woman at the soccer game yesterday."

Nodding toward the island, Maggie said, "You might want to sit down, Georgina."

"Why?"

She squared her shoulders. "Because Carly Smith is Lia's sister and your niece, Heather."

"What?" Jacqueline's question exploded into the room.

Georgina's mouth worked, but no sound came out. Then she shook her head as though to clear it and turned to David. "I-I don't understand. Heather is alive?"

He hoped she was. "Yes," he said. "I planned to tell you when . . ." He didn't know when he planned to tell her, he hadn't thought that far ahead.

"How long have you known?" Jacqueline asked.

"Not long."

"If Carly Smith is Heather, why didn't she come to me? Where has she been all these years?" Georgina asked. She didn't give him time to answer before she asked, "Why did she run away in the first place?"

David dipped his head to Maggie. "Would you mind telling Georgina what Heather, or rather Carly, told you? In the living room, maybe? I need to talk to Jacqueline."

"Wait," Jacqueline said. "I'd like to hear the story."

He'd wanted to question her about Austin King, but maybe it'd be better to see her reaction when Maggie came to his part of the story. "Okay."

He motioned for the two older women to sit on one side of the island. That way he could watch them. As Maggie told Heather's story, Georgina's face went from shock to disbelief while Jacqueline showed no emotion at all. When she came to the part about Heather meeting Austin King at the party, Jacqueline shook her head.

"I don't remember anyone by that name," she said.

Maggie pulled a paper from her purse and handed it to the two women. "She had an artist sketch how Austin King might look now. Do either of you recognize this man?"

Jacqueline barely glanced at the paper before shaking her head, but Georgina looked closer. When she raised her gaze, a frown creased her brow. "I know it's not him, but this one with the receding hairline . . . right around the eyes, it looks a tiny bit like Jim Rankin." She nudged her friend. "Don't you think?"

Jacqueline took another look and shrugged. "Maybe . . . I don't have any use for Jim, but it's hard to believe even he would be involved in human trafficking."

David reached for the sketch. If he imagined the man in the sketch being completely bald, he supposed a case could be made for the likeness of the older man.

Maggie looked over his shoulder, and he held the paper so they both could see the sketch Georgina referred to.

"I saw him just this morning." Maggie shook her head. "I can't believe it could be him, either."

David looked up at Jacqueline. "Was he at the party that night?"

Jacqueline shrugged. "I don't have a clue. It was so long ago."

This was getting him nowhere, and he handed the sketch back to Maggie and stood. "I'm going to see if Eric's had any luck." He also wanted to dig out Lia's file and check her phone records. "Jacqueline, do you remember if Lia called you the day she died?"

She rubbed her forehead. "Maybe. I had hired her to take publicity photos at the store, and so we were in contact almost daily back then."

"Did she ever ask you about Austin King?"

"Today is the first time I heard his name."

33

"You should have left the cop behind." Blade felt like punching both of them. He yanked Jasmine's purse from Gibson's hands and riffled through it, pocketing the cash. The rest he'd leave to burn in the fire. He paused when he saw the hotel key. She'd been staying at the Westin. Nice digs. Jasmine had done well for herself. Too bad she wouldn't live to enjoy it. "And you let him see your faces?"

The two men shuffled their feet and stared at the floor. One of them looked up. "You told us to get the woman. He got in the way."

And now the mess had to be cleaned up. "Did you move the kid?"

"She's going with the last load."

"Why didn't you move them all at one time?"

"Twenty kids? The scanner says the cops are looking for a van. They would pull us over for sure."

"How about Rankin?"

"He'll die in the fire."

Blade nodded. Rankin had become a liability. "No bullet holes for the coroner to find."

That had been his instructions from Grey.

"No, it'll look like he got caught setting the fire."

"Good. Burning will be good enough for the cop and the woman too." But before Jasmine died, he wanted to make sure of two things. She knew what would happen to her niece and who was going to kill her.

34

CARLY LEANED HER HEAD against the wall. As long as she didn't move her shoulder, she could tolerate the throbbing. Lexi slept draped across the two of them with her head in Carly's lap. The girl must really trust Logan to be able to sleep. She envied Lexi and smoothed her hair, checking the barrette to make sure it was secure.

She'd thought she had all her bases covered. RLT knew where she was and so did Jamie. They could pinpoint her location to the house where they were being held. But until she missed her check-in call or they moved her out of the Memphis area, no one would know she was in trouble. She should have given RLT a specific itinerary, but she hadn't known exactly where her search would take her.

Jamie had called Carly while she was in the hospital, so her friend probably wouldn't call again until tomorrow. Or was it already tomorrow? In the dark, it was hard to judge how much time had passed. Off and on they'd heard cars come and go in the drive, the last time just a few minutes ago.

"Do you think the men are gone for good this time?" Her voice sounded loud in the dark room.

"Probably not both of them. And who knows, there could have

been others already here when we arrived," Logan said. "The door has a rubber gasket at the bottom, blocks sound and light from the hallway. I didn't find any windows."

An invisible band tightened around Carly's chest. Houses weren't built with rooms without windows unless someone had turned the rooms into cells. "This must be where they hold the girls they traffic. How about the room joining it? The one Lexi mentioned."

"That door is locked. If we could find a weapon, it would help, but there's not a stick of furniture in here. And they took my gun and badge. Surprised they didn't take my shoes."

They were in a bad situation. No way would their captors let them walk out of here alive. "The girl Lexi talked to. I wonder if they moved her."

So far no one had answered Logan when he asked if anyone was there. Carly's suspicion that he was in on the kidnapping had faded to the point that she almost believed she could trust him. Moot point since she had no choice.

"I figure they took her, and probably more, in some of that traffic we've been hearing," Logan said. "We need to make a plan."

"You still have my dagger?"

"Yeah. Just wish it were bigger."

"Then they probably would have found it."

"Why do you carry it? And why do you wear a GPS tracker?"

"I didn't realize you heard me tell Lexi about it." He'd been busy scouting out the room and she'd kept her voice low.

"Well, I did. Mind explaining?"

To explain she would have to tell him her story. Yes or no? The question seesawed in her mind.

"If you won't explain, tell me who you really are."

Carly didn't think her throat could get any drier, but it did. She would give almost anything for a drink of water.

"Why don't you trust me? Or is it all cops you don't trust?"

Lexi whimpered in her sleep. Carly rubbed her back and the girl settled down. If only she could see Logan's face and read it, see if his eyes were as sincere as his voice. "I don't trust anyone, especially cops."

"You trusted Madeline Starr."

"She promised not to tell what I told her."

"Why did you trust her to keep her word? What's different about Maggie?"

"I don't know . . . we just connected."

He huffed a sigh. "I was hoping you'd trust me enough to tell me yourself . . ."

"What are you talking about?"

"Maggie told me that you're Heather Morgan," he said gently, "and that a man by the name of Austin King sold you into prostitution."

Carly was stunned into silence. She couldn't believe Maggie had told him. She'd promised. "Why did she tell you?"

"She was afraid for your life and wanted me to find you before the traffickers found you, for all the good it did," he said. "Trust me, Carly. Or whatever your name is."

She twirled a lock of Lexi's hair around her finger. "It's Carly," she said after a long silence. "Heather died the night you took me to the party, and I met Austin King, and he promised me a modeling career."

Logan sucked in a quick breath. "And you thought I had something to do with it."

"I saw you talking to Austin King. And your mother too. I wouldn't have trusted him otherwise."

"I did not set you up. I probably talked to most of the people there, and I wouldn't even remember that particular party except it's the last time I saw you until now. And my mother would never have any dealings with someone involved in trafficking."

He defended his mother, just as she suspected he would.

"Look," he said, "when we get out of this, I'll take you to see her. You can ask her yourself."

She bit her lip, confused by her conflicting thoughts. "How much did Maggie tell you about me?"

"Only who you were and what King did. She said the rest was your story to tell, but you don't have to tell me if you don't want to."

If Logan was possibly going to die for trying to save her, he deserved to know why. "You were right all along, you did know me."

Once she started telling him her story, the words spilled out of her. When she finished, Logan's silence was worse than the darkness. Then his fingers touched her arm, and his hand covered hers.

"No wonder you don't trust cops," he said, his voice husky. "I'm sorry."

"For years I've wondered if you set me up. Or your mother. She didn't like me. But looking back, if I'd been your mother I wouldn't have liked a weird girl like me, either. Can't believe the way I used to dress."

He chuckled. "I didn't think you looked so bad. Of course I was going through a period of rebellion against my mother's control back then. And I had no idea you were only seventeen."

"I can't believe you were twenty and just trying to break the apron strings." This was the way she remembered Logan. Lighthearted. Fun. Able to laugh at anything. A car door slammed and Carly stiffened. "They're back. What are we going to do?"

"Wake Lexi, then let's see if we can get them to open the door. While I distract them, the two of you run for it."

"Leave you behind?"

"If I can get away, I'll be right behind you."

Maybe he *was* in cahoots with their captors, and he knew they wouldn't hurt him. *No!* If he was one of them he would not help them escape. *Trust him.* She straightened up and gently shook Lexi.

The girl jerked awake. "Is my daddy here?"

"I'm afraid not, honey," Carly said. "We're going to make a lot of noise, and when the men come, Logan is going to help us get away. So, when I say run, I want you to hold on to my hand and run. Got that?"

"Yes ma'am. But I'm scared."

"Me too, Lexi." A peculiar odor reached her nose. "Do you smell that?" she whispered.

"Gasoline," Logan said grimly. "They're going to burn the house. You have to get Lexi out of here."

Keys jingled outside the door.

"Maybe we won't have to cause a commotion," he said. "When they brought us in, this room was right across from the front door. Be ready when I rush them. Run for the outside and then keep running."

The door swung open, revealing the silhouette of a man. Yelling like a banshee, Logan charged forward, tackling him.

Carly grabbed Lexi's hand. "Run!"

Logan and the man crashed to the floor, and the thud of blows hitting their mark filled the room.

She and Lexi dashed for the hall. Suddenly, a beam of light blinded her. Carly tripped and stumbled to her knees, taking Lexi with her. Heavy footsteps pounded the floor, and someone snatched Lexi away from her.

"No! Help me!" Lexi screamed.

Carly struggled to her feet. Strong hands shoved her back to the floor and she looked up and locked gazes with her captor. Her heart slammed into her ribs. *Blade!*

He narrowed his eyes and leaned over her. "I told you if you ran away, I'd find you, Jaz. Now I have your niece, and you know what's in store for her."

Carly head-butted him, aiming for his nose. The crunch of cartilage breaking let her know she'd hit her target.

Blade swore.

She rolled away from the kick that was certain to come. Where was Logan? A boot slammed her rib, and she doubled over, groaning. *Must. Get. Away.* Carly scrambled to her feet and ran to the door. *Where is Lexi?* She scanned the empty hallway. No! Lexi couldn't be gone!

Pain ricocheted through her skull. Carly struggled to hold on to consciousness.

35

MAGGIE TRIED TO FOCUS on Georgina and Jacqueline's questions, but David's words kept chasing through her head. *"I worry that the law will always come first with you."* No more than his police duties. And once she'd given her word to Carly, being a lawyer had nothing to do with whether she broke a confidence. It was the way she was wired. Did David even know her?

She hated this barrier between them. Maggie looked up to find Georgina looking expectantly at her. She must have asked a question. "I'm sorry, could you repeat that?"

"You said Heather is a counselor. Where?"

"At a drug rehab near Nashville."

"I still don't understand why she didn't get in contact with me. I'm her aunt."

"Hopefully you'll get a chance to ask her." She looked up as David walked back into the kitchen holding a sheet of paper.

"Jacqueline, I found Lia's phone records for the day she died and they show she called your store three times that afternoon."

"You're kidding." She shook her head. *"I* didn't talk to her three times. Someone else at the store must have."

"Could it have been Jared?" Maggie asked.

"You'd have to ask him," Jacqueline replied. "Would you like me to call him?"

"I'd appreciate it."

While Jacqueline talked with her son, Maggie booted up Carly's computer. The tech could have missed something. First she checked Carly's contacts and scanned the list. Mostly business. When she came to a Laura Abernathy, MD, Maggie paused. That name was familiar. She hunted for the medicine bottle she'd brought from the hotel. When she found it, she looked to see who the prescribing doctor was. Laura Abernathy.

Maggie googled the name. She was a psychiatrist in Nashville. Maybe Carly had confided in her about the GPS tracker. Maggie searched for a home phone number to call. Not finding one, she called the office number. When an answering service picked up, Maggie explained their situation and asked for Dr. Abernathy's home number.

"I'm sorry, I can't give that to you, but I can pass the word."

Maggie motioned David over. "Is she on call tonight?" Otherwise it would be morning before word got to her.

"No."

"Can you hold just one second?" She handed David the prescription bottle. "This Dr. Abernathy might know something, but I need you to talk with the answering service."

David nodded, and she spoke to the operator again. "I'm putting a Memphis police lieutenant on speaker with you. Once you confirm his identification, could you patch him through to the doctor on call?"

"No, but I can relay the message to the doctor, and he can get back with you."

"This is Lieutenant David Raines," he said. "Do you need my badge number?"

When he'd given her the information she asked for, the operator said, "I'll get this to the doctor, and you should hear from him right away unless he's in an emergency."

"Thanks," David said as he handed her phone back.

She read the frustration in his eyes, making her want to help him so bad she could taste it. "We're going to find her, David." She slipped her arm around his waist and he leaned into her.

"I have to keep believing that."

He jerked back when her phone rang.

"Hello?" Maggie said and put the call on speaker.

"This is Dr. Peters. The call service explained your situation and that you're attempting to get in touch with Dr. Abernathy."

"Yes. Can you help us?"

"I have her cell number." He rattled it off.

"You don't happen to know her patient Carly Smith?" David asked.

"No, I'm afraid not. But that number should get you in touch with the doctor."

David dialed the number and put the call on speaker. It rang four times before a groggy voice answered. "Dr. Abernathy."

"This is Lieutenant David Raines with the Memphis police department," he said. "I'm calling about a patient of yours. Carly Smith."

"Is Carly all right?"

"She's been kidnapped, and I understand she wears a GPS tracker."

"She does."

"Do you have the app to locate her?"

A sigh came from the phone. "No. But her friend Jamie Parker should have it."

"Do you have the friend's number?"

"I'm afraid not."

Maggie gripped the table as David ended the call. One more roadblock. She quickly checked Carly's contacts again and found Jamie Parker. "Try this number," she said.

A minute later, David shook his head. "She doesn't answer."

36

IN THE DARKNESS that engulfed them again, Carly jerked on the doorknob, and when it didn't move, she pounded the wooden door.

"Save your energy," Logan said.

His voice came from across the room, and she dropped to her knees and crawled toward him, her shoulder throbbing with each beat of her heart. "Are you okay?" she asked.

"Yeah. Other than having a jackhammer drilling my head. How about you?"

She touched her shoulder. Her fingers were sticky when she pulled them away. "I think my stitches have torn loose."

"Try to keep your arm still. Where's Lexi?"

"Gone." She rubbed her sore ribs. "Blade took her."

"Blade?"

"The pimp I told you about."

"We have to get her back," Logan said. "But how did he know you were in Memphis?"

"I don't know, unless one of the people I've questioned about Austin King got in touch with him."

His feet scuffled, and then she heard him grunt and heave himself up. "Give me your hand and I'll help you up."

She felt the air with her right hand until she connected with him. "Slow, please."

Carly held her left arm close to her body and let him pull her up, sending her head into orbit. "How can you be dizzy in a dark room?"

"Yeah, I know what you mean."

"How are we going to get out of here?"

"The door opens outward, and I'm hoping—" He stopped. "What's that noise?"

The room fell silent and she cocked her head, listening. Crackling came from outside the room. "Fire!"

"We have to get out of here." He moved away from her.

"Don't leave me." Her voice rose to a high pitch.

"I'm here." He was closer. "Take my hand."

She followed the sound of his voice, bumping into his arm. Carly grabbed his hand and held on as he inched forward.

"The door should be right here."

"If only we could see." The darkness was like a blanket that smothered her, but at least the smoke couldn't get into the room, not the way it was sealed off. At least not until the fire ate through the Sheetrock.

He tapped his hands against the wall, the hollow sound echoing in the room. "Here's the door."

A faint odor of smoke reached her nose. "If we open this, it'll cause a backdraft. We'll die."

Logan pulled her away. "Got to find that other door and break it down. Might be a way out of the house in the other room."

He dropped to the floor, pulling her with him, and they crawled across the room. "I think the door is to our right," he said, helping Carly to her feet.

Again, she stuck to him like glue. If they got out of this alive, she owed him an apology for ever thinking he was the bad guy in all of this.

"Here it is." He placed her hand on the wood.

She tapped on the door. "Doesn't sound solid."

"No, I think it's hollow," he said. "I'm going to let go of your hand so I can ram it and maybe crash through it or knock it off its hinges."

The crackling in the hall grew louder. Carly coughed. Smoke was seeping into the room from the ceiling. She sensed Logan's energy as he launched himself at the door. The dull thud told her he hadn't gotten through. "Find the center," she said. "If it's hollow, the middle will be the weakest spot."

"Good idea." A few seconds later, he slammed against it again. "One more time," he said.

The third time she heard the wood splinter, and the screech of nails as they separated from the frame made her want to cry with relief until she heard him hit the floor. "Are you hurt?"

"I don't think I broke anything," he said.

She grabbed the doorframe to steady herself and almost fell when the two-by-fours crashed to the floor. "Did it hit you?" she cried.

"Just barely."

Inside the room, dim light filtered from the fire in the ceiling.

She scanned the room, looking for the window. "There," she said, nudging him. "Do you think that's a way out?"

"Let's find out, but we better crawl again. No telling what kind of booby trap they've set."

She dropped to the floor beside him, and they crawled across the room.

Logan stood first. "It is a window!"

From what little she could see, the room looked bare, but the light was growing. She coughed as smoke filled the room. In the half-light he jerked off his jacket, wrapped it around his hand, and slammed his fist against the window, shattering the glass.

"No," she groaned. Plywood stood between them and freedom.

A flaming piece of wood fell from the ceiling, and she stomped it out. "What are we going to do now?"

"Same thing I did before," he said.

More bits of flaming wood rained down as smoke poured from the ceiling, stinging her eyes. She inched closer to Logan while he knocked out the jagged edges of the glass encased in the window frame.

He slammed his shoulder against the plywood. This time there was no splintering of the wood.

"Can we use the two-by-fours in the doorframe?" she asked.

"Good idea."

They hurried back to the door they'd just come through, and Logan dragged the frame across the room, prying one of the two-by-fours loose. A flaming piece of ceiling dropped behind her, and she stomped it out.

Logan rammed the board against the top of the window until it gave, then he repeated the process, inching downward until the plywood gave way and fell away from the window.

"Let me see how far a drop it is," he said and poked his head outside. "It's about five feet to the ground. You'll have to climb through the window and hang on until you can drop."

"With my shoulder, I can't hang. I'll have to jump."

"Let me go first and I'll help you from the ground." Logan climbed out the window, and she heard him drop to the ground. "Anytime you're ready," he called back.

With fire licking the Sheetrock, Carly was more than ready.

37

THE DRIVER SCARED HER, and Lexi huddled against the window as the SUV made yet another turn. Where was Coach Logan? And the lady who smelled like her aunt? Tears burned the back of her eyes. The driver said if they cried, he'd give them something to cry about.

The older girl in the seat beside her leaned over. "Stay close to me," she whispered. "And pretend you're asleep."

Lexi looked up. Natalie had been in the room next to her at the house. Kind eyes smiled down at her, and Lexi teared up again. Natalie was the only one who had even looked at her. The other girls acted funny, like they didn't know what they were doing. Must have been that pill the other man gave them. When he turned around, she'd spit it out. She bet Natalie did the same thing. "Where are they taking us?"

The SUV slowed and Natalie put her finger to her lips and shook her head. Lexi rose up so she could see. They were at a stoplight. When it changed to green, they made a left turn onto the interstate ramp. *No!* He was taking them farther and farther away from her dad. How was she ever going to get home?

38

A PALE MOON cast eerie shadows as Logan's strong arms helped Carly to the ground. When she turned around to face him, admiration glinted in his eyes. Then he grabbed her good hand and pulled her with him as they ran to safety.

"We made it," Logan said. He unwrapped his hand and shook the glass from his jacket and then offered it to her.

"I'm not cold." Carly glanced over her shoulder. The whole house was engulfed. "We better find a phone and call the fire department."

"Wait . . . what's that?" He cocked his head. "Do you hear that?"

All she heard was falling rafters and crackling flames. Then, she gasped as a faint cry for help reached her ears. "Someone's in there."

"You stay here," he said and ran toward the house.

No. Wherever Logan was, that's where she wanted to be. She caught up with him at the back door.

"I told you to stay put. The room is engulfed!"

Adrenaline pulsed through her body. "You may need help!"

"No! Stay back!" Logan jerked open the back screen.

Carly hesitated. Then a scream jolted her into action. She couldn't

222

walk away and let someone die. Logan had saved her life and she owed him.

Inside the burning house, the fire sucked the oxygen from the room. Smoke swirled around them. A man lay slumped on the floor, flames eating his clothes.

Logan used his jacket to beat the fire out. It hadn't reached the table yet, and Carly yanked the tablecloth off. "Can you wrap him in this?" Her lungs burned, and she covered her nose and mouth with her hand, trying to filter the air.

He rolled the groaning man in the tablecloth, smothering the remaining flames. "Got to get him outside."

Together they used the tablecloth to carry the man out the back door. "A little farther out in the yard," Logan said, panting.

A minute later, he said, "This should be far enough."

They gently laid the man on the ground. "Is . . ." Coughing cut her words off. "Is he alive?"

"I don't know."

He peeled back the tablecloth and gasped. "Jim Rankin?" he said. "What's he doing here?"

Carly shuddered at the charred skin on the man's chest and legs. The poor man. Why had he been left to die? Her gaze traveled to his face, and she froze. Fisting her hands, she took a step back. *No!*

His eyes fluttered open. "Help me," he whispered.

Carly struggled for air. There was no mistaking the man was Austin King.

Lights swept across them.

"Get behind me," Logan said and stood, planting his feet. "It could be our captors returning."

She stood frozen, her legs unable to move until Logan pulled her behind him. She couldn't stop staring at King. She'd forgotten so many details of his face. The sketches were so wrong.

"It's a pickup," Logan said.

The truck braked to a stop a good hundred yards away, and two men spilled out. They appeared oblivious to Carly and Logan as they pulled on black slickers.

"We need a hook and ladder," one of them yelled as he grabbed an axe from the bed of the truck. The other man took out his cell phone.

Logan breathed a long sigh. "Volunteer firemen."

"You sure?" Carly said.

"Pretty sure," he said and stepped forward. "Over here! Got a man who's been burned pretty bad."

The men stopped and stared their way, then the man with the cell phone made another call before jogging over to Logan and Carly. The other man ran back to the pickup.

"Got an ambulance coming," the shorter man said. He took one look at the man on the ground and quickly punched in another number. "Need a helicopter to transport a burn victim to the Med," he said into the phone. Then he looked up and frowned. "You okay, ma'am? You're looking mighty pale."

No, she was not okay. Fog swirled through her brain, and she couldn't hold a thought longer than a second. Carly shifted her gaze back to Austin King, not believing she'd just saved the life of the man who sold her to Blade. She hugged her arms to her waist. If she let go, she would fall apart.

"A little smoke inhalation . . . and she's been through a lot." Logan said when it was apparent she wasn't going to answer, and then he identified himself.

"There's a fire truck on the way," the shorter man said. "I'm Gordon McCoy, fire chief of our volunteer fire department, and live just up the road. Smelled the smoke and came to investigate. The other guy is a paramedic. Is anyone else inside?"

"I don't know," Logan replied. "We'd barely made it out when we found him."

The paramedic arrived with a bag and knelt beside King. He shook his head. "He's bad, going into shock. We need a helicopter."

"One's on the way," the fire chief said.

Immediately the paramedic went to work getting an IV started, and the fire chief turned to Logan. "What were you doing here?"

A gust of wind blew the smoke from the house away from them, chilling her as Logan filled in the fire chief. Carly's legs wobbled. She couldn't stand much longer and looked around for somewhere to sit. Spying a fallen tree at the edge of the yard, she stumbled to it and sank down on it, not caring that it was wet. She braced her head in her hands. It was impossible to corral her thoughts as even the simplest sentence slipped away unfinished. Thirst gnawed at her burning throat, and she licked her cracked lips.

What time was it? In the moonlight, Carly checked her arm for her watch and remembered Snake had taken it, thinking it was a smart watch. It had to be well after midnight.

She didn't know how much time passed before the yard filled with fire engines or the helicopter landed. At some point, Logan returned and put his jacket around her shoulders. After an ambulance arrived, he broke away from the firemen and hurried toward her with a phone pressed to his ear. "I have David Raines—"

"Lexi!" She grabbed his arm. How could she have forgotten Lexi? "I have to let him know how to find her."

"Calm down. I have him here." He handed her the phone. "He knows about the GPS chip, but not how to track it."

She grabbed the phone. "David, I'm so sorry. I tried to keep him from taking her, but you can find her. She has the chip!"

"How do we track it?" David asked.

"Call RLT Security in Nashville." Carly pinched the bridge of her nose. Why wouldn't her brain clear? "I can't think of the number right now, but just google it."

"Was Lexi all right when you last saw her?" David asked.

The girl's screams for help echoed in Carly's ears. "Yes," she whispered. "They hadn't hurt her, but please, hurry. Find her."

"I will. Thanks for giving her the chip," he said, his voice breaking.

"I hope it helps. Did Logan tell you to look for a dark-colored Tahoe? That's what they used when they kidnapped us, and they may still be using it."

She handed the phone back to Logan and listened as he spoke to David again.

"No," he said. "I don't know what Jim Rankin was doing in the house. Can you let my mom know I'm okay? And tell her about Rankin. She was very close to his wife."

A shiver went down her back. Was Logan's mom involved as well? She looked up when she realized Logan had said something to her.

He nodded toward the drive. "The ambulance is here to take you to the hospital to be checked out," he said.

"No, take me to David Raines's house. I want to be there when Lexi gets home," Carly said and jumped up. When she took a step, the ground rushed up to meet her.

Logan swept her up in his arms like she weighed nothing. "You are the most stubborn person I've ever met," he said and strode across the grass to the waiting ambulance.

She didn't have the strength to wiggle out of his embrace. Or the desire. She felt safe in his arms. He gently deposited her on a gurney sitting beside the ambulance and stepped back, his eyes locked into hers. Weak-kneed as she was, it was good he didn't stand her on the ground.

A woman approached, a stethoscope hanging around her neck. "I'm Amber," she said, offering a smile. "Can we take your jacket off?"

Carly shivered. She was so cold.

"I have a blanket to wrap around you," Amber added. When Carly nodded, the medic peeled the jacket from her shoulders.

"Ah." She grunted and gritted her teeth.

"You're bleeding," Logan said.

"I think Blade tore the stitches loose."

"Would you lie down?" Amber said. "We need to get an IV started and get you to the hospital."

"I don't—"

"You don't have a choice," Logan said. "You're going."

She stared into his concerned face, and her throat tightened. Carly fought the tears that threatened. If she started crying, she was sure she would never quit. All fight left her and she stretched out on the gurney. The double take from Logan almost made her laugh.

He leaned toward her. "You are not only the most stubborn woman I've ever met," he said, his voice low and husky, "but one of the bravest."

"I'm not brave. Just determined to live." His rich baritone triggered a response in her heart she hadn't felt in sixteen years. A response she wasn't ready to deal with, and she shut it down.

"Not everyone would rush into a burning house to save someone they don't know. You're a hero in my book."

Logan's tender gaze almost made her believe him. Could it be possible . . . ? She shook her head, breaking the hold he had on her heart. "If I'd known who he was, I would have let him die. The man we saved is Austin King."

39

ERIC FOUND THE NUMBER for RLT Security and David quickly called. He identified himself and said, "I need to speak with a supervisor."

"Maybe I can help you."

When he explained what he wanted, the tech said, "I'm sorry, but that information is confidential unless you have the password."

Red tape. Everywhere they turned, red tape stopped them. And he should have realized he would need a password to get into Carly's RLT Security account. He just hoped he could reach her. "I don't have it at my fingertips. Can you hold while I get it?"

"Why don't you retrieve it and call me back?"

David jotted the tech's extension on a piece of paper and disconnected. "We need the password," he said to no one in particular as he searched for the number Logan had called him from. He put the call on speakerphone.

"Hello?"

"Logan?" David said.

"Sorry, this is Fire Chief McCoy."

He identified himself and then said, "If Sergeant Logan Donovan is still at the fire scene, I need to speak with him."

There was a pause, and then the man said, "I see him. Hold on a sec."

David drummed his fingers on the table until Logan came on the line.

"Have you found Lexi?" he asked.

"No. I need the password for the account with RLT Security," David said.

"Carly's here. Let me ask her." In less than a minute he was back on the line. "She doesn't remember it. But she said her friend Jamie Parker has it." Logan rattled off a phone number.

It was the same number Maggie had found on Carly's computer. "Parker isn't answering her phone. Ask Carly if her friend has another number where she can be reached."

"No," Logan said when he came back on the phone. "She only has a cell."

"Thanks—"

"Wait! You need to know that Jim Rankin is Austin King."

"What?" He listened as Logan filled him in. "That's hard to believe. Why do you think they tried to kill him?"

"I don't know," Logan replied.

"Was he able to tell you where they're taking Lexi?"

"He's been unconscious the whole time," Logan said.

David disconnected and turned to Maggie. "Georgina was right when she thought the sketch looked like Jim Rankin."

"You're kidding. Was he able to tell you where Lexi is?"

David rubbed the back of his neck as he relayed what Logan had told him.

"How about Carly? Did she give you the password for the RLT Security account?"

He shifted his attention back to the tracker. "She doesn't remember it. And Jamie Parker doesn't have another number."

"Call her again," Maggie suggested.

He scrolled down, hit redial, and counted the rings. One more and it would go to voicemail. David started to end the call when someone answered.

"Hello?"

"Is this Jamie Parker?"

"Yes?"

David put the call on speaker and then identified himself and explained what had happened. "Carly said to call you—that you could give me the password to her RLT Security account. I need to know the location of the GPS tracker."

There was no answer on the other end of the line.

"Are you still there?"

"Yes. If Carly is safe, why do you need it?"

He bit back his frustration. "Carly gave the tracker to my daughter. And she's been kidnapped. Please, I need to know where she is."

"How can I be sure you're David Raines?"

He heard her typing on her computer. "I can give you my badge number."

"I don't know . . ." Parker was silent again. "If you've seen Carly, then you know she wears something all the time. What is it?"

David glanced helplessly at Maggie and Eric.

Maggie spoke up. "It's a bracelet. Lily gave it to her."

"That's good enough," Jamie said. She gave him the password. "But hold on a second while I open the app. I'll give you the tracker's location." More clicks on the computer. "Do you know of a place called Hernando?"

"Yes, it's a small town south of Memphis."

"The app says the tracker is at a motel . . . I'm going to send you a screenshot rather than attempt to tell you what's on the map. Send it to this number?"

"Yes." Seconds later the photo came in, and he shared it with Eric. "Thanks," he said into the phone. "Would you keep me posted if it moves?"

"Definitely. What hospital is Carly in?"

"Regional One," he said and hung up.

"You go," Eric said. "I'll contact the De Soto County Sheriff."

In less than ten minutes, David was checking his side mirror as he swerved into the left lane on I-55, speeding past a slower-moving car. In the passenger seat, Maggie grabbed for the armrest. "Sorry," he said.

"No! Just go." She loosened her grip. "I wish we could have gotten the tracking information earlier."

"Me too. But we have it now." Eric had contacted Jamie again after they left, and she had called RLT Security and given permission for the tech to locate the tracker and keep David up-to-date on its movement. He jumped when his radio came alive.

"Lieutenant Raines, my DeSoto County deputies have invisibly deployed to the motel in question."

David punched his mic button. "Were any of the orders given over the radio?"

"Affirmative."

"Please advise your dispatcher not to relate any other information concerning this case over the airwaves." David gripped the steering wheel and pressed the gas pedal harder. He didn't have his siren going, but the blue lights flashed off and on.

"Ten-four."

"What's wrong?" Maggie asked.

"If the kidnappers have a scanner and know the local sheriff department's frequency, we just got shot out of the water."

"But how could they—" She shook her head. "I don't know why I asked that. Vanessa Driscoll said these traffickers have contacts all over Mississippi as well as Tennessee."

"Yeah, like Jim Rankin. Who would have thought an attorney who was a Memphis city councilman would be involved in human trafficking? Check with Eric and see if the tracker has moved location."

"He said he'd call—"

"Check anyway." He wanted to know the instant that tracker moved.

On the outskirts of Hernando, Blade pulled the Tahoe around to the back of the seedy motel and nosed his SUV toward the two end rooms where a white fifteen-passenger van sat parked. He'd wasted an hour making sure no one was following him. Gibson kept an eye on the five girls.

"When are we pulling out?" Gibson's slow Texas drawl broke the silence.

They all needed a few hours of sleep before they left. "Seven in the morning. I want to make the coast by two."

"Do you think the boat is ready?"

"It'll be ready. Once we get the girls to the house, we wait until dark to move them to the boat." A crew had been working day and night to modify an old yacht with a room to stash the girls when they transported them to Miami.

Blade checked his rearview mirror to see which of the girls was sniffling. It grated on his nerves. "Button it up," he yelled. If he found whoever was crying, he'd make an example of her.

This would be his last run now that he'd gotten his revenge on Jasmine. Revenge. Satisfaction welled inside his chest. No one escaped from him and lived to tell about it. It'd taken eight years, but he was a patient man. He'd known one day Jasmine would show up in her hometown, and he'd be here, waiting to make her pay.

It was why he'd asked for the syndicate to move him to Memphis and taken a job transporting girls to the coast. It'd cost him a bundle of money, but the look on Jasmine's face had been worth it. He hadn't decided whether to ship the niece out in the refitted boat when they got to the coast or leave her body somewhere.

He touched his nose with his gloved fingers. It still throbbed from her head butt. He curled his lip. The house with her body in it should be nothing but cinders by now. He hoped her last thoughts were of her niece. Revenge could be sweet, especially when it was a long time coming.

Blade pulled in beside the van and parked. The rest of the girls were in the adjoining rooms with Ramirez watching them. Blade turned until he faced his group. "You're getting out here," he said. "If you try to run, I will find you and you will wish you'd never been born."

He nodded for Gibson to stand guard and make sure they went straight into the room, and then pulled out his latex gloves and climbed out and stood where he could see them. Most of them passed by him with their gaze averted. Except one. The older girl stared defiantly at him before she pulled the detective's kid in front of her and put a protective hand on her shoulder. She would be one to watch.

They'd moved the girls out of Rankin's farmhouse and to the motel in Hernando five at a time to keep from arousing suspicion. In the morning, they would load fifteen of them into the van and the remaining five would ride in his SUV—no need to draw attention by having more people in the van than was legal. His gaze followed Jasmine's niece as she adjusted the barrette in her hair. It was the third time he'd seen her do that.

"Boss!"

Ramirez had bugged Blade about something every time he turned around. "What do you want now?"

"The cops! They're coming!"

"What are you talking about?"

"Just heard on the scanner—the cops know we're here. And they know about the Chevy!" He jerked his head toward the Tahoe.

Blade swore. How did the cops find them? *The kid kept adjusting her barrette . . .* "Get the cop's kid out here. And then get the girls into the van." Good thing he'd worn gloves every time he'd driven the Tahoe since he'd have to leave it behind. "Make some of them sit on the floor—I don't want more than fifteen people visible."

Ramirez disappeared into the room on the end. Less than a minute later, he brought the kid to him as Gibson hustled the other girls toward the van. "What do you have in your hair?" Blade demanded.

"Nothing. Just my barrette."

He snatched it out of her hair.

"Give that back to me. It's mine!"

Blade turned it over and held it up to the light. A tiny chip? His chest threatened to explode. He grabbed the girl, shaking her. "Where did you get this?"

"I-I—"

He shook her again. "Where did this come from?"

She kicked him in the shins. Then she twisted out of his hands and took off running.

"Get her," he yelled and started after her himself, but a shout from Gibson stopped him.

"They're getting away."

Blade turned as the older girl he'd worried about earlier broke for the road with three more in tow. Just then, Ramirez caught the cop's kid.

"Let me go!" She fought, kicking and screaming.

"Shut her up," Blade hissed, and Ramirez clamped a hand over the kid's mouth.

"Ow! She bit me!"

The sound of sirens reached Blade's ears. "Put her in the van. Gibson! We have to get out of here!"

"What about the others?"

"We don't have time to run them down."

He climbed in the driver's seat while Ramirez set the squirming kid on the floorboard.

"But they can identify us," Gibson said as he hopped into the van.

"Can't be helped. We'll just have to disappear once we get these girls to the coast." Blade rubbed the barrette against his pants. His fingerprints weren't on record anywhere, and he wanted to keep it that way. Then he tossed the GPS tracker out the window.

"Let's go!"

40

MAGGIE GRIPPED THE ARMREST again as David raced off the exit ramp, barely stopping at the yield sign. Two o'clock in the morning and traffic was almost nonexistent at Hernando. *Please let us find Lexi alive and well.* The prayer played through her mind over and over. "How far away are we?"

"About a mile," he said. His phone rang and he answered without looking at the ID. "Raines."

He listened while someone talked. "No! How long?"

"What is it?" she asked. "What's happened?"

He shook his head at her and listened again. "I'm two minutes away," he said and hung up. "Lexi is gone."

"How?" This couldn't be. They were so close.

"They probably had a scanner. The DeSoto County deputies found four of the girls hiding in a culvert. Maybe one of them knows something."

Maggie rubbed her forehead. How could the kidnappers get away? She leaned forward as he turned into the motel parking lot and drove around to the back where work trucks filled the lot.

The motel looked as though it'd been built in the sixties and catered to construction crews. A dozen patrol cars lit up the area with their flashing blue lights. But it was the girls who got her attention. They sat on the curb, huddled together with their heads down. A female deputy stood guard. None of the girls looked like Lexi, but Maggie couldn't see their faces to know for sure—maybe she was still here.

As soon as David parked, she hopped out and followed him as he hurried to the group and showed his badge to the officer. All four of the girls looked up. Maggie swallowed down the bitter taste of defeat. Lexi wasn't one of them.

"I was hoping they were wrong." David's voice cracked. "Where can I find who's in charge?"

"Lieutenant West is in the room on the end," the officer said, pointing to the last room.

He nodded and glanced at Maggie. "Go," she said. "I'll talk to the girls."

At least she hoped she could talk to them. She wasn't police. "I'm Madeline Starr," she said to the female officer. "Can I speak to the girls?"

"You're with him, so I suppose it's okay," she replied, nodding toward David's retreating back.

"Thank you." The curb was L-shaped, and she sat down opposite the girls, who appeared to be in their mid-to-late teens. All except one turned vacant eyes to her. She suppressed a wince. They'd been drugged and were still under the influence. Maggie studied the one with clear eyes. She appeared to be the oldest. On her right hand was a tattoo of a cross, and silver studs lined her ear. "Hi," she said. "I'm Maggie Starr."

Instead of anyone responding, three pairs of eyes turned to the older girl. "What do you want?" She crossed her arms, staring belligerently at Maggie.

She tried to figure out why the girl was so angry. They'd saved her, after all. She smoothed a wrinkle from her dress pants. *Oh, wait.* Dress pants, suit jacket—Maggie was still in her courtroom clothes. "I'm not a social worker, I'm an attorney, and I'm looking for a young girl who was taken tonight. Pretty sure she was with you earlier."

The girl's demeanor changed instantly. "You're not with the police?"

Maggie looked over her shoulder to see if the deputy overheard them. She didn't want to be hustled away. If the deputy was listening, she didn't show it. "No. I'd just like to know your name, and information on the young girl that was here."

"You're a friend of Lexi's?"

"Yes. What's your name? And how did you know hers? Were you held in the same room with her?"

"My name's Natalie," the girl said, dropping her arms. "I was in one room and Lexi was in another, but we could talk under the door."

"Do you know how the men knew we were coming?"

Natalie bit her bottom lip. "They heard it on a scanner. And then they got all mad about a barrette in Lexi's hair. Yanked it out. That's when I took off and brought these other girls with me."

"You're not drugged. How did—"

"Before we left the house, they gave me a pill. I pretended to take it, but as soon as they turned around, I spit it out. I figure Lexi did the same thing."

Natalie was a smart girl. "Can you tell me where the men are taking the girls?"

"I heard them talking about a boat when they thought we were asleep. But I don't know where."

"Do you have any family around here?"

Natalie's face closed up. "No."

Maggie stared at her a minute, then turned to the other girls. "How about you three?"

Natalie crossed her arms over her chest again. "They don't have anyone, either."

"You know if you don't give me your families' names, you'll all have to go into foster care."

"Foster care isn't that bad," one of the other girls said softly.

Maggie stood and fished a card from the inside pocket on her jacket. "If you change your mind, or if you just need to talk to someone, call me. I'll try to help you," she said, handing it to Natalie.

The girl looked down at the card then back up at Maggie. Splotches of red crept into her face as she pressed her lips together. "Thanks, I will," she croaked. Then she looked away, swiping her eyes with the back of her hand.

A few steps away, Maggie stopped and turned around. "I'll check on you tomorrow." She wasn't sure, but it looked as though Natalie's face was wet when she nodded.

Maggie hurried to the room where David had disappeared. She found him holding a plastic bag in his hand. "Find anything?" she asked.

He looked up. "A deputy found the barrette in the parking lot."

"Prints?"

His shoulders slumped, and he shook his head. "How about you? Did the girls know anything?"

"Three of them are too strung out to know what's going on. But the one called Natalie mentioned a boat. She didn't know where it was."

"That's what the deputy told me."

Maggie wished there was something she could do to help the girls. Maybe once Lexi was found, she could talk to social services. She scanned the area, noticing a man who didn't look like police. She nodded toward him. "Motel manager?"

"Yes. But he hasn't been much help. Said a man with a Texas accent rented the room and evidently used a license plate number from one of the vehicles parked out front. Vans come and go at all hours, and he didn't notice anything unusual."

"What next?" she asked. The energy she'd seen in David earlier was gone.

"Probably need to take you home."

She crossed her arms. "No. I'm staying with you."

"Don't you have appointments today? Or court?"

"Nothing important. I'll call my assistant. She'll reschedule everything."

"Let's check on Jim Rankin, then. If he's part of the trafficking ring, maybe he knows where they're taking the girls."

If he was? According to what Logan had told them, Rankin was Austin King, so Maggie was dead certain the city councilman was in the middle of the ring. Her question was why his cohorts had attempted to murder him.

41

BLADE GLANCED at the sky. It would be daylight soon, and more people would be on the road. The morning news would lead with the story of the cop's kid being kidnapped and their escape from Hernando. It would be too risky to be on the road in this van.

"Find the closest town," he said.

Gibson took out his phone, and a few minutes later, he said, "We're close to Yazoo City. About twenty-five miles from the interstate."

"What's the population? And see if there's a car rental." He needed a place big enough to rent another van. He waited while Gibson looked up the city demographics.

"About 11,000 people. And there are two car rental places."

Should be big enough for what he needed. "We'll stop there and lay over until dark," he said. Maybe a town that far from the interstate was a good idea. "Find us a motel, one where the clerk won't be too nosy."

An hour later, he had the girls unloaded and divided into two groups in adjoining rooms while he'd gotten a separate room so he could sleep. "If another one of these girls escapes, you'll pay with your life." He looked each of them in the eye. "Got that?"

"You don't have to worry," Gibson said, with Ramirez nodding in agreement.

Blade set his alarm for eight o'clock. Car rental places should be open by then.

42

An ATTENDANT pushed open the hospital door and entered the room, holding a tray. "Good morning. Here's your breakfast."

Carly found a smile. "Thank you."

She wasn't hungry and fingered the tape securing the IV in her arm. Her other arm was in a sling again. She'd been admitted to the hospital for observation after the wound had been restitched, and at least they'd allowed her to put on a pair of scrubs when she refused the hospital gown. The nurse hadn't known it but another minute in her smoky clothes, and she would have agreed to the gown. Whenever she moved her head, she got a whiff of smoke from her hair.

"Thinking of escaping?"

She hadn't seen Logan turn from the window where he'd been looking out. "What do you think?"

He gave her a tired smile. "Don't. I'm not up to chasing you down again."

"You don't have to stay here, you know. Go home and get some rest. I can get an Uber once they discharge me and go back to Haven House to pick up my car before I go to the hotel." Warmth filled her chest that he was sticking so close to her.

"With this Blade guy on the loose, you're still in danger."

"I doubt he'll come to the hospital. Besides, the forensic artist I worked with said his picture would be plastered on every floor." Carly smoothed a wrinkle from the sheet.

The artist had come to her room before eight and worked with her until Carly was satisfied with the likeness. She leaned back and stared at the ceiling. She hoped they caught Blade soon. He'd left her to die in the fire and wouldn't be happy to learn she hadn't.

Logan lifted the lid covering her food. "Are you going to eat this?"

She looked to see what was on the plate. Two strips of limp bacon, powdered eggs, and toast. "Why don't you eat it?"

He grinned. "Split the bacon with you."

"You can have it all," she said. "Are you working a twenty-four-hour shift?"

"No."

"But you were in my hospital room yesterday morning." And had been with her since the kidnapping except for when she was in the ER.

"I was off-duty then. And I'm sticking with you until I'm certain Blade or his bosses don't send someone after you again."

She eyed his clean khakis and shirt. It wasn't what he'd worn yesterday. "How did you get a shower and new clothes?"

"I went home when you first came into the hospital since they wouldn't let me stay with you."

"Lucky you. And really, you don't have to babysit me."

He walked to the vinyl chair beside the bed and sat down. "But I do. We still don't know who we're dealing with."

"Did you get a look at Blade?"

"No. I was too busy fighting, and after being in the dark so long, my eyes didn't adjust very fast."

The likeness the sketch artist had drawn was based on how Blade looked eight years ago since she didn't get a good look at him either. All she could remember was the hatred in his eyes when he snatched Lexi from her. "I hope it's better than what I came up with on Austin King. I was really off base on his sketch. Is he still alive?"

"Last I heard, he was." Logan unhooked his cell phone from his belt and texted someone.

"I hope he doesn't die, at least not until he tells us where Blade took Lexi."

His phone chirped, and he read the text and suddenly sat up straighter. "He's still hanging on. And he's asking for you."

She gripped the sheet. "What? Why?"

"I don't know. But it might be a chance to find out what he knows and maybe where they're taking Lexi. Are you up to it?"

Carly was up to it and more. She swung her feet off the bed. She wanted to tell Austin King what a vile person he was before he died. "Do I have to stay hooked to this thing?" she asked, nodding at the IV pole.

"Yep. But I'll help you with it. Don't you want a wheelchair?"

"No wheelchair." She stood too quickly and had to wait for her head to stop spinning before she took a step.

"You sure you can walk? I really don't want to have to catch you again."

Pulling herself up straight, Carly gripped the pole, steadying herself. "I'm good."

"Will it hurt you if I hold your good arm?"

Her head swam. This was harder than she'd expected. "We can try it."

Logan slid his hand under her elbow, clasping it. "You okay?"

She nodded. He was close enough for her to smell his after-shave—a heady, light woodsy scent. He'd saved her life. That was why her heart was pounding like a jackhammer. It had nothing to do with how close he stood to her.

Carly rolled the IV pole out of the room. Then she groaned.

"You okay?"

"I didn't know we were at the end of the hallway." The nurse's station and elevator had to be a mile away. Halfway there, her legs threatened to crumple. "Maybe . . ." she said, panting, "a wheelchair wouldn't be such a bad idea."

"It's at the nurses' station. Either I carry you—"

"No! I can make it. Just let me stop a second." She leaned against him just as a nurse stepped out of the room across from them.

"Ms. Smith, what are you doing?"

She tried to straighten. "Going to see someone."

"Why aren't you using a wheelchair?"

Carly glanced at Logan and he snickered.

"Because someone is too stubborn. Could you get us one?" he asked.

She refused to look at him again for fear she would start laughing and end up at his feet. When the nurse returned with a wheelchair, Carly sank into it. "Thank you," she said. Now she dreaded seeing the I-told-you-so in Logan's face.

"Want me to push you or are you going to keep playing the independent card?"

"Push me. Please," she added. "I'll pull the pole along."

They rode the elevator to the bottom floor, and after they were admitted to ICU, a nurse directed them to a room at the end of the hall.

"Are you Heather Morgan?" the nurse asked. "That's who he keeps asking for."

Carly stiffened. Hearing that name always undid her. "Yes," she said faintly.

"It's not going to be pretty," she said. "He has burns over 40 percent of his lower body. Parts of his chest and neck are also burned."

Carly nodded. She'd never seen a burn victim before, and could only imagine.

"The hospital doesn't normally allow visitors during the critical phase of treatment, but he keeps asking for you. So if you want to 'suit up,' I'll take you into the room."

"Can't Logan go with me?" Her nose twitched. Something smelled terrible.

"I'm afraid not. We're stretching it to allow you in."

Logan locked the wheels and helped her put on a paper gown before handing her a mask. He came around in front of her and knelt by the wheelchair. "It's pretty bad," he said, looking over his shoulder. "Are you certain you're up for this?"

"I thought you wanted me to—"

He held her gaze, his amber eyes soft. "Not if it's going to make you come unglued."

Carly gripped the arm of the wheelchair. Unglued was not the feeling she felt. For sixteen years, she'd waited for this minute. Dreamed of what she'd say to the man she'd harbored such hatred for. The man who had ruined her life. The man who was responsible for Lexi's kidnapping. Falling apart wasn't happening. Why he wanted to see her was what gave her pause.

She straightened her shoulders. "He can save Lexi," she said and looked up at the nurse. "Push me in."

Inside the room she realized the smell that she'd noticed was charred flesh. Breathing was difficult. She looked at Austin King and wanted to look away.

The area from his knees to his feet lay exposed, the skin raw where it wasn't black. A sheet covered the middle of his body where the fire had skipped, but above his stomach, his shoulders and arms mirrored the legs. How could anyone live with that much damage?

She shuddered and tamped down the nausea that crept up from her stomach. Above his head a monitor beeped his heart rate, and Carly zeroed in on the T waves crawling across the screen.

"Mr. Rankin." The nurse leaned over and spoke in his ear. "Heather Morgan is here to see you."

Carly dropped her gaze and focused on his face that was untouched by the fire. The image etched in her mind bore little resemblance to this man. She probably would not have recognized him if she'd passed him on the street. He was completely bald, and time had not been kind to Austin King, or rather Jim Rankin. That was what Logan had said his real name was. He wasn't on a vent but some other type of machine. The nurse removed the mask over his nose and mouth and replaced it with an oxygen tube in his nose. She spoke to him again, and his eyes fluttered open.

"Heather?" he wheezed. "Where . . . is she?"

"I'm right here." His eyes found hers, the gaze so intense, she couldn't move.

"You . . . came."

Carly leaned forward. "Yes."

"Have . . . to tell you . . . I'm sorry. About you . . . About your sister. Panicked when she called . . . Can you . . . forgive me?" he said, his voice breaking.

She jerked back. Forgive him? Never. He ruined her life. Killed her sister. Kidnapped her niece. "How can you ask—"

"I'm . . . "—he sucked in air—"dying. Want . . . them to pay . . . Please tell . . . me you forgive—"

"Where is my niece?" she demanded.

"They . . ." His eyes clouded. And then closed.

She balled her hands. "Don't you die until you tell me where my niece is!"

He didn't respond, and she wanted to shake the words out of him. Was he dead? No, the monitor continued to beep a steady if rapid heart rate. She should have known nothing good would come from Austin King.

"Can you forgive me?" His words sprang into her mind, and she gritted her teeth. No way. Maybe if he'd told them where Lexi was. But he hadn't. He didn't deserve forgiveness.

"I'm sorry," the nurse said. "The pain medication has knocked him out. Do you need my help getting out of the room?"

"No." Carly turned the wheelchair and a moan came from the

bed, and she cut her eyes toward King. The man was in unimaginable pain. She gripped the armrest, remembering all those years in captivity when she'd been in pain.

"Wait . . . must tell you . . ." The whispered words halted her. "Help . . . girls . . . A . . ."

She could barely hear his mumbling and rolled to the bed. "Please, where are the girls?"

"Boat . . . done . . . horrible things . . . so sorry . . ."

43

LOGAN TOLD HIS MOTHER goodbye, ended the call, and then glanced around the empty ICU waiting room. It'd been much different an hour ago during visiting hours. He turned his attention to Carly. "You okay?"

She nodded. "What did your mother want?"

"To see if I'd heard anything. She's concerned about Lexi. And you."

Carly gave him a sour look. "Lexi, I believe, but she has no use for me."

"You're wrong about that. She asked about you, and I told her you were okay, that the doctor is discharging you later today." When she frowned again, Logan said, "She also offered for you to stay at the house, but I told her you planned to return to the Westin."

"Good," she said. "Maggie offered to let me stay with her if I want to leave the hotel."

"Maggie has a nice place," he said. "Would you like some coffee? Eggs, maybe, since you didn't eat earlier? I think they serve breakfast in the cafeteria until nine thirty—another fifteen minutes."

"I want Austin King to give us some answers," she said. "What do you think he was trying to tell me?"

Carly had told him what Rankin said, or as much of it as she could remember, but little of it made sense. "I don't know. It sounded like he was trying to tell you about the boat they're taking the girls to. Maybe he'll be clearer when you go back in."

"I wish they'd let you go in with me." Carly glanced toward the ICU doors and folded her arms across her chest. "I can't believe he had the nerve to ask me to forgive him. I'll see him rot in the ground first."

Concern filled him . . . and something else. It was the something else that set his heart racing.

She looked up and caught him staring at her. "What is it?"

"You look so angry."

Instantly her face became impassive, her brow relaxed, and the hard line of her mouth softened. "Better?"

"It would be if I thought it were natural. How do you mask your expressions so quickly?"

"I used to practice hiding my emotions in front of a mirror. It was the only control I had in my life."

She'd experienced things no human should. "I can't begin to know what you've gone through, but I hate to see anger holding you hostage."

"It's not holding me *anything*." She lifted her chin. "What if he'd sold your sister into the sex trade? Wouldn't you be angry?"

"Of course I would." His jaw tightened. "And you have every right to be outraged—"

"You bet I do. That man sold me into slavery. Eight long years of it. Some days I didn't even know if I'd survive." Her eyes narrowed. "Why does it matter to you whether or not I forgive him?"

Why did it matter? Like a thunderbolt, it hit him. Although they'd only dated a short while, she'd made a deep impression on him. He'd seen her heart the day she took a homeless person inside a fast-food restaurant and fed her. After that, he hadn't been surprised to learn she helped out at a food kitchen. He did not want to see bitterness destroy her . . . or any chance they might have together.

She held up her hand. "Forget it. I'm done talking about this."

Probably just as well. If he kept pushing her, she'd dig in her heels. It was the way she'd been when he met her the first time all those years ago.

Funny how her core personality was still there, even after everything she'd been through. He was still surprised it took as long as it had for him to figure out who she was. Even their sparring the first day should have tipped him off that Carly Smith was Heather Morgan.

When he'd known her sixteen years ago, her concern for others, and her independence, and yes, even her stubbornness had been what attracted him to her. That and the beauty that even heavy makeup and jet-black hair couldn't hide. Her Goth look should have been a clue to her age, but he'd been into a little rebellion himself.

Carly looked up from her magazine. "Do you think I'll be able to talk to him again?"

"I imagine so if he wakes up. He's in pretty bad shape." From the doorway, he'd watched the readings on the monitor, not liking the way Rankin's heart rate jumped from fifty to a hundred and fifty and then back down. His blood pressure was low as well.

"You honestly think I should forgive him, don't you." Her gaze challenged him.

"It doesn't matter what I think," he said.

"But I want to know."

Logan scratched his jaw and squirmed in his seat.

"That's what I thought," she said.

"But I haven't answered you." *Could* he forgive if it had been Geri? The thought curled his fingers into a fist. "I—"

The ICU doors opened and Rankin's nurse beckoned to Carly. "I'm so glad you're still here. He's awake again and keeps asking for you. I thought it might calm him down if you came back and talked to him again."

He wasn't too sure of that. If Carly steadfastly refused to forgive Rankin, it might make things worse. "Doesn't he have family?"

"No one in Memphis. I think he has a brother flying in from California."

He wasn't sure it would be good for Carly if she went back, but before he could express it, she said, "I'd like to talk to him again."

"Are you sure?" he asked.

"Yes. He knows where they took Lexi, and I'll do anything to get her back. And don't worry. I'm not going to make it worse."

He wheeled her through the ICU doors, and she suited up again before he pushed her to Rankin's room at the end of the hall. He'd seen the man's burns from the doorway earlier, and he was in no hurry to see them again. Even from where he stood, the odor had been bad, but not as bad as he'd expected, probably because the burns were still fresh. In a day or so when debridement started, it would be worse. If he lived that long.

"It might go better if you speak softly to him," Logan said.

"I'm not going to jump down his throat," she said dryly.

King lay with his head turned toward the door, and his eyes widened when he saw Carly. "You came back."

He sounded stronger. Maybe he'd survive this yet.

"Yes," she replied.

"Thank you." He stared at her. "I would have never . . ."—he sucked in air through the cannula in his nose—"known you if Grey hadn't—" King grimaced and moaned. "Hurts so bad."

In spite of what he'd done, she received no pleasure from knowing he was in pain. "Who is Grey?"

"I didn't . . ." He stopped and breathed again. "Know Blade . . . was going to take your niece. Stupid thing to do . . . Tried to get him to release—"

"Where is she?" Carly said, leaning forward.

"Grey won't . . . like it when he . . . finds out."

He was in his own world. She wondered if he even heard her. "Who is Grey?" she asked.

"They shouldn't have done this." His words slurred.

"You keep talking about someone named Grey. Who is he?"

"They . . . shouldn't . . ." A scream tore from his lips, and the nurse rushed in.

"You better leave."

"Nooo!" he cried. "Get . . . the doctor . . . stop . . ."

Carly frowned. His mind was slipping away. "What are you trying to say?"

He mumbled something, but she couldn't make out the words.

"So tired." He focused on breathing again, sucking oxygen through the cannula.

"Where is Lexi?" Carly asked again, impatience sharpening her words.

King roused, his eyes fixed on her. "I didn't know . . . have to believe me."

She stiffened and pressed against the back of the wheelchair. "Then why did you?"

He blinked. "Why . . . what?"

He was losing it. Carly rolled a little closer to the bed. "Lexi, the eleven-year-old girl that was kidnapped. Where is she, King?"

Rankin's heart rate spiked, and alarms shrieked from the monitor. "No. Please . . ." He shrank back from Carly.

In an instant the room was full of nurses, and Carly backed away from the bed and out into the hallway to where Logan waited.

Neither of them spoke as he wheeled her through the ICU, stopping at the doors to remove her gown and mask. Carly propped her head in her hand. "I didn't expect him to react like that when I called him King," she said.

"Something certainly triggered fear in him. Even from where I stood, I could see his expression. He looked at you like you were the angel of death."

She'd blown it. "They'll never let me back in to see him, and we won't find out where Lexi is." She licked her lips. Her mouth was so dry. "Could you get me some water?"

A water cooler stood in the corner, and he found a cup. "Ice water or not?" he asked.

"No ice."

Logan's phone dinged with a text. "It's David. He wants to know where we are."

While he answered, she leaned back in the wheelchair with her eyes closed.

"You okay?"

"Frustrated," she said, opening her eyes. "Who do you think this Grey is?"

"No clue," Logan said. He stood with a cup of water in his hand.

"Maybe he's the mastermind." She replayed their conversation. "I was trying to break through whatever fog he was in. I didn't know calling him King would send him off the deep end."

"I think his past is eating at him."

She took the cup of water he handed her. "It should."

He glanced back toward the room. "I wish there was something I could do or say to help you, but I can't even imagine what you went through because of him . . ."

Carly rubbed the locket on the bracelet around her wrist. Only someone who'd lived through it could understand her anger. Someone like Lily. But she had forgiven her captors.

How did she do it? *Because she was stronger and had more faith. She believed in forgiveness instead of judgment.*

Carly lifted her chin. She wasn't Lily. No way did Austin King deserve forgiveness.

Lily's voice whispered in her ear. *"None of us deserve it."*

44

WHILE THE OTHER GIRLS SLEPT, Lexi kept a watch on the man who had driven them as he dozed in a straight-backed chair. She didn't see how he could sleep like that with the chair rocked back on two legs against the door. The curtains had been pulled, but a tiny bit of light slipped through a split. Even though it was daylight, the room was deathly quiet except for the sounds of breathing.

Lexi had been in the middle of three other girls. But when she'd pretended she needed to go to the bathroom and came back to bed, the girl on the outside had rolled over in her place. Now Lexi was on the edge. Right next to the telephone.

Her stomach growled, reminding her she hadn't had anything to eat since lunch yesterday. When Natalie had complained earlier that everyone was hungry to the man who acted like he was in charge, he'd laughed, and when she complained again, he'd slapped her and told her to get used to it.

Lexi missed Natalie. She was the only one who tried to talk to her. The others were drugged or maybe they were too scared to say anything. She looked at their guard again. His head had dropped to his chest and he was snoring.

She pulled the blanket with her as she rolled over on her side and stared at the phone on the bedside table. It was so close. She tried to swallow, but her throat was too tight. Lexi wanted to pick the phone up, call her dad, but it was like she was frozen and couldn't move. What if the man woke up? *Jesus, help me.*

Her tongue stuck to the roof of her dry mouth. She kept her gaze on the man and inched her hand to the table.

"El balón es mío."

She snatched her hand back and pretended to be asleep. He mumbled something else in Spanish that she couldn't understand, and she peeked over her shoulder at him. He looked like he was still asleep. Then he chuckled. Her muscles went slack. He was talking in his sleep like Uncle Frank did sometimes.

Lexi took a shaky breath. She eyed the phone again, and this time she grabbed for the receiver and slid it under the blanket. The phone gave a light beep when she pressed the first number and she quickly pressed the other numbers. It rang. One, two, three . . .

The chair legs slammed to the floor, and she quickly ended the call. Lexi sensed movement and closed her eyes, praying he would not walk to her side of the bed. When she heard the bathroom door close, she looked over her shoulder and didn't see him. Maybe her dad would answer this time. She punched the first two numbers and heard the commode flush. *No. Not enough time.* She put the receiver back and pulled the cover over her head just as the bathroom door opened.

45

DAVID PLACED HIS HAND on the small of Maggie's back as they climbed the steps to the entrance to Regional One. They'd come to the hospital earlier but had been unable to get any information on Rankin and had returned to David's house for Maggie's car and a little rest.

When Logan had texted him that Jim Rankin had asked to see Heather, David wanted to hear in person what he'd told her. He hoped Rankin knew where Blade was taking the girls and was willing to tell Carly.

At the top of the steps, he held the door to the Med open for Maggie. She touched his arm, and he looked down into her troubled blue eyes. He was pretty sure he was the cause of some of the trouble in them, and he squeezed her hand. "You okay?"

"I was going to ask you the same thing," she said.

"I'll be better when we get Lexi back." His cell phone rang and he pulled it off his belt. His brother. "What do you have, Eric?" he asked.

"Carly Smith worked with a forensic artist on a sketch of the man she calls Blade—no last name. No hits from the facial recognition software. We're distributing the poster to all law enforcement agencies in Mississippi, Tennessee, Arkansas, and Louisiana."

"How about the van he used to transport the girls?"

"When the deputies canvassed the motel residents, most didn't want to get involved, but two people reported seeing a dirty white van parked at the end of the row. DeSoto County deputies set up roadblocks on the major roads, but evidently the van had already slipped out of the county. We've sent every sheriff's department from here to the coast a be-on-the-lookout for a white fifteen-passenger van containing a group of girls and three men." Eric stopped and blew out a breath. "It would help if we had a license plate number. I worry that they found a place to hole up in when it got to be daylight. Or he'll rent a different van."

But if they holed up until dark, it would buy some much-needed time. Especially if Jim Rankin gave them the information on where the boat was docked. David thanked his brother and disconnected.

"Any news?" Maggie asked as they walked to the elevator.

"Afraid not." David punched the down button and relayed what Eric had told him. When an elevator didn't immediately appear, he checked the lighted numbers above the doors. One elevator was on the third floor and the other on the fifth. He jabbed the button again, multiple times. When the doors finally opened, they got in and rode in silence. Except for a couple of people, the waiting room was deserted. "Wonder where Logan and Carly are." He took out his phone.

"Maybe they're still in with Rankin," Maggie said.

He texted Logan.

Where are you?

In ICU. On our way out.

David showed Maggie the text and she pointed to a corner of the room. "Why don't we sit over there and wait for them?"

He followed Maggie to the sofa and sat next to her. And just like every other time he got still, images of Lexi bombarded his thoughts. David stood and walked to the refreshment area, but his thoughts followed him. He squeezed his eyes shut, warding off the tears that burned the backs of his eyes. When Maggie slipped her arm around his waist, he drew her into his embrace and almost came undone.

"What if we don't find her?" he whispered against her hair. "Right now she's looking for me to come and save her. And I don't know where she is."

"We're going to find her," she said.

"You don't know that."

"Look at me," she said.

He lowered his gaze. Hope shone bright in her eyes. If only he had her faith that this was going to turn out all right. The memory of his words last night assaulted him. "I'm sorry—"

"Shh," Maggie said. "It's okay."

"No. I'm sorry for what I said. This isn't your fault."

"Or yours," she said.

"But it is. I'm a cop and I didn't protect her." He should have been able to keep his family safe.

"No one is to blame except the evil person who took Lexi. We are going to make it through this."

He traced his thumb along her jaw, drawing from her strength. "Thank you," he said.

The swish of the ICU doors caught his attention, and he looked around as Logan wheeled Carly Smith through them. "They're back."

He caught Logan's eye and waved him over. Logan bent down and said something to Carly, and she looked his way and nodded.

When they reached their area of the ICU waiting room, David leaned forward. "Did he tell you anything?"

"No," Carly said. "He might have, except the first time we went back, he went to sleep. The nurse thought it was the medication. This last time he had a crisis."

David sat down next to the wheelchair. He'd never really taken a good look at his wife's sister, but in spite of her lighter hair and complexion, he could see a resemblance to Lia in the shape of her face and mouth. The dark circles under her eyes reminded him of Lia when she was tired. She held the arm that was in a sling close to her body. "So they got you stitched up again?"

"Yes."

David turned to Logan. "Any word on the bullet they dug out of her shoulder?"

"Nothing other than it's a .22."

"That's not a gun professionals would use," David said.

"I know, and it's puzzling."

David turned back to Carly. "Heather—Carly—" He held his hands up. "I don't know what to call you . . . but your name doesn't matter. I want to thank you for helping Lexi."

"I'm Carly," she said. "Heather just doesn't fit anymore—it belongs in another life. And I'm sorry the GPS tracker didn't help."

"It helped to free four girls, at least," David said. "And we know they're taking them to a boat somewhere. Just don't know where."

Carly's shoulders slumped. "A lot of times that's the way they get the girls to Miami where the buyers are. They put false bottoms in the boats and stack the girls on top of each other. Like sardines. We have to find them before they reach that boat."

A band squeezed his chest, cutting off his air. He hadn't let himself think of what would happen if Blade got the girls to the boat. "I don't think he'll take them straight to a boat—moving that many young girls in daylight on a waterfront would draw a lot of attention. I figure once he gets to the coast, he'll find a motel to stay in until it gets dark."

"Unless he's rented a house," Maggie said.

David raked his hand through his hair. He should be out looking for the van instead of sitting here doing nothing.

Maggie touched his arm and he flinched.

"Why don't we take a walk?" she asked. "Work off a little of your steam. Maybe we can pick up some food for everyone."

"Go," Logan said. "I'll call you if I hear any news at all."

David stood. He didn't like being the one waiting. But Kevin Scott was in charge of the investigation, and he would do a good job. It was just so frustrating to not be able to help find his own daughter. Getting some fresh air might help his mental outlook.

He and Maggie rode the elevator in silence, and then when they walked out the door, she asked, "You want to walk east? There's a breakfast café that way. It should still be open."

He didn't know that he could eat anything, but he needed the fuel for his body. "Sure."

They walked a few blocks in the nippy air with the sun on their faces. Morning traffic passed them by, and he couldn't understand how the world could go on like nothing was wrong. Maggie slid her hand in his and he squeezed it. "Thanks for sticking with me," he said.

"Nothing to thank me for. The café is just ahead—Mike's."

When they reached the café, he opened the door for her. David didn't remember ever eating here. "How did you find this place?" he asked after they sat in a booth.

"My assistant eats here all the time. Sometimes she brings me biscuits and ham. The food is really very good."

They ordered the breakfast special and a couple of ham biscuits to take back to the hospital. When the food came, David barely tasted it, his mind on Lexi. "Where could they be?"

"No word from the Mississippi Highway Patrol?"

"Nothing. How can a van with sixteen girls disappear?"

"I don't know. It's like they're invisible."

He drummed his fingers on the table and then checked his phone to make sure it was turned on. A missed call showed on his screen. "I don't remember missing a call," he said. "Unless it came in when I was talking to Eric."

263

He clicked on his recent calls. The missed call showed up about the same time as Eric's. "It's a 601 number. That's somewhere in Mississippi. Could be a call from one of the Mississippi sheriffs." He tapped the call button, and after five rings, he was about to hang up when someone answered. "No-El Motel. How may I help you?"

His heart ratcheted up a notch. "This is Lieutenant Raines with the Memphis police department. I received a phone call from this number. Is there any way you can connect me with the room?"

"What's the room number?"

"I don't know."

"I'm afraid I can't help you then."

Was it possible Lexi had managed to call him? "Whoever called would be in a white van traveling with several girls. Do you have someone like that staying with you?"

"Let me ask the manager."

The operator put him on hold. "The manager remembers one van like you're talking about. I'll put you through to the room."

"Before you do, what city are you in?"

"Yazoo, Mississippi," she said.

No one answered and the call went to a voice mailbox. David disconnected and punched his brother's number in. "I think Lexi tried to call me."

"What? Where was she?" Eric asked.

David told him what had happened and the name of the motel. "Can you fax the sketch of Blade to the manager, see if anyone recognizes him?"

"On it. And I'll send the local police to check it out."

As soon as he relayed the fax number to Eric, David hooked his phone on his belt. "I'm going back to the hospital."

46

WITH NO IV POLE to worry her, Carly relaxed as Logan wheeled her toward the ICU waiting room. The IV was gone and she'd been discharged. The nurses had even allowed her to wear the scrubs until she could get to her clothes at the hotel.

"Thanks for being my . . ." She paused, trying to find the right word. Her brain was so foggy. "Chauffeur." Carly shook her head. "No, that's not the right word."

"How about Prince Charming?"

She couldn't stop the laughter that burst from her lips. "If you're going in that direction, more like Jiminy Cricket," she said, referring to the animated cricket that had been Pinocchio's conscience. "I was thinking along the lines of transporter."

"I like Prince Charming better."

His voice had dropped an octave, spiraling her heart rate. She'd felt the attraction between them before. His long gazes. Sometimes lingering touch. Picturing a calm lake wouldn't work this time. Logan had somehow chipped a hole in the wall she had erected around her heart, and she needed to find that hole and seal it up again. She fought to regain control of her emotions. *Focus on finding Lexi.* That thought sobered her.

The waiting room door opened as they approached, and he wheeled her through. "Same place?" he asked, all business.

Carly nodded, her cheeks burning. His interest had only been in her imagination. What an idiot she was, thinking he could be interested in someone who was damaged goods. She forced her thoughts to the man in the ICU. Logan called him Jim Rankin, but she still thought of him as Austin King.

"None of us deserve forgiveness." Lily's words replayed in her head. God had extended his mercy and forgiven her much, but she hadn't done the things Austin King had. "Austin King is responsible for Lexi being kidnapped and probably my sister's death as well."

"Whoa. Where did that come from?"

Heat warmed her cheeks. Had she actually said that? "Sorry. I was just thinking out loud."

He nodded. "Since you mentioned it, I'm wondering if he actually had anything to do with Lexi's kidnapping," Logan said. "He didn't seem to know it was going to happen."

"So he said. I don't believe him."

She locked the wheels and stood, almost wishing for the IV pole to steady her legs. When she was certain of her balance, Carly walked to the refreshment center in the corner and poured a cup of black coffee. Logan followed her. She took a sip and made a face.

"Strong?"

"I think it can walk better than I can."

"Let me see if I can make a fresh pot."

She dumped the coffee in the sink and then moved aside as he rummaged in the drawers under the counter, finding a filter and package of coffee. "Why don't you eat one of those protein bars someone donated?" he said.

Carly chose a powdered doughnut instead. Right now she wanted something dense and sugary, not food that was good for her. The image of Austin King haunted her. She pushed it away only to have another one take its place. She tossed the doughnut into the trash.

Logan emptied the coffeepot and set it on the burner. After he filled the brew basket with coffee, he flipped the button to start the cycle before turning to her. "I can't totally know how you feel, but I'm angry too."

He stood inches from her, his amber eyes locked into hers. She wanted to look away, but she couldn't. She wasn't imagining the desire in his eyes. Her heart almost stopped when he smoothed a lock of her hair with his hand, then traced her jawline.

"And not just for what's happened to you and Lexi," he said softly. He tipped her face up, his thumb trembling as he gently brushed it across her bottom lip.

Carly gripped the front of his shirt, tugging him closer. Logan took a ragged breath and cupped her face in his hands. She closed her eyes as he bent his head closer. His lips covered hers, sending an electric shock through her body. Moaning, she leaned into the kiss, her heart beating so hard he had to feel it.

When he released her, she sighed and laid her head against his chest, inhaling the scent of him. Like a fresh spring day. She never thought love would stir in her heart again.

"Sixteen years ago," he whispered against her hair, "you and I had something going for us. If you hadn't been kidnapped, we might be married now with a couple of kids."

She raised her head, looking at him. "Why didn't you ever marry?"

His smile was tender as he stroked her hair. "Even though you were only seventeen—and for the record, I really thought you were twenty—I knew you were the only woman for me. When you disappeared, my world crashed. Searching for you is what got me into the police academy."

"You're kidding."

The coffee gurgled behind them. "You ready for that coffee?" he asked.

Not really. Carly was quite content for him to hold her, but when she heard the sound of the door opening, she stepped back and turned around. The rotund physician she'd met at Haven House stood just inside the room. His eyes widened when he noticed her. "Dr. Adams?" she said.

"Ms. Smith." He walked toward the refreshment center. "How wonderful to see you after all you've been through."

"Thank you," she said, frowning.

"Vanessa told me about the kidnapping," the doctor added. "Is your doctor keeping you for twenty-four-hour observation?"

"No. He discharged me just a bit ago." She nodded toward Logan. "This is Detective Donovan."

The two men shook hands. "So where will you go? Back home to Stillwater?" Dr. Adams asked.

"Not until we find Lexi," Carly said.

"Are you still at the Westin?"

"How did you know I was staying there?" she asked.

Dr. Adams poured a cup of coffee. "You told me at Haven House, after you left the hospital the first time and almost passed out."

Oh yeah . . . He'd wanted to call an ambulance.

"She'll be moving from there later today." Logan pointed to his black bag. "Do you have a patient here?"

Dr. Adams sipped his coffee. "Yes, and I heard Jim Rankin had been brought in. He's my neighbor, and I wanted to check on him before I see my patients."

"He's not doing too well," Carly said.

"Your sketches didn't resemble him very much."

"No, I was working with very old memories." She was surprised at how far off she'd been on his features, but when she saw King at the farmhouse, it had been crystal clear who he was.

"Anyway, I was shocked to hear of his involvement in human trafficking," the doctor said.

"I'm sure a lot of people are."

"Were the two of you able to talk with him at all?"

"I was. The nurses wouldn't let Logan go in. Rankin didn't make a lot of sense, and I'm still trying to piece his words together," Carly said and looked around for the wheelchair. "Maybe he'll be more alert when I talk with him again."

"Stay right there," Logan said. "I'll get your carriage."

The doctor set the cup down and nodded to Carly. "Well, I think I'll just take a quick peek at him. I'd like him to know I'm here." He stopped at the doors. "I'll be right back and let you know how he is."

Carly sank down in the wheelchair, glad to be off her feet. Logan parked her by the sofa where they'd been earlier and sat across from her. Her lips still tingled where he'd kissed her. But the biggest shock was the way she'd responded. For eight years, she'd avoided relationships because she believed her past had ruined any chance for love. The question now was, could Logan look beyond the life she'd lived? She didn't see how he could. Maybe even now he regretted kissing her.

"Feel better?"

She stretched her shoulders, wincing when the stitches pulled. "Yeah."

"I meant it earlier when I said you are the bravest woman I know."

Carly ducked her head. She wanted to tell him she wouldn't hold him to the kiss. Or what he said about what could have happened years ago if she hadn't been kidnapped. Logan poured her a cup of coffee and she slowly sipped it. A caffeine rush would be nice about now.

A few minutes later the ICU doors opened, and she turned to look. A nurse stood in the doorway, scanning the room.

"Ms. Morgan," she said when she saw Carly. "I was afraid you'd left. Mr. Rankin is in and out of consciousness, and he's very agitated, but he keeps asking for you."

269

Carly nodded and glanced toward Logan. "Go with me?"

"As far as they will let me."

Images of Austin King from earlier bombarded Carly's mind, and she steeled herself for seeing him again. But when she rolled into the room, her gaze fixed on his burned body and she faltered. His eyes were closed, asleep maybe, and he looked so pale. The monitor over his head still beeped although much slower than before.

Mercy. Forgiveness. She curled her fingers, making a fist. Her years on the streets hadn't been her fault. But hatred was a sin too. And she had plenty of that.

Could she forgive him? The thought rankled inside her. The man was responsible for no telling how many girls being sold into prostitution. She rubbed the gold bracelet on her arm. *"If you don't forgive . . . it will eat you alive."* Lily's words wouldn't go away. Carly clenched her jaw until it hurt.

She couldn't do this. She put her hand on the wheel of her wheelchair to turn around when someone stepped out of the bathroom. "Dr. Adams, you're still here," she said, glad to avert her eyes.

"Yes. I don't think he ever realized I was here. I wish I could stay longer." He picked up his medical bag. "But I have patients—"

"Heather," King rasped. "You came. Thank you."

She shifted her attention to him.

"Have . . . to tell you . . ." His blue eyes bored into hers. "I'm . . . sorry."

Carly barely nodded.

"Please . . . can you forgive me?" His whispered words fell into the room where only the sound of the slowing monitor remained.

Just tell him what he wants to hear. Her heart resisted. But did she really want him to go into eternity without forgiveness? "Tell me where Lexi is," she said.

His gaze became unfocused. "Lexi? . . . Blade took her . . . Annie . . ."

She didn't want more names. Carly wanted a location.

"I'm sorry . . . for . . ." His eyes closed briefly, then he struggled to raise his head. "Got to . . . tell . . . forgive me . . ."

Her heart beat so hard, she could hear it in her ears. She rubbed her hand over Lily's gold bracelet.

"I . . . I forgive you," she said. Even though Carly didn't know if she meant it, just saying the words lifted a burden from her.

"Thank . . . you . . ." He closed his eyes. "Feel so weak . . . *Annie* . . ." His breathing grew shallow. Suddenly an alarm blasted into the room as his heart rate flatlined.

Dr. Adams set his medical bag down as the RN rushed in.

"He's coding!" The nurse turned to the doctor.

"Draw 1 mg of epinephrine," he said as Carly backed out of the room and more nurses rushed in with a crash cart.

47

BLADE'S CELL PHONE RANG, waking him from a shallow sleep. "Yeah?" he said without looking at the ID.

"You fool. You've made a mess of everything."

It was Grey, and Blade sat straight up in bed, sleep forgotten. "What are you talking about?"

"Which one do you want first? The woman? Or the cop's kid?"

How did he find out about the kid? He never intended for Grey to know—a pain hit his stomach and he fumbled for antacids. He must have talked to Ramirez or Gibson. "What about the woman?"

"She's in the hospital, but nothing serious. And she and the cop got Rankin out of the house."

"That's impossible. The whole house was on fire when we left."

"I'm telling you, they're alive."

His stomach soured, knowing Jasmine had gotten away. "Where are they?"

"The Med."

Grey mumbled something under his breath, probably swearing. Blade gripped the phone. If he rented a car, he could be in Memphis by three. She would not escape this time.

272

"Where are you?"

"Yazoo City. I rented a new van with dark-tinted windows. We're leaving in ten minutes."

"All right. Get the girls delivered to the house, and from now on Gibson and Ramirez report directly to me. I'll clean up your mess here."

No. He would clean up his own mess.

Pounding sounded on his door, and his heart slammed against his ribs.

"It's me! Manny!"

"I'll call you back," he said into the phone and then jerked open the door. "What's wrong?"

A stream of Spanish spewed from Ramirez's mouth.

"Speak English!"

"Police are coming!"

"What are you talking about?"

"The phone rings and I don't answer. I go ask the woman at the desk about it. She say some Memphis cop was asking about a white van with kids."

Blade's mind raced. If it was Raines, it would not take the cop long to find the motel—if he hadn't already. Even now, deputies might be surrounding them. "Who's with your girls?"

Ramirez's eyes widened. "No one—I had to tell you."

Blade shoved him aside and charged out of the room. One of the girls was running out the door. "Stop!" He spied Lexi as she ran toward the office, and he sprinted after her while Ramirez went after the other girl. A woman walking to her room stopped and stared at him. "She's"—he circled his finger—"special needs. I'm afraid she'll hurt herself."

Her mouth formed a small O.

Just before the office door, he caught Lexi by her shoulders and jerked her off the ground. "You scream or say one word, and I'll wring your neck," he hissed in her ear. "Do you understand?"

She nodded, and he smiled calmly in case someone was watching. "That's a good girl," he said through his teeth.

When he reached the van, he opened the door and shoved her inside, then turned to Ramirez. "Are the others secure?"

He nodded.

"Get them loaded one or two at a time so we don't draw attention. Then you're going to drop me off at a car rental."

Once the girls were inside the van, he returned to his room with Gibson. "The GPS is programmed with Rankin's house address, and Ramirez is driving. You ride in the back with the girls. Drive them straight to the house. It's on the Bouffa River, and keep them there until nightfall."

"Why wait? I thought the boat was at the house."

"Because I said so." He did not like Gibson questioning his orders. The Texan should know that boarding the girls on the boat in broad daylight with the neighbors looking on would bring the police in a heartbeat. He'd wanted to go to a different house than the one on the river, but it was the only property Rankin owned that wasn't registered to him. Instead, it was in his dead stepson's name. Tracing the house to Rankin would be all but impossible.

"The cabin cruiser is in the boathouse, and the registration number and name have been changed—just in case the cops figure out we're using Rankin's boat." He leveled a hard stare at Gibson. "Don't mess this up."

"When have *I* ever messed up?" he said.

Blade narrowed his eyes at Gibson. He really didn't like his attitude. "I want to get one thing straight. You answer to me, not Grey."

Gibson broke eye contact first. "Okay, but where are you going, Boss?"

"Back to Memphis. I have a little matter I need to take care of."

48

LOGAN WHEELED CARLY past the nurses' station in the ICU. "Let's wait here a minute," she said. "Maybe he'll pull through."

"Are you sure?" he asked.

"Yes." From the wheelchair, she had a direct line of vision. One nurse applied chest compressions, and Dr. Adams placed an oxygen mask over his face. The crash cart arrived and Carly flinched when the doctor applied the paddles to his chest.

"I think it's time to go," Logan said.

Carly tore her gaze from the room. Seeing them work on King was harder than she'd thought, and she nodded.

Logan pushed her toward the waiting room. "I'm glad you forgave him."

"For all the good it did. He didn't tell us where they were taking Lexi. And who do you think Annie is?"

"I don't know, but you did all you could," he said and wheeled her through the doors.

The first person Carly saw when they rolled through the doors was her aunt, and then her uncle Frank. Maybe Logan would take her back to the ICU. Before she had the chance to ask him, Gigi looked up from the magazine she was reading and her mouth dropped open.

"Heather?" she said, rising from the sofa. "I can't believe it! It really is you."

She gripped the cup in her hand and searched their faces, especially Frank's, for any sign of revulsion. Surprisingly, there was only concern. "I would prefer for you to call me Carly."

"Yes, of course." Her aunt hurried to her side. "I'm so glad you're back and you're all right."

Frank joined Gigi. "Absolutely. We worried for so many years. It's really wonderful to have you back."

"Please, do you mind sitting on the sofa?" Carly said. Looking up sent pain through her neck.

"Oh yes, of course," her aunt said and sat in the chair closest to the wheelchair. "Are you all right?"

She wasn't sure how to answer that question. She'd like to say she had a bullet wound, had been kidnapped and almost burned alive, and Lexi was still missing, and no, she was not all right. Instead, she mustered a tiny smile. "I'm recovering."

Frank patted Carly on her good shoulder. "Of course you're not okay. Georgina doesn't always know the right thing to say," he said and sat beside his wife. "We're so sorry for all you've been through."

Who was this man and where was the Frank she remembered? The Frank who couldn't stand her when she was a kid.

Logan leaned over and caught her eye. "Can I get you something to drink? Coffee maybe?"

"No thanks." She was coffeed-out. Carly handed him the empty cup and leaned back in the wheelchair, massaging the back of her neck with her good hand. She did not want to deal with her aunt and uncle right now.

"When you get out of the hospital," Gigi said, "we'd like you to come and stay with us."

"Yes," Frank agreed. "We have plenty of room at the farm."

This was exactly what she didn't want to deal with.

Her aunt leaned forward. "It will be a good place for you to reconnect with Lexi when she's found."

"I-I appreciate your offer," she said. Their concern confused her. "But I have a job near Nashville. I'll be returning there as soon as this is over."

"You have business you need to attend to here," Frank said. "There's the trust, you know. You need to get all of the paperwork straightened out, claim your inheritance."

Carly pressed her fingers to her temples. This was too much to take in. Movement at the entrance to the waiting room caught her eye. David and Maggie had returned, and David was on his cell phone. He looked upset as he stopped near the door.

"What's wrong?" she asked when Maggie was near enough to hear her.

"David thinks Lexi tried to call him," she said.

Across from her, Gigi gasped and Frank leaned forward. "What happened?" he asked.

"David will tell you once he gets off the phone." She sat next to Carly. "I want to know if you got anything more from Jim Rankin."

Carly shook her head. "We went back in after you left, but nothing he said made sense. He mentioned someone named Annie. And then he coded."

"Annie?" Maggie repeated. "That was his late wife's name."

Logan snapped his fingers. "I don't know how I forgot that," he said. "She and my mom were good friends."

"Were they able to bring him back?" Maggie asked.

"I don't know." Somehow she didn't think Rankin had survived. "Dr. Adams is in there with him."

"Dr. Adams? What's he doing here?"

"He has patients here, and he said Rankin was his neighbor." Carly looked up as David pocketed his phone and approached them, his face grim. "What happened?"

"I missed a call from a motel in Yazoo City. My gut says Lexi tried to call me."

"Yazoo City is off I-55," Logan said, "and I-55 is the shortest route to Biloxi from here."

"I know," David said. "Eric alerted the Yazoo City PD, but when they got to the motel, there was no sign of the girls. They're processing the motel now and Eric has the Coast Guard searching the marinas on the coast for unusual activity too."

Maggie took out her computer. "I'm going to see what I can find on the internet about Jim."

While Maggie worked on her computer, Carly slumped in the chair. Logan took her hand, gently cupping it in his own hand. It seemed no matter what they did, and no matter how many breaks they got, nothing worked out. She looked up to find David watching her. Heat crawled up her neck. "I'm sorry I didn't come to you when I first got back in town."

"Why didn't you?" he asked.

"*I* don't understand that, either," Gigi said.

"I didn't know if I could trust you." When he started to say something, she shook her head. "I've seen too many crooked cops . . . but I realize now that I made a mistake in not trusting you and Logan."

Logan squeezed her fingers. "It's understandable after what you've been through," he said.

"But it doesn't get Lexi back." She turned as the doors to the ICU opened and Dr. Adams walked out, his head down and his shoulders slumped.

"Dr. Adams," Carly said. "How is he?"

He looked up and shook his head. "He . . . didn't make it. He's dead."

49

BLADE PULLED AWAY from the car rental. The man there had acted like there was something wrong with paying cash for the Dodge Charger. Although once Blade produced a fake driver's license and paid for insurance, the problem went away. He checked his watch. Noon. Gibson and Ramirez should be out of Jackson and on Highway 49 by now. If the two men hadn't messed up.

They wouldn't. Not if they wanted to live, and they knew it. They wouldn't be reporting anything to Grey, either. A traffic light caught him, and he drummed his fingers on the steering wheel. The four girls they'd lost in Hernando rankled him. He could've easily gotten four thousand dollars for each of them. But maybe he should focus on the positive—he'd escaped with fifteen of them and the cop's kid. A thought niggled at the back of his mind. Blade would bet the cop would give more than fifteen thousand to get her back. Maybe there was a way to milk this situation. Get the cop's money and still sell the kid to the cartel. He'd have to think about it.

Would the light never change? Blade glanced at the car beside him, and the back of his neck prickled. Dark sedan with a spotlight on the mirror? His gaze traveled to the driver and his breath caught in his chest. The man was staring, and he had a frown on his face.

279

Blade forced himself to nonchalantly tip his head and smile. Just like a normal person. When the light changed, he eased away from the light instead of flooring the gas pedal like he wanted to. He watched in the side mirror and breathed easier as the car made a left turn. At the next light, he turned right even though it took him away from the interstate. Double arches caught his eye, and he pulled into the McDonald's drive-thru lane.

No way the guy could have gotten his license plate, but it wouldn't hurt to make sure he didn't double back and try to follow him. Blade's sixth sense for trouble had served him well in the past. Now wasn't the time to stop listening to it. "Large coffee, black," he said when the disembodied voice asked for his order. When he drove around and paid, he smiled at the teenage boy at the window. "Say a person wanted to take the scenic route to Memphis. What road would he take?"

"Beats me, mister. Hold on a sec." He turned and called to someone over his shoulder, "Hey, Bill, this guy doesn't want to take 55 to Memphis. How would he go?"

Bill came over to the window. "If it was me, I'd take Highway 51. It's just a little piece on the other side of the interstate. But if you have plenty of time to kill, you can go in the opposite direction over to Highway 61—a lot more scenic."

"Thanks," Blade said and accepted the cup of coffee he'd ordered. "I think 61 sounds like what I'm looking for."

He pulled out of the parking lot and retraced his path to Jerry Clower Boulevard, and watching in his mirrors, he traveled it until he came to a sign that pointed to I-55. Twenty minutes later he crossed under the interstate and continued on until he reached Highway 51 then drove north. He was certain no one had followed him and planned to get back on the interstate at Pickens.

His cell phone rang. "Yeah?"

"Why haven't you called me back?" Grey asked, his voice steely.

"I haven't had time."

"Can you cut loose from Gibson and Ramirez?"

"Maybe. Why?"

"Carly Smith talked to Rankin, and I need to know what he told her."

"So you want me to come back and take care of *your* mess."

"Don't get smart with me. How long will it take you to get to Memphis?"

"Maybe two and a half hours."

Silence filled the airwaves. "So, you were headed back to Memphis?"

"Yeah."

"You were assigned to get the girls to Biloxi, not go off on some vendetta of your own. The syndicate is not going to like that."

Blade didn't like Grey's tone. "Since you apparently want me to come back and kill Jaz, you better be glad I'm a step ahead of you."

"Don't kill her yet. Just snatch her and bring her to Rankin's cabin in Shelby Forest. But leave the cop out of it."

When had the cop become sacrosanct? "Why not just go ahead and kill them both? You were going to kill them together in the fire."

"No, you weren't supposed to take the cop—he was collateral damage. Thanks to you, this is getting too much publicity," Grey said. "How far are the girls from the coast?"

He checked his watch and gauged where the van should be. "About three hours."

"One of the girls you left behind in Hernando informed the police about the boat, so the Coast Guard is looking for it. They don't have a name or where it's moored, but they'll be watching for any suspicious activity. Have Gibson lay low in the house until dark, then smuggle the girls in one or two at a time. They can pull out under the cover of darkness."

"Gotcha." Like he hadn't already thought of that.

"How did she know about the boat, Blade? Did you talk in front of her?"

He clenched his jaw. Gibson and Ramirez must have talked about the boat when they thought the girls were asleep.

"The syndicate won't like it if you fail."

"I won't fail."

"I'm sure you won't. By the way, your face is plastered all over the news, and it's fairly accurate, so you better do something about your appearance."

Blade gripped the steering wheel until his knuckles turned white. He'd always been so careful not to get arrested and didn't have a rap sheet *anywhere*. No fingerprints, no photos. No one even knew his real name. How could a picture of him be circulating? *Jasmine*. She must have worked with a police artist. "Why are you just now telling me this?" No wonder the cop at the traffic light had stared.

"Does it matter? You know now."

Blade had been watching his back around Grey for years. The man complained to the higher-ups about Blade every chance he got. He wasn't stupid. Right now Grey needed him, but once he brought Jasmine to the cabin, Grey would not care who recognized him. "Any other information I need to know?"

"No. Just get the woman to the cabin."

"Got it. I'll text when I have her."

Grey ended the call. Blade glanced in the rearview mirror and raked his fingers through his hair. He had to find a disguise. A small strip mall came into view on his right, and he whipped into the lot. A Dollar General stood off to one side. Beside it, a beauty shop and barbecue place, and on the end, a fuel center. He parked in front of the beauty shop. *Walk-ins Welcomed*. That'd be a start.

Half an hour later, he walked out of the shop with a buzz cut. It'd taken some fast-talking and a lie that he was cutting his hair because a friend was going through chemo before the stylist would agree to shave off his wavy black hair. What happened to hairstylists who cut your hair the way you wanted it without question? He ran his hand over the half-inch stubble. Jasmine would pay for this.

His next stop was the Dollar General, where he bought a black eyeliner pencil. Then in the gas station restroom, he used the pencil to enhance the hair over his lip, making a more pronounced mustache. He didn't have to create a scruffy beard since he hadn't shaved since yesterday. Once he had the mustache penciled in, he examined his reflection.

Not bad. And certainly not the way he'd looked half an hour ago. He kind of liked the widow's peak that made him look almost evil. He capped the eyeliner and stuck it in his jacket. Might need it for a refresher later.

Before he got back on the road, he took the burner phone he'd bought at the fuel center from his jacket. It would do for any calls he made looking for Jasmine. After he left Pickens behind, he drove the two-lane road until the next crossover to I-55. Back on the interstate, he set his cruise control on seventy so he wouldn't get pulled over for exceeding the speed limit. He checked the time again. Almost one.

Blade pressed the home button on his phone until a "What can I help you with?" message popped up. "Phone number for the Med in Memphis," he said.

After a few seconds, the automated voice said, "I found five places for the med. Tap the one you are looking for."

He scanned the list. All pharmacies. "None of them, you idiot." He pressed the home button and tried again. "Phone number for the Med hospital in Memphis."

The reply came back even quicker. "I couldn't find any matching places."

Blade swore. He'd never heard the hospital called anything but the Med. He chewed the inside of his cheek then tried once more. "Hospitals in Memphis."

This time a list of five hospitals popped up. He quickly ruled out three of them and, using the burner phone, dialed the first one that might possibly be the Med.

"Regional One. How may I help you?" the operator said in a bored tone.

What was Jasmine calling herself now? "Carly Smith. Can you tell me which room she's in?" he asked, and then added, "I'd like to send her a card."

He wasn't sure if the operator would give him her room number. There was a pause, and he thought about hanging up in case there was an alert for anyone inquiring about Carly.

"Says here she's been discharged," she said.

"Thank you." He ended the call. So she *hadn't* been badly injured. Where would she go? He remembered the hotel card that had been in her purse. He dialed his hacker.

"Got another job for you. Check the Westin Hotel in Memphis for a Carly Smith. I need her room number."

"Sure. Anything else?"

He thought a minute. Even if she hadn't checked out, she might get a different room. "Let me know if the room number changes. Can you do that?"

"You have to ask?"

"Call me when you have something. Oh, and if she's not at the Westin, check the other hotels."

Fifteen minutes later, his phone rang. His hacker. "You have it?"

"You doubted me? Room 321."

"Thanks. Let me know if that changes."

50

After Dr. Adams left, Maggie stared intently at the text her administrative assistant had just sent. Really, Mr. Conley? Evidently the building developer was calling every half hour, insisting that he must see her today. She wasn't even his lawyer but was representing his son in a driving-under-the-influence charge that involved an accident that injured another person. His was one of the few cases she took where she knew her client was guilty, but his father was friends with her father, and sometimes these cases were unavoidable.

Not that she was trying to get him off, but the young man was truly repentant and wanted to get help with his alcohol problem. It was his third DUI, and he wanted to take the deal she had brokered with the DA—twelve months at a minimum-security facility where he could continue his education and get help for his alcohol problem. Conley wanted the alcohol treatment, but he didn't want his son to have a prison record.

Maggie wasn't sure what the rest of the day would hold, but at some point, she needed to shower and change clothes. She could do that at the office, and maybe she could see Conley then. She texted her secretary and asked Shawna to see if Conley would be available to come on short notice. She slipped her phone in her pocket and leaned forward to catch what Georgina was saying.

"I just can't believe Jim had any part in this."

Maggie felt the same way, and the shock of learning what Rankin was capable of had not worn off. She glanced around the room, her gaze settling on Logan and the way he had a protective hand on Carly's arm. Maybe something good would come from this. She shifted her gaze to David, who was studying Carly.

"Tell me everything Rankin said when you were with him," he said.

Carly's thin frame slumped in the wheelchair. She had to be exhausted, and evidently Logan recognized it as well.

"I wasn't in the room," he said, "but Carly filled me in. He rambled. Kept saying he was sorry and he wanted her to forgive him. Mentioned his wife."

"Annie," Carly said in a small voice.

"She died a few years ago," Maggie said. Carly looked as though she could pass out any minute.

David turned to her. "Did you know her?"

"Not really," Maggie said. "But she wasn't the type of person to be involved in any of this."

"I would've thought the same thing about Rankin." David's cell phone buzzed, and he checked it. "It's Eric." He spoke with his brother, and then he pocketed his phone. "Nothing new." He glanced around the room. "Looks like there's no reason for us all to hang around here."

Logan nodded. "I thought I'd take Carly by the hotel so she can shower and change and get some rest."

"Where are you staying?" Frank asked.

"At the Westin," Carly replied.

"Why don't you get your clothes and come to our condo?" Georgina said. "We're staying in town until Lexi is found. It's not far from here."

Carly shook her head. "Right now, I'd be more comfortable at a hotel. At least until we get Lexi back and these people are in jail."

"And I'm sticking with her until then," Logan said.

Georgina approached the wheelchair and appeared undecided about what to do. Then she leaned over and hugged Carly.

"I'm so glad you're back, and at some point, I hope you'll let us help you," she said.

"Yes," Frank agreed, patting Carly on the arm. "As soon as things are back to normal, promise you'll come to the farm for a couple of days. We'd like to catch up on things, get to know you again. There's a mare at the barn who would be mighty happy to see you."

"You still have Candy?"

It did Maggie good to see Carly brighten up.

"Yep," Frank said. "She has a little gray in her coat, but she has plenty of spirit left in her."

After the Wilsons left, Maggie turned to Carly. "I hope you'll get some rest while you're at the hotel. You too, Logan. You've both had a bad twenty-four hours."

"I don't know if I can," Carly said, "but I'll try. And thanks for everything." She looked up at Logan and nodded, and he wheeled her around toward the door.

"Oh, wait." Maggie pulled out a plastic baggie from her purse containing the Westin hotel key card and the GPS tracker. "You'll need your key to get into your room. And here's the barrette, but it looks like a car crushed it. I'm afraid it's a lost cause. Not sure about the tracker."

"I forgot I'd given the key to you, but I'm glad you had it. The other key was in my purse, and who knows where that is." Carly figured her purse either burned in the fire or Blade had it. Either way, she'd cancelled her credit card and put a hold on all checks. With no proof of identity, it would be a hassle to get another key card from the hotel.

Carly slipped the mangled barrette from the baggie and pried the chip loose and slipped it in her pocket. "When I get to the hotel, I'll check and see if it will charge."

Maggie smiled at her. "I don't think you should stay at the hotel if there's any chance Blade has your key."

"I haven't even thought about him having the key to my room. Now I'll have to change rooms, maybe even hotels," Carly said with a sigh. "Makes me tired just to think about it."

"Why don't you grab your clothes and stay with me?"

"Thanks, but I would rather stay at a hotel until Blade is caught. After that, I may take Gigi and Frank up on their offer. I'm not sure why, but they're trying so hard to connect. Maybe I should give them a chance—it'd be nice to see my horse again, and other than Lexi, they're the only family I have."

Maggie squeezed her hand. "They're reaching out to you because you're family."

"Yeah, and that's what's so strange. I never got the feeling before that they wanted me."

David cleared his throat. "When this is all over and we have Lexi back, I'd like for her to get to know you."

Carly sat up straighter in the wheelchair. "Really? I was afraid you wouldn't—"

"You're her aunt. You can tell her things about her mom no one else knows," David said, smiling.

"It's going to be okay." Maggie leaned over and hugged Carly, getting a whiff of smoke from her hair. A shower would probably feel pretty good to her. She spied the takeout box. "Oh, and take those ham biscuits from Mike's Café with you."

"Thanks," Logan said. "We haven't eaten."

After they left, David eyed her. "Do you need to go to your office?" he asked.

She'd almost forgotten the message from Shawna and took out her phone. "My administrative assistant texted me that one client insists on meeting with me today if at all possible. But I hate for you to be by yourself."

"I'll be fine," he said, palming his hands up. "Go take care of whatever you need to, and then try and get some rest yourself. I'll be at Eric's office in case something comes in." He crossed his arms. "I'd go to the coast if I thought it'd do any good."

"You think you can find the boat?"

"No. That's why I'm staying here until we have something concrete. That boat could be anywhere from New Orleans to Mobile. I'm afraid even the Coast Guard won't find where it's moored in time."

"Maybe they'll get lucky." She squeezed his hand. "My meeting won't take long," she said. "And then I'll join you at Eric's office."

When they separated outside the hospital, Maggie called Shawna and told her to set up an appointment with Conley as soon as possible. After the fiasco at the motel in Hernando, David had driven Maggie back to his house so she could get her car, and they'd come downtown separately. Her car was parked in the lot at her office and she was glad for the walk. The crisp October air would clear her head before she met with her client. Hopefully.

When Maggie stepped inside her office, Shawna said, "Good afternoon. Any news?"

"I'm afraid not."

"I'm sorry. I've been praying all night that Lexi would be found safe. My church is praying too."

"Thanks." She knew God answered prayers, but sometimes not the way she wanted. Maggie wasn't going there. Either way, she knew God was with Lexi no matter what was happening.

But what if they didn't find her before she was put on a boat to Miami? God had not kept Carly from being sold . . . No. She blocked the rest of the thought as her stomach churned. *Focus on something more positive.* Lexi was resilient. She'd found a way to call her dad earlier. She might even be able to escape the men.

"Mr. Conley will be here in a half hour, if you want to change," Shawna said.

"Definitely." Her office had a shower, and she kept several changes of clothes. "If he comes early, tell him I'll be with him shortly."

Half an hour later, when Shawna escorted Lucas Conley into her office, Maggie felt halfway decent and definitely fresher.

Conley extended his hand. "Thank you for seeing me."

"What's so important that it couldn't wait?" she asked, keeping her voice pleasant. It had better be good.

He cleared his throat. "My son and I have talked, and he wants to take the plea deal. He's already made restitution to the young woman in the other car."

This was worth taking time for. "I think that's the best decision he could make. He'll get rehab while he's there." It was a win-win. If it'd gone to court and they lost, the judge could have sentenced the boy to five years. "I'll get the paperwork started this afternoon."

"Thank you," he said.

"It's what I'm here for." She leaned forward. Conley was a developer and operated in several states. "How's your business doing?"

"Really good. I have several houses started on the property I own down on the Gulf Coast. I can't believe how that area has exploded. People are buying the houses before I can get them finished."

She stared at him. What if Jim Rankin had a house on the coast? Could that be where Blade was headed with the girls? "How could I find out if someone owns property on the coast?"

Conley pointed to her computer. "Look it up online. Each county has a portal where you can search for property and owners. I can show you."

Maggie moved her mouse and the computer woke up, then she moved so he could sit in her chair. After a few keystrokes, he was at a real estate document access page.

"Just put the person's name in and hit search. If he owns any property, it'll show up." Conley stood. "And I have to get back to work."

"Thanks. You've helped me more than you can know."

After he left, she sat behind her computer again and looked at a map of the coast. Like David said, the boat could be anywhere from New Orleans to Mobile, and the same thing was true for any property Rankin might own. Since she had the Jackson County, Mississippi, page already open, she started with it and typed Jim Rankin's name in the grantee space. While the site searched, she popped a hazelnut coffee pod in her Keurig. When she returned to her desk, she saw that there was no property belonging to him.

Maggie stared at the blinking cursor. Then it dawned on her. Of course there wasn't. He wouldn't buy property under his nickname. This time she typed in James Rankin and sipped her coffee while she waited. Three properties near Ocean Springs. Now she was getting somewhere. Should she call David? No, not yet. She wanted to play her hunch out to the end and googled Harrison County. Nothing there. Next she tried Hancock County and got hits on two properties. She dialed David.

"You finished already?" he said.

"I am." She studied the computer screen. "Where are you?"

"Eric's office."

"I'll be there in twenty." Something nagged at the back of her mind as she disconnected. *Annie.* What if Rankin bought property in his wife's name? She sat behind her computer again and went through the search, using Annie Rankin's name. Nothing.

What if he used her maiden name? But what was it? Logan had said his mother had been friends with Annie. Maybe she would know.

Maggie scrolled down her contacts and called Jacqueline.

She answered the phone with a question. "Have you found Lexi?"

"No, I'm afraid not. But I have something you might help me with. What was Annie Rankin's maiden name?"

"Jefferies, but why do you want to know?"

"I'm playing a hunch. Thanks. I'll let you know as soon as we find Lexi."

Maggie repeated the search, typing Annie Jefferies into the form and two properties popped up. She snapped a picture of her screen with her phone. Now it was time to go see David.

When Maggie arrived at the glass and brick building in East Memphis she parked on the right side, near Eric's office, then grabbed her computer and hurried inside. David was waiting for her in the lobby, and after she signed in, he escorted her to a conference room where Eric had set up. A corkboard held several photos of girls. A shiver went through her. One of the pictures was one she'd taken of Lexi.

"We're about to leave for the coast," David said.

"You decided to go down anyway even though you don't know where they're taking the girls?"

"We have an idea," Eric said. "Found three properties near Ocean Springs."

Her shoulders sagged. And she thought she'd found something. Wait. They only found three? "Did you find the property in his wife's name?"

"What?" David turned to her.

"I found where he bought two more houses in Annie's maiden name," she said, showing him the photos on her phone.

"Good job!" Eric said. His phone beeped and he grabbed his jacket. "The plane's ready."

"You want to come with us?" David asked.

"Try and leave me here."

51

CARLY'S LEGS TREMBLED as she and Logan stepped off the elevator on the third floor of the Westin Hotel. Logan took her arm and guided her around the housekeeper's cart parked in the middle of the hall. She'd talked him into letting her shower and change before moving into a different hotel. Even if Blade had her key, he had no way of knowing what room she was in.

"I can't wait to get a shower and shampoo my hair. The smoke odor is getting to me."

"Is it okay to shower with your shoulder like it is?" he asked.

"They put a waterproof bandage on it. It won't be easy with one arm." She waved the key Maggie had given her in front of the door, and the light flashed red. Carly groaned. "This key doesn't work. And I don't think I can go all the way back to the front desk."

"Hold on a sec." Logan stepped back to the open door where the cart was parked. "Hello?" he said, knocking on the door. "Ah, there you are. My friend's key isn't working. Could you let her into her room?"

When the housekeeper stuck her head around the door, Carly recognized her from the first day she checked in. "Remember me?" she said.

The woman narrowed her eyes slightly then nodded. "Yes. You have been gone two days."

"I know—I've been in the hospital." She held up her card. "My key isn't working, so could you let me in?"

"Sure. Hold on a second."

The housekeeper used the card on the lanyard around her neck and waved it in front of the lock before she pushed the door open. "There you go. You can get a new key at the desk."

"Thanks." Logan shot Carly a look that indicated he wanted to go in first, so she stepped back.

"This won't take long." He opened the closet door and then briefly disappeared into the bathroom. "It's all clear," he said and turned around.

She stepped inside the room and let the door close behind her. Carly didn't remember leaving her things scattered over the bed, then remembered Maggie telling her they had searched her room when they couldn't find her. She moved a pair of jeans and plopped onto the bed. "This feels good," she said, leaning against the headboard.

Logan held up the to-go box he'd brought from the hospital. "Why don't you eat something before you shower?"

The only thing she'd had to eat since lunch yesterday was a bite of doughnut at the hospital, and in just the past few minutes her stomach had protested the lack of sustenance. "Think you could get us a couple of drinks from the vending machine I saw when we got off the elevator?"

"Yes, ma'am. Be right back and don't let *anyone* but me in."

"Don't worry."

It didn't take Logan long to get the drinks and return to the room. When he knocked, she padded to the door and asked, "Who is it?"

"It's me, Logan."

She leaned her head against the door, chuckling softly. "How do I know it's you?"

"Come on, Carly, I'm hungry. Just look in the peephole."

Still laughing, she opened the door. "I couldn't resist."

He tapped her on the head with one of the drinks. "As long as you're sure who it is every time, I'm fine with it."

Carly saluted. "Yes, sir." She opened the microwave. "I zapped the ham biscuits, so they're warm."

Holding her arm close to her body, she climbed on the bed with her food and a napkin and sat cross-legged. "I wish I could make biscuits like these," she said after biting into one.

Logan took the corner chair and propped his feet on the edge of the bed. "You can't?"

"Mine can kill at thirty paces."

"I don't believe that," he said.

"No, I'm a horrible cook."

"Not a deal breaker," Logan said.

His grin held the promise of so much more. Carly swallowed down another bite, and then as thoughts of Lexi bombarded her, she laid the biscuit on the napkin.

"What's wrong?"

She shook her head, fighting back tears. "How can we be having such a normal conversation with Lexi out there, who knows where? We need to do something. We have to find her."

He put his feet down and sat beside her on the bed. "You've done all you can do, Carly," he said, gently putting his arm around her shoulders. "It's time to put it in God's hands."

The heaviness in her heart grew until it exploded into physical pain that spread through her chest. She couldn't fight the tears any longer and collapsed against his chest, tears running down her cheeks.

"It's okay," he said, smoothing her hair. "It's all right to cry."

His tenderness undid her, unleashing even more tears. Logan cradled her in his arms and spoke soothing words until she'd cried herself out. Carly couldn't remember ever crying this way before, not even in Dr. Abernathy's office when she was going through therapy. When the tears subsided, she wiped her face with the back of her hand then blew her nose into the napkin. "Thank you," she whispered.

He lifted her chin until she was looking into his eyes.

"You're entitled to cry sometimes," he said softly and kissed her forehead before releasing her.

Carly took a shuddering breath. "You surprise me. I don't remember you being this . . ."

"I'm older, learned a lot in the last sixteen years."

She loved the way the skin around his eyes crinkled when he smiled. "What's next?" she asked as he shifted back to the chair.

"You mean besides you finishing your food, getting a shower, and then resting?"

She crossed her eyes at him. "I don't have time to rest."

"Yes, you do. The FBI is on the case, and Homeland Security has come in."

She'd forgotten that trafficking fell under Homeland Security's jurisdiction. Exhaustion did funny things to the brain.

"Why don't you finish eating and then get a shower? It'll make you feel better," he said.

She took another bite of the ham biscuit then laid it down. "I think I'll take the shower first. Maybe I can eat this later."

He nodded. "While you're showering, I'll go down and get a new key." Logan grabbed the Do Not Disturb sign. "And I'll hang this on the door."

"It'll take me at least fifteen minutes to get rid of the smoke and dry my hair."

"You got it."

She walked to the door and locked it behind him, then flipped the security anchor above the handle. That should keep her safe enough. Then Carly turned the shower on as hot as it would go and grabbed her clothes. Nikes or boots? Boots. Logan had given the dagger back at the hospital, and she felt safer knowing it was within reach.

She pulled the tracker from the pocket of the scrubs and slipped it in the small pocket in the jeans she planned to wear.

52

BLADE RODE THE EMPTY ELEVATOR up to the third floor, checking his appearance in the mirrored doors. He pulled off the baseball cap and ran his fingers over his buzz cut. Jaz would pay for making him cut his hair.

He'd arrived at the hotel early enough to locate the security cameras in the garage and smear petroleum jelly over the lens, being careful to keep his face hidden with the cap visor. Now to do the same for the one in the elevator. Once he covered the lens, he slipped the tube of jelly into his pocket.

He'd been in the lobby when Jasmine and the cop entered the hotel and noticed right away her left arm was in a sling. He'd even been close enough to hear her say she wanted to get a shower. He'd been afraid the cop would stick with her, but just a few minutes ago, he'd seen him get off the elevator and figured Jasmine was probably taking that shower.

Blade had a couple of minutes at most to get into her room and get out, but he needed a way to get her to open the door. When the elevator doors opened on the third floor, a housekeeper with her cart waited for him to get off.

"No, I punched the wrong button," he said, giving her his warmest smile. His fingers curled around the switchblade in his pocket, his gaze on the master key dangling around the housekeeper's neck. She pushed the cart inside the car. As soon as she turned her back to him, Blade wrapped his hand around her mouth and pressed the knife against her neck. "Say one word and you're dead. Understand?"

With eyes wide in terror, she nodded.

"I'm going to release you, but when the doors open, push your cart back into the hallway and come with me. If you do or say anything, I'll slit your throat before you can get away. Got it?"

When she nodded again, he pushed the button that opened the door and walked out beside her, his hand firmly on her elbow. Blade kept his head ducked and looked in both directions. Two people were coming their way and he felt the woman tense.

"They can't save you," he said. "When they go into their room, I want you to knock on the door at 321."

Once the couple disappeared inside their quarters, Blade and the housekeeper approached 321, and he stood to the side while she knocked. Jasmine didn't answer. Probably still in the shower and had more than likely double-locked the door with the latch. He grabbed the Do Not Disturb sign. Guests thought they were so safe, like there was a lock he couldn't get past. "Open the door."

Once the housekeeper flashed her key card in front of the laser, he pushed the door, but the bar on the security lock kept it from opening. Keeping the knife at her throat with one hand, he used his other hand to slide the Do Not Disturb sign between the door and the frame until it bumped against the lock.

He nudged her. "Pull the door almost closed."

When she hesitated, he pressed the knife against her skin. "Don't make me kill you."

She pulled the door almost closed, and he used the plastic sign to push the bar on the lock open. It had taken less than five seconds to get inside. And just like he'd figured, from the sound of a hair dryer, Jaz was in the bathroom.

Blade shoved the housekeeper onto the bed and sliced the sheet into strips and hogtied her. He didn't know how much time he had, but it couldn't be much before the cop returned. Just as he put his hand on the bathroom door, it opened.

Jasmine's eyes widened. "No!"

He shoved the door back on her, knocking her off balance, leaving her nowhere to run. "You didn't think I'd let you go, did you?"

He lunged at her. She jerked her hand up, holding a can of hairspray. He tried to backpedal, but he wasn't fast enough, and she sprayed his face.

"Ahh!" He couldn't see and swiped at his burning eyes.

She slammed the can against his already sore nose and ran past him. Blade shook off the pain that shot through his face and grabbed at her body. Latching onto her ponytail, he jerked her back.

Jasmine screamed and turned on him, kicking and flailing her arms.

He grabbed the arm that had been in a sling and squeezed her shoulder. Moaning, she slumped to her knees. He quickly splashed cold water in his eyes, clearing them, and then he yanked Jasmine up and threw her over his shoulder. Good thing Grey didn't want Jasmine dead just yet. Killing her was too easy. She was going to pay for hurting him.

53

THE DESK CLERK handed Logan two key cards just as his cell phone rang. It was David. "Everything okay?" he asked.

"Yeah. I just wanted to let you know my brother is flying us to the coast in his plane," he said. "We have five locations for property belonging to Jim Rankin down there."

"Keep me informed."

"I will. Maggie is going too, so let Carly know and keep an eye on her."

He'd definitely do that. Logan checked his watch. Fifteen minutes, Carly had said, and it'd barely been ten. It would be awkward to return to the room before she finished. And since he doubted she could dress that quickly, he might give her another five minutes. A gift shop caught his eye, and he wandered over to it, smiling when the first thing he saw was a vase filled with different-colored roses.

Carly needed something to brighten her day. Which color? Too soon for red, but he could certainly see their relationship heading in that direction. He'd never known a woman as strong and courageous as she was. And open to God's prodding. She thought she hadn't forgiven Rankin, but he'd seen her face when she spoke the words. In that instant, she'd meant them and would come to realize it.

"Can I help you?"

The clerk's voice startled him, and he looked up. "I was thinking of giving a friend a rose, Lindsay," he said, reading her nametag. "But I don't know what color . . ."

"Are you in a relationship with this person?"

He lifted his shoulders in an iffy shrug. "Not quite—but we were once."

"Oh," she said, raising her eyebrows. "So, you're making up?"

"No, we lost touch for a few years."

She pointed to a pretty light yellow bud. "Well, a yellow rose says, 'I care,' and I don't think you want the light pink, it's more for sympathy." She tapped her lip with her forefinger. "Wait! I have the perfect flower for you," she said and motioned him to another vase filled with daisies. "A daisy symbolizes a new beginning."

He liked that. "I'd like a dozen," he said.

She beamed at him. "Perfect!"

Logan left the gift shop with his bouquet and feeling lighter than he had in days.

When he stepped off the elevator, he glanced at the oddly parked housekeeping cart. When a door clanged shut to his left, the skin on his neck prickled. Frowning, he hurried to Carly's room. The door was slightly ajar.

With his heart thumping in his throat, he shoved it open. The housekeeper lay squirming on the bed. She attempted to talk through the gag in her mouth. Logan untied her bonds. "What happened?"

"A man. He has a knife and he took the woman."

Had to be Blade. "When?"

"Just now. You didn't see him?"

The door he'd heard closing. He'd taken Carly down the stairs. Logan yanked out his phone and dialed 911. "Officer needs assistance at the Westin Hotel on Beale. Assailant is armed and dangerous."

He turned to the housekeeper. "Help will be here in a minute," he said and bounded out of the room. When he reached the stairwell, he jerked the door open.

"Let me go!"

Carly's voice sounded hollow in the stairwell. They were two flights down.

"Shut up or I'll shut you up!"

Logan descended the steps two at a time. "Let her go!"

His answer was the slamming of another door.

54

SMALL AIRPLANES were not David's favorite mode of transportation, but today they were in a race against time. Every second Lexi was in her captor's hand, she could die. He looked out the window toward the ocean. The white sand gave way to tannish water that deepened to blue past the barrier islands. Near the islands, the setting sun glinted off a shiny cabin cruiser. He turned his gaze back to the shoreline and spotted a marina with boats. He nudged Eric in the pilot seat. "Could Rankin's boat be there?" he asked, speaking into his mic.

"I doubt it. His property is inland, and I figure if the boat isn't at the house, it's moored on the bay side," Eric replied, pointing in a different direction. "A Coast Guard officer is meeting us at the airport. He'll update us when we land."

His brother appeared to be handling the flight well, but he was used to small planes. David glanced back at Maggie, who gripped her armrest. She didn't like flying any better than he did.

"We're approaching Ocean Springs Airport to the left," Eric said through the headphones. "The Gulf is on the right."

David's stomach dipped as Eric rolled the plane toward the airport and nosed it down. Once they were on the tarmac, he released the death grip on the armrest.

US Coast Guard Lieutenant Andrew Morrison met them inside

the terminal. "When we didn't find a boat registered to Rankin, we followed your suggestion and searched boat registrations for Annie Jefferies in all three counties," he said. "Found it registered in Hancock County. But we haven't found the boat yet. Officers are combing the marinas in all the coastal counties."

"How about private property?" Eric asked.

"Not enough manpower," he replied.

"Did the county set up road checks for the van?" David asked. They were so close.

"Yes, but only on the main highways. If the kidnappers know this area, they could easily bypass the roadblocks."

"Rankin's property—did you locate all of his houses?" Maggie asked.

The lieutenant nodded. "Unfortunately, that hasn't panned out, either. The three houses he owns are currently rented to legitimate people, and the same with his wife's property. Is there any other name he could have used to buy property?"

"I can't help you there," David said. He felt so helpless. What if they were on a wild goose chase?

Maggie took out her phone. "Let me call Jacqueline Donovan," she said. "She was Annie's friend."

David waited impatiently while Maggie found Jacqueline's number and called her. After they talked a minute, she glanced toward him and shook her head.

"Thanks," she said into the phone. "If you think of anything, give me a call." Maggie slipped her phone in her pocket. "Sorry. I thought it was worth a try."

"Where do we go from here?" David asked.

"There are four harbors on Biloxi Bay, and we could use your help to check out the marinas. The airport has agreed to let you use the courtesy car," Morrison said, handing him a list. "We're checking every boat, making sure the number on the bow matches the name."

Eric studied the aerial map of the county. "You think they may have changed the boat's name?"

"It's possible. Ready to go?" Morrison handed David the key to the courtesy car.

"Can I help?" Maggie asked.

"I'm sure they could use the manpower," David said. "But if you want to stay here and rest, I understand."

"I'd rather be useful," she said as her phone rang. "It's Jacqueline." She quickly answered, "Did you remember something?" She listened, and then said, "Yeah. I remember Mark from school. Thanks!"

Maggie disconnected. "Jacqueline said she was mistaken. Jefferies wasn't Annie's maiden name. It was her first husband's name. They had a son together, Mark. After her husband died, she married Jim. Not long after she was diagnosed with cancer, she found papers indicating he'd bought a piece of property a few years ago on the Bouffa River in Mark Jefferies's name. If she hadn't been so critically ill, Annie would have divorced Jim over it."

David frowned. "Why?"

Maggie looked disgusted. "One, her son was dead, and two, he never told her about the property because it was where he took his girlfriends."

What a lowlife. David thought he'd known the affable city councilman. He'd never seen the sleazy side of him. He turned to Morrison. "How fast can you check the records?"

"I have it right here," he said, showing him the county record on his tablet. "I'm putting it into Google Earth now."

"I wish it was real time," David said, "so we could see if the van is there."

They were soon looking at a satellite view of the property. Morrison backed it off until they could see the roads leading into and out of the area. "Looks like there's only one road in, and the river."

"That's a good thing," Eric said. "Unless the kidnappers panic and start shooting the girls."

David refused to let that thought take root in his mind.

"Gulfport has an excellent SWAT team," Morrison said, taking out his phone.

What if the team tried to block him from being there? No. Wasn't happening. David folded his arms across his chest. "I'm going in with them."

"No surprise there," Morrison said, and then he turned to Maggie. "But you'll need to stay here."

While Morrison called the Gulfport SWAT Division, David squeezed Maggie's hand. "I'll keep you posted."

She nodded and squeezed his hand in return. "Be safe."

"Let's go," Morrison yelled. "The SWAT team is on their way."

55

LOGAN SAT DOWN behind one of the computers in the Westin Hotel's security office with the security guard. "Have you found anything yet?"

Gonzales, the guard, shook his head. "Nothing so far."

Carly had been gone fifteen minutes and Logan had nothing. He started the security tape from the camera that was aimed at the area around the elevator on the third floor and fast-forwarded the tape to three o'clock. In the video, the housekeeper pushed her cart to the elevator, and when it opened, she appeared to wait for someone to step off. But no one did.

Then she rolled the cart into the elevator and the doors closed. Seconds later, the doors opened again and she pushed the cart back out and emerged with a man by her side. He wore a baseball cap and a jacket and had his head ducked, making it impossible to see his face.

He turned to Gonzales. "Is there another camera I can check? I can't get a good look at this guy."

"Check the elevator cam," Gonzales said.

Logan switched to the elevator camera and viewed the tape. The feed showed a man with his face hidden by a cap, then everything went blurry.

"What?" he muttered and turned to Gonzales. "You see this?"

Gonzales looked over at Logan's video. "It looks like someone smeared something over the lens."

"That's what I figure. Can you get someone to check out the elevator camera?"

He paused his video and quickly dialed a number. After he dispatched a guard to the third floor, he started his video again. "Hey! This one in the garage is blurred as well."

Logan quickly switched back to his original video and picked up where the housekeeper and the tall man came into view. He kept his gaze glued to the video, watching as the man stood at a door, then it looked as though the housekeeper unlocked the door and the two disappeared inside. The tall man had to be Blade.

He fast-forwarded the video until Blade came out of the room with Carly slung over his shoulder. Logan's chest tightened as the two came toward the camera, Blade with his head down and turned away from the camera. He'd evaded cameras before.

Seconds later, Logan leaned forward, tensing as he appeared on the video entering Carly's room, then coming out and running toward the stairwell. If only he'd gone back to the room five minutes earlier. A text dinged on his phone and he checked it. Maggie.

Arrived in Gulfport. Have a lead. Everything good on your end?

Instead of texting, he quickly dialed her number. "No. Blade has Carly."

Maggie gasped. "No!" A brief silence followed. "She has the GPS chip. Have you checked with RLT Security on her location?"

"No. Do you have their number and someone to talk to?"

"I'll text the information to you."

"Thanks," he said. "Have you found Lexi?"

"Maybe. David and Eric have gone with the local sheriff to check it out."

"Keep me posted." Seconds after they disconnected, Maggie texted the number and a name. Time was lost when the tech was not available, but Logan convinced another tech to work with him. His greatest fear was that Carly had never charged the chip and it was dead, but within minutes, the tech had a location.

"She's on Tennessee 388," he said and gave him an address.

"Keep me updated." Logan calculated the direction he needed to go as he hurried to his car. Where was Blade taking her? Shelby Forest and Millington were the only locations that came to mind.

Rush hour was in full force, and Logan wove in and out of traffic until he reached the ramp on I-40. He'd just exited onto Highway 51 when his phone rang. "Donovan," he snapped.

"We lost Carly Smith's location. Either she turned off the GPS or it died."

"She wouldn't have turned it off," he said. "What's the last location you have?"

"Looks like she's near Shelby Forest and the Mississippi River. But I don't have an address."

That was near his family's cabin, but why would Blade take Carly there? Could he have a cabin in the area? "Got it," Logan said. "Let me know if you pick her up again."

In this traffic it would be getting dark by the time he got to the state park. If only there was a quick way to get there, but there wasn't. He should know, he'd made the trip to the family cabin often enough. *Family*. His mouth went dry. Carly had believed his mother was involved in her kidnapping. No way. But whoever took Carly knew they were at the Westin Hotel, and he'd told his mother that's where they were going.

A traffic light caught him and he dialed her number. His mother answered on the third ring. "Where are you?"

"What?" she asked. "Is something wrong?"

"No. Are you at the store?"

"No, I'm running errands," she said. "What's going on? Have they found Lexi?"

"No. Have you been to the cabin lately?" Sometimes he wished he didn't think like a cop. What was he thinking anyway?

"The cabin? Why would you ask that?"

"No reason." Was his mother being evasive? A horn blew and he looked up. The light had changed, and Logan shot forward.

"Is it true that Jim Rankin was involved in human trafficking?" He hesitated. "Yes," he said.

A small gasp came through his phone. "I didn't like the man, but it's hard to believe he'd stoop that low. Although it could explain how he lost so much money gambling and still afforded his fancy lifestyle. Madeline Starr just called wanting to know about Jim's property on the coast."

"It's connected to the case," he said. "What did you tell her?"

"That his wife, Annie, was a friend of mine, and that she'd told me about property he'd bought on the coast as well as a cabin near ours in Shelby Forest."

Logan's GPS told him to turn left onto Tennessee 388.

". . . was a good woman. Are you listening to me?" his mother asked.

"Yes, you were talking about Rankin's wife. Wait—did you say he bought a cabin at Shelby Forest? Do you know the address?"

"No, but it's half a mile past our place. He saw the property once when we had a barbecue at the cabin. I think he and George went in together and bought it."

"George?"

"Dr. Adams."

The doctor's words flashed through his mind. *"I heard Jim Rankin had been brought in. He's my neighbor, and I wanted to check on him before I see my patients."* Not half an hour later, Rankin was dead.

He rubbed his face. It was hard to imagine that Dr. Adams was involved in human trafficking. Doctors saved lives not ruined them, and the man volunteered at the safe house. But what better way to know what was going on. "Mom, I have to go. I'll call you later."

Logan dialed the coroner's office and asked for Dr. Caldwell. When the coroner answered, Logan told him to double-check Rankin's body, to look for an overdose or anything unusual. Then he clicked off and floored the gas pedal.

56

BLADE HAD THROWN CARLY in the trunk of his car and driven for what seemed like hours. She squirmed around to find a more comfortable place. There was none. The car hit another pothole, jarring her.

At least he'd been too rushed to tie her hands when he tossed her in. Her shoulder throbbed where he had gouged his fingers, but she didn't think the stitches had broken again. That was the least of her worries.

The car jostled her as it swung wide and then sped up. Where was he taking her? If only she could see, but it was dark in the trunk. And where was the glow-in-the-dark handle she'd read about for the safety trunk release? Not that she could open it and jump out, as fast as he was traveling, but if he ever slowed down . . .

She ran her hands across the roof of the trunk, and a stiff wire poked her finger. He'd cut the handle off. Carly slumped back on the floor. Think. Regroup. Because she was not going to let Blade kill her. At least not without a fight. He had to be stopped before he killed more innocent people.

Along with the deal about the trunk release, Carly had read that all cars were made so that the trunk was accessible through the back seat. She was laying the wrong way. Turning over meant pain.

She gritted her teeth and wiggled around until she faced the back seat. Sweat ran down her face, and she gasped for air. After resting a second, Carly explored the frame, pushing against it. The seat moved forward slightly, letting in a little light and air. Good. She didn't push it again—she didn't want to attract Blade's attention.

His cell phone rang and she held her breath, her ears straining.

"What do you want?" Blade asked.

Yes! She could hear him.

"I had to make sure no one followed me . . . Twenty minutes . . . See you there."

Evidently they were twenty minutes from where he was taking her and someone else was joining him. She had to escape before reinforcements arrived. Clenching her jaw, Carly flipped over on her back. If he ever slowed, she could grab enough of the release cord and open the trunk. She probed the hole, finding the stiff wire again. Had to be careful and not pull on it too hard—she didn't want it opening too soon.

While she waited, Carly took stock of her situation. The dagger remained in her boot as a last resort, and she felt her pocket. The GPS chip was still there. But was it even still live? Would Logan think of it? She couldn't depend on him to rescue her.

Blade had immediately locked her in the trunk, so security video would only show one driver when the car exited the parking garage. Logan would be looking for a car with two passengers. And once again, the sketch the forensic artist had drawn was so far off.

Blade's appearance had shocked her. Nothing would have made her believe he would shave his head or look so scruffy. In all the years she'd known him, he'd prided himself on his good looks. He would blame her for that too.

The car slowed. Go now or wait? It gathered speed. Too late, but next time it slowed she'd be prepared. Blade's driving became erratic, turning first one way and then another, until her head reeled. She swallowed down the bile that rose from her stomach. If he was trying to make her sick, he had succeeded.

The road noise changed from pavement to . . . gravel? She tried to estimate how much time had passed. Surely the twenty minutes he'd said. Carly had to escape now. She grasped the trunk release wire, waiting until the car slowed once more. The car hit a pothole, jerking her finger, and the trunk lid popped open.

She raised up. They were in a wooded area. Blade drove the gravel road fast, hitting the ruts and throwing her around. She scrambled to her knees, ready to dive out if she could just keep her balance. Suddenly the car slammed to a stop.

Carly dove out of the trunk and rolled. Pain sent stars to her eyes.

She climbed to her feet and bolted away from the car. Behind her the door slammed. She ran for the thicket of trees to her right. If she could make it there, she could hide.

A log lay across the road and she jumped it, coming down sideways on her ankle. Even before she felt the pain, she knew she'd twisted it, or worse. She hobbled to her feet and broke for the woods.

Blade caught her before she reached the trees and pinned her arms to her sides. She kicked at him and screamed again.

"Yell all you want," he hissed in her ear. "Nobody will hear you." The cold blade of his knife pressed against her neck. "If you move again, you're a dead woman."

She stilled, knowing he'd cut her throat if she even sneezed. "What do you want? Why did you bring me here?"

"Someone wants to see you."

"Who?"

"Why don't we go find out?"

Carly limped back to the car.

"I ought to make you walk to the cabin," he said as he opened the passenger door and shoved her inside. He locked her door before he slammed it shut. "You'll regret it if you try to run again."

315

She grabbed the door handle. Locked. He'd engaged the child locks.

Blade settled in the front seat and started the engine. "Put your seat belt on."

"You're worried about my safety?"

He looked over at her and curled his lip. "Still got that attitude, I see. We still have a ways to go, and I don't want to hear the seat belt alarm."

"I hope you don't think you're going to sell me into prostitution again."

"Hardly—you're a little old for my clients. They prefer something more along the line of your niece."

She curled her fingers into a ball and stared out the side window so he couldn't see the fire that was bound to be in her eyes. "I'll do anything you want," she said. "Just let her go."

"Too late for that, honey. She'll be in Miami this time tomorrow."

Her stomach clenched. She had to keep her head if she was going to get out of this and save Lexi. Carly grabbed the armrest as he hit one hole after another.

The trees got denser as they traveled deeper into the forest. They passed a few cabins that reminded Carly of the date she'd had with Logan when he'd brought her to their cabin for a picnic with his family. Back then it seemed fifty miles from nowhere. If that was where they were, even if the chip wasn't dead, the signal wouldn't get past the dense forest. Logan would never find her.

She had to find a way to get Blade to relax his guard. But she needed more than that. Maybe if she rattled him, she could gain a tiny edge to exploit. "How did you get stuck in Memphis?"

He ignored her question, but red crept up his neck and his jaw hardened.

"I'd like to think I was partially responsible for your demotion."

He jerked the car onto another road. "Just keep talking. It will make taking care of you all the more fun."

"Did they move you to Memphis right after I escaped?" she needled. "Or did you lose more girls?"

The red spread to his face. "For your information, I asked for Memphis so I could be there when you came back." He glanced toward her. "What happened with your shoulder? You tick someone else off?"

"You should know—you're the one who shot me."

His face went blank. "Not me. I prefer a knife," he said as he turned into a clearing with a cabin sitting at the edge and killed the motor.

She wasn't a fool. He didn't plan for her to come out of this alive. She scanned the area, looking for a way of escape. Maybe the woods . . . "Whose cabin?" she asked.

"You ask too many questions." He climbed out of the car and kept the gun trained on her as he walked around to her side. When he opened the door, she exploded from the seat, butting him in the stomach. Blade bent double and Carly ran.

57

LOGAN GRIPPED THE STEERING WHEEL. The sun had dropped below the horizon, and darkness would soon be closing in. He needed help. The Shelby County sheriff's number was stored in his phone, and he voice dialed it. "I need to speak with Sheriff Hunt," he said when dispatch answered.

"What's up, Donovan?" the sheriff said when he came on the line. "You ready to lose at the firing range again?"

"No," he replied. "I believe I have a hostage situation, and I need manpower."

"Where?" Hunt's voice turned serious.

"Meeman-Shelby Forest area." He explained what was going on.

"And you think this Dr. Adams is holding Smith hostage?"

"I won't know until I get there, but I'd like backup." He gave him the address of his family's cabin. "It's the next cabin after ours."

"Where are you?"

"Fifteen minutes from the location."

Hunt grunted. "My nearest deputy is half an hour away. It'll take me a little longer. I'll text you my phone number in case you need to update me."

"Thanks." A minute later the sheriff's text with his cell phone number chimed on his phone.

Logan reached his family's cabin in less than the fifteen minutes he'd told Sheriff Hunt and parked in the back. Rankin's cabin was only half a mile away, and Logan planned to hike the short distance. Part of him wanted to drive as close as possible, but then he would have to park on the side of the road. His car would be a dead giveaway with the spotlight mirrors, plus he was pretty sure that Blade knew his car.

He took a small .22 caliber automatic from the console and stuck it in his belt behind his back. Just in case. After he eased the door open, he adjusted the service revolver on his side, then jogged to the road and turned toward the Rankin cabin.

Darkness was creeping in. There were advantages to it being dark—he wouldn't be easily seen, but then neither could he see anyone else.

58

CARLY RAN, every step sending knife-like pain through her ankle that was swollen tight against her boot. A shot rang out behind her, then more gunfire with bullets splitting the dirt in front of her feet as she zigzagged across the clearing. She'd expected a knife, not a gun.

"Those were warning shots." The steely voice didn't belong to Blade, but it was familiar. "One more step, Carly, and I won't miss."

She didn't relish being shot in the back. Carly stopped and turned around, facing her shooter. Her head spun, and she blinked her eyes.

"That's a good girl."

Keeping the gun trained on her, Dr. Adams knelt beside Blade's body and grabbed the gun in his hand. "Now walk this way," he said, tucking the automatic in his waistband.

"You?" She shook her head to clear it. Maybe this was just a bad dream.

He backed up to the porch. "Move."

No. It wasn't a bad dream. It was a living nightmare. She stumbled past Blade's body. "You killed him?"

He shrugged. "When Blade took your niece, he became a liability. The syndicate does not tolerate stupidity."

Pulling her gaze from the dead man, Carly covered her mouth with her hand. Slowly she shifted her gaze from Adams to the open cabin door. He'd been here when they arrived? Fog filled her brain. Why couldn't she think? Buy time. She took her time climbing the steps to the porch where he waited. "Why did you have him bring me here?"

"Come on, Carly . . . you're smarter than that. Rankin told you something. I want to know what it was and who you told. Get inside."

She flinched as he pressed the gun to her side. Carly was smart enough to not tell him anything. Once he had what he wanted, she was dead.

59

LOGAN WAS ALMOST TO THE CABIN when a shot rang out. He dropped to the ground, yanking out his gun as two more shots followed. Then he heard a man order Carly to stop. Adams, he presumed. He crept closer until he spied a Dodge Charger parked in the drive.

He swept his gaze to the cabin and raised his gun when he saw Adams and Carly standing on the front porch. The doctor had a gun pressed to her side. If Logan fired, Adams would shoot her.

Logan glanced back at the Charger. A body was on the ground beside it. He texted the sheriff.

> Help. Have hostage situation and a body in the yard. Send an ambulance.

Carly hobbled inside the cabin. Her ankle throbbed—it couldn't take much more abuse. "Nothing Austin King said made sense. You've made a big mistake."

"I don't make mistakes." Adams closed the door and then waved the gun toward the sofa. "Sit there and tell me every word he said and how much of it Donovan heard."

She limped to the sofa and sank onto the cushions, then scanned the open-concept room for exits. A door led out of the kitchen. To her right was another door, probably to the bedrooms. Two options—the kitchen door or the entrance she'd come through.

Her ankle throbbed through her boot. No, she had one other option. The dagger.

Adams paced the room. He stopped and turned to her. "What did Rankin tell you?"

She fingered the gold bracelet around her wrist. "Which time?"

"Quit stalling and tell me what he said, his exact words—all of them."

"I'm not sure I can remember."

Adams pointed the pistol at her knee. "Perhaps a shattered kneecap will help you."

She flinched. He'd do it too. "Let me think."

Carly closed her eyes and recited what she remembered. *"I'm dying . . ."* She stopped and opened her eyes. "He wanted me to forgive him."

"What else?"

She rubbed her temples and replayed the scenes in the ICU . . . "He said he didn't know you were going to take Lexi and that he tried to stop you. It's why you tried to kill him."

"I knew nothing about your niece until it was too late to do anything about it. That was all Blade's doing."

Rankin had talked about Blade and Grey. She leveled a gaze at him. "*You're* Grey. He wanted to make you pay for what you did to him. But he was one of yours—why did you leave him to die in the fire?"

"He was getting soft, wanted us to turn the girls loose. What else did he say?"

Carly shook her head, trying to clear it. "He asked for a doctor, and I thought he was telling the nurse to get . . ." She pressed her hand to her mouth. "He was trying to tell me it was you—how did I not figure that out?"

"Indeed. Where was Donovan when Rankin said that?"

She glared at him and said nothing.

He lifted the gun again. "I asked you a question."

"He was standing at the door, but he didn't hear anything."

Adams sighed. "It doesn't matter. I'm sure you've told him everything he said." He pulled a phone from his pocket.

She eyed the small phone in his hand. "What are you doing?"

"I'm calling Donovan, and you're going to get him here."

"You're crazy. I'm not going to get him killed."

"Too late for that." He took out another phone and scrolled through the screen then dialed a number. While he was distracted, she slipped the dagger from her boot and palmed the knife in her hand.

Once it rang, Adams stepped closer to her, holding out the phone. "When he answers, tell him where you are and that you need him."

Carly grabbed the phone and threw it against the wall. The unexpected movement gave her precious seconds. She sprang from the sofa and dashed for the door.

60

HUNKERED DOWN at the rear of the Charger, the vibration from his phone startled Logan and he ignored it as the front door flew open. Carly shot out of the house with Adams on her heels.

Logan stood and raised his gun just as Adams grabbed her. In the failing light he was afraid he'd hit Carly and eased his finger off the trigger. The doctor's eyes widened when he saw Logan.

"Throw your gun out in the yard and walk this way," Adams yelled. "Or I kill your friend here."

Logan's shoulders slumped as he calculated how long it would take the sheriff to get here. Too long.

"Don't think I won't do it," the doctor shouted.

Logan had no doubt Adams would kill her. Him too. He was helpless to do anything where he was, but if he could get into the house, he might get the drop on the doctor with the .22 tucked behind his back. And it wasn't like he had a choice.

"I'm coming," he yelled and tossed his service revolver a few yards away from the car. He had to stall Adams long enough for the sheriff to get here.

He moved from behind the car. Between darkness falling and the shadows from the trees that loomed over the cabin, Logan could barely see what Adams was doing.

"Keep your hands where I can see them."

He complied and slowly walked past Blade to the cabin. Did the man's hand just move? He looked at the body again but it was still. He must have imagined it. Then Carly moaned, and he shifted his attention.

"Just let her go," he said. "You'll never get away with this. You're a part owner of the cabin. The sheriff will know it was you."

Adams barked a laugh. "My name is nowhere on the deed. And I will pull your murders off. There is nothing tying me to *any* of this, except what you heard Rankin say."

Logan slowed his steps. He had to keep him talking, give the sheriff time to get here. "How do you figure to get away with it?"

Adams held up his gun. "This belongs to Blade," he said, nodding to the body in the yard. "He worked with Rankin so he was familiar with the location of the cabin. It was a natural place to stash Carly's body. And then you showed up, so he had to kill you too."

He motioned Logan closer. "Everyone knows I was coming to Shelby Forest to hunt and I just happened upon him. Too late to save you, but I managed to outwit him and shoot him. I'll be a hero."

It didn't matter whether it was true or not—in his own deluded mind, the doctor believed because he was an upstanding citizen, a physician, that he would get away with their murders.

"You know why you won't get away with it?" Before the doctor could answer, Logan continued. "Because we have the bullet from Carly's shoulder, and I'm betting it will match one of your rifles."

"You're barking up the wrong tree. I didn't shoot her. Not yet anyway. Now get inside," he said, backing up and pulling Carly with him.

Logan stepped up onto the porch and slowly walked inside. He couldn't grab the gun hidden in his waistband without Adams seeing him.

Suddenly Carly swung her right hand around. A flash of silver streaked toward Adams's throat. The doctor jerked back and the small blade missed him.

Logan yanked the .22 from his belt, but Adams held on to Carly, using her body as a shield. He put the gun to her head. "Drop the knife," he said.

The look of desperation Carly sent him before she dropped the dagger was like a sledgehammer to his heart.

The doctor waved his pistol toward Logan. "Put your gun down."

Logan's blood thrummed through his body, his nerves stretched taut. He gripped his .22. Again, he couldn't shoot Adams without risking Carly's life.

A board creaked behind Logan. He cut his eyes to the door just as Blade lurched through it, a Bowie knife in his hand.

When Adams swung his gun toward Blade, Carly jerked away from him and ran toward Logan.

The doctor fired just as Blade threw the knife. The bullet struck Blade dead center of his chest and he collapsed.

With his ears ringing from the gunshot, Logan dropped to his knee, zeroing in on Adams. He fired, and a red stain spread across the doctor's chest. Adams raised his gun, and Logan fired again. The doctor fell to the floor. Logan kicked the gun from his hand and turned to find Carly.

She lay on the floor, the knife in her chest.

No!

"Carly, can you hear me?"

Blood gurgled in her chest.

"Logan . . ." She closed her eyes.

"Stay with me! Help is on the way."

Footsteps pounded on the porch. "Freeze!" a voice commanded.

Holding his hands up, Logan looked over his shoulder. "I'm a cop. Sergeant Logan Donovan. My badge is on my belt," he said. "She needs an ambulance."

Sheriff Hunt appeared in the doorway. "Donovan! What happened here?"

"Later. Is the ambulance here?" Logan cradled her in his arms. Carly couldn't die. "She has a knife wound. And I don't know how to help her."

"Should be here any minute." Hunt flipped on a light then knelt beside Adams's body. "This one is dead." He moved to Blade. "Got a faint heartbeat here," he said.

"Blade threw the knife, then Adams shot him," Logan said. "And I shot Adams."

Carly was too still. He placed his finger on the inside of her wrist. Way too slow. "Where's that ambulance!"

"It's coming."

61

A FULL MOON ROSE as David waited behind a tree near the boat-house. He'd like to be on the boat, but that assignment went to two members of the SWAT team. The houses on either side of Rankin's house had been evacuated, and the rest of the team had been deployed in the woods around the house. The van had been sighted among the trees near the back of the property. Everyone had instructions to wait until the SWAT team could take down both men without endangering the girls.

David's hand tensed on his Glock as the back door opened. A light flashed down the path to the steps that led to the boathouse, and then the shadowy figure of a man and two smaller ones came into view. He lifted a pair of field binoculars to his eyes. His heart leapt into his throat. It was Lexi and another girl. So they planned to take the girls down two at a time.

"Let me go!"

It was Lexi's voice. *Don't antagonize him!* Then she kicked him in the groin and broke loose when he doubled over. He let loose a string of Spanish.

"Run!" Lexi grabbed the other girl's hand and pulled. The girl didn't move, just stood frozen. Lexi dropped her hand and ran to the end of the dock and dove in just as the SWAT team exploded into action.

David raced to the pier as two members tackled the man. Seconds later an explosion shattered the quiet as a flash bang went off inside the cabin. The water was black and he couldn't find Lexi. "Can you see her?" he yelled.

Eric raced to his side. "Where'd she go in?"

"Right here! It's so dark I can't see anything in the water." They couldn't lose her now. Not when they were so close.

David handed his Glock to Eric and yanked off his shoes and then dove into the water, searching for his daughter. He felt for her arm, for her hair, her clothing, anything. He surfaced and Eric was shining a light around him. "Have you seen her?"

"No. She hasn't come up." Eric's voice cracked.

Where could she be? David dove again, and again found nothing. He surfaced to lights shining over the water.

"She's not here," Eric said.

He was about to go down again when he heard coughing. "Lexi?"

"Daddy?" Her voice came from the other side of the dock. She coughed again. "I knew you'd find me!"

He swam around the dock and found her clinging to a wooden crossbeam. She was safe.

62

When Logan arrived at the ER, a guard at the reception desk kept him from entering the exam rooms. "Look, I'm with the Memphis police department. I need to get in there," he said. The medics had stabilized Carly before they whisked her to the hospital.

"Just calm down," the receptionist said. "The doctors are working on her, and they'll let you in to see her as soon as they can. Have a seat over there." She pointed to a waiting area with magazines and a TV.

Logan paced the waiting room, watching the clock on the wall tick off the minutes with no word. A news report flashed on the TV, breaking the story. His cell phone rang and his mother's name showed on the caller ID. He spent the next ten minutes convincing her he was okay and for her not to come to the hospital. And no, he didn't know how Carly was, only that she was alive the last time he saw her.

After he talked with his mother, he approached the receptionist behind the desk again and asked about seeing Carly. She shook her head and told him he could go back when the doctor said he could.

An hour passed of pacing back and forth in the waiting room. He looked up as the Wilsons came through the entrance to the ER.

"How is she?" Georgina asked.

"Yes, how is she?" Frank echoed.

"I don't know. No one will tell me anything. How did—"

"Your mother called. We dropped everything and came."

"Have you heard from David or Maggie?" Frank asked.

"No. They'll call when they have something to tell us."

"What happened?" Frank asked. "Your mother said something about a knife wound."

"Yes. When the paramedics treated her, they indicated the knife may have nicked her lung," Logan said.

Georgina wrung her hands. "Is she going to be all right?"

"I don't know," Logan said, glancing toward the ER doors. "There might be more damage."

His cell phone rang, and he jerked it off his belt. "It's David." He wasn't sure he wanted to answer—he couldn't take any more bad news.

"Answer it," Georgina said.

He pressed the green button. "Hello?"

"We got her!" David yelled. "Lexi is all right."

Chill bumps raced over his body. "She's safe," he said to Georgina, and then he listened as David described what had gone down. Relief turned his muscles to mush, and he sat down. "That's great," he said over and over. Carly would be so happy to know her niece was all right. If she lived long enough for him to tell her.

"So, how's everything there?" David asked.

"Sergeant Donovan," the receptionist called.

Logan turned toward her.

"You can go back now."

He nodded and hurried to the doors. "Can I call you back?" he asked David. "I have a lot to tell you, but first I want to check on Carly."

"Is she okay?"

"I hope so."

63

CARLY GAGGED AND BIT DOWN on whatever was choking her. She tried to spit it out. It was still there. She couldn't move her hands and struggled against the restraints. Bells went off.

"Ms. Smith, you're in the hospital, and you're on a ventilator. You can't take the tube out."

Hospital? She just got out of one. Carly turned toward the voice, and the movement sent pain shooting through her body. The fuzzy image of a man bent over her. *Please, take it out.*

"Don't try to talk," he said as he loosened the restraints. "As long as you leave the tube alone, I'll leave your hands free."

She nodded, trying to assure him she'd do as he said.

"You have a collapsed lung, but you're breathing mostly on your own now. It'll be out soon."

A hazy memory floated just out of reach. Blade . . . Dr. Adams . . . Logan . . . *Lexi* . . .

A knock broke into her thoughts, and the nurse turned his head toward the door. "Looks like you have company."

Logan appeared at the side of the bed and took her hand. "Can't you stay out of here?" he asked, giving her a tender smile.

She tried to say her niece's name.

Logan squeezed her hand. "Just listen, okay?"

She nodded, drinking in his eyes, the lines in his face. He'd saved her life again.

"David called. They have Lexi and she's fine."

Tears sprang to her eyes. Her niece was okay?

"Don't cry." He wiped her cheeks with a tissue.

The memory became clearer. Blade kidnapping her. Dr. Adams . . . the overhead monitor went crazy again.

The nurse came immediately. "I'm going to give you something to calm you down," he said.

She shook her head violently. "Mmnnn!"

"Can you hold up on that a second?" Logan asked and then turned to her. "I've seen you do it before. Can you calm yourself without medication?"

Carly nodded. Anything to keep from being knocked out again. She went through her routine with the lake. Her throat relaxed and she quit fighting the tube. Her heart rate returned to normal, quieting the alarms.

"Good." Logan squeezed her hand again. "You're safe now. Dr. Adams is . . . he won't ever bother you again. And Blade is in custody."

Lexi. She wanted to know all about her and pinched her brow, willing him to tell her more about her niece.

"You want to know more about Lexi?" When she nodded, he laughed. "I'm getting pretty good at reading your expressions, but I'm afraid I don't know much—I was in too big a hurry to see how you were."

She frowned at him again.

He took out his phone and then hesitated. "Your aunt and uncle are in the waiting room. If it's okay with your nurse, could they come see you and hear what David has to say?"

Gigi and Frank were here? She tensed but caught herself before she shook her head. They had been nothing but nice to her since they discovered her identity. It was just so hard to forget their troubled history. But a new life stretched before Carly. Did she really want to drag the past into it?

"You don't have to," Logan said. "I shouldn't have asked. It's just that they're so worried."

She fluttered her hand, trying to let him know it was okay.

"I'm not sure what that means," he said. "Think you could write something?"

When she nodded, he found a paper and pen and she scrawled "yes, they can come."

"Be right back," he said and disappeared out the door.

A few minutes later Gigi and Frank smiled tentatively at her. "I'm so glad you're safe," her aunt said, squeezing her hand.

Frank nodded from behind Gigi. "We've been so worried about you and Lexi."

Carly gave a thumbs-up, and then she turned to Logan and pointed to his phone.

"I'm calling now," he said.

Once he had David on the phone, he put the call on speaker. The story her brother-in-law told sent chills over Carly's body, especially when he came to the part about Lexi diving into the river. Before Logan disconnected, David promised to bring Lexi to the hospital to see her. Carly blotted her tears with the tissue Logan handed her. Her niece was safe. And so was she. It really was a new beginning.

64

THE LATE-AFTERNOON SUN cast a golden glow on the trees as Logan's car ate up the miles from Memphis to Senatobia. It'd been a week since Carly was released from the hospital. He glanced toward Carly in the passenger seat as she stared out the window at the passing trees.

"You're sure about this?" he asked. "You know Maggie doesn't mind if you stay another week with her."

"I know, but she needs her place back." Carly smoothed a wrinkle from her jeans. "David is coming to dinner tonight, and they don't need me hanging around. Besides, it's time I got to know my aunt and uncle again. And I want to see Candy."

"The mare you raised?"

"I was surprised when Frank told me he still had her, but then horses live thirty years or more sometimes. Candy is one good thing I remember about living with them." She chuckled. "Of course the tension between us wasn't all their fault. They were so different from Mom and Dad . . . Frank had so many rules."

"And you were a teenager," Logan said with a laugh. He didn't know why he was uneasy about this. "I just wish it'd been the Memphis condo instead of their farm."

"It's only about thirty miles," she said.

"Why the farm, do you know?"

"It was Frank's idea. He knew I wanted to spend time with Candy. He thought the farm would be a better atmosphere, and I can take care of the trust while I'm there. I haven't told them yet, but Maggie is handling all the legal work," she said. "Oh, and Lexi is coming for the weekend—she has a horse at the farm too."

"How's it going with her?"

"Wonderful. She's so much like her mother. I can't believe how easy it's been to get to know her."

He shot her a smile. "I bet she's a lot like her aunt too," he said.

His GPS instructed him to exit off the interstate and take a left at the bottom of the ramp. "Did I tell you Jim Rankin's autopsy showed a massive dose of morphine? Everything points to Adams administering it. And, Blade turned informant," he said after he turned. "He's already rolled over on a couple of higher-ups, one that I'm sorry to say is a police officer."

Out of the corner of his eye, he saw Carly shiver her shoulders. "You're kidding. Does that mean he'll get off?"

"No, it means he'll be in a nicer prison and maybe have a lighter sentence. But even if he gets less time, he'll be an old man before he gets out. Would you like to know what his real name is?" When she nodded he said, "Arthur Clark."

"Hardly fits him. Did he say who shot me?"

"That's the odd part. He claims he doesn't know anything about it, that your shooting must have been something Adams did on his own. But before he died, Adams claimed he didn't shoot you, either. We're comparing the bullet taken from your shoulder to the rifles Adams owned and should get that report back anytime."

Logan didn't like loose ends. What if someone other than Adams wanted Carly dead? But who? He didn't have a suspect, and he had to consider it had been either random or gang activity.

"It's so surreal, thinking that someone wanted to kill me," Carly said then sat forward. "The farm is just up the road—next drive on the right."

Logan's GPS piped up that they were arriving at their destination on the right, and she laughed. "Told you."

She turned and looked toward the farmhouse. "Oh my, it looks like it always did, except for maybe a new coat of paint."

He parked and came around to Carly's side as Georgina and Frank came out of the house.

"Where's your bag?" Frank asked.

"In the trunk," Logan said and popped the lid. He took her bag out and handed it off to him.

"We're putting you in your old room," Georgina said. "Lexi always stays in her mom's."

Logan held Carly's arm as they climbed the steps to a wraparound porch.

"These looked so steep when I was a kid. We dared each other to jump off the top step."

"And that's why you ended up with a broken arm," Frank said wryly.

"It was kind of neat to get everyone to sign my cast when I went back to school that week, though," Carly said with a laugh. "And I got out of washing dishes too."

She stopped in front of the security door. "You got rid of the screen door."

"Afraid so," Georgina said. "After there were a few break-ins in the area, Frank thought it best to put these security doors up, but personally, I miss hearing that screen slap the frame when I go out," she said. "You have time before supper to go out to the barn, if you'd like."

She looked longingly toward the red building, and he hoped she would take a pass. The barn looked a good quarter mile away and Carly already looked tuckered out.

"I think I'll rest until dinner." She turned to him. "You'll stay, won't you?"

Logan thought of the paperwork waiting for him at the office, but the way her eyes entreated him, he couldn't say no. "Sure." He could catch up tomorrow.

After dinner, Logan waited in the den while Carly went upstairs with Georgina. Frank had built a fire and Logan backed up to it. He glanced around the room, noticing Frank's gun safe. "Do much hunting?" he asked.

Frank shook his head. "Not so much anymore. Most hunting is in winter, and I don't like being cold."

Logan walked to the glassed gun cabinet. It was locked. "Is that a Weatherby 30.06?"

"Yeah." He made no effort to show Logan the gun.

"Nice. Interested in selling it?" Logan had a Weatherby when he was a teenager.

"I hadn't thought about it."

"If you ever want to, let me know." He looked closer at the guns. "Is that a Browning .22?"

"You know your rifles," Frank said. "That's a collector's item and one of the last models to be made and assembled in Belgium. You can't find a better rifle for hitting the target." He glanced toward the stairs. "I'm glad we have a few minutes by ourselves to talk."

Logan cocked his head. "About what?"

"When Carly was released, we were there. I noticed she had a prescription for painkillers."

"So?"

Frank shot another look toward the stairs. "She told us a little about when she escaped, how she had to go into rehab. What if she gets on drugs again?"

"I don't think that's going to happen."

"You don't think the pain medication they gave her in the hospital will trigger a backslide?"

While anything was possible, Logan didn't see that happening with Carly. "I'm glad you're concerned about her, but when you've been around Carly a little longer, I think you'll see you don't have anything to worry about."

Just then voices from the stairway drew his attention.

"Don't mention I brought this up," Frank said. "I don't want her to think I don't trust her."

"Sure." He turned as Carly followed her aunt down the steps.

"Would you like to walk to the barn with me?" Carly asked. "I've gone about as long as I can without seeing Candy."

"It's awfully chilly," her aunt said. "Why don't you wait until morning?"

"But I want Logan to meet Candy," Carly said. "And he won't be here in the morning."

"It's not that cold," Frank said and handed her a puffy down jacket. "But wear this. And don't enter the last stall. We're boarding a stallion for a couple of days."

"He's very high-strung," Georgina added.

Frank shook his head. "No, Phantom is just plain mean."

"We won't bother him," Logan assured them.

Outside the air was nippy and the moonless night allowed the stars to stand out against the black sky. "I had forgotten how far out in the country we are," Carly said, slipping her hand into his. "You can't see the stars in town like you can here."

"Your hand is cold," he said and rubbed her fingers, warming them.

A nicker came from the barn, and she laughed. "That's Candy! I'd recognize that nicker anywhere."

She pulled him by the hand to the barn. A black horse with a white star on her forehead stretched her neck toward them, and Carly went to her immediately.

"Hey, girl. Do you remember me? I've missed you." The mare nudged Carly with her nose. "No, I can't take you out of the stall tonight, but tomorrow morning I will."

"You're not going to ride her tomorrow, are you?"

"I wish," she said. "No. I'll spend tomorrow getting reacquainted with her. Help me find a square of hay."

He helped her look and they found a bale in the side hall and peeled off a couple of flakes.

"What kind of horse is she?" Logan asked as she tossed the hay in Candy's stall.

"She's an Arabian. It's all Frank ever kept when I was a kid."

Pawing came from the end stall, and Carly wandered down to it. "Oh, wow. He's beautiful."

Logan followed her. The jet-black horse tossed his head and flared his nostrils as he pawed the ground again.

"Would you like some hay?" She held out a handful of grass, and the horse stretched his neck out to snatch it from her hand. When he looked expectantly at her, she moved closer. "You'll have to come to the door if you want more."

"Maybe you better not," he said. "Frank said he was mean."

"I don't think he's mean at all." She held out another handful just out of reach. After a minute he took a step toward her. "That's a good boy." After another handful, he eased up to the stall door and she rubbed his forehead. "You're not bad," she murmured.

He hadn't seen Carly like this before. Relaxed. Enjoying herself. Coming to the farm had been a good idea, after all. He brushed a piece of straw from her hair, and she turned toward him, her eyes wide and her lips soft. He held her gaze as electricity arced between them, his heart filling his chest to bursting.

As much as he wanted to kiss her, he didn't want to push her into something she wasn't ready for. The stallion nudged Carly, breaking the spell. Logan pulled her to his chest and wrapped his arms around her. "You're vulnerable right now, and I don't want to take advantage of you."

"You kissed me once," she said, disappointment ringing in her voice.

"I shouldn't have," he said. "And right now, it's not because I don't want to, but you need a little time to process everything that's happened." He kissed the top of her head. "We better go back in. I should go back to Memphis, and you need to get some rest."

When they reached his car, he kissed her lightly. "That one doesn't count," he said. "Would you say good night for me to Frank and Georgina?"

She nodded and he placed another kiss on her forehead. "I'll call you in the morning."

As he drove down the lane, he looked in his rearview mirror, his breath hitching as the light from the porch bathed her in a soft glow.

65

WHEN THE DOORBELL RANG, Maggie swept her gaze around her apartment. Dinner was ready. The table was set . . . she still debated whether she'd made the right choice not to light the candles. She didn't know what she was so nervous about. Lexi was safe and they'd resolved the issue of possible conflicts with their jobs. David had acknowledged he'd been wrong to get angry, and his reaction had been from the stress of Lexi's kidnapping. But nothing more had been said about marriage.

Maggie glanced at the video feed just as David checked his watch and then rang the doorbell again. *Are those roses in his hands?* Her heart fluttered as she opened the door. "Come in," she said.

His smile warmed her heart but did nothing for her nerves.

David held out the red flowers as he stepped inside. "I know you saw these on the camera, so they're not a surprise."

"Thank you," she said, her voice breathy as she took the flowers. "Let me find a vase."

"Where's Carly?"

"She went to stay a few days with her aunt and uncle in Senatobia," she said over her shoulder. "Has her case been officially closed?"

He nodded. "I don't think we'll ever know who shot her that

first night." He pressed his lips together. "Just like we'll never know for sure who killed Lia."

"Don't you think Rankin did it?"

"Ninety-nine percent, but unless ballistics match the bullet that killed her with one of Rankin's guns, there's no proof."

Maggie was thankful he'd come to terms with Lia's murder. She squeezed his waist then went to find the vase.

David watched her arrange the flowers, jingling the change in his pocket, and she shooed him out on the balcony. He was in a strange mood.

Once she finished, she grabbed a sweater. Her fingers trembled when she opened the French doors. His back was to her as he looked out over the city lights. Taking a deep breath, she joined him. Overhead the velvet sky twinkled with a host of stars.

"I love it out here," he said, turning to her.

"Me too." He caught her gaze and held it, making her want to melt into his arms.

A breeze lifted a lock of her hair and blew it across her face. David gently brushed it back. "Would you miss it too much?"

"Miss it . . ." Her eyes widened when she saw the ring in his other hand and then the question in his eyes.

"I love you, Madeline Starr. Would you do me the honor of becoming Mrs. David Raines?" he asked softly.

He got it right this time. She looked up into eyes so blue they reminded her of the Caribbean. "Are you sure?" she asked. "I can't promise I'll always share information with you."

He dipped his head until it touched hers. "I'll trust that you'll share what you can," he said.

She breathed deeply. "Then, yes, I love you, and I'll marry you."

David pulled her close, and she slid her arms around his neck.

66

SOMEWHERE A ROOSTER CROWED, and Carly burrowed deeper into a bed that was too comfortable to leave. He crowed again, sounding as though he was right outside her window, and she blinked away the last dregs of sleep. A rush of memories sent her heart racing. Blade. Adams. Logan . . . Every morning when she first woke up, she relived that day.

She was safe. And she was at her aunt's farm to recover. That's why the bedroom smelled of lavender. And why it seemed familiar. Carly sat up and stretched, being careful with her wounds.

Although some things had changed since she'd stayed here last, the wood armoire and dresser were the same. The sliding barn doors over the closet were new. On the window, burlap curtains hung from brass rods adorned with horseshoes. The theme continued with horseshoe tiebacks.

What time was it? She found her new cell phone on the bedside table. Ten o'clock? That couldn't be right. She looked again. But it was. Gigi had never allowed her to sleep this late when she was a kid. There were some perks to being an adult.

Coffee. Now that she was fully awake, she needed caffeine. She climbed out of bed and stretched, wincing when a twinge of pain shot through her. She was healing but still sore.

After a quick run through the bathroom, Carly slipped into the robe her aunt had laid across the bed last night. She cinched the robe and descended the stairs to the kitchen.

"Hello, sleepyhead," Gigi said. Her oversized purse sat on the granite counter. "Coffee maker and pods are by the sink."

"Thanks for letting me sleep in," Carly said.

"Was the bed comfortable? It has a new mattress."

"It was great. I love the changes you've made," she said and found a mug. Carly chose a hazelnut blend from the carousel and popped it into the single-serve brewer. "Are you going somewhere?"

"Garden club meeting. I wouldn't go except I'm the president and the vice-president is out of town. I should be back a little past noon."

"Don't hurry on my account. Is Frank around?" Maybe he was going with Gigi. She'd like to have what was left of the morning to herself. Get reacquainted with Candy.

"He's at the barn. He got a late start, but he should be through feeding shortly." She picked up her purse. "When I return, we'll go over the paperwork for your trust, and as soon as you're up to it, we'll go to the bank in town and have the trust dissolved and the funds transferred to your name."

"There's no hurry. Why don't we wait until tomorrow?" She wasn't ready to tell her aunt and uncle that Maggie was taking care of the legal matters with the trust. "How much money are you talking about?"

"About two million dollars."

Carly almost dropped her cup. "Did you say . . ."

"That's how much Frank said was in there the last time I asked," Gigi said, beaming. "There have been no withdrawals since you left. With the interest compounding annually, the money added up."

It was too much for her to take in. "Thank you for taking care of it all these years."

"You can thank Frank. I don't know if you remember, but I am horrible at numbers. Years ago I turned it over to him and the man at the bank." She checked her watch. "I have to run. Eggs are in the fridge and cereal is in the cupboard."

After Gigi left, Carly scrambled an egg and made toast. When she finished, she went upstairs and changed. Each day she'd grown a little stronger, and while she didn't want to ride today, she thought she was strong enough to lunge Candy in the small exercise pen. Or not, when a twinge pinched her shoulder as she slipped on a sweatshirt. She could groom her, at least.

The sun felt good on her face as she walked to the barn. "Frank?" she called. He didn't answer. She patted Candy on the neck and then checked the stalls. Evidently he'd already fed, since hay had been tossed into each stall. In the end stall, Phantom kicked at the wall.

Logan looked up from the computer as David stopped by his cubicle. "How was last night?"

David's face turned a bright shade of red. "How'd you know about last night?"

"When I took Carly to Senatobia, she said you and Maggie were having dinner together."

"Oh. It went well." A smile tugged at his mouth, and then he grinned big. "She said yes."

Logan high-fived him. "Great! When's the date?"

"Haven't set that yet," he said.

An email dinged on Logan's computer and he checked it. "It's the ballistics report."

David leaned over his shoulder as he opened the email.

"Do you see that?" David asked.

The report stated that the bullet that killed Lia came from a .38 revolver belonging to one of the guns they'd found at Rankin's home. "This has to be hard for you," Logan said.

David gave a bare nod. "At least now we can have closure," he said, his voice breaking.

Logan read further into the report. "No match to Carly's bullet."

He couldn't figure it out. After Blade swore he hadn't shot Carly, Logan had been certain Adams was the shooter.

"We may have to accept it was a random shooting," David said. "What caliber did you tell me the bullet was?"

"A .22 long rifle."

"I don't like it." David rubbed his chin. "That's an unusual choice for a murder weapon, especially gang related."

"My thoughts too. What if someone is still after her?"

David's cell phone rang and he grinned. "Maggie," he said and answered it. "Good morning."

His face grew serious. "You're kidding. Hold on a sec." He turned to Logan. "Have you talked to Carly this morning?"

"No." He'd been waiting for her to call him. "Why?"

"Maggie discovered something, and she's been trying to get ahold of her. Carly's not answering. Let me put the call on speaker."

"What's going on?" Logan asked.

"Before she left for Senatobia, Carly asked me to handle the legal matters involving the trust." Maggie's voice filled the cubicle. "I talked with the co-trustee at the bank in Senatobia yesterday, and he was evasive, so this morning I called and talked with the bank president. He looked into the financial records for the trust, and it looks like there have been withdrawals," she said. "And the trustee didn't show up for work today. It appears Frank and the bank employee have been embezzling from the trust. And now Carly isn't answering her phone."

"What?" Logan's mouth went dry. The gun cabinet at Frank's house flashed through his mind. He jumped up. "Frank has a .22 rifle."

◆

The horse in the stall next to Candy's nickered, and Carly turned, catching a glimpse of Frank in her peripheral vision. "There you are," she said and turned to face him. "I thought I might lunge Candy."

Frank stared at her, an odd expression on his face.

"Unless you want to start working on the paperwork for the trust."

"No." His voice had an edge. "I don't want to work on that."

He came closer to her, his hand down by his side. Was he hiding something?

"What are you holding?" she asked, stepping back as he invaded her space.

His hand came around so fast she barely saw the horseshoe on the end of a steel rod. The rod whistled past her ear as she jumped out of the way. "What are you doing?"

She backed away from him, keeping her eye on the rod. Her chest tightened, cutting off her breath. It was just like the tieback in her bedroom.

The stall door stopped her. Behind her, Phantom pawed the ground in his stall.

"You just couldn't die, could you?" he said.

"Why are you doing this?" The slide bolt that latched Phantom's stall door dug into her back.

"The trust, why else?" he said. "I never thought you'd come back."

"You'll never get away with this."

Phantom snorted, drawing Frank's attention. Carly slid her hand behind her back, her fingers searching for the knob on the bolt. She had not escaped Blade and Adams to die at Frank's hands.

"Of course I will. I told you last night to stay out of Phantom's stall." He brought his attention back to Carly. "But you wouldn't listen. You came out here, and slipped into his stall, and he pawed you to death."

He raised the metal horseshoe over his head.

She grasped the bolt and jerked it out of the u-clamps holding it. When it came free, she jumped to the side, pulling the stall door open. The horseshoe whistled past her head and slammed into the wooden door.

The stallion reared in his stall. Frank came at her again. Using the self-defense moves she'd learned, Carly grabbed his arm with one hand and the back of his neck with her other. At the same time, she wrapped her leg around the bend of Frank's knees and shoved him. The stallion reared again. Frank's knees buckled and he tripped over the back of her leg, landing under Phantom's hooves.

With the horse's high-pitched squeal in her ears, she ran toward the house, stopping only when flashing blue lights raced up the drive, their sirens wailing at full blast.

67

A MONTH LATER

Carly leaned back against the seat as Logan stopped for a traffic light. She felt his gaze on her and turned toward him, her heart aching when their eyes met. Tomorrow she was returning to Stillwater, leaving him behind.

While he'd visited her often at Maggie's condo after the fiasco in Senatobia, he hadn't kissed her again. If he had, she wouldn't be leaving.

"Thank you for all you've done for me, and for today," she said. Her aunt had called early this morning, reminding her she had left a suitcase behind, and Logan had offered to drive her to the farm.

He returned his gaze to the light. "Not a problem. Are you really up to seeing Georgina again?"

She nodded. "I'm done with running. She called me after Frank was released from the hospital to the county jail. We talked a long time, and she apologized for what he'd done. The bank insurance will replace the quarter million he stole from the trust, and I think he'll spend his remaining years in prison."

The light changed, and she leaned back when he pressed the accelerator. She tried to count how many times he'd saved her life.

"You're awfully quiet," he said as he took the ramp onto I-55.

"Just thinking about last month."

"We'll certainly have stories to tell our grandkids one day."

Her heart tap-danced in her chest.

"That didn't come out quite right," he said quickly. "I meant, grandkids, respectively."

"So you don't think we would make good grandkids together?" she teased.

Red crawled up his neck. "Do you?" he shot back.

Carly couldn't deny the attraction she felt for him, and in the last few days, she'd come to realize how much he meant to her. The problem was, he hadn't given her any indication since the day at the hospital that he felt the same way. She wasn't about to risk rejection.

"I don't know," she said faintly and looked out the window. The hickories and oaks were the only trees still holding on to their leaves.

"Feel like walking a little?"

"What do you have in mind?"

"Arkabutla is just off the next exit, and it's not too chilly. We could take a few minutes to enjoy the lake," he said. "Give you a good memory of your time here—replace some of the bad ones."

And give her a little more time to be with him.

"Let me call Gigi and let her know I'll be a little later getting there."

While she made the call, they exited I-55 at the Coldwater exit and drove the short distance to the lake. After they entered the state park, Logan said, "There's a place where I used to fish that I want to show you."

She sat back as he drove to Hernando Point and parked next to a grove of trees that stopped just at the shoreline. He came around to her side of the car and opened the door. "I'm not an invalid now. I could have gotten out on my own."

"I know that, Ms. Independent, but it's the gentlemanly thing to do."

She laughed and then breathed in the crisp November air. It was just the way she liked autumn. "This is my favorite time of year," she said. "The trees are like Joseph's coat of colors, and the sky—it's never this blue in any of the other seasons. I'm glad we stopped."

"Me too." Logan laced his fingers in hers and pulled her toward the shoreline.

The afternoon's golden glow imprinted on her brain. This *was* a memory she'd keep.

"Smell that air?" he said. "It has a hint of the winter that's coming."

She breathed deeply. "I don't like winter. It reminds me of endings."

"But after winter is the spring." Logan slipped his arm around her waist and drew her to his side. "And spring means new beginnings, just like daisies."

He'd told her about the daisies he'd bought at the Westin. She leaned into him. New beginnings. That was a thought to hold on to.

"How do you feel about going out with me?"

Carly's heart skipped a beat. He'd surprised her. "It's a little late for that question—I'm leaving tomorrow."

"Nashville isn't that far."

She ducked her head. "I don't exactly have the pedigree your mother always wanted for you."

"My mother doesn't pick the women I date," he said. "And your pedigree is just fine with me. Her, too, now."

Carly laughed then turned sober as she stared out over the water. "I bring a lot of baggage into a relationship," she said softly.

He turned her around and tipped her face up. His eyes said he wanted to kiss her . . . "No," Logan said softly. "You bring courage and strength."

Her insides melted as he traced his finger along her jaw, keeping his gaze glued to hers.

"I'm not sure you're ready for this, but I can't let you leave without telling you how I feel. I can't promise to never disappoint you, but know this—I will never intentionally hurt you. I love you, Carly Smith, and I'll wait however long it takes for you to love me back and become my wife."

Her heart soared to the blue sky above, and she slipped her arms behind his neck. "Thank you," she whispered. "But you don't have to wait at all. I love you, Logan Donovan. And if that's a proposal, my answer is yes."

ACKNOWLEDGMENTS

As ALWAYS, to Jesus, who gives me the words.

To my family and friends who believe in me and encourage me every day.

To my editors, Lonnie Hull DuPont, Kristin Kornoelje, and Julie Davis, thank you for making my stories so much better.

To the art, editorial, marketing, and sales team at Revell— Michele Misiak, Karen Steele, Erin Bartels, Hannah Brinks, and Cheryl Van Andel, thank you for your hard work. You are the best!

To Julie Gwinn, thank you for your direction and for working so tirelessly with me and for being my friend.

To Carole Bullard, Susie Harvill, and Advocates for Freedom (advocatesforfreedom.org), thank you for bringing the plight of human trafficking victims to my attention. I had no idea. Your tireless efforts on their behalf amaze me.

NOTE FROM THE AUTHOR

HUMAN TRAFFICKING, also known as modern-day slavery, exists in the twenty-first century, even in the United States. Illegal profits made from human trafficking are estimated to be in excess of $150 billion a year. And so many people have no idea it exists.

What can we do to stop it?

Educate yourself. Information about human trafficking and how to identify a victim can be found at humantraffickinghotline.org.

Talk about human trafficking with your friends, law enforcement, elected officials—anyone who will listen.

Get involved with your local nonprofit organizations dedicated to stopping human trafficking.

Patricia Bradley is the author of two series—the Logan Point Series (*Shadows of the Past, A Promise to Protect, Gone without a Trace*, and *Silence in the Dark*) and the Memphis Cold Case novels (*Justice Delayed, Justice Buried, Justice Betrayed*, and *Justice Delivered*). Bradley is the winner of an Inspirational Choice award and a Carol finalist. Bradley is cofounder of Aiming for Healthy Families, Inc., and she is a member of American Christian Fiction Writers and Romance Writers of America. Bradley makes her home in Mississippi. Learn more at www.ptbradley.com.

Meet

Patricia
BRADLEY

www.ptbradley.com

 @PTBradley1

Patricia Bradley Author

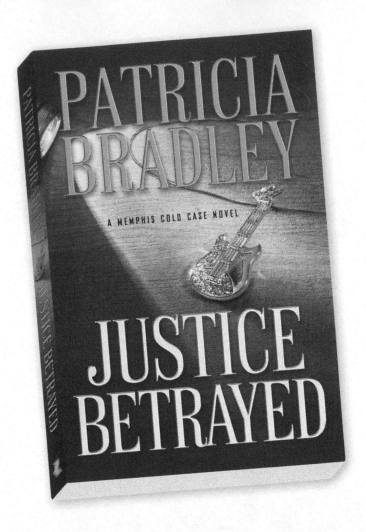

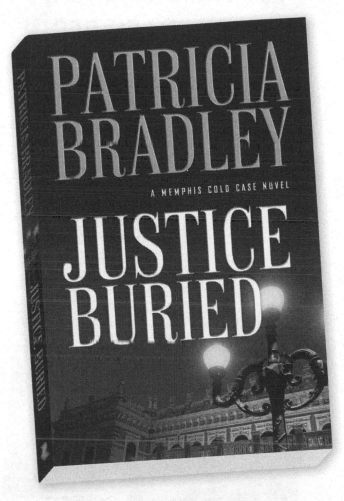

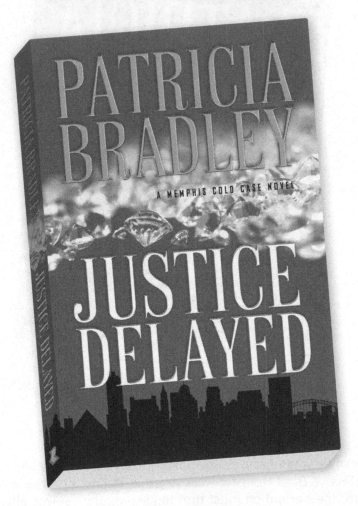

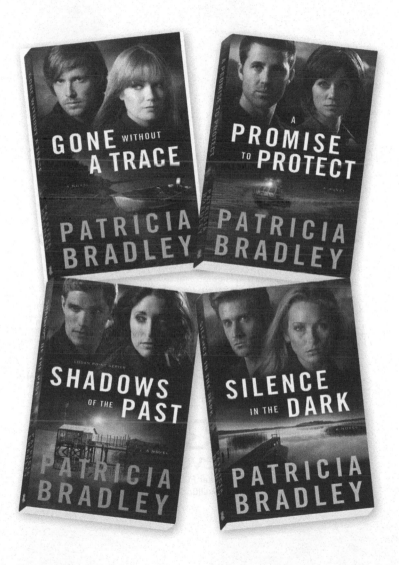